A BABY FOR CHRISTMAS

She crept to the door and tried to peer through a small pane, but a light layer of frost clouded the glass.

The soft cry came again.

Turning the flimsy lock, she sucked in her breath and slowly opened the door. A crack at first. An inch. Then two. She couldn't imagine what in God's name had prompted her to do that. Even Murphy would have thought that she was nuts.

Then, there it was. On the floor, right outside the door. Not a raccoon or a skunk, but a basket. A big handwoven basket, the kind her aunt had used to hold skeins of yarn. A red bow was tied around the handle. And inside was a baby, swaddled in white fleece.

PRAISE FOR JEAN STONE'S PREVIOUS NOVELS

"Stone is a talented novelist whose elegant prose brings the Martha's Vineyard setting vividly to life. . . . A very good read." —*Milwaukee Journal Sentinel*

"Stone's graceful prose, vivid imagery and compassionately drawn characters make this one a standout."—*Publishers Weekly*

"Jean Stone is a truly gifted writer. I wish I could claim her as a long-lost sister—but I can't. I can merely enjoy her wonderful talent." —nationally best-selling author Katherine Stone

"A wrenching and emotionally complex story. Sometimes, if you are very lucky, you can build a bridge across all obstacles. A very touching read." —*RT Book Reviews*

"A very smart and well-written book." —*Fresh Fiction*

"[A] cheeky debut. . . . As delightfully campy as an episode of *Desperate Housewives*." —*Publishers Weekly*

A VINEYARD CHRISTMAS

JEAN STONE

KENSINGTON BOOKS

www.kensingtonbooks.com

KENSINGTON BOOKS are published by

Kensington Publishing Corp.
119 West 40th Street
New York, NY 10018

All Kensington titles, imprints, and distributed lines are available at special quantity discounts for bulk purchases for sales promotion, premiums, fund-raising, and educational or institutional use.

Special book excerpts or customized printings can also be created to fit specific needs. For details, write or phone the office of the Kensington Sales Manager: Kensington Publishing Corp., 119 West 40th Street, New York, NY 10018. Attn. Sales Department. Phone: 1-800-221-2647.

Kensington and the K logo Reg. U.S. Pat. & TM Off.

ISBN-13: 978-1-4967-1662-0
ISBN-10: 1-4967-1662-0
First Kensington Trade Paperback Printing: October 2018

eISBN-13: 978-1-4967-1663-7
eISBN-10: 1-4967-1663-9
First Kensington Electronic Edition: October 2018

10 9 8 7 6 5 4 3 2 1

Printed in the United States of America

In Memory of
Esme Willis
1919–2016

A kind and gracious lady who loved being
surrounded by books.
I will always be grateful that she welcomed
me into her life.

Acknowledgments

Thanks to the people of Chappaquiddick for their welcoming spirit and their awesome potlucks; to the hardworking folks at the Edgartown Library; to the many other wonderful islanders I now have as neighbors and friends; to my agent, Loretta Weingel-Fidel, who has never given up on me; and mostly, to my longtime editor, Wendy McCurdy, who called me on a snowy winter day and quietly asked, "Would you like to write a Vineyard series?" Answer: Yes. I believe I would.

Chapter 1

The turnout was better than Annie had expected. It was, after all, a bitter, see-your-breath kind of morning, with a brisk December wind whirling around Vineyard Sound. But sunshine was vibrant against a bright blue sky, painting a perfect backdrop for the evergreens and colorful lights that decked the lampposts along Main Street, the storefronts, the town hall. Around the village, the traditional Christmas in Edgartown celebration was underway: on her walk to the elementary school gymnasium, Annie had witnessed the beloved parade of quick-stepping marching bands; mismatched, decorative pickup trucks; and a Coast Guard lifeboat perched atop a flatbed trailer that carried Santa himself, who waved and shouted "Ho ho ho!" while tossing candy canes into the cheering curbside throngs.

The atmosphere inside the gym was equally festive as "Jingle Bells" and "Joy to the World" scratched through the ancient PA system. Browsers and shoppers yakked in high-pitched voices and jostled around one another—many were armed with reusable bags silk-screened with the names of island markets, banks, insurance agents. By day's end, the bags would no doubt bulge with knitted scarves, island jewelry, specialty chocolates, and, hopefully, one or two of Annie's handcrafted soaps.

From her station behind a table under a basketball hoop, Annie wore a hesitant smile. The Holiday Crafts Fair had been open less than an hour, but she'd already sold seven bath-sized bars and a three-pack of hand-shaped balls she called "scoops" because each was the size of a scoop of sweet ice cream. Her cash pouch now held fifty-two dollars—not bad for her first endeavor in making boutique soaps by using wildflowers and herbs that grew right there on Martha's Vineyard.

But as happy as the earnings made her, Annie mused that fifty-two dollars was hardly a sign she should quit her day job. Then a middle-aged woman in jeans, an old peacoat, and a felt hat with a yellow bird crocheted on the brim approached the table. *An islander*, Annie knew. A year-rounder, like Annie was now. She'd seen her somewhere in town—the post office, the movies, the library. With the days growing shorter and colder and the streets less cluttered with tourists, faces were becoming familiar. The woman in the peacoat examined Annie's wares, which were wrapped in pastel netting and tied with coordinating ribbon: pink for beach roses and cream; yellow for buttercup balm; lavender for violets and honey.

At the far end of the table, a young woman sniffed a scoop of fox grape and sunflower oil: Annie had gathered the buds, then added the oil for velvety smoothness, the way her teacher, Winnie Lathrop, had showed her.

"How much?" the young woman asked as she adjusted a basket on the crook of her arm. It was a big handwoven basket, the kind Annie's aunt had used to hold skeins of yarn. This one, however, held a sleeping infant, snugly wrapped in a thick fleece blanket.

Annie smiled again, the ambiance and the people almost warming her spirit and her mood. "Four dollars. Ten dollars for a three-pack of mixed scents."

The young woman, who looked barely out of her teens, had short, pixie-ish chestnut hair and sad, soulful eyes that were large and dark and looked veiled with sorrow. She set down the scoop, readjusted the basket. Then she picked up a piece of cranberry and aloe oil that was tied with red ribbon. She did not speak again.

Wincing at the snub, Annie wondered if she'd ever learn not to take the actions of strangers personally. "As hard as it is for us to believe, not everyone will love you or your work," her old college pal, her best-friend-forever, Murphy, had once told her after a tepid review of one of Annie's books. "Forget about them. They're pond scum anyway."

"Annie Sutton!"

Startled to hear her name, she quickly spun back to the present. Only a few people knew she now lived on the island; fewer knew who she was or that she had a backlist of best-selling mystery novels. She turned from the ill-mannered young woman and politely asked, "Yes?"

The caller's hair was as silver as the foil bells made by the first-graders that the custodian had hung from the gymnasium rafters. She wore a smart wool coat that fit her nicely—a Calvin Klein or Michael Kors. Her well-manicured fingernails were painted red and matched her lipstick; her purse might have been a Birkin bag—a real one, not a knockoff. She'd most likely arrived that morning on the *Grey Lady*, the special "holiday shopping" ferry that had come from Cape Cod straight into Edgartown for the festive weekend.

"You're Annie Sutton? The writer?"

Annie's cheeks turned the same shade as her beach roses and cream. "Guilty." An often-rehearsed, engaging grin sprang to her mouth. She hoped it was convincing.

The woman's eyes grazed the table. "And now you're a soap maker?"

"Just a hobby."

"Well, goodness, I hope so. When's your next book coming out?"

That, Annie wanted to reply, *is a good question*. But she could hardly say she was reassessing her life, that she had lost her inspiration to write, that she was now on a healing sabbatical. If the news ever went viral, Trish—her patient, yet perfectionist editor—would never forgive her. "Soon," she said, aware that several browsers at her table had shifted their focus from her products onto her, and that other shoppers were drifting her way. In her peripheral vision, she noticed that the young mother remained standing, silent, her head slightly cocked, as if she were listening. "Actually," Annie continued, shaking off silly discomfort, "I'm still working on it. It's the first book in a new mystery series."

"Well, hurry up. Your readers are dying to read it!" The woman put a hand to her mouth and giggled. "Yes, we're *dying* to read your next mystery. That's a pun. Get it?"

Annie nodded and said she did.

The woman picked up nine three-bar sets and plunked them down in front of Annie without checking the scents. "I'll take these. The ladies in my book group will adore them. Will you sign the labels?" She juggled her big purse and pulled out a credit card.

Annie had pierced a small hole for the ribbon on each oval-shaped paper label, which had an illustration of the island, the name of the flowers or herbs she had added, and a frilly typeface that read: *Soaps by Sutton*. There was no blank space for a signature. Embarrassed, she turned over each label and penned: *Happy Holidays! Annie Sutton*. It had not occurred to her that Annie-the-soap-maker would be "outed" at the fair, that she'd be asked to dish out her autograph.

"I love your books, too!" another voice called out. "Will you sign a bar of soap for me?"

"Me, too?"

"Me, three?"

The requests shot out from a line now swollen with reusable bag–toting patrons.

"Do you live on the Vineyard?" another voice hollered.

Annie sat up straighter on the metal folding chair. "I moved here at the end of the summer," she replied, summoning full celebrity persona now, the one she'd cultivated at Murphy's insistence.

"Did you buy a house?"

"No, I'm renting a guesthouse—a cottage—over on Chappaquiddick."

"I love Chappy!" someone else cried. "Whereabouts are you?"

"North Neck Road." She cleared her throat and spoke loudly and pleasantly, as if she were at a book reading.

"Does your new book take place here?"

"Is it an autobiography?"

"A murder mystery?" a different voice cried. "That would be a terrible autobiography!"

The crowd tittered, then another woman asked, "Will you be finished with it soon?"

The chattering rushed at her, the voices drowning out the PA system's "Jingle Bells." Annie remembered a time, not long ago, when she'd prayed to have a few fans of her books. *Be careful what you wish for*, she reminded herself, trying to keep her rising anxiety at bay. She forced a laugh, rang up another sale, signed another autograph, and sadly wished that this day were done. "My first book was the closest I've come to writing about my life. That was hard enough."

"Was that the one where your character was adopted?"

"Yes," she said, then collected more dollars, signed more labels. "It was before I started writing mysteries; I can assure you that no one in my life has been murdered!" Not that she would have minded learning that her ex-husband had met his demise.

The crowd laughed along with her, except for the girl with the sad, soulful eyes, who simply wandered away.

If this were an ordinary off-season Saturday night, Annie might have stopped at the Newes for a bowl of chowder and a glass of chardonnay on her way back to Chappy. But the 275-year-old, brick-walled, fireplaced pub would be packed with the weekend wave of merry, but tired, shoppers—mostly women with their friends, having lots of fun. She would hate being alone.

With the fair finally over, she stepped outside, took a long breath of the crisp night air, and willed herself to feel, if not completely happy, then at least content: there was no good reason not to. Yesterday, Earl Lyons—the white-haired, robust caretaker for the estate where she rented the cottage—had loaded four cartons of her soap into his pickup truck, driven onto the small ferry over from Chappy, and helped set up her table at the fair. He'd said he'd be glad to come back if she needed any leftovers hauled home. But now, carrying a single bag that held only a handful of unsold soaps and a fat envelope of cash and receipts, Annie decided to walk. Maybe the exercise would help her figure out if she'd found a new trade, after all—and help her shed what was beginning to feel like a dose of Christmas blues.

She put on her alpaca mittens ("The warmest you'll ever find," Earl had advised when he'd offered helpful hints about the island), then pulled the matching knit hat over her straight, silver-black hair that barely skimmed her shoulders. Though the night air was calm, the trek to the boat would be chilly, and the crossing downright cold: the miniature ferry that navigated the 527-foot channel from Edgartown to Chappy offered no shelter for passengers, only a three-sided glass cubicle where the captain stood. More like a motorized raft than an actual boat, the one running that winter was called the *On Time II* and only held three vehicles, or an SUV and a UPS truck, or some other meager configuration. Benches that hugged the sides could seat up to twelve walk-ons, though Annie hadn't seen that many people on the boat since tourism predictably had plummeted after Columbus Day weekend. A slightly larger *On Time III* crisscrossed the *II* in season, but was in dry dock now, taking its turn for maintenance, getting prepped for the next onslaught in the spring. There was no sign of an *On Time I*, though surely it once had existed.

Leaving the school grounds, she walked on past the new library to the fire station, where their original cast-iron bell, circa 1832, was displayed on the lawn. Like much of the village, the bell was decorated with hundreds of enchanting holiday lights.

She turned onto Peases Point Way, then crossed the street to avoid the graveyard, something Murphy would have found ridiculous.

Annie sighed. God, how she missed her best friend. She knew that the loss, the grief, were at the core of her glum spirits. Murphy once said: "Men can come and go in life, but best friends last forever." At the time, Murphy's hand had been clutching the stem of a glass of pinot noir, having come over after calling Annie at midnight with a rare need to escape from her "workaholic husband" and her "rambunctious boys." The two of them had smiled, clinked glasses, and taken another sip, neither of them having any idea how suddenly and sharply cancer would snap the "forever" of their bond.

Peases Point Way connected to Cooke Street, where Annie took a right and headed toward the harbor. But at South Summer Street, she changed her mind and turned left instead. She passed the eighteenth-century, gray-shingled building that had once been a poorhouse, but where the *Vineyard Gazette* had been located for over a century now. On the opposite side of the narrow street was the gracious, stately Charlotte Inn, known for its old-world charm. Annie jaywalked across the road, climbed the three front stairs, and stepped into the foyer.

A woman in a sleek black dress stood at the mahogany reception desk.

"I know the terrace isn't open in winter," Annie said, "but may I sit at a table if I only want wine?" She pulled off her hat and shook out her hair.

"Are you alone, or will someone join you?"

"It's just me," Annie replied, keeping her tone carefully neutral. The woman was just doing her job, she reminded herself. *She isn't mocking me for the fact that I'm alone.*

They moved into a candlelit room that was filled with diners who were conversing in intimate tones. Then, as if guided by the universe—or, more likely, Murphy—the hostess led Annie to a small table that had a view of the terrace. Annie thanked her, sat down, and gazed out at the redbrick courtyard. The wrought iron tables were gone, as were the navy umbrellas, which, early last summer, had shaded Annie and Murphy as they'd whiled away a sunny day. They'd been wearing flowered sundresses and open-toed sandals that showed off fresh pedicures. The sunlight had brought out the red in Murphy's shoulder-length hair. As usual, they'd shared plucky conversation about some things that mattered and many more that didn't. It had been a celebratory weekend, a girls' getaway to mark their fiftieth birthdays—Annie's had been in February; Murphy's, in April.

And now, on this December evening, Annie ordered a Chambord Cosmopolitan instead of her usual chardonnay. She and Murphy had sipped Cosmos that afternoon—Murphy claimed that vodka dressed up with Chambord and orange liqueur showed more enthusiasm than wine. "We made it to fifty; we deserve to live a little," she'd declared. A full-time behavioral therapist, the mother of twin boys (the rambunctious ones), and the wife of a well-respected Boston surgeon (the workaholic), Murphy prided herself in maintaining a positive attitude and mostly agreeable relationships with her family, friends, and an assortment of alcoholic beverages.

"If I drink this, I'll get drunk," Annie had said. "You know I can't drink the way you do."

Murphy asked the waitress to bring Annie more cranberry juice on the side. "Now," she said, turning back to her friend, "tell me about your next book."

Annie sighed. "I'm struggling with it. It's about two women who work in a museum where there's a huge art heist. And a dead body or two. I love the concept, but the plot isn't gelling."

"It will. You're not much of a drinker, but you've got the gift of blarney. Whether you're Irish or not."

Of course, Annie had no idea if she was Irish, French, or Tasmanian, though her dad often said she must be Scottish because of her black hair, hazel—not blue—eyes, and "outdoorsy" complexion, whatever that meant. Her mom and dad had adopted Annie when she was six weeks old; she'd never learned her heritage, not even later, when she'd had the chance.

"The truth is," Annie had explained, "my characters were best friends in college and are reunited when one gets a job at the museum where the other one volunteers. They're not us, though. Neither one of us knows squat about art history. And my characters are smarter, richer, and much more beautiful."

"No!" Murphy had screeched. "They can't possibly be smarter or more beautiful! But I do think the story sounds terrific. If you feel stuck, maybe you need a break. Even better, a vacation!" Then she'd grown uncharacteristically pensive. "Let's get serious. What's on your bucket list?"

"Stop! We're only fifty. It's too soon for one of those."

"No it isn't, Annie. Think about it. What would you want to do if you weren't such an infernally sober stick-in-the-mud? If you shake things up a little, you might reignite your creative genius."

Annie had a good laugh at that. Still, she wondered if her friend was right. Murphy, after all, knew her like no one ever had. Not like her parents. Not like her first husband—her first love—Brian. And certainly not like the next one, Mark, the man she'd wasted too much of herself trying to please. "Okay," she said. "If I had a list—which is not to say that I'll make one—the first thing I would do would be to move here. Live on the Vineyard. At least for a while."

"Where you met Brian."

"A thousand years ago. But even then, I knew this place was more than romantic: it's magical." Annie had chosen to set two of her mysteries there. While doing the research, she'd fallen in love with the island again, not only for the breathtaking landscape, but also for its diversity of people, its immense support for art and culture, and its rich, unforgotten history—all of which combined to form an inspiring community.

"Do it," Murphy said in a serious whisper. "Make the move. It's time to open up your life." Annie knew that was Murphy's way of saying it was time to move on, time to shed the baggage of too many losses and disappointments. In hindsight, Annie wondered if her friend had had a premonition.

A month after that wonderful weekend, Murphy was diagnosed with a rare, swift-moving cancer. Carving out time between her family, work, and chemo treatments, she helped Annie find the cottage on Chappy, then, with her bald head cocooned in a gaily striped turban, she went with her the day that Annie moved. She said she needed to see Annie settled, to know that she was safe. That had been on Labor Day. Four weeks later, Murphy died. And Annie's heart had been irrevocably broken.

In some ways, Murphy's death had been Annie's greatest loss; no one was left now to help her navigate the day-to-day waters of life. But thanks to her advice, Annie was following her dream. She was here. On the Vineyard. Surrounded by unending beauty and the gentle rhythm of the place she now called home. And she knew that if she dared to leave, her old pal would come back to haunt her in her spunky, rap-on-the-knuckles kind of way.

Gazing out the window now, from the terrace up to the night sky, Annie saw the Milky Way, its wide, white ribbon shimmering like a twinkling sash. Just then, a comet streaked across, as if delivering a message of faith, hope, and love. With the curve of a soft smile, Annie felt her tears glisten like the stars. "I'm trying, my friend," she whispered to the heavens, up to Murphy, who surely was there.

Chapter 2

Annie woke up in the morning to loud sounds of something thumping on her front porch. Rising too quickly out of bed, she was halted by a fierce wave of dizziness. Outside, the thumping continued. When her balance returned, she slid into fluffy slippers and pulled a quilted robe over her flannel pajamas. The Vineyard in winter was no place or time for a woman—single or not—to dress like a vamp.

Moving into the main living area, she padded across the hardwood floor and the braided rug, then opened the door that led onto the porch. A man in a black hoodie and a red-and-black-checkered woolen shirt lumbered up the steps, his gait weighed down by the armful of wood he was carrying. It was Earl, of course. Judging by the sizable stack already amassed, he'd made several trips from his pickup that morning.

"Happy Sunday!" he said, his blue eyes twinkling in the chilly air. "Hope I didn't wake you!" He pushed on the screen door, stepped up onto the porch, and arranged the logs atop the already substantial pile.

"No problem. But what's the hurry? I thought I had plenty to last me awhile." But even as she said it, a chill ran through her, and she realized it was well past time to stoke the wood-stove for the day.

Earl shook his head. "Forecast says a blizzard's on the way. Looks like a nor'easter. Likely it'll hit Wednesday or Thursday."

Nor'easter, Annie knew, was a word that could make the heartiest New Englander shudder, thanks to the roar of winds, the huge accumulations of heavy snow, and the structural damage it often left in its ravaged wake. "Oh," she replied, "in that case, I'd better make coffee."

He chuckled. "And I'd be grateful for a mug when I'm done here."

She toted some logs into the living room and set them between the antique rocking chair and the woodstove. She opened the small cast-iron door and laid in a new fire with a lattice of a few logs, kindling she'd crafted from empty paper towel tubes stuffed with sheets from last Sunday's *New York Times*, then two more logs—and lit it. Folding her arms, she stood back and assessed her work. For a girl who'd been raised in Boston, she was doing a pretty good job of roughing it.

Once the flames caught, she closed the stove door and got to work making coffee with the old-fashioned tin percolator. "Better learn how to do this stuff now," Earl had suggested when she'd moved in. "When winter hits, the power can go out here for long stretches at a time. Your oven, your microwave, and anything with a plug will be useless. But if you master the woodstove, you'll have a way to heat up stew and make a decent cup of coffee. And stay warm."

She'd been an eager student.

With the coffee underway, she quickly showered and made herself *presentable*—a word borrowed from her mother, to whom those things had been important—by dressing in clean jeans, a long-sleeved white tee, and her favorite pink cardigan. She combed her wet hair behind her ears and marveled at how, at this midlife age, in this magical place, not using a blow dryer was perfectly acceptable. It also reinforced her determination to live a healthier, quieter life, no longer on the edge of other people's expectations.

Back in the kitchen, she checked the time: ten o'clock, the usual hour when Earl found a reason to drift by the cottage in search of a mid-morning snack, so he was right on schedule.

Setting cinnamon rolls on a plate, she inhaled the aroma of the coffee perking. The fire warmed the room from the over-stuffed sofa to the small oak table, from the corner desk to the wall of bookcases Annie had packed with her favorite volumes. The desk and bookcases were the only new items she'd bought for the furnished cottage: she'd sold most of her belongings before moving. *Except the bed*, she thought now, as she set out a couple of napkins. She'd had Earl hoist the owner's bed into the storage space over the garage; hers was high and sturdy, with a luxurious, deep mattress that guaranteed a good night's sleep. And held a few nice memories from her youthful days with Brian.

Earl cracked open the door. "I smell java."

"Come on in. Cinnamon rolls to go with it."

His stocky, still-muscled body worked its way through the door as he shed his wool shirt and peeled back the hood of his sweatshirt. Like most islanders, Earl dressed in layers, always prepared for anything from a sunny day to blustery, gale-force winds. Annie would bet that behind the seat of his pickup, he kept a yellow slicker and an extra pair of socks.

He sat down at the table on one of the pair of red corduroy–cushioned chairs. Though his visits were typically brief, Annie was grateful for his company, and for his help in teaching her about the Vineyard, its people, and its ways. A native islander, he knew most people there and how to get things done. When Annie had mentioned she wanted to learn how to make soap, he'd kindly driven her up island and introduced her to Winnie.

He eyed the pastry now. "Got a full cord on the porch now. That ought to get you through the first good chunk of winter."

Annie nodded. "Thanks." She had no idea how long "a chunk" was to Earl, but trusted that he knew what he was doing.

"And you can always call if you need more."

"Which won't do me a whole lot of good, seeing as how you hardly ever answer your cell phone."

"I'm trying to get better at that. Honest." He helped himself to a roll, took a hefty bite, chewed slowly, then smiled and nodded as if declaring his approval.

She was about to mention that though she knew his cell number, she also knew that many houses on Chappy were secluded, and she had no idea how or where to find him if the cell tower ever went down.

But before she got the words out, Earl asked, "So, how was the fair? I heard the *Grey Lady* has made all its trips so far, which must have been good for yesterday's business." Some people hadn't been convinced the ferry would make it safely into the harbor: a boat big enough to hold a couple of hundred folks hadn't docked in Edgartown for over half a century. The naysayers had claimed the inlet was too small, the water was too choppy off season, the plan was far too risky. But the folks on the Board of Trade had overruled them after a successful test run last March. The same folks who must now be preening with delight.

Annie set down two steamy mugs and sat opposite him. "The fair was amazing. I never dreamed I'd do so well. I came home with only five bars and three scoops."

He chuckled again, the same way Annie's dad had often chuckled. Though Earl was half a foot shorter and wider than her dad, his hardworking yet easy demeanor often reminded her of him. "Now that it's getting colder, I've been thinking that if you want to make more, I could put a propane stove in the workshop. I don't think Roger would mind."

Roger was Roger Flanagan, Annie's landlord. He owned the three-acre waterfront property that sprawled up a wide, velvet lawn, merged into a maze of walking trails that meandered through tangles of scrub oaks and pines, and met up with North Neck Road, the bumpy dirt lane now serving as Annie's legal address. The showpiece of the property was a posh seasonal home that faced the harbor. The guest cottage was halfway up the hill; a four-car garage with an adjoining workshop, where Annie made her soaps, blocked her view of the water. But from her front window she could see the flagpole-high nesting platform for ospreys that her landlord had installed; Earl had said it was a welcome respite for the once-endangered birds, and would give her a unique view in the spring. "A far cry from Boston," he'd added.

She smiled now and wrapped her cardigan closely against her, not because she was cold, but because sometimes she wanted to hold in the warmth she felt whenever her mood momentarily lifted, as it did when she reflected on how lucky she was that, in spite of her losses, she really, truly did live there now. She really, truly had this new life. She'd become so accustomed to having to overcome obstacles, Annie sometimes worried that all she had now, including her book-writing career, was absolutely too good to be true. Murphy would have set her straight about that.

"As much as I love making soap," she said to Earl now, "I have to get back to work on my manuscript. Apparently I have a few fans, not to mention a publisher, who expect me to be productive."

He scratched the scruffy whiskers on his chin. "Well, at least if you have the heater, you'll know you have something to do if you're stuck inside and get tired of writing. We don't often have wicked winters out here, but we're overdue. Claire thinks we're in for a doozy." Claire was his wife, whom Annie still hadn't met. She'd once caught a glimpse of their son, John, on the *On Time* ferry; he was an Edgartown police officer who, according to Earl, often "hopped over" the channel to check up on his parents, as if they needed checking up on: they were, after all, "only seventy-four." He'd also told her that John was divorced with two daughters who lived with their mother off island in Plymouth, and who visited on occasion, though not often enough.

"Being 'stuck inside' suits me just fine," Annie said. "Writers need lots of solitude. It's one of the reasons I jumped at the chance to live on Chappy. It's quiet and remote here."

He sipped his coffee, his heavy, white eyebrows weaving together, forming a tapestry of the wisdom of his years. "Solitude can be good, Annie; isolation, not so much. And out here, well, we can have challenges."

She took a bite of a cinnamon roll, a little worried by Earl's words. She knew there was no store on Chappy in winter, no gas station, nothing in the way of services except the volunteer fire department and a couple of EMTs; she had no idea what other challenges a Vineyard winter might entail: she only hoped her isolated writer's life would not turn into Stephen King's novel *The Shining*, or that those creepy twins would not pop up in her secluded place.

Dabbing at a few bits of cinnamon that had fallen onto her napkin, Annie hoped that when she'd rented the place, she hadn't let her romantic notions overrule plain common sense.

Monday morning, armed with a list of nor'easter essentials that she'd made after Earl had left the day before, Annie drove her six-year-old Lexus onto the *On Time* and ferried over to Edgartown. Before she'd left the city, she'd considered trading her car for something more island-appropriate, but she'd run out of time. With the impending weather, she hoped she wouldn't regret it: her car did not have all-wheel drive.

Her first stop was the supermarket for fresh and canned

food, ingredients to make and bake an abundance of goodies, and three cases of water. Then she went to Granite—Edgartown's anything-anyone-could-ever-possibly-need-except-food store—where she purchased an LED lantern, and a snow shovel and road salt in case Earl couldn't reach her.

Outside in the parking lot, members of the high school hockey team were selling Christmas trees. She knew that a small one would fit perfectly in the living room in front of a window. A month earlier, submerged deeply in grief, she'd decided not to acknowledge the holidays at all. But when Annie had shown Winnie her first completed soaps, Winnie had said they were quite good and would be welcome at the fair. Annie had been reminded of her dad's unwavering habit of starting each day with a smile—*No matter what*, he'd say. She'd known that if she gave into her sorrow, she'd spend Christmas Day in tears, so she'd pasted on a smile and signed up for the fair. And now, the spruce beckoned her, too.

She dragged it to the makeshift checkout booth and hoped that she remembered where she'd packed her ornaments. Nostalgia aside, it might be fun to decorate the tree if she did get stranded in her home.

Now, with the spruce anchored to the roof of her car, Annie went back into Granite and bought a tree stand. Then she drove to the library and checked out a few bestsellers. After that she swung by the liquor store for wine in case it turned into the doozy of a winter that Claire Lyons portended.

Later, Annie would worry about gifts, not that she'd be giving many: Winnie and Earl . . . that was it. She'd already mailed alpaca socks to Murphy's husband and checks to Murphy's boys, because they were nearly twenty-two, and she no longer knew the things they liked. As she pulled up behind the short line for the *On Time*, Annie resisted the impulse to feel sad about her small gift-giving list; she would not, could not, allow that. For the next few days, she would focus solely on staying positive and being productive, no matter what Mother Nature had in store.

When she finally arrived home, she lugged the tree inside and set it in the stand. Then, instead of decorating it or cooking or writing, she made a pot of tea, curled up by the woodstove, and dove into one of the library books, her favorite guilty pleasure. It was well past midnight before she went to bed.

Tuesday morning—ahead of the meteorologists' predictions—it started to snow. It was a light, fluffy "dusting," a "teaser of things to come," the Boston television meteorologist commented with a sly look.

The "things to come" came quickly, with heavy snow and incessant, howling winds. Annie stayed burrowed, reading, for that whole first day and half the next. By Wednesday afternoon, after having consumed nearly two of the library books and never stepping out of her pajamas, the charm of the nor'easter had abated, and she began to feel edgy. Taking a shower helped. So did tying back her hair, donning clean sweats and fuzzy slippers, and spending the rest of the day cooking and baking as if she had a family of ten. But the aromas of chicken soup on the stove and beef stew simmering in the Crock-Pot, combined with brownies in the oven, followed by more cinnamon rolls, soothed her like a warm down quilt. They also provided a pleasant diversion from the fact that the cottage, too, was shivering.

Somehow, she made it to bedtime. She crawled under the covers with just one thought: *Tomorrow I will write. Tomorrow, whether or not it's still snowing, I will stop procrastinating, relax, and get back to work.*

Soon, she fell asleep.

Until, during the night, when she was awakened by a horrific bang.

Her eyelids popped open.

Her arms, her legs, her whole body stiffened.

Her heart started to pound.

The wind, she told herself. The wind must have loosened some shingles. Or slapped the screen door on the porch.

Other sounds followed: footsteps.

Footsteps?

Really, Annie?

But, yes, she thought as she drew the comforter up to her neck, she was fairly certain the sounds were footsteps, crunching through snow.

Her eyes scanned the darkness in the bedroom. She had no idea what time it was. Two, three, four o'clock? She had no clue what to do. So she waited. And listened. To . . . nothing. Only the infernal wind as it rattled the scrub oaks and pines.

Several moments passed. Then several more. And Annie knew she would not sleep again until she had investigated.

Sucking in a shaky breath, she emerged with caution from her bed. She slid into her slippers. Pulled on her robe. Lit a small candle so as not to turn on the lights and startle . . . whatever.

Whomever.

She tiptoed from the bedroom.

Panning the flickering light around the living room, she saw only darkness. But then . . . an unfamiliar shadow. Standing in front of her. She stopped abruptly, too scared to scream. Her heart threatened to burst out of her chest.

But then an aroma wafted toward her. Not one of chicken soup, beef stew, or luscious baked goods. The scent was spruce; the shadow was the tree, standing in front of the window that looked out onto the porch.

Quietly, she groaned.

Once she regained her bearings, she sneaked toward the kitchen area, still not knowing what the sound had been. It was cool in the room, but not freezing: a low fire still glowed in the woodstove.

Then, more noise. That time, it was not a bang. It wasn't footsteps. It was a muted sound, almost like a whimper. Maybe a raccoon was trapped on the porch. Or a skunk. The Vineyard was known for those. *Oh, great,* she thought and warded off full-blown panic.

But no matter what it was, Annie needed to know.

She crept to the door and tried to peer through a small pane, but a light layer of frost clouded the glass.

The soft cry came again.

Turning the flimsy lock, she sucked in her breath and slowly opened the door. A crack at first. An inch. Then two. She couldn't imagine what in God's name had prompted her to do that. Even Murphy would have thought that she was nuts.

Then, there it was. On the floor, right outside the door. Not a raccoon or a skunk, but a basket. A big handwoven basket, the kind her aunt had used to hold skeins of yarn. A red bow was tied around the handle. And inside was a baby, swaddled in white fleece.

Chapter 3

Annie stood rock-still and stared down at the basket. A baby? *Really?*

She reached back and flipped on the light switch; the radiance confirmed what she had thought.

"Well," she said. "Well." She stepped around the basket and peered out the screened windows. Beyond patches of ice stuck between the mesh, she could see the wind still blowing and snow swirling everywhere. But on the ground she also saw the indentations of footprints—not man-sized ones like Earl's boots would have made, but smaller. Going in both directions. She couldn't see too far; the porch light only revealed about twenty feet. The footprints then disappeared into the darkness.

The baby whimpered again. Annie turned back, which was when she noticed a brown paper shopping bag next to the basket. What was more captivating, though, were the eyes that looked up at her. They were the same large, sad, and soulful eyes as those of the young woman at the holiday fair. The same eyes, the same basket—though the red bow had been added.

"Well," Annie repeated. "Hello, you. What are you doing here? And where in God's name is your mommy?"

The baby started to cry.

"Damn," Annie said. She walked back to the screen door and stared out, as if something might have changed in the last fifteen seconds. But all she could see was snow.

The baby cried harder. Annie walked over, bent down, and studied its little face, its chubby cheeks nearly as red as the bow. She touched one lightly; it was as bone cold as the night. She quickly picked up the basket. "Well," she said again, "I have no idea who you are or where your mommy has gone, but we need to get you inside where it's warm."

Back in the living room, she turned on the lights, set the basket by the woodstove, and crouched next to it. Cupping her hands under the fleece, she lifted the baby and slid off its tiny hoodie. Beneath it was a thick crown of silky, dark hair, the same shade as the sad eyes. "Shhh," Annie whispered as she pulled the baby close and gently rubbed its back. "Shhh. Everything will be fine."

Of course, she had no idea if that was true. Just as she had no idea what to do with a baby. She'd never had one, never even had been around them, except for Murphy's twins, who Murphy had taken care of as easily as if they'd come with a tutorial.

The only thing now about which Annie was fairly sure was that this baby was cold and terribly upset. She didn't think it was a newborn: it seemed too big and too alert. So apparently the mother had not just given birth, wrapped the baby up, laid it in her version of a manger, and mistaken Annie's cottage for a stable.

With the bundle in her arms, Annie paced, her eyes fixed on the window, watching for the mother to return. Whoever she was, maybe her power had gone out or she'd run out of wood. Maybe she'd dropped off the baby, then raced back to her place for extra blankets before she would return and beg Annie to let them stay the remainder of the night. Or . . . maybe she'd needed an appendectomy and had called the *On Time* captain for emergency transport and knew it would be cumbersome to bring the baby with her.

Even with Annie's vivid imagination, neither scenario made a whole lot of sense.

As she paced, the baby's crying grew quieter, more pitiful. "You poor, sweet thing," she said. She couldn't say, "You poor, sweet girl," or "You poor, sweet boy," because she had no idea what gender it was.

Touching the baby's soft cheek again, trying to convince herself it was getting warmer, Annie straightened the blanket around the little pink chin that had a perfect dimple deeply sculpted in the center. As she fussed with the fleece, a piece of paper slid from between the folds: it was a receipt from Stop & Shop, one of only a few chain stores allowed on the island. She turned it over—a handwritten note was scrawled on the back. But Annie couldn't make out the words without her glasses. "Damn," she said again.

The library book that she'd been reading was on the end table next to the rocking chair; her glasses sat on top. Fearful she'd drop the baby if she let go with one hand, she hung on tightly, sidled to the chair, and gingerly sat. She put on her glasses and, while the baby still cried in her arms, she studied the note. The handwriting was clear, the intent concise:

Her name is Bella, after my grandmother. Please take care of her for a couple of days, because I can't. I left you some supplies.

That was all. No signature. No phone number. No exact timetable as to when she would return. No other information, except Annie now knew the baby's name—Bella—and that she was a girl.

With frustration rising, Annie turned the receipt over again; there was only the imprint from the store register: Baby formula. Diapers. A red bow. The customer had paid with cash.

Then she had a disturbing thought. "Did you add the bow to make her look like a Christmas gift?" she asked the absent mother. "As if your baby was the equivalent of a scented candle or one of my soaps?"

Leaning back in the chair, she tried to think clearly. Slowly, she started to rock. And baby Bella stopped crying. Annie looked into the shining black eyes again. "My God," she whispered. "Is that really what your mommy wants you to be? A Christmas gift for a couple of days? Like a weekend in the Bahamas?"

Bella gurgled. She gazed squarely at Annie, her small mouth revealing a tiny, almost tentative smile.

Annie melted. "Well, you can't stay here. I don't have a spare bedroom."

Bella gurgled again. Annie lifted her to her shoulder and rubbed her back again. "Bella, Bella. Whatever will we do with you?" She would start, of course, by calling Earl. If he couldn't help, at least he could call his son at the police station. John would take care of the problem, because it was his job to preserve and protect, or however that slogan went. All Annie needed was to get to her phone, which was on the nightstand in the bedroom, plugged in, and charging. But first, she had to figure out how to stand up from a moving rocker while holding a small baby.

With her right elbow resting on the arm of the chair, she leaned on it and tried to boost herself up. That didn't work.

She leaned to the left; that didn't work either.

Bella let out a whimper that sounded one breath short of a full-fledged cry.

Leaning back a little, Annie slid down a little and stretched out her right foot, grateful she had long legs. Flattening her instep, she hooked the handle of the basket and managed to drag it toward her, then gingerly set the baby back inside. She stood and went into the bedroom. And the crying began again.

Annie cringed. She picked up her phone: the time on the screen read 3:51. Should she call Earl now, or wait until daybreak? Of course, day never really "broke" during a nor'easter, especially on Chappaquiddick, where there were no streetlights to brighten the gray air. No car headlights. No nothing. Just the infernal isolation that only days ago Annie had craved. She gazed at her phone as if it would tell her what to do. She decided that, her insecurities aside, it was almost four in the morning, far too early to phone anyone. But what would she do with a baby until the hour was "reasonable" for her to summon help?

Then she remembered the paper bag out on the porch. It must hold the "supplies" the mother had mentioned.

Slipping her phone into the pocket of her robe, Annie walked past the screaming infant and retrieved the bag.

"Okay," she said above the noise when she returned and squatted beside the basket again. "Let's see what Mommy left for you."

Inside were two twelve-packs of diapers, which seemed to Annie like a lot, but who knew? She found a couple of things she knew were called "onesies," a pink pacifier, a box of something called "rice cereal," a plastic baby bottle, and a few cans of formula clearly marked for ages three to six months. At least she now knew Bella's age, or at least her age range. The formula, however, felt frozen.

But when was Annie supposed to feed the baby, how often, and how much? What was the right way to put on a diaper?

How often should the baby sleep, and when should she wake her up? Why hadn't the mother left some instructions? Then Annie remembered one time when she and Murphy were on the phone and Murphy said she had to hang up because it was time to wake the babies from their nap.

How had she known? Had that been in the tutorial as well?

Closing her eyes, Annie inhaled and exhaled slowly. The reality was she had no business trying to take care of a small baby. No business whatsoever. No matter how early the hour, this definitely constituted an emergency. And she needed help.

She looked back at her phone and scrolled through her list of contacts for Earl's information. At least he and his wife had had a child; though their son was somewhere in his forties, they'd know how to take care of a baby far better than she did. She touched Earl's number and held the phone up to her ear. It took a few seconds to register that nothing happened. There was no indication of ringing on the other end. No beeps, no chirps, no nothing. Though the power was still on, the cell tower must have been knocked out. Blown over. Somehow gone down in the wind.

"Okay," Annie said again. "Okay." She took another of the deep yoga breaths she'd learned at a class she'd attended a decade ago when her life had imploded. "Relax. All you need is to go onto the Internet and find a video on how to take care of a three-to-six-month-old baby. For God's sake, there must be a million on YouTube."

She went to her desk and booted up her laptop. But the Internet, like the cell service, was down. Which meant that not only were Annie and Bella alone, but Annie would have to figure out a way to fend for them both. Unless the baby's mother came back with the blankets Annie had dreamed up or returned from the emergency appendectomy.

"Fat chance," she muttered into the darkness, then returned to the rocker and plunked back down.

A short time later, the scent in the room clued Annie in on the reason Bella was crying. If she could only call Murphy, she could get a quick lesson in changing a diaper. "Some friend you turned out to be!" she cried up at the ceiling, as if Murphy's ghost were hovering in the beams. Then Annie remembered hearing her friend once say that babies cried when they were hungry, tired, or in need of a change. "Or bored," Murphy had added. "That's the hardest kind of crying to make go away."

Right then, however, while the "why" behind the crying was quite clear, the next step would not be simple for Annie. The truth was, unlike most reasonably well-adjusted, fifty-year-old adults on the planet, she'd never changed a diaper. So perhaps it was better that no one was there to watch.

She looked over at the baby, who didn't look as if she'd be the least bit helpful.

So, without Earl, Murphy, or the Internet, Annie would have to be in charge. She would need to tackle this the way she wrote a book: one word, one sentence, one chapter, at a time. *Baby steps*, she thought, then stifled a laugh at her perfect choice of words.

The first question was: *Where to do this?* Standing again, she leaned over and scrutinized the basket. Even if she were able to maneuver around the handle, she could tell that it was neither big enough nor flat enough for the baby to lie comfortably while Annie attempted the monumental task. And the bow would be in the way. But she couldn't very well set Bella on the kitchen table—that didn't seem either healthy or safe. Which left the cold, hard floor. Or Annie's coveted bed.

Looking back at Bella, Annie said, "Don't worry. I'll figure this out. You don't know me, but I'm not entirely stupid. Top five percent of my high school class. Three-point-seven-nine college GPA. Author of five published novels, the last two of which reached the bestseller list. Oh, and I used to teach third grade, but I think most of my students were potty trained."

The baby responded by crying. Louder. Obviously, she was not impressed.

Then Annie remembered the pacifier. Quickly retrieving it from the bag, she stuck it into Bella's mouth. The baby looked at her a moment, sucked on the plastic apparatus, and promptly spit it out.

"Alright, then," Annie moaned with unmasked exasperation. "I get it. We'll get you changed. Then get you fed, in case you want that, too. Easy-peasy, right?"

Accompanied by a symphony of cries, she went into the bathroom and found a clean towel and facecloth. She dampened the cloth with warm water, then snatched another towel—just in case. Using pillows as borders and two layers of towels, she set up a makeshift changing table area on her bed. When she went back into the living room, she picked up the baby and pulled a clean diaper from one of the packs. Then she walked into the bedroom, unwrapped the fleece, and lay Bella down.

"Waaah," the baby squealed.

Not to be dissuaded, Annie held the new diaper between her teeth, used one hand to undo the old one, the other to clean Bella with the damp facecloth, then her third hand to . . . *Right,* she thought. *Even real mothers only have two hands.* But somehow, fueled by perseverance, she managed to get Bella relatively back together.

The crying stopped for all of one minute.

"Food," Annie said. She carried her back to the kitchen, peeled open a can of formula, unscrewed the plastic bottle with her teeth, rinsed off the nipple and—*Damn,* she thought, *this needs to be heated.*

She deposited Bella back in the basket. She located a small saucepan and added water. Then she spooned the frozen formula into the bottle, set the bottle in the pan of water, then put the whole *shebang*—one of her dad's favorite terms—on a burner on the woodstove, hoping she was doing the right thing. After a few more minutes of hearing the endless crying, she tested the temperature of the formula, took another yoga breath, picked up her charge again, and settled into the rocking chair, where the baby quickly nestled in Annie's arms and eagerly ate her breakfast. Or lunch. Whatever it was.

Bella only took half the liquid, then burped—twice. What seemed like only seconds later, her bottom moving in tiny wriggles, she emitted a distressful wail, and Annie quickly realized that another diaper change was needed. That time, she tackled the chore without hesitation, then they went back to the rocker, where Bella—apparently lulled by the slow rocking, the full tummy, and the clean diaper—fell sound asleep on Annie's chest.

Silence.

At last.

Less than an hour had passed since Annie had opened the door and found the unexpected gift, yet she felt as if she'd run a marathon. She leaned back, closed her eyes, and savored the warmth of Bella's little body resting against her, the little heart beating a gentle thump-thump. The silence felt blessed, as if the drama had been worth the wait.

Annie had wanted to have children. But her first husband, Brian, had been killed in an accident when he was only twenty-nine and a drunk driver slammed into him. Both Annie and Brian had been elementary school teachers, devoted to kids, helping them learn, watching them flourish, the little people growing into distinct individuals. She and Brian would have had several wonderful children, born out of love and joy. That had been their plan.

As for her second husband, Mark, well, he had seemed like a good idea at the time.

Mark had come in a great-looking package that Murphy had warned her to be wary of. But by then both of Annie's parents had died, too, and she wanted more in her life than teaching, more in her life than emotional pain. And heavy-duty loss. She wanted to have fun, which Mark was terrific at providing.

But whenever she brought up the subject of kids, he said, "Not yet, hon, okay? I want to feel financially secure before we bring kids into this crazy world."

Like everything else he'd said, she'd believed him, silly her.

Mark was in real estate, buying and selling commercial properties, garnering deals all over the world. They lived in a big, beautiful apartment on the affluent Brookline-Boston city line—the kind of address where she'd never thought that she would live. Annie was, after all, a middle class kid who'd gone to a state college and had reached her childhood dream of teaching eight- and nine-year-olds.

And though she'd never craved costly clothes, she soon amassed an enviable wardrobe. Mark bought her a "luxury" car, and, at his suggestion, she hired a twice-a-week cleaning woman. Annie had regular mani-pedis and needless massages and often accompanied her husband to client dinners, where she enjoyed the gourmet food and the imported wine and laughed at anecdotes she tried to tell herself were amusing. A few times, during school vacations, she traveled with him and brought back items to show her students: a silk shawl from Thailand, a Carnival costume from Brazil; French Santon fig-urines from Provence.

Caught up in the whirlwind of busy, busy days and nights, Annie had been tricked into thinking her marriage was solid. She "ran" the household because she was home more often than Mark; he handled their finances because he made lots of money and was "so good" with it.

But, as Murphy often reminded her, *tempus fugit*. Time flies.

Before Annie realized the impact of that warning, she had turned forty, her chances for children rapidly diminishing. Then, one afternoon, Mark called from his office.

"I'll be tied up tonight, babe. Probably late."

For some reason that Murphy later referred to as *primal instinct*, when Annie hung up that day, she had a sudden vision of thousands of red flags, the warnings she'd been denying that something in their world was—had been from the beginning— terribly wrong for her. She clutched her stomach, skipped dinner, and went to bed at seven thirty.

Her primal instinct had been right. Mark did not come home that night. Or any night thereafter. By the time Annie filed a missing persons report, he was gone. Very gone. The only thing the police learned was that he'd left a tsunami of debt—all of which he had put in Annie's name. That's when she knew it was time to stop crying and find a solution. She was too embarrassed, and had too much pride, to file bankruptcy.

After years of hard work and determination, she'd finally paid off the debt with the advance from her last book. Through it all, she'd forged ahead, and, most importantly, she'd kept smiling. As her dad had often said, "It's hard to cry when you wear a smile."

Bu now, with this baby, this warm, tiny stranger resting against her, Annie felt consumed by loss. She rocked back and forth, wondering how she could have lost something she'd never been allowed to have: a child like this, one who needed her not just for sustenance and care, but for love and nurture, if only for a couple of days.

With gentle tears and a tender aching in her heart, Annie pulled Bella a little closer and bent her head to hers. After a while, she closed her eyes and, like Bella, she fell asleep.

Chapter 4

Francine ate her last protein bar. She'd tried to hold off a while longer, but she couldn't help herself. She was hungry. Starved. Who knew she'd get caught in a blizzard? Who knew it would snow so damn long?

Who knew anything anymore?

Like what she should do next.

Like where she should go.

Like why she was still there.

She shivered. From the upstairs window, she could see . . . nothing. Except swirling, twirling white stuff blinding her view.

She huddled back under two white comforters that probably cost more than she'd made in a month waiting tables at the Sunrise Café. She didn't care that they smelled musty. It was a smell she'd grown used to, having spent so much time on the Cape.

Sooner or later, she'd need more food. And she'd have to figure out her next move. She wondered how long she could survive without eating again. Or drinking. She hadn't planned it this way. But the storm had started too soon. And she'd been trapped on Chappaquiddick because she'd assumed the ferry had shut down.

If she couldn't find something else to eat, starving to death might be a solution. Out here, no one would find her until summer, when whoever owned the house she'd broken into and where she was camped out would arrive for the season in their Range Rovers and BMWs, with their kids and their big dogs and their attitudes. The "attitude of entitlement," they called it at the Sunrise. She supposed it was worse on the Vineyard because of all the gigantic houses she'd seen from the water. Like the one where she was hiding now.

Back home, her father hadn't been very good at feeling entitled. He had never reached his full potential, she'd heard her grandfather shout at him before the old man died, though not before he'd cut them all out of his will: her father, her mother, and her.

Francine had always known she'd never been entitled. The fact that she now had only eighteen dollars left to her name was proof positive of that.

At least she knew Bella was safe now. And better off without her.

Hours later, Annie awoke with a kink in her arm, a crimp in her back, and an unfamiliar stirring on her chest. It took a moment for her to realize it was . . . *Bella.* The cuddly baby who had shown up in the night.

"Who are you?" Annie whispered. "And how did you wind up in my lap?"

She thought about the young woman—the girl—from the fair. "How much?" That was all Annie had heard her say. Had she wanted to buy Annie's soap to give as a Christmas gift? Except for the baby, she'd been alone. No girlfriend, no boyfriend, no one who might have been her mother. Or sister. Or grand-mother named Bella, which might mean something. Or noth-ing. There was only the note and its pleading words:

Please take care of her for a couple of days . . .

But how long was *a few days*? And where was the rest of the baby's family? Did she only have her mother? Her name might be a lead, but Annie doubted if she Googled BELLA, MARTHA'S VINEYARD there would be many hits.

In a feeble attempt to put those concerns aside, Annie

stood up, miraculously not dropping the baby. She stoked the fire, heated a bottle, and fed and changed Bella, almost, she thought, with the ease of a true new mother.

"Applause, please!" she instructed Murphy, who she hoped was still hiding up in the ceiling.

When Murphy did not cooperate, Annie lifted tiny Bella's hands and clapped them together, while oohing and aahing the way adults often did that made them look ridiculous but that babies seemed to relish.

The rest of the day passed in a blur. Bella slept often, for which Annie was grateful, though she would not have minded spending more time holding her. But Annie was productive: She dusted the cottage, which did not need dusting. She ironed a few shirts, which did not need ironing. She tried to read, but could not get engaged. She did not attempt to write.

Between tasks, she checked the snow accumulation (a lot, and still not winding down), the wind velocity (still high), and the possibility that phone service had returned (it had not). But, whether she liked it or not, her worries overrode her concentration. Would the formula outlast the storm? Would the diapers? And—worst of all—what if the mother had no real intention of returning?

Beneath those practical questions, though, one greater conundrum lurked: *Why Annie?*

But no matter what the questions, or the answers, Annie knew that Bella did not belong with her. Bella was a living, breathing little baby, not a stray cat to whom Annie should give shelter. When the storm was over, if the young mother didn't show up first, Annie would tell Earl the story, and he would help bring Bella to the police.

When the snowy light of day slipped into the darkness of late afternoon, Annie heated stew for dinner and some cereal for the baby, who had already gone through half of the formula. She tried not to dwell on the sizable dent that had been made in the pack of diapers. Instead, she prayed that they'd sleep through the night and be greeted by a sunny morning and the missing mother standing on the porch. It would be a happier ending than seeing Earl standing there.

Bedtime arrived with no sign of the storm abating or of help arriving, so Annie carried the basket into the bedroom. She feared the floor might get too cold in the night if she set the basket there, but with its lovely curved base, an elevated spot no doubt would be dangerous. Then she focused on the nightstand. Pulling open the bottom drawer to provide support, she emptied the middle one, lined it with the fleece blanket, and snuggled Bella inside. Perfect. Annie put on her pajamas, went to bed, turned off the lamp, and closed her eyes.

And the baby started to cry.

Annie sighed. "You win. Let's read."

A copy of every novel she'd written sat beside her bed for nights when sleep refused to come. Turning onto her side, she reached over and grabbed one—her first: *You Let Me Go.*

"Well, this is appropriate," she said with a laugh. "In a dark-humor kind of way."

Bella responded with a tiny wail.

Opening the book, Annie turned to the prologue. It had been a long time since she'd read what truly was the closest she had come to an autobiography. She ran a finger over the words, remembering how she'd struggled to get started, to keep it simple yet engaging. And realistic at its core.

She looked over at Bella again: the cries had ceased, and the baby stared at Annie, as if she were poised to listen, eager to hear a sliver of what her future might hold if her mother went back on her word.

Annie cleared her throat, returned to her book, and read:

I was the only kid in my class who was adopted. When I was in fourth grade, I thought that was cool. I hadn't yet considered that my real parents hadn't wanted me. Then, one day on the playground, Bobby Briggs told me they hadn't.

She read the first chapter, then moved on to the second. It was fiction—well, some of it. Bobby Briggs had been real, but she'd changed his name. And though time had tempered the trauma of that day on the playground, her doubts about herself and her feelings of *but-what-if-she-had-kept-me* had taken longer to fade. But they had. Writing the book had helped purge her of the rest of those emotions, bringing closure and, more importantly, forgiveness.

With those comforting thoughts, and Bella quiet again— her eyes closed, her breathing steady and calm—Annie put the book back on the nightstand. Then she turned off the light and slid under the comforter. But it was hours before she fell asleep.

By morning, the snow had finally stopped; sunlight filled the cottage with welcoming warmth. The only thing missing from Annie's wish list was Bella's mother standing on the porch.

Annie had been up for a while. She'd already changed and fed the baby, who was back in the basket on the floor by the Christmas tree. Coffee perked on the woodstove; Earl would arrive momentarily to plow the driveway. She'd heaped cinnamon rolls onto a plate so he could enjoy one or two while she told him a story he might not believe. After that she would wrap up little Bella, and they'd go off to the police station with Earl. Then she would get back to her baby-free life.

She was peering out the window, watching for Earl, when Bella giggled. Annie turned and saw that the baby was laughing and smiling, wiggling her little arms up toward the unadorned branches of the tree. *After she's gone I'll have time to decorate,* Annie thought. It was too bad Bella wouldn't be there to see the results.

"You're such a sweet little girl," Annie said. "I'm sure that the nice police officers will take good care of you, and your mommy will be back soon. And hopefully you won't have to put up with a bully when you reach fourth grade."

Then, in an instant, like the day that Mark had called to say he'd be home late, a sick premonition washed over Annie, the taunting words of Bobby Briggs jumping into her mind:

"If you weren't so ugly and skinny and stupid," Bobby said, *"your real mother would have kept you."*

The memories rushed back of the pain that had gripped her heart and head and stomach and had come all at once, causing her to throw up right there in front of all the other kids.

Though nearly forty years had passed, Annie once again felt those same sensations. As her gaze drifted down to Bella, she could almost hear the taunts of the other kids on the playground, she could almost see their fingers pointing at her, she could almost hear their high-pitched laughs. Pressing a hand against her throat now, Annie tried to breathe, her stomach rumbling and tumbling the way that it had on that awful day.

Her mother hadn't wanted her.

Despite Annie's hard work to purge and to forgive, that was a truth that would not go away.

Just then Earl's pickup crunched down the driveway, its narrow plow blade slicing into the snow, pushing it to one side. That's when Annie knew she could not tell him about Bella. If he took the baby to his son, John, the *police officer*, John would put Bella in protective custody, because what kind of mother would leave her baby with a total stranger, let alone during a nor'easter? Bella had been cold out on the porch. What if she'd died of hypothermia before Annie had found her?

Annie began to hyperventilate.

Once John had the baby, he no doubt would not wait the "couple of days" for the mother to come back on her own. He'd set Bella up in foster care, and she'd be in the dreadful "system." When Annie had been a teacher, she'd seen kids that had happened to. Some were fine, but others . . .

And though Bella's mother had been irresponsible, would she be given any credit for being too young to know better?

The predictable answer was: *No*.

Nor would there be any assurance that Bella would not be left to wonder if her mother had given her up because she was ugly. Or skinny. Or stupid.

Watching Earl's plow clear away the remnants of the storm, Annie knew she wasn't ready to give up on Bella's mother either. If Annie could find her first, maybe she could reunite her with the baby before any real damage was done.

When the pickup churned to a stop at the stairs that led onto the porch, Annie pushed open the door, stepped outside, and waved.

Earl rolled down the window and said, "Morning!"

She took a deep breath, the crush of her memories slowly easing. "Morning, yourself! Nice day, isn't it?"

"Peachy. You got coffee on?"

Annie stood on one foot, then the other, and prayed Bella wouldn't let out a scream. "Actually, I'm sorry, but I ran out. And I'm so busy working, I haven't bothered to worry about it."

"Good thing you charged up your computer last night."

"What?"

"Your computer. I said it was a good thing you charged it up last night. Power's out. Or haven't you noticed? Went out at six this morning."

She shook her head. "No. I was still asleep. The woodstove kept us cozy through the night." She flinched right after she said *us*. Earl looked at her oddly, but didn't ask if she was alone. Maybe he thought that a man—a lover?—had come from out of nowhere and was camped out inside.

"Well, then," he said, "I'll finish up here and be on my way. Lots of driveways to take care of. Not that any of the owners will be here until June, but gotta keep 'em clear in case of emergency."

She nodded. "Right. See you later then. And thanks." She closed the door, leaned against it, and let out a long, lingering sigh. Then she moved over by the Christmas tree, picked up Bella, and held her close for a long time.

Annie decided to stay in for the rest of the day, to keep out of Earl's sight. Even if he were plowing driveways on the other side of Chappy, she could not take the risk. And she needed to be home in case Bella's mother came back.

But in order to remain sequestered, Annie had to figure out how to improvise with the dwindling baby supplies.

When she finally put Bella down for an afternoon nap, Annie prowled through the refrigerator, hunting for some type of "people food" that a three-to-six-month old could digest. Certainly not the stew, the freshly baked brownies, or the cinnamon rolls. She did have sweet potatoes—maybe she could cook one and mash it with the old-fashioned, handheld eggbeater that she'd seen in the utensil drawer. Then she remembered she had a few bananas—hadn't Murphy mashed bananas for her boys? Was it worth a try? Or would it harm Bella?

She shook a frustrated fist up to the ceiling. "Help!" she cried in a low whisper, so as not to wake up Bella.

When Murphy didn't reply, Annie peeled a banana, dropped it into a bowl, and started mashing. Somehow, the fruit seemed like a safer bet than the sweet potato. She congratulated herself on that sensible assessment.

When her task was complete, she addressed the diaper situation. She headed for the linen closet and started rooting through it, wishing she'd paid better attention when she'd been a Girl Scout. There must have been a badge for taking care of babies. But Annie had been more interested in crafts, and she'd wound up making jewelry out of beads and wires, and sewing tablecloths and matching aprons and giving them to her mother as birthday and Mother's Day gifts.

It was not surprising that she'd chosen to teach third grade. In her pre–Bobby Briggs years, life had been magical—the lucky infant awarded to the perfect couple, Bob and Ellen Sutton, the only child who was doted on and loved. She had, after all, been born in 1968, when people still believed that perfect couples existed.

In many ways, the Suttons had been exactly that. They'd attended the Anglican church of their British ancestors, were involved in the parent-teacher organization, and took an active interest in Annie's schoolwork. Ellen volunteered in the school office two afternoons a week; otherwise, she stayed home and cooked and cleaned as if it were the 1950s. With a smile and a wave, Bob went off to work at his small insurance company every day. A single martini—extra dry, no olive—greeted him each evening, followed by a pot roast dinner or tuna casserole. They'd never had pizza until Ellen suggested it for Annie's ninth birthday party. Until then, refreshments had been limited to cake and ice cream.

"The world is changing," Ellen said. "Girls want different things." Bob said no one could argue with that. After all, Ellen now smoked his cigarettes and had traded her housedresses for polyester jumpsuits. Her favorite TV show was also different, having swung from *The Partridge Family* to *The Mary Tyler Moore Show*.

At the party, ten of Annie's classmates (all girls) gobbled up the pizza, then Ellen brought out several shades of fingernail polish. They had a blast, and everyone agreed that Ellen was a perfect mom. But the day after Annie's party, the perfect mom ran off with Mr. Dorey, the vice principal of the elementary school.

Stunned and confused, Annie thought it must have been her fault. But her dad said no, that strange things happened now because of a combination of Vietnam and Watergate and a woman named Helen Gurley Brown. Annie hadn't understood, but she supposed his explanation was plausible because he was so smart.

As for him, he continued to start each day with a smile, as if their lives hadn't been shattered. Together they figured out how to do the laundry, and Annie taught herself how to cook. On Friday nights, Bob brought home pizza.

A few weeks later, Annie came home from school, and there was her mom, standing in the kitchen wearing a housedress, making dinner, as if she'd never left. "Women's liberation is a fad," Ellen said. "I can't imagine what I was thinking."

Annie's dad seemed to take her back without question, not that either of her parents would have said otherwise.

But though life in the Sutton house had resumed its happier, predictable time, something inside Annie had been bruised. She sometimes wondered if she'd been permanently damaged by having had two mothers abandon her. She'd never learned what her mom had done during those weeks away, or why she had returned. Maybe knowing would have hurt more—and maybe that fear had been the real reason why, years later, when Annie's birth mother had tried to come back to her, too, Annie had read the letter once, then put it safely away. *Out of sight, out of mind*, her dad would have called it, had he known.

"Bingo!" she exclaimed now as her hand landed on what felt like flannel. She pulled out a set of sheets and deemed that they'd make perfect diapers. She didn't know how she'd get them to stay together, but there was always the Gorilla Glue she'd brought from home. If Annie had learned anything over the years, it was how to survive when the odds were stacked against you.

By the time Bella woke up, Annie was ready. She fed her some cereal and a taste of the banana. At first, Bella wrinkled her nose; Annie waited for a scream. But then the little mouth turned up in a smile, then opened wide, as if wanting more. Annie patiently alternated cereal with the banana. Bella seemed to enjoy it all, despite the mess caused by "grown-up" spoons that were too big for her and left the food smeared all over her face. Annie wiped it off as best she could, but knew she must give her a bath.

After warming water on the stove and using the dishpan and a bar of her beach roses and cream—the softest soap she'd made—she washed the baby from tip to toe. Bella gurgled and giggled, and didn't once let out a cry. When they were done, Annie decided to wait until later to try one of her "custom" diapers. She'd experimented enough for one day.

Then, as she finished taping the store-bought diaper, the power surged and shocked the cottage back to life. Annie scooped Bella up and lightly danced across the room, resetting the clocks and plugging in her phone and computer. She felt wonderfully, inexplicably optimistic, as if she, too, had been recharged. Then Bella threw up all over them both.

Chapter 5

Diapers. Formula. Cream for the diaper rash Bella had developed, no doubt from the clumsy way Annie had tried to clean her. Staring at her list the following morning, she suspected it should be longer, but how on earth would she know what to add?

By nine o'clock, she'd dressed in her favorite pink sweater and jeans again, managed to get Bella ready, poured coffee into a thermos, picked up the basket, and walked out of the cottage.

But when she opened her car door, she realized she didn't know where to put the baby, who had not come equipped with a car seat. Wasn't it a law to use one? And did babies go in the back seat, facing front? Or were they supposed to face backward now? Annie stared into the back of her Lexus, doubting that a simple seat belt could secure the basket well enough to save Bella from anything. So she set it on the floor in the front passenger seat, where at least she could keep a watchful eye.

The water was quiet and calm; crossing the channel on the small ferry was smooth. Bella didn't cry. Thank God.

"So far, so good," Annie muttered as the captain unhooked the restraining strap and Annie wheeled out onto Dock Street.

First stop was the supermarket for the essentials. She also

tossed a couple of baby toys and a teething ring into the shopping cart, though she had no idea if Bella was teething.

Next was the town hall, where she hoped to find someone who might know Grandma Bella. She parked at the Old Whaling Church and looked past the Dukes County Courthouse down Main Street, which looked even more festive now, thanks to the snow.

Sitting for a moment, Annie wondered how she should start the conversation with the town clerk. She could ask if anyone knew an island woman named Bella, or perhaps Isabella, or something similar. She could say she was a long-lost relative, that she remembered that the woman lived there, and wanted to look her up.

Yes, she decided. That seemed innocent enough.

But then, *No*. How could she claim to have a relative if she did not know her last name?

Besides, she couldn't very well bring the baby inside. What if someone recognized her? Or what if someone recognized the basket? The girl had toted it into the holiday fair only a week ago. Even if no one had known her before, surely she'd been seen in town that day.

Then the first line of the letter that Annie's birth mother had written sprang to her mind: *They made me let you go.*

Ugh. Years ago, she'd read the letter from her birth mother so many times that she'd once known it by heart. If she concentrated, she was sure she still could recite it. Instead, her thoughts moved back to Bella.

Had Bella's mother been running from someone who was trying to force her to let her baby go, too? Had she been seeking refuge when she'd showed up at Annie's, then, for some reason, changed her mind and left only the baby?

Annie studied the town hall, its gleaming white exterior a vibrant contrast to the endless green garlands and strands of white lights that adorned it. Then a small doubt began to fester: what if the people inside, like Earl's son, would feel the need to uphold the law? They were islanders, but Annie was a wash-ashore. A come-from-away. One of *those*. If they knew Bella's family, they might put the baby back into the same situation her mother had been trying to save her from.

"Too chancy," Annie said. She needed a different approach. What about the hospital? Could she find out if Bella had been born there? It was doubtful anyone would tell her. But if she went to the *Gazette* and prowled through back issues—from three to six months ago—she might find Bella's birth notice.

Tapping the steering wheel, pondering that option, Annie realized that if she went to the newspaper office, her presence might raise curious eyebrows among the journalists who'd no doubt been trained to spot news. Which meant that in order to search for a birth announcement, it would be safer for her to go home and scan the paper's website, out of sight of potentially snooping eyes. As long as the Internet felt like connecting.

Of course, if she and Bella went home, Earl could be there.

If Annie were a mad dog, she might have growled.

She didn't growl; she simply sat there. And continued tapping the wheel. She chewed her lower lip. Then, finally, a solution: if she drove up island, maybe Winnie would help. Winnie was older than Annie by at least a decade. She'd been raised among her unpretentious Wampanoag people, and seemed to carry their quiet wisdom deep within her DNA. Winnie would help without judgment or the need for too much explanation. If she was working at the ferry terminal in Vineyard Haven, was busy with her family, or had gone out shopping, at least the drive would enable Annie to stay occupied until the sun went down and it was safe to go back to Chappy.

The journey up island to Aquinnah was long, and the roads were rural, winding, and hilly, blighted by hard-packed, icy patches, made worse by the blustery winds that shot billowing spirals up into blue sky. They reminded Annie of the sparkling clouds that had burst from the snow-making machines at Wachusett Mountain the weekend she and Brian had gone skiing. It had been their first Christmas together since they'd been married; they'd been young, happy, filled with life. The trip was their gift to each other: they were fresh out of grad school and had little money. Brian's sister had said they shouldn't splurge on a ski trip when they needed things like proper dishes and suitable draperies. But Annie and Brian had each other, and that was enough for them. After he was killed, she was grateful she had memories instead of dishes or draperies.

Annie hated that memories of Brian surfaced like that—in instant, unexpected blinks that came and then were gone. But though the years had faded the images and dulled the intensity of the emotion, Annie knew she'd once been happy, and that she'd once been loved. Those feelings had helped her through the dark days after Mark, when she'd felt like such a loser.

Glancing down at the basket, she wondered if the baby's young mother had ever had a glimmer of happiness. Somehow, it seemed doubtful. Maybe she was too young.

With a small sigh, Annie looked back to the road, which was bordered by ribbons of stone walls that now were topped with snow that looked like thick vanilla frosting. To the west, she could see the graceful hills that arced down toward the quaint fishing village of Menemsha, known for its breathtaking sunsets; to the south she saw the rolling vista of an eighteenth-century sheep farm that swept out to the ocean. Whenever Annie came up island, she drank in the serenity. That day, however, she quickly pulled her eyes back to the pavement. She knew she must pay full attention to her driving; after all, she had precious cargo in a basket on the floor.

At last, she turned down the rutty, well-traveled road to Winnie's cedar-shingled house, which was huddled on the sacred tribal land where Winnie and her brothers had been raised. Winnie's husband had died several years ago; she now lived in the house with her daughter and son-in-law and their two children, who were in elementary school, and with one of her brothers, his wife, and their teenage son, none of whom had been around on the weekdays when Annie had been there taking lessons. Winnie once told her they'd built additions onto the house whenever the quarters felt cramped; they'd even installed propane heat—a luxury compared to years ago when, before the first frost appeared, they'd wrapped the base of the house in seaweed that served as winter insulation.

Pulling into the driveway, she noticed that a path had been shoveled to the small stone house where root vegetables were sheltered after the harvest. Winnie's studio was next to that, and then a round brick kiln, which now puffed smoke through a stovepipe that rose up through the top. As Annie turned off the ignition, a large, shaggy dog galloped toward the car, his fluffy tail wagging, his pink tongue hanging out of one side of his mouth in a panting, welcoming greeting. Best of all, Winnie's old van was parked next to the porch, so she was probably home.

Winnie was tall and square, with a long, gray braid that snaked from behind her neck, over her shoulder, and down her ample breasts. Her skin was the color of the coppery clay of the Gay Head Cliffs, which made her white teeth almost glow whenever she smiled, as she did when she opened the side door and signaled Annie to the house. "Greetings, Annie Sutton. What the devil are you doing way up here the day after a blizzard? And what the devil is in that basket?"

Annie laughed and proceeded to the porch. It was great to see Winnie again; she'd felt comfortable with her from the first day they'd met. "Don't worry. This is definitely not a Christmas gift for you. Although I meant to bring yours. But I'm afraid I got sidetracked with the blizzard and with . . . this." She nodded toward the basket.

"Well, come on in. Around here, we rarely turn away a friend. And never one of those." She was clearly not referring to the basket, but to its cooing contents.

"Tea?" Winnie asked. "Got to keep an eye on the kiln, but there's always time for tea."

Annie nodded. "I'm so glad you're home. I didn't know if you'd be at the terminal."

"Regular day off. Add that to two days off thanks to the storm, and I feel like I've been on vacation." She gestured for Annie to follow her into the kitchen. "You picked a perfect time, because I shooed my brood into the fresh air. Gave them a list and sent them down island for supplies. Christmas decorations. A tree. Anything I could think of. We were cooped up together too long; you'd have thought we'd invented the term *cabin fever*. Now, give me that sweet baby before you let me talk forever. You never said you had one of these."

Annie set the basket on top of the long wooden farm table that looked to have been lovingly hewn by hand. She hadn't been in the house before, only in the studio, but wasn't surprised at the warm, homey feeling it emitted. A number of chairs were clustered around the table, a testament to the big, multigenerational family. Annie picked Bella up and handed her over to more experienced arms. "Her name is Bella. And if she were mine, it would be a true Christmas miracle."

"Well, you seem too young to be a grandmother, though I suppose anything goes these days."

The drive up island should have given Annie plenty of time to decide what to tell Winnie, how to explain what had happened, what kind of help she'd ask her for. But the road conditions had demanded her attention and, more than likely, she hadn't wanted to think about it. But now, safe in Winnie's kitchen where she could almost think straight, she wondered if her escape from Chappy and not having gone to the police had made the situation worse. And if she had screwed up. Big time.

She stared at the floor, and then, as if she were no older than Bella, Annie started to cry.

"Oh, boy," Winnie quietly said. "There's a story here, isn't there? Well, if you put the kettle on, I'll hang on to the baby. You're welcome to talk when you're ready. If that's why you've come."

By the time Annie finished telling the story, Winnie was the one in tears.

"I don't want to do anything wrong," Annie continued. "I don't want to break the law. But I keep hoping the mother will come back for her. I think it's too soon to turn her over to the police, or even to tell Earl, who might feel obliged to tell his son. The mother said she'd be back in a couple of days; I want to give her that chance. Today, however, marks day number three, and I'm starting to get very concerned."

They sat at the table, drinking hot tea from Winnie's special blend of herbs that she grew and dried herself.

"And you know the island," Annie continued. "I don't. I'm sure there are ins and outs and ways of doing things that I'd never think of. Ways of finding people. Or at least, of finding people who know people."

"You think the mother's an island girl?" Winnie asked.

"I have no idea. All I really know is that she saw me at the fair, then found me on Chappy. If she lives on the Vineyard, why would she come to me?"

"If she went to the fair, do you think she came over on that special boat out of Hyannis?"

"The *Grey Lady*? Who knows? She was alone, so it doesn't seem like she came for a fun day of shopping. Besides, I had the impression she didn't have much money."

"But if she had a car, she couldn't have come that way. The *Grey Lady* is passengers only."

"Well, I only saw footprints, not tire tracks."

"With or without a car, she could have come in on the Steamship Authority into Vineyard Haven. There's one every hour and fifteen minutes—more often, if you count the freight boats. So she could have come anytime."

Annie closed her eyes. "I know."

Winnie stood up, walked around the table, placed a hand on Annie's shoulder. "You sit for a while. I have to tend to the kiln. It will give me a chance to think this through."

Annie took Bella from her, and Winnie left through the back door.

Chapter 6

After Annie had finished another mug of tea—without having come up with any bright ideas—Winnie returned.

"Let's suppose Bella's mother is still on Chappy," Winnie said as she settled back down at the table. "She went to your house on foot in the middle of the night, during the storm no less, so she must live, or was staying, close by. Have you canvassed your neighborhood?"

"No. I've been too worried I'd run into Earl."

"Right. But I have a thought."

Annie had put the sleeping baby back into the basket, which she now nervously rocked.

"You said the girl at the fair was young. How young?"

"I have no idea. Maybe seventeen. Eighteen. I have no one to compare her with."

Winnie broke into a smile. "Well, we might. Lucas, my brother Orrin's boy, just turned nineteen. If that little baby's mother lives on the island, chances are they were in school together."

"But you're way up here. A long way from Edgartown."

"There's only one public high school. And there's the charter school. Lucas went to the public one."

"The big one on Edgartown–Vineyard Haven Road?"

"Yes. I think they have several hundred students. The charter school, a lot fewer. But Lucas would probably know her. Most of the kids know each other if only by sight, even if they're not in the same class. There are so many activities, it seems like sooner or later, they run into one another. Anyway, he's home from college on winter break."

"That's great, but I wouldn't want to tell him why I'm trying to find her. I have a strong feeling that she's an unwed mother." Annie didn't know if that term was still used; it always made her think about Donna MacNeish, the woman who'd given birth to her so many years ago. "If Bella's father is an island boy, I don't want to go public with information that isn't mine to share."

"I agree. But we can look in the yearbook. Lucas must have one. He graduated last year."

Annie rocked the basket a little more. "Well . . . I only saw her briefly . . . but Bella has her mother's dark hair and her sad, soulful eyes," she said. "Even at her age, there's a striking similarity between them."

"Good. That's a place to start." She signaled her toward the hall. "We have enough bookshelves in the living room to start a library. Sooner or later, all our books wind up there. Let's check it out before the clan gets home."

Sometimes, when least expected, Annie's heart could start to race as if something—or someone—had triggered an internal panic alarm. She didn't know why this was one of those times; she only knew that when she stood up, her heart pounded as hard as it had the night Bella had arrived. But, as she wrapped her sweater tightly around her and picked up the basket, she heard herself say, "Okay. Lead the way."

The living room was enormous. The focal point was a wide fireplace that was beautifully crafted from the same brick as

Winnie's kiln and a mantel that looked like it had been hewn from the same wood as the table.

"When I was a kid, this room didn't exist," Winnie said. "We all lived in the kitchen. My parents' bedroom was downstairs where I sleep now; there was only one real bedroom upstairs; my brothers slept there. My room was the storage closet at the top of the stairs. It didn't have a window, but I could close the door and get away from them." She said it matter-of-factly. "Now we have this wonderful room and a few more people. But everybody still likes to hang out in the kitchen." She laughed. "I guess it's like that in most families."

"I guess," Annie said with her practiced smile. Then her eyes traveled around the room: one long wall held shelves and shelves of magnificent pottery—pitchers, mugs, and dishes of all sizes. Some of the pieces were wheel-thrown, kiln-fired, and glazed with soft shades the colors of sea glass; others were more fragile pinch pottery, crafted from clay that had been shaped and pounded, then dried by hand, revealing vivid earth tones in reds and golds, and browns and grays—colors that had been hidden within the clay. Winnie once told her that if those pieces were fired they would lose their radiance.

"I'm working on my collection for the spring fair," Winnie said. "It's hard to believe with all the snow outside, but it will be here soon enough."

The distraction helped ease Annie's anxiety. "And your jewelry pieces are for the fall shows?"

"Right. I hate working around the kiln in summer. Too hot!" She laughed again. "Which reminds me. That baby's basket looks like the ones that Nancy Clieg makes. Was she selling them at the fair?"

Annie scowled. "I have no idea." She'd been so busy trying to look relaxed, she sadly hadn't noticed any of the other vendors.

Stooping down, Winnie examined it. "I can't be sure, but it sure looks like one of Nancy's."

"Do you know her?"

"She lives over in Menemsha. I'd go see her for you, but . . . well, we once had an issue over a piece of land, and let's leave it at that. But I'll give you her address before you leave. Maybe she'll remember if Bella's mother bought it." She turned and gestured toward the opposite wall, which was about thirty feet long and had shelves stuffed with books, floor to ceiling. A ladder was on one end: it was attached to a row of tracks that spanned the whole length of the wall. Winnie grinned. "Welcome to our library."

"Wow. You weren't kidding."

"We might even have one or two of your volumes in there. My sister-in-law is a big fan. Now let's get to work. I'll tackle the top; you start on the bottom. You're younger than I am, so you probably can squat without falling over."

Annie doubted that Winnie had ever "fallen over." But she was grateful for the help and the companionship. Not to mention that she felt as if she were in heaven when faced with all the wondrous volumes. A quick scan said it all: novels, histories, biographies, politics, and on and on—indeed, a veritable library. She moved to the far end of the wall, crouched, and got to work.

Nearly two hours had elapsed without a single sighting of a high school yearbook when the front door opened and footsteps clamored into the hall. Voices yammered, boots clunked onto the floor, long zippers could be heard gliding down crinkling nylon parkas. The silence had been broken.

"Food!" someone shouted.

Bella let out a wail.

"They're back," Winnie groaned. She climbed down from

the ladder. "Sorry we haven't had any luck. You'll stay for lunch? It's long past time to eat."

They returned to the kitchen, where Annie was greeted with an assemblage of faces, which, like Bella's and her mother's, resembled one another. Annie wondered, not for the first time, if she, too, resembled her birth family.

Winnie quickly introduced the five adults who'd crammed into the kitchen: a teacher, a nurse, a carpenter, Winnie's brother the fisherman, and Lucas—the college student who might know the missing mother.

"You left the kids at story time?" Winnie asked.

"Yup," the son-in-law, the carpenter, replied. "They'll be done at four. I gave them lunch in the car. Sandwiches from The Food Truck in Menemsha."

"You stopped at Orange Peel?"

"Yup. Three loaves of multigrain, as ordered."

The Orange Peel Bakery had become the go-to destination for breads and cookies crafted from nature's ingredients and baked in an outdoor oven; its tasty products had received kudos even from the *New York Times*.

"I'll heat the chowder from last night," Winnie's daughter announced. "Then it's every man for himself." She was the teacher and clearly knew how to take charge. Annie recognized that as a trait from her former life; she also knew she could not turn down chowder and Orange Peel's multigrain.

"And I'll get the baby changed," Winnie announced, then whisked Bella from the basket, grabbed the bag of things Annie had bought, and disappeared into another room.

"Sweet baby," the daughter said. "Beautiful eyes. Adorable dimple. Yours?"

"I wish," Annie replied. "I'm sitting for a friend." Congratulating herself for her fast thinking, she stepped past the men and began to help set the table.

"You're the writer, aren't you?" Winnie's sister-in-law, the nurse, asked. She was a good deal younger than Winnie's brother; their marriage was his second.

"I am."

"Working on a new book?"

"Always." Then she had a thought. "In fact, Winnie's helping me with some research." She turned to Lucas. "You graduated from the island high school, didn't you?" The boy nodded. "Do you have a yearbook? I'm trying to get a quick picture of the inside of the school—the classrooms, the activities—and looking at a yearbook would really help." A white lie might turn out to be kinder than the truth.

"Sure," he said. "Got one in my room. Somewhere." He put his hands into the pockets of his sweatshirt.

His mother looked at him. "Maybe you'd like to go find it for Annie?"

"Oh," he said, "sure. I think it's in my closet."

Annie finished setting the table, while the others found their places and sat down.

With the happy commotion around her, by the time they'd finished eating, Annie still hadn't checked the yearbook that Lucas had set beside her. And it was nearly dark.

"You and the baby will stay here tonight," Winnie announced. "It's too late for you to head back to Chappy. The roads will be slick and hard to see. Dangerous. We'll set you up with an air mattress in the living room. Tomorrow, you can go home by way of Menemsha and pay a visit to Nancy Clieg. Tonight, you can help us decorate the tree—we might or might not have enough lights and ornaments for whatever monstrosity they came home with this year. Then we'll all play rummy. It's our Saturday night tradition."

It was a wonderful way to end a wonderful day: Annie felt as if she'd known the Lathrop family for years. When Winnie's son-in-law won the last round of rummy—"He always does," his wife complained—everyone, except Winnie and Annie went to bed. Winnie collected remnants of the tree decorations while Annie sat by the fireplace and pored over the yearbook. But page after page of senior photos yielded no one who looked remotely like Bella's mother. Nor did any of the students in the group shots of underclass kids. It was a dead end.

"I will not allow you to get discouraged," Winnie said. "When the time is right, you will know what you need to know."

With the last of the evening's tea gone, Annie checked on Bella, who was sleeping peacefully in her basket. Then she lay down on the air mattress that they'd set next to her. "Good night, Winnie," she said. "Thank you for everything."

Winnie turned off the twinkling tree and whispered into the darkness, "Good night, Annie Sutton. And for your information, you would have made a fine mother. You already love a baby you don't even know."

Annie closed her eyes, let Winnie's words sink in, and tried not to feel the old, familiar ache sneak back into her heart.

Frozen with fear.

A long time ago, when she was thirteen, Francine had sat in the movies with Jason Arroyo, whom her grandfather would have shot if he'd known they were together because he was from Puerto Rico and therefore, according to Gramps, was not their kind. In truth, he probably would have shot both of them. It wasn't as if they were going to get married, but if they were, Francine knew they'd have to run away.

She'd really liked Jason. He had held her hand while they watched the previews of the coming attractions. One was for a real scary movie. She didn't remember the plot, only the terrifying music playing—loud—in the background while the title slashed over the screen: Frozen in Fear.

That was how she felt now. When it was three o'clock in the morning and Annie Sutton still hadn't gotten home with or without Bella, and Francine couldn't move because she was so scared.

Jason had moved away before the end of that school year, and Francine never heard from him again. But she wished he were there now to hold her hand.

Chapter 7

The morning was cloudy, but the temperature was warmer; the forecast promised some melting on the icy roads.

After a hearty breakfast of fresh farm eggs and cranberry scones, Annie bundled the baby once again and carefully set the basket in the car. She made sure Bella was facing her: Annie enjoyed glancing over at the baby, hoping to be rewarded by one of her sweet, small smiles.

"Keep me posted," Winnie said, tucking a bag of scones into Annie's bag. "If you need me, you know where I am. And good luck with Nancy."

Annie thanked her again, waved, and drove off. Because GPS wasn't dependable up island, she'd written the directions to Nancy Clieg's house in the small notebook she kept in her purse—a writer's habit, so she was always ready to jot down a tidbit or two. The notebook now rested, open, on the passenger seat. With any luck, Annie would finally find one piece of the puzzle.

Following South Road to Beetlebung Corner, she turned at the old white church onto Menemsha Cross Road—a narrow country lane that wound through tall, lichen-coated oak trees and what looked like ancient pathways. At North Road, she went left, then found the turnoff that led to Nancy's cottage. Like many island homes, it featured a "peek" of the harbor; true waterfront properties seemed reserved for family homesteads that went back many generations or for seasonal people with unlimited resources.

Annie parked and carried Bella up the front walk. She crossed her fingers as she knocked.

Nancy greeted her with a raised eyebrow and a suspicious expression. She had tangled gray hair and deep lines at the corners of her mouth and eyes that spoke of years of close concentration.

"I heard you make beautiful baskets," Annie said. "I'm trying to find out if you sold this one at the fair."

In less than a second, the woman shook her head. "Fake," she said, her small eyes darkening. "Christ. People steal everybody's ideas nowadays. They think they can make a buck the easy way."

Annie was dumbstruck. Whatever she might have thought Nancy would say, it certainly wasn't that.

"Look at this," Nancy grunted, then pointed to the edge where the handle met the basket. "It's a piece of crap. I'd be ashamed to take money for a job like that. You'd best not keep that baby in there when she gets much bigger. That handle's going to give out."

Thinking quickly, Annie said, "I'm not surprised. I showed it to Winnie Lathrop, but she didn't think it was up to your standards." The woman wouldn't know it was a lie; Annie felt it never hurt to try to spread goodwill. "But do you know who made this . . . fake? If it was someone on the island?"

"Not if they know me. And most people do. Nope. More than likely, it's someone on the Cape. I heard there were copycats in a souvenir shop in Provincetown." She shook her head. "Yup. Piece of crap. Now if you'll excuse me, my breakfast is on the stove." The door started to close.

"Wait!" Annie cried, tightening her grip on the basket that might give out at any time and send Bella somersaulting down the hill toward the Coast Guard station in the harbor. "Do you have any of your baskets here? Can I buy one?"

The door stayed half-open. Nancy scowled again and said, "You have cash? Eighty-five dollars. That's a discount. I sold them for a hundred at the fair."

It was just past noon when Annie and Bella—safely in her brand-new basket, the old one tossed haphazardly into the back seat—made it to the *On Time*. The Lexus was fifth in line, an anomaly for late December, when lone vehicles crossing on the ferry were common. But it was a beautiful Sunday, and last-minute shoppers no doubt had scuttled off Chappy to finish their holiday shopping.

Parked behind an SUV that blocked her view of the harbor, Annie closed her eyes and wondered if she should get Bella a gift. Nothing big, of course. Nothing . . . permanent. Or costly. Nothing that might be misinterpreted as an attempt to claim the baby as her own. But if they were still together Christmas morning, it would be nice to mark the occasion with a visit from Santa.

With her thoughts drifting to what she could give her, the last thing Annie expected was a loud rap on her window. She jumped. Her eyes sprang open. And, of course, Bella let out a screech.

A woman stood on the passenger side—Bella's side—of the car. Her face was so close it was nearly pressed onto the glass. She had white, flyaway hair, startling pearl-gray eyes, and a thousand lines etched across her fair skin. She stared inside the car and rapped again.

Annie knew she had to respond. She turned the key in the ignition and lightly touched the power button, opening the window only a few inches.

"Hello?" she asked.

The woman scrunched her face, deepening the thousand lines. "Annie Sutton?"

Oh, God, Annie thought. *Not another book fan.* She smiled. "Yes. How may I help you?"

Luckily, the SUV in front of her inched forward. The *On Time* must have arrived, the vehicles must have disembarked, and the first three in line must have moved onto the flatbed for the next journey across the channel, which would last less than two minutes. Annie knew if she didn't pull up behind the SUV, the driver behind her would get justifiably annoyed.

She pointed toward the ferry, then shifted the Lexus into drive. Unfortunately, the intruder skipped along next to her.

"You're renting the Flanagan place?"

"Yes." There was no point denying something she apparently already knew.

Then the woman's hand squeezed into the four-inch gap. Annie resisted the urge to push the power button up. Instead, she stopped the car, tapped the button down, reached across the passenger seat, and extended her hand. The woman shook it and smiled. Then her pearl-gray eyes dropped down to the basket. "Cute baby. Yours?"

Annie's heart quickly thumped into its warning mode. "No. I'm babysitting for a friend."

"Someone in Edgartown?"

Her thoughts flickered like the twinkling lights on the Christmas tree at Winnie's. If the woman was headed back to Chappy, chances were she knew everyone there—Earl had told her the population was less than two hundred year-round. Chances also were that the woman would know Bella did not belong there—if, in fact, she didn't. And, with Annie's luck, she might also know everyone in Edgartown. So Annie simply said, "No. She lives up island."

The woman nodded. "Well, welcome to the Vineyard, anyway. I'm surprised I haven't run into you before. I'm Claire Lyons. Earl's wife."

A lump of golf ball proportions popped into Annie's throat. "Oh," she squeaked, "Earl's terrific." She should have said more, but the lump was in the way.

Claire rapped on the door, startling Annie again. "You'd better move," she said, and at first Annie thought it was a threat meant to shoo her from the island, to send her back to Boston. Then Claire pointed a long, gloved finger toward the water, and Annie saw that the SUV had driven onto the ferry and that the captain was waiting for her to board.

"This is precisely why some people prefer not to have babies," Annie joked half-heartedly. She looked down at Bella, who was toying with her bottle—*taking her sweet time*, Murphy would have said with a laugh.

But Annie wasn't laughing; she was eager to get Bella fed, changed, and resettled in her safe replacement basket, which, Nancy Clieg's grouchy personality aside, really was much nicer than the one the baby had arrived in.

After having been startled by Earl's wife, Annie knew she needed to get serious about finding the girl; she planned to start by spending what remained of the daylight hours scouring Chappaquiddick for clues. She decided that if she'd made no progress by the end of Christmas Day, she'd go to the police the next morning. It would be the right thing to do. Until then, she'd be giving Bella's mother a few more days to show up. And relishing some baby time for herself.

But Bella clearly felt no urgency. She rested in the crook of Annie's arm and closed her eyes with disinterest. Annie had no idea if she should keep trying to feed her or assume she simply wasn't hungry.

"Three minutes," Annie said in a low, but firm, voice. "If you don't finish this in three minutes, we're going out on our

mission and pray we don't run into Earl." She wondered if
birth mothers had more patience, if they instinctively knew
the boundaries between putting their babies' needs first and
not letting them take control. She thought about the six weeks
between when she'd been born and when the Suttons had
taken her home. She had no recall of those weeks; she only
knew she'd been removed from the hospital and placed in foster care until the paperwork was completed, until Donna Mac-
Neish had signed the final papers, attesting that no, she did not
want her baby, she had not changed her mind.

It was a thought that, despite it being ancient history, still
managed to make Annie well up.

But there was no time for welling up right now.

Sliding the bottle from Bella's tiny mouth, Annie eased her
to a sitting position and said, "I wonder if my foster mother
had more patience than I do."

When she was as sure as she could be that Bella was finished, she re-bundled both of them and headed for the door,
hoping to find something—like footsteps in the snow, or some
sign of anyone who might be trying to hide.

It was the kind of caper she and Murphy had liked to do.
Of course, capers did not always work—like the time they'd
followed Murphy's brother-in-law, who'd claimed he was
going to London by himself, without Murphy's sister, who was
his wife. Naturally, they'd suspected he was cheating . . . until he
caught them, red-handed and red-faced, stalking him when he
arrived back at Logan. As expected, he was not alone, though
his companion was a cocker spaniel puppy that he'd traveled to
England to buy as a surprise for his wife's birthday. The women
were suitably embarrassed and professed that they were ashamed,
but Murphy convinced him that their hearts had been in the
right place. After, they'd all laughed about it over chardonnay.

But that was then, and this was now. In only a few minutes,
Annie was gingerly driving down Chappaquiddick Road,

scoping out every driveway and building she saw. She passed the community center, Pimpneymouse Farm, and the fire station, then traveled all the way to Wasque Point, which she'd heard pronounced *Way-squeee* by a local fisherman. The road was tightly restricted thanks to the hefty snowbanks that hugged the sides but thankfully acted as convenient cushions each time her car lost traction and swerved in the wrong direction.

Yes, she reminded herself. *Next year I will buy a more suitable vehicle.* It was her first official acknowledgment that she wanted to stay on the Vineyard forever.

But there was no time for thinking about that, either.

When she reached the deserted strip of road that sloped down to the nature preserve that skirted the east side of the coastline, Annie stopped. She knew there were no homes out there, only piping plovers, which, like many other islanders, might have flown south for the winter.

Though she'd once heard a tourist describe Chappy as mostly "scrub and sand dunes," she had learned that was far from the truth. Chappaquiddick—the Wampanoag word for "island unto itself"—was rich with sunrises and red cedar woods, rare nesting birds and white-tailed deer, unspoiled marshes and spectacular blue herons. And it was quiet. Like now, when the thick quilt of snow silenced the land, when Annie had not seen a single vehicle or a single person, let alone Bella's young mother.

In fact, she'd barely seen a house. Most places were set back from the road; the few that were visible seemed unoccupied, closed up for the winter, without a single column of smoke curling from a chimney or a single coal-eyed snowman standing in a yard. She wondered if Earl and Claire's house was isolated from its neighbors.

Propping her elbows on the steering wheel, she cupped her face with her hands and considered how, even in today's high-tech world, it wasn't hard to disappear. She thought about Mark, how the police had searched for him those first few weeks, then were diverted to more pressing cases. Months later, his file was converted from paper to digital, then relinquished to the cloud, or to wherever the server had sent it back then, out of sight, out of queue. "It's not exactly a cold case," the sergeant had explained. "But we must be realistic. It doesn't look as if your husband wants to be found."

She wondered now if that were true for Bella's mother, too.

A soft whimper rose from the basket on the floor.

"Bella, Bella, Bella," Annie said. "How on earth will we ever find your mommy?"

When she received no answer, Annie turned the car around and headed back to her cottage. She was discouraged: the next day was Monday, Christmas Eve; Tuesday would be Christmas. Wednesday would mark a full week since Bella had arrived on her porch. If the mother hadn't returned by then, that was the day Annie had marked to bring Bella to the police. Annie worked well with deadlines, and worked in a timely manner, though at the present time, her editor might not agree with that. Nor would fans whose e-mails sat in her bulging in-box awaiting responses, or others who had noticed her lack of recent posts on social media. And though Annie was not a quitter, she knew she had to honor the deadline regarding Bella that she'd set: Wednesday, December twenty-sixth. Maybe it was because she couldn't shake the feeling that Bella's mother wasn't coming back. Or maybe it was because the longer Bella stayed with her, the more Annie felt her old wounds being pried more widely open.

Just before she reached the cottage, Annie heard Murphy whisper: *It's okay to say, "enough is enough."* Thank God; her old friend hadn't deserted her. Annie knew she shouldn't be surprised. Because Murphy was the only one who'd known almost all of her demons.

"You're right," Annie said. "As usual." She supposed she could take some solace in having tried to do the right thing by honoring the young mother's request, by waiting those "couple of days." She did know she was grateful that she hadn't been caught or been arrested. Yet.

But seconds later, when she pulled down her driveway, Annie saw Earl's pickup. And then she saw him, sitting on her porch.

Earl stood up and meandered toward the Lexus in his slow, lumbering gait. As he grew closer, Annie felt her cheeks flush. Had his wife told him about Bella? He would never believe that Annie was babysitting for a friend: he knew that the only other friend she'd made on the island so far was Winnie. And he'd know that Winnie's clan would hardly need someone to babysit because, first, they did not have a baby, and second, if they did, they had plenty of relatives to take care of one of their own.

She turned off the car and shifted into park, her eyes never leaving the red-and-black wool jacket that was moving closer. She was reminded of the time her father had caught her smoking outside Brigham's Ice Cream, where the kids liked to hang out until the manager shooed them away. How was she to know her father would have picked that night to stop on the way home from his lodge meeting for a pint of rum raisin— her mother's favorite? Annie had simply been trying to be cool, standing with her friend Lisbeth, talking with the boys who were seniors at the high school where she and Lisbeth were only sophomores. She'd never dreamed her dad would show up . . . never dreamed that he'd walk past the group and make eye contact with her. He did not say a word, not then, not until she got home and he sauntered up the sidewalk in front of their house to greet her the way Earl was sauntering toward her now. She wondered if Earl would say he was disappointed in her, the way that her father had, the way that had left her in tears and more upset than if he'd grounded her.

But Annie was over fifty now, not fifteen. And Earl was her friend, not her father. She straightened her spine and wondered why it was that the child within often remained there, teasing the adult with unsteady emotion anytime certain buttons were rebooted. Murphy once said it was so shrinks could make a living.

Earl stopped a few feet from the car.

Annie opened the door and got out.

"Been off island?" he asked.

She dropped the keys into her pocket. She closed the door quietly behind her. "Yes. Off this island, anyway. I was in Aquinnah. Up at Winnie's." At least her heart wasn't thumping like a racehorse at the gate.

"Well, you know, Chappy's technically no longer an island," he said. "Not since the breech was closed in 2015. It broke open again later that winter, but by the following January it had filled in again."

It might have amused Annie to listen to Earl's small talk if it weren't for that infernal elephant in the room, which, in this case, was a baby in the car. "That's right," she replied, "I forgot. But I had a wonderful time with Winnie and her family. I spent the night there. They're such a fun-loving family." She wondered how long she should leave Bella in the car with the door closed and the windows up. It was a far cry from summer, but did cold weather affect a sleeping baby the same way excessive heat did? Thankfully, Bella hadn't been on the porch long enough that first night for Annie to find out.

"Yup. They're a good bunch," he replied. "Done a lot for the tribe."

Annie shifted on one foot, then the other, then averted Earl's eyes altogether. She wondered if he expected her to invite him inside for coffee. Or cinnamon rolls. He wasn't usually there this late in the day. *Yes*, she decided, *Claire must have told him.* Maybe, with a little luck, he'd let Annie mind her own business. "So," she said, "I guess I can still get some work done before nightfall." She looked up at the sky as if searching for inspiration.

"Writing the book?"

She nodded. "I'm finally getting somewhere with it." In addition to telling Nancy Clieg that Winnie had said the basket wasn't up to her standards, and to telling Claire that she was babysitting for a friend, Annie had now told three lies in the same day. That did not feel terrific.

Earl scratched at what looked like a two-day growth of whiskers on his chin. Then he said, "Do you read it to her?"

Annie gulped. "What?" Her voice came out in a whisper.

"To that baby in your car. Do you read what you're writing to her? It's a girl, isn't it?"

She bit her lip. "Well. Yes. But no. I don't read it to her. She's just a baby." There was no sense pretending Bella wasn't on the floor of the Lexus. But Earl didn't need to know the details. Did he?

Trying to act innocent, Annie strolled to the passenger side, her thoughts clanging together. What would she do if he asked for proof that Bella belonged there? She had the note, but would that be enough? *He hardly knows you. He only met you a few months ago.* How would he know she didn't have a sister or a relative who needed help with babysitting? Then Annie remembered: He'd know because over coffee one morning, she'd told him she was alone in the world. A grown-up orphan with no siblings and no close—or even distant—relations. And that her best friend had just died. She hadn't mentioned her birth mother, because Annie didn't think the woman counted. And besides, she might be dead now, too.

She pulled on the handle and opened the door. *Stay cool,* she thought. *You've done nothing wrong.*

But she felt his eyes on her as she reached inside.

"Need some help?" he asked.

That's when she realized he had quietly moved and was now standing directly behind her. And that his voice was patient and kind, much like her father's had been. Though she mostly talked to Murphy these days, she thought about her dad a lot, too. She'd been closer to him than to her mom, especially after the incident with the vice principal. Love, she knew, never really left the heart or the mind.

She wondered what her father would advise her to say. Would he be disappointed in her for what she'd been trying to do? Then Annie looked down at Bella, whose eyes were wide open, looking brightly around as if searching for something . . . or someone. When her sight landed on Annie, she broke into a big smile. For the second day in a row, Annie began to cry. "I do," she whispered to Earl. "I really do need help."

Earl walked around her, leaned down, and hoisted the basket from the floor of the car. Without saying a word, he trudged back to the porch and let himself into the house. Annie closed the car door, wiped her eyes, and followed his tracks up to the porch.

Chapter 8

"Well," Earl said, when she'd finished sharing Bella's story, "how 'bout that."

Annie laughed with relief. "You sound like Winnie." She'd put hot water on for tea, though she probably had drunk enough up island. She'd then picked Bella up and was still holding her, had been holding her the whole time that she'd talked, guarding her, she supposed, keeping her close as if Earl might want to snatch her and whisk her off to the police.

"Claire said she met you at the *On Time*."

"I did. She was very nice. But I lied to her, Earl. I said I was babysitting for a friend." Annie liked Earl. Despite her guilt, she trusted him. It wasn't only because he sometimes reminded her of her dad; it was also because of all he'd done for her since she'd arrived. How he'd gone out of his way to show her that, beneath its celebrity and its beauty, the Vineyard was really about good neighbors in a caring community. But Annie didn't know if she could also trust his wife, who had eyed Annie with suspicion. Or maybe Annie's conscience had made her think that.

"I have no idea why the young woman picked me," she continued. "For one thing, I know nothing about babies. Maybe my cottage was the first place she found during the storm where she could tell a fire was burning in the woodstove, and that someone was living here, probably safe and warm. Or at least safer and warmer than she and Bella were right then." She stood up. "Care to take her while I fix the tea?" She needed the reminder that she trusted him.

"You bet," Earl said, extending his arms. "Been a while since I've held one of these beauties."

"I learned pretty quickly that they don't break. Which was really good news to me."

He took over while Annie filled two mugs, set them on the table, then put a few chocolate chip cookies on a plate.

"So what's your plan now?" he asked as he swiftly moved Bella to his left arm and helped himself to a cookie. He was clearly a father and a grandfather, comfortable with a baby in his arms. Her dad would have loved holding a baby, too, if she and Brian had only known the urgency for them to have one before he and, soon after, her dad died.

She sat again, with so many feelings spinning together. "I thought I'd wait until the day after Christmas. If Bella's mother isn't back by then, or if I haven't found her, I'll go to the police. Part of me—the novelist part that always secretly longs for a happy ending—hopes that because of all the *fa-la-la* of the holiday, the young woman will feel sentimental and will come back for her. There's probably a better chance of that than of me finding her. Because if she's still here on Chappy, I'm afraid she's well-hidden."

Earl chewed, swallowed, took a big gulp of tea. "If you want, I can check with the ferry captains. See if any of them remember if a young woman came over with a baby, then crossed back alone. It might sound like a long shot, but they know everyone who lives on Chappy year-round. Anyone who doesn't belong sticks out like a sore thumb. We might at least learn if she's still here, or if she's gone back to the main island or to wherever she's from, to take care of some other, more pressing business. As if anything could be more pressing than this." He snorted sarcastically at his last remark, then wiggled his little finger until Bella grasped it.

Annie wanted to tell him she'd be grateful if he talked to the captains, but her stomach started to churn. She broke a corner off a cookie and took a small bite. "I appreciate the thought, but I'm afraid if you ask anyone, it will set off an alert that something dreadful has happened . . . that a mysterious young woman left a baby here. I think they'd feel obligated to contact the police right away."

"Good point. Well, then, will you at least let my Claire help out? She'd love to have a little one around. Even if it's only for a couple of days."

Annie didn't know how to respond. She didn't want him to think she didn't like Claire—good grief, she did not even know her—but she had to think about Bella first. "I'm sorry, Earl. I'm just so worried that the more people I involve . . . well, that it will drag them into this and make them partly responsible, too. If I get into trouble for not turning Bella over right away, I'd hate to make anyone else an accomplice." She thought that sounded plausible without hurting his feelings. Then she smiled. "Of course, I guess present company is now excepted."

Earl stood up, held Bella to his shoulder, and swigged the rest of his tea. Then he slipped a couple of cookies into his pocket. "Don't worry about me. As for my wife, well, I get what you mean. That girl left her baby on your doorstep, not ours. And, yup, the fewer folks who know, the better. But I'll tell you what. Tomorrow is Christmas Eve. Why don't you come to the house and celebrate with us? Claire doesn't need to know what's really going on, but she'd love to have a baby there; our holiday will be pretty quiet. When John's girls were here, we always went to the party at the community center, but Claire says without our grandkids it's hard to see people having fun with theirs. So we stay home. Once in a while a neighbor drops by, which is nice. In any event, don't worry, I'll back you up."

"Thanks, Earl. I'd enjoy that. But what about your son? Will he be there?"

"I don't know. Sometimes he covers so other guys on the force can have the night off. Unless he's on duty, though, he'll probably come. But I won't breathe a word of truth to him, either. Scout's honor."

"But you'd be lying to your family."

"Only by omission. When a baby is involved, I don't think that counts." He winked, then softly patted Bella's head. "Now, wrap up this little one and put your coat back on. We're going on a hunting trip. It'll be dark soon; folks will be turning on their lights. We can see who's home. If our little mother's still on Chappy, she can't be too far. Not if she walked through that nor'easter. Besides, I know every house that's occupied this time of year—if our girl is squatting, chances are, she'll have a light on. And I'll know if she doesn't belong there."

"Summer people don't turn off their electricity?"

"Not usually. Their caretakers might need it. Or they keep it on for their housekeepers. Lots of folks have cleaners go in every few weeks to keep up with the dust and the spiders and the mice. Squatters come in all sizes, you know." He handed Bella to Annie and pulled on his jacket. "If the girl is here, we'll find her. And she can join us for Christmas Eve, too."

At the top of the driveway, Earl turned left onto North Neck Road.

"Why this way?" Annie asked.

He rubbed his chin again. "If we're right to think she's not far from you, maybe she's in one of the waterfront houses here. She might have thought she'd have more room to hide. Anyway, let's give it a shot. You ever come down this way?"

She shook her head. "I thought it might be too bumpy for my car. Whenever I go for a walk, which isn't often enough, I stick to the main road. Besides, everything in this direction is private property, isn't it? Like the Flanagan place. Every time I cross the channel, I can see the beautiful houses on the water. They always look so empty, like a Rolls-Royce or a Bentley, just sitting there, idling, waiting for their masters to return."

Earl laughed. "You really are a writer, aren't you?"

Annie grimaced. "I don't know where that came from. I'm certainly not a poet. Maybe I've already spent too much time on the Vineyard."

"Never!" He chuckled, then stopped at the beginning of what looked like a driveway that hadn't been plowed. It was bordered on both sides by thickets of trees; no footprints were visible in the snow. "It never ceases to amaze me when someone buys a property worth millions, but won't spend a few bucks to keep it clear in case of fire. They forget that sparks can fly from neighbor to neighbor and burn down more than one house." He sighed, then pointed down the hill. "Your next-door neighbors are down there. The Littlefield property. They sank a ton of cash into renovations a few years ago. But both parents are dead now—the kids are squabbling about selling it. Nobody wins. In the meantime, no one keeps an eye on the place. They don't even have an alarm system. A couple of them come and go, on and off, in summer, but don't seem to care much about their inheritance. As I recall, they once seemed smart enough. But . . ." He shrugged, took his foot off the brake, and shifted back into first gear. "Anyway, our girl isn't here. No footprints. No lights."

They drove to the next driveway, which had been plowed.

"Looks like Taylor's been around." He turned down the wide path; Annie assumed that Taylor—whoever that was—was in charge of that particular property: apparently, the market for caretakers was strong on Chappy. They rounded a curve, then another, and Earl's truck abruptly came grill-to-grill with another black pickup.

He stopped and said, "Speak of the devil. You wait here. I'll do the talking."

Annie had no intention of getting out, but watched as both men did. They met in the middle of what looked like dueling pickups and shook hands. Taylor wore a heavy knit cap and an L.L.Bean parka that looked just like Earl's.

"Seen a lost cat?" Annie heard Earl ask. It took a moment to realize he'd made that up as a reason why they'd gone down the driveway.

"Haven't seen much of anything," came the reply. "'Cept a nasty hawk that I'm pretty sure has been going after the chickens at the Alvords' coop."

Earl scanned the property. "Could be leftover tourists. They gotta eat, too."

Taylor shook his head. "Nah. Those two-leggers are long gone. They think Chappy shuts down after Columbus Day." Then he nodded toward Earl's truck. "'Cept her, of course. She staying the winter?" Taylor took off his hat, and a mass of auburn hair tumbled out. Annie blinked. She hadn't thought Taylor had seen her. Nor had she imagined that Taylor was a woman. The basket was out of sight between her feet; Annie reached down and smoothed the blanket around sleeping Bella.

"Looks like she's with us for a while," Earl said, then gave Taylor a small salute. "Later, neighbor. Got a cat to track down." He headed back to the truck, and Taylor headed toward hers.

"Keep an eye out for that hawk," she called back to him. "You have my permission to shoot it."

Chuckling again, Earl got into the truck, threw the shift into reverse, and deftly maneuvered the curves of the driveway as if he did it—backward—every day.

Once he reached the road, he drove what might have been the length of a football field, then steered between two redbrick pillars and down a long driveway that also had been cleared, but had a coat of fresh powder on top. Clearly, the work had been finished before the snow had stopped. "This place changed hands last year for over eight million. Never have seen anyone around, but rumor has it, it's a movie star. As if we don't get enough of those."

Then a house came into view. Like the Flanagans', it was big and wide and had gray cedar shingles and an enormous porch that looked like it encircled the perimeter. A five-bay garage with what could be a second-story guest apartment stood off to one side. But the only signs of life were the soft footprints of rabbits and deer, not those made by a young woman who had abandoned her baby—*yes,* Annie thought, *that was what it felt like now.* And no lights were on, upstairs or down.

"Another dead end," Annie said. "If Bella's mother is here, it doesn't look like she's been outside since the storm stopped."

"Yup," Earl said, turning the truck around and heading back toward the road. "Let's go out as far as the golf course tonight. We can scout more tomorrow. I have errands off island in the morning, but I can come by after lunch."

The rest of the houses on North Neck were as dark as the sky had grown, with no signs of a squatter. By the time they were finished, Bella started to cry, as if she, too, were ready to give up on having a happy ending.

★　★　★

The car was back. Francine had no idea why it had been gone all night. She'd waited and she'd worried, but it hadn't come back until afternoon.

Then it was gone again.

And a truck had showed up.

Then the car came back.

Now the truck was gone.

She pushed her hands against her temples, the blood coursing inside her head, hammering harder and harder, hurting more and more.

She'd planned to make her move last night, when nobody was around. But she'd fallen asleep. When she'd woken up, it was daylight. Too late. So she lay there waiting. Watching. Still frozen, though the numbness had started to feel normal.

She must have even fallen asleep again because the sky looked as if it was growing dark. Unless they were in for another stupid storm.

She wondered why Annie Sutton had been gone all night. Had she taken Bella somewhere else, like Boston or New York or any of those cities where rich people like her went? Like where Gramps had threatened to make them move so Francine's father could reach his potential? It had never happened; her father had killed himself first.

Maybe Annie Sutton had dumped Bella at one of those hospitals where people were now allowed to dump babies—the unwanted, the unloved, no questions asked.

Bella, little Bella, deserved better. Which was why Francine had found Annie in the first place.

She pulled the covers over her head again. She knew she could not do what she needed to do. Not yet. Not until she knew. If Bella really was all right.

It hadn't been part of her plan. But neither had been breaking into a big house and freezing to death.

Chapter 9

It did not feel like Christmas, not like the Christmases of long ago when Annie had spent hours baking with her mother, watching old holiday movies with her dad (*It's a Wonderful Life* and *Miracle on 34th Street* were his favorites), then helping to deliver almond cookies and cherry tarts (also her dad's favorites) to the neighbors and the mailman and the newspaper boy. It didn't even seem like the more recent Christmases she'd spent with Murphy and her husband and the boys, when she and Murphy stayed up long past midnight, sipping brandy Alexanders and wrapping gifts, while Murphy's husband left them to their gossip and went to bed.

Unlike all of those, this Christmas was quiet. Except for the wind that was still blowing into the evening.

"Enough with the wind!" Annie cried cheerfully as she slid a tray of candy cane cookies into the oven. They had been her mother's specialty, back before everyone had access to the recipe through Instagram: she'd dyed half the dough red, rolled out thin logs of white and red, and twisted them together into candy cane shapes, and then, once they were out of the oven and cooled, she squeezed green frosting out of a tiny hole in a cloth bag and decorated the "hook" with what looked like a wreath. Those cookies were the one thing that Annie made every year—when she'd been with Brian, when she'd been with Mark, since she'd been alone. They helped her feel festive and connected to the ones whom she had loved. This year, she would wrap some for Earl—she suspected he'd enjoy them.

Despite moments of nostalgia, Annie tried to keep smiling. Having shared her dilemma with Winnie and now Earl, having each of them agree without hesitation to help her, without trying to convince her to go to the police, meant a lot. It meant she had found two friends whom she could trust. Good friends—the kind who weren't easy to find.

She picked out a few of her handmade soaps for Claire, wrapped them in red tissue, and tied them together with silver ribbon. She wondered if she should bring something for John. What was an appropriate gift for a police officer that someone had been trying to avoid?

"Good question," she said with a snicker.

Dragging a chair to the sink, she climbed onto it, opened the overhead cabinet, and unearthed a few snowmen-themed tins. Maybe she'd make a double batch of cinnamon rolls and split them between Earl and John; she could also give Earl the extra pair of alpaca socks she'd bought, like the ones that she'd sent Murphy's husband, Stan. After seeing Winnie's magnificent library, she'd already decided to give her a signed edition of a young British nature writer, Lou MacFarlane's, latest work. It wasn't on a topic Annie typically read, but after her first novel was published, she promised herself that whenever she saw an author signing books, she'd buy a copy and have it signed. She'd logged in too many hours sitting at one of those tables in bookstores, praying someone would pick up one of hers, or simply stop to say hi. Over time, she'd wound up with an eclectic collection of volumes, from poetry to cookbooks, from thrillers to nature—like the one that she'd give Winnie.

With Bella contentedly examining Annie's measuring spoons, the baking underway, and the modest gift list finalized, Annie wondered if she could make something Bella might like, something that could go with her wherever she ended up, a small reminder of a woman who'd sheltered her during a blizzard.

With a giant sigh, she knew she was being sentimental—a telltale sign of the season. *Good for me*, she decided. At least she was cheerful on her first Vineyard Christmas, when she could have been, *would* have been, otherwise.

But what could she make Bella? When Murphy's boys were babies, she'd given them each a small stuffed bunny: beige for Danny, yellow for Derek. They had kept them for years, until they'd fallen apart. It was too late to shop, so Annie went to the linen closet again on a quest for ideas. In just a few minutes, she knew what to do. But first, she had to finish the baking. Then she would finally decorate the tree.

With a batch of candy cane cookies in the oven and another one cooling, Annie retrieved a long plastic container from under her bed: it was loaded with shiny ornaments, glimmering tinsel, and strings of lights from Christmases Past.

"We need to be sure that Santa will find us," she told Bella.

Then she strung and hung and adjusted; she stood on a chair and positioned the angel on the top, while the baby quietly watched, mesmerized, the whole time. When Annie plugged in the lights, Bella's mouth opened; she cooed and rattled the spoons.

Then Annie resurrected her third-grade teaching skills and began to make Bella's gift. Plucking a section of the *Times* from the kindling box and scissors and a marker from the junk drawer in the kitchen, she smoothed the newsprint on the

floor and drew a template of a baby lamb—like the ones that
romped and grazed up island. Then, using a white fleece jacket
she'd planned to donate to the thrift shop, and shredding leftover fabric for stuffing, Annie made a sweet little companion
for Bella. From old felt pieces she'd found in the box of ornaments, she cut out a red mouth, black eyes, and little black
hooves, which she didn't know if sheep had. As a finishing
touch, she cut a small bit of ribbon from the red bow on Bella's
basket and shaped it into a heart for the lamb's chest—like the
heart on her childhood Raggedy Ann doll.

When she started stitching, she kept her back to Bella so
the baby wouldn't see what she was making. It was foolish, of
course, but thankfully, Murphy didn't comment. A few times,
when Annie looked over her shoulder, she realized that Bella
was too interested in looking at the tree to bother with what
she was doing.

Annie smiled; she couldn't remember when she'd had such
heartwarming fun. So it made no sense that when she was finished, without a hint of a warning, Winnie's words sprang to
her mind:

*You would have made a fine mother, Annie Sutton. You already
love a baby you don't even know.*

She drew in a sharp breath as another memory flooded
back. Dropping the needle and thread, Annie closed her eyes,
her old demon rising from the ashes of her past.

It was still hard to believe that she'd had an abortion. She.
Annie Sutton. Of all people.

She and Mark had been married less than a year: she'd
known he'd be angry that she was pregnant; he'd told her several times it was too soon. But one night over wine and a mis-
placed diaphragm, an accident happened. Annie pondered on
it, prayed on it, talked to Murphy about it. And then Annie
made the decision not to tell Mark. The next time he left the

country for a business meeting, she scheduled the procedure. Murphy went with her to the hospital.

"It's too soon," Annie repeated Mark's words as they sat in the waiting room. "It's not just about him, either. I honestly think he's worried that it's too soon for me. Too soon after Brian's accident, you know?"

They were excuses, which Murphy must have suspected. But after a few more "Are you sure?" remarks, her friend nodded, took her hand, and said nothing more.

Several years later, when Annie's bio-clock (as Murphy called it) began to tick loudly, she stopped taking the pill. She didn't tell Mark. And yet, she never got pregnant again. In the dark corner of her mind that she reserved for truths too painful to consider, Annie added the big one: God was punishing her for having had the abortion.

But now, with her wonderful mood threatening to slide, to feel those sad, long-buried feelings once again, her cell phone, blessedly, rang.

"Auntie Annie! Auntie Annie!" came the stereo voices of Murphy's twins.

Of course it's them, Annie thought. *Murphy is working her magic.* She looked up to the ceiling and blew her friend a kiss.

"We've got you on speaker," one of the boys said, "so don't say anything you don't want Dad to hear. He's standing right behind us."

"Hello, Annie," Stan, called from the background.

"Hi, you guys." Annie quickly moved to the kitchen, grabbed a bottle of wine, and poured a glass. She took a quick sip, smiling again, silently praising that instant gratification sometimes had its place.

"Thanks for the loot!" It had always been hard to tell the twins apart, whether on the phone or in person. They had

Murphy's red hair and Stan's tall, solid build, and both had their parents' giant personalities. "We're going to save it for our birthday so we can go to O'Malley's and get viciously drunk."

"I heard that," Stan said.

Annie laughed. "I was hoping you'd do something more sensible, like put it toward grad school."

"Oh," one of them replied with fake disappointment. "Yeah, I suppose we could do that." They were scheduled to graduate from Boston College in May: Danny was headed to grad school for astrophysics; Derek to med school to become a surgeon, like Stan. Murphy had raised brilliant boys. She'd once confided to Annie that she never guessed she'd have kids who "were so amazingly well wired together." Annie never understood what that meant, but supposed it was based on something Irish.

They chattered a few more minutes, then said they were off to a party. "Merry Christmas, thanks again!" were their parting words before turning the phone over to Stan.

"The boys sound good," Annie said. "How are they really doing?"

"Actually, not bad. For our first Christmas without her. You know how they've always bolstered each other, whether one failed to ace a test or one of their teams lost a game. Murphy always loved that. She would have loved to see them now." His voice grew somber, tired.

"How about you?" Annie asked. "How are you doing?"

"I'm doing crappy, but thanks for asking. Thank God I have work. And the boys. Did I tell you the hospital gave me a promotion? Chief of Neurosurgery, can you imagine?"

"Oh, Stan, that's wonderful."

"At first I thought they felt sorry for me. Then I realized how much work is involved. I was probably the only sucker who'd accept."

"Stop it. I'm sure you earned it. Murphy would know that."

"Yeah," he said, "yeah, she would."

The conversation fell into silence, then Annie said, "It's still so hard to believe she's not here. I really miss her, Stan."

"Me, too, Annie. She'd be happy for you that you're on the Vineyard, though. One time toward the end, when she was sitting in the chemo chair trying to be patient—which, as you know, wasn't easy for her—she said she was so happy you'd moved there. She said the island was your happy place and that you, of all people, deserved some happiness."

A bounty of emotion swelled in her again. "I do love it here, Stan. And I survived my first nor'easter, though the infernal wind has whipped up again tonight."

"Wind off the water can be most interesting."

"Especially when you're in an old cottage that, charming as it is, provides a constant chorus of creaks and groans." As if in response, a strong gust shook the kitchen window. "Sometimes," she added, "I feel her presence here. It makes me feel good. Not so alone."

Stan gave a small laugh. "That's strange, because I feel her here, too. Leave it to our Murphy to learn how to be in two places at once."

Annie laughed, too. Then she wondered if she should tell him about Bella, but decided not to. Stan deserved to have this conversation be about him, the boys, and his late wife. Not about Annie and her little drama that had nothing to do with them.

He thanked her for the socks; she told him about the wonderful alpaca farm on Oak Bluffs. They talked awhile longer, then ran out of things to say. Annie promised to be at the twins' graduation in May, and they wistfully said good night.

Fueled by having connected to people she loved, Annie picked up the messes she had made around the cottage, grateful for Stan and the twins, for Winnie and Earl and for Bella, and for her belief that there could still be many wonders yet to come in her life. She knew she'd learned that optimism from her father.

It was after midnight when Annie finally snuggled Bella into the bureau drawer, then crawled into bed and pulled up the covers. She was exhausted, yet felt wonderful. She hadn't realized how much she'd dreaded this Christmas until now, when she no longer did.

Looking over at Bella, she knew that this baby was a gift that she'd been given, if only for a short time. A gift of experiencing unconditional love, of total dependability, of utter trust. This was what a baby brought, along with diapers, crying, and spit-up. That was what Annie had missed out on for reasons she'd never learn, but she knew it was time to accept the fact.

She closed her eyes, wondering, not for the first time, how many babies she and Brian might have had, how much laughter and love they would have shared, if that accident had never happened. But love, she now knew, came in different ways, like with sweet little Bella, fast asleep in the small nightstand drawer.

The day after Christmas would come soon enough; until then, Annie would keep searching for Bella's mother as best she could. Winnie was right, Annie did love Bella, but Bella was not Annie's; just as Bella had shown up on Annie's doorstep and not on Earl and Claire's.

At last, her thoughts guided her peacefully into sleep until—suddenly—a loud bang shot through the night.

Her eyes flew open, as they'd done before.

She knew in an instant that the sound had come from the porch door. As if it had been opened. By someone. Or something.

Her body went rigid; she sucked in her breath.

Then she heard footsteps. Again.

And another bang.

Then . . . silence.

Had she been dreaming? It was possible, but . . .

Her eyes darted over to Bella. But it was so dark, Annie could not see her. So she held her breath and listened until she heard the baby's soft sleeping sounds.

It must have been the wind, Annie told herself. The door must have blown open, rattled, then slammed back against the windows. It was only a coincidence that it sounded like something else.

She had no idea what the odds would be for that.

But she hated to think about what she really thought.

That it was *her*.

That she'd come back.

Squeezing her eyes shut, Annie tried to relax, tried to breathe quietly, steadily, the way Bella was doing. *It will be fine*, she said as in a mantra. *It will. It will.*

She knew she should investigate. But in the living room, the fire would still be casting a low glow, and she'd left the tree lights on. If someone—if *she*—were on the porch, Annie would be spotted as soon as she stepped out of the bedroom. If she looked out into the night, however, she would not see anything—or anyone—in the darkness, not until she'd walked clear across the room and turned on the outside lights.

But before she'd be able to see outside, she would be clearly visible through the living room windows. Because they had no curtains. Because here on Martha's Vineyard, people trusted that their neighbors respected their privacy.

Holding her breath again, Annie continued to listen. But all she heard were the symphony of creaks and groans that she'd been hearing all evening and the eerie hoot of a distant, snowy owl.

So she stayed motionless, under her covers. And hoped that she wouldn't have to give Bella up. Not yet. *Please, Murphy*, Annie whispered. *Not yet.* And not in the middle of the night when good things usually didn't happen.

Chapter 10

Annie had no idea how she'd fallen back to sleep. But first thing in the morning, she looked onto the porch. The outside door was closed. Whatever had gone bump in the night must have been in her dreams. Still, she must remember to ask Earl to check the latch on the porch door. She didn't want to spend another night with her imagination working overtime.

By the time Bella awoke, Annie had showered and dressed. She breezed through her mom-chores with surprising ease, then spread her favorite quilt in front of the tree and set Bella on it. She gave her the things she'd picked up at Stop & Shop: the teething ring and some baby toys—a set of plastic keys, a rubber caterpillar, and, God help her, a ball that could transform its colors and "dance" to the songs of farm animals.

She sat next to Bella, who touched the ball and giggled, clearly more interested in that than in the other things. Annie tapped a button: the ball turned red and jumped around while a cow sang a verse about giving chocolate milk. Bella giggled again as if she understood. When Annie tapped the ball again, it turned green and bounced to a tinny voice that belonged to a mouse who sang about living in a hayfield behind a barn. With another tap, the ball glowed yellow and jiggled and a duck

quack-quacked so loudly that Annie barely heard the knocking on the door.

"Annie!" a voice called out. "It's Winnie!"

Pulling herself up off the floor, Annie went to the door.

Winnie was alone. She wore a red Santa hat and carried a
white pillowcase decorated with green felt holly leaves and
berries made of red glitter. "Merry Christmas!" she exclaimed.
"Are you two having a party?"

Annie laughed and let her in. "We're playing with . . . something. I don't know what you call it. This stuff's new to me."

Glancing down, Winnie quickly said, "It's what my grandkids call a wiggle biggle. They all had one. They said it was
magical."

"A wiggle biggle. I should have guessed. Though it's hardly
magical."

"It is, according to them." Winnie handed her the pillowcase.
"From my crew. A bit of everything for a Merry Christmas."

"Thank you, Winnie. But you shouldn't have. Really."

"It's not as much as it looks like. Just a few things that are
part of our holiday tradition. And something special for the lit-
tlest angel." She reached into the pillowcase, withdrew a flat
object wrapped in pink tissue, and handed it to Annie. "We all
had a hand in making this. But it was Lucas's idea. He still has
the one I made him when he was a baby."

Annie opened the tissue. Inside was a large ring that
looked like it was made from a twig or tree branch. Pink and
white feathers dangled from the perimeter. "It's beautiful. Is it
a dream catcher?"

"Yes. A special one. For a baby. The feathers are attached to
a willow hoop. It goes over her crib—if the poor thing ever
gets one. It should be hung high enough so she can't touch it,
but close enough so it will catch her dreams and keep them in
the circle of her life. My family has always believed that the
dreams we had as babies always remain with us."

Annie felt a twinge of wonder again about those six weeks when she'd had no one—no birth mother, no adopted parents, just foster people who tended to her physical needs. Had she dreamed back then? Then she realized that though having Bella around was fun, she wasn't crazy about the way the baby's presence kept dredging up thoughts of her own past. She cleared her throat. "It really is beautiful," she repeated. "I'm sure it will mean a lot to Bella, wherever she goes."

"Well," Winnie laughed, "if you're going to hang out with Native people, you're going to have to learn our lore." She handed Annie a few more gifts: a jar of honey from the three hives her brother tended on their land; a box of tea made from their herbs; and a pale blue and green pottery mug that Winnie made.

Annie was touched. Uplifted. And grateful for the presents, but mostly for the gift of friendship.

Then Winnie got down on the floor and pushed the button on the wiggle biggle: the toy lit up pink; a pig emitted a rendition of oink-oink as it leapt in little circles. Bella's tiny giggles bubbled up. "Babies are so precious," Winnie added.

Knowing that if she responded, she was sure to cry, she went to the table and retrieved the book for Winnie and a package of candy cane cookies. "For you," she said. "From me. Or I guess I should say 'from us,' because Bella watched me make the cookies before she took her nap." She handed Winnie the gifts. "But I can't believe you drove all the way out here from Aquinnah. And I can't believe you found this place again!" Winnie had been to the cottage once when Annie had run out of soybean oil while she was making soap; she'd dropped some off while en route to Edgartown to deliver jewelry for October sales in shops.

"When you've lived here all your life, you know how to find most things. Well, most places, anyway. People, not always. Speaking of which . . ."

"Open your gift first."

So Winnie did. "MacFarlane! I've heard of him, but never read one of his books. Thank you, my friend."

"I'm not sure if you have any more room in your book-case . . . but it's autographed. I met him at a signing."

"I shall read it. And treasure it. But enough procrastinating. Tell me where things stand with Bella's mother."

Annie filled her in on her useless attempts. She also told her about Earl, and how, so far, they'd struck out, too.

"If anyone can find her, Earl Lyons can," Winnie said. "It's good that you decided to tell him. But I wonder if the girl's already left Chappy. Unless she lives here."

"That seems doubtful, don't you think? From what I understand, most people who are here after Columbus Day live here year-round. And everyone knows everyone, or so I'm told. If she needed to keep Bella a secret, there would be easier places to do it than Chappaquiddick."

"What about the ferry captains? Of course, you wouldn't know who'd been on duty, because you don't know when she crossed. Actually, you don't know much of anything, do you?"

"No. Only that she was on the Vineyard sometime between the Holiday Crafts Fair and the night of the blizzard. A grand total of three days." Annie sat down and poked the wiggle biggle, which responded with a kitten's mew. Bella cooed and reached out to touch the surface that now glowed silver as it jiggled.

Annie sighed. "I've promised myself I will notify the police the day after Christmas. If I haven't found her by then. Or if she hasn't come back to us."

"You don't have to explain to me why you're stalling," Winnie said quietly, "but I have a feeling there's a lot more to this story."

"Not to Bella's story, but to mine. I'm stalling because I was adopted, Winnie. I want to give her mother a fair chance to change her mind. Otherwise, if down the road, she regrets what she has done, it might be too late."

During the hour that followed, Annie told Winnie about her parents, and her wonderful childhood, but how she'd sometimes felt something was missing. Then she told about her marriages, about the empty days and nights she'd had since then, and about how, after Mark's demise, writing books had saved her sanity and rescued her from financial ruin.

Winnie listened with kindness. "I guess most of us don't make it to adulthood without a knotted-up story behind us. But now, I see how good you are with Bella. Yet you didn't have children? Ignore the question if it's too personal."

"It's not. And no. I did not have children. My first husband died too young; my second didn't want them."

"So it was not because you were adopted?"

"I don't think so. I've always loved kids; I used to be a third-grade teacher." She toyed with the edge of the quilt, which was one of her favorite possessions—something she'd never get rid of no matter how much she downsized. Her mother had made it as a wedding gift for Annie and Brian. She'd used squares of fabric left over from dresses and skirts that she'd made for Annie when Annie was a little girl: polished cotton Sunday dresses, pleated wool skirts for school, even the buttercup-colored satin gown she'd worn to the eighth-grade semiformal dance and afterward, at Brigham's, had spilled a chocolate frappe on.

"When I was married to my second husband, I had an abortion," she blurted out suddenly. It was the first time since Murphy that Annie had shared her humiliating secret. "So maybe you're right. In my mind, I blamed him. He kept saying we should wait to have kids. Maybe I was too willing to let the time go by because, deep down, I was afraid that if I had a baby, I'd abandon her, the way my birth mother had abandoned me."

She knew that last thought had come from the special corner, the safe harbor, in her mind.

"Is that how it happened? Your mother abandoned you?"

"It's what I'd chosen to believe. I wrote about it in my first novel, though I pretended it had happened to my character, not me."

"But that wasn't the real story?"

"No." Then Bella began to cry. Annie picked her up and held her, as if she were her own.

"When I turned thirty," she continued, "my birth mother wrote to me. I didn't respond." She lowered her eyes. "The timing was all wrong. My adoptive parents had recently died—first my dad, then, six months later, my mom. If I'd reached out to Donna—that's her name—it would have felt as if I were trying to replace the Suttons, as if they hadn't mattered to me. I couldn't do that. I loved and respected them too much."

Winnie slowly nodded. "Maybe you were trying to protect their memory, the way they'd protected you. There's nothing wrong with that." She reached over and took Annie's hand. "We are all people, Annie, and people are complex. Our stories make us who we are. Yours explains a lot—you have a kind, sensitive soul. And Bella is lucky that her mother brought her here. Because you know the importance of protecting those who need it."

Annie shrugged. "Maybe it was just a coincidence that Bella landed here. Or a lucky guess on her mother's part. But I'm sure anyone would have done what worked best for them; what they thought would be best for the baby."

"I have a feeling you don't tell many people about your past," Winnie said.

"No. I'm a fairly happy person; I've never considered the past as baggage. Maybe that's because I've never wanted to deal with the discussion. Or with judgment."

Winnie stood up. "Well, you don't have to worry about any of that here. You're among people who care about you, Annie. The longer you live here, the more you'll come to know that. Most island people don't judge one another." Then she smirked. "Of course, there's always a rogue or two."

Annie smiled, stood up, and gave her a hug. "Thanks, Winnie. For everything. Mostly for understanding."

"And thank you for trusting me. But for now, I must get back to my sleigh. I have other deliveries to make."

She was halfway out the door when Annie had a sudden thought. "Wait!" she called out. "How did you know Bella would still be with me? How did you know I hadn't brought her to the police?"

Winnie glanced back, her mouth turned up in a smile. "Guess it must be magic. Like the wiggle biggle." She put her hand on the porch door, then looked back at Annie. "By the way, do you know the latch on your screen door is broken?"

Annie stared at the latch. An icy chill ran down her spine; the tenderness of the morning swept away. She wanted to tell Winnie about the noises in the night, but she'd already taken too much of her time. It was Christmas Eve; Winnie had things to do. So Annie just said, "Oh. Well, thanks. I'll have Earl take care of it. He'll be here soon. I'm going to their place tonight for Christmas Eve."

"Well then, good luck. Have you met Claire yet?"

"Briefly."

Winnie nodded. "Okay, well, be careful. She's Earl's wife, but . . ." She nodded again as if agreeing with herself, thanked Annie for the gifts, then went on her way.

Annie waved as the old van sputtered up the driveway. She wondered why on earth Winnie had said that about Claire. Perhaps she'd had an odd altercation with her, the way Annie had at the dock. Picking up the dream catcher, Annie touched the delicate feathers. She thought about how intuitive Winnie was about people and their needs, how she could convey a message even by leaving things unsaid. If her words about Claire were meant to be a warning, Annie knew she should be mindful of them.

Chapter 11

By the time Earl arrived for their hunting expedition, Annie had eaten half a sandwich, and Bella was up from her nap. It was after two o'clock: she'd begun to think he had forgotten.

"Sorry I'm late. I had to stop at the florist and the drugstore and fill up a few jugs with gas just in case another storm decides to brew. Not to mention it felt like August in town. Impossible to get through traffic at the triangle."

The triangle was where customers of the post office, a few banks, and other shops converged and often became entangled, even off season. She'd once commented that it was strange, in today's world, that neither he nor Winnie liked using cell phones. "I, for one, have gone without one nearly as many years as there are scallops in Poucha Pond," he had explained. "And, don't forget, we haven't had reliable service as long as they've had it in America. At this stage of the game, I can survive without one. Maybe Winnie feels the same." It was an understandable reply. And it was why Annie simply smiled now and said, "Don't worry about being late. Bella and I had a surprise visit from Winnie that kept us busy."

He nodded and picked up Bella's basket. "Sorry I missed

her. Did I ever tell you one of her uncles was in business with my dad?"

Annie zipped her jacket and slipped on her gloves. "No. Doing what?"

"Carpentry. They teamed up in the early seventies when the housing boom hit the island. Thanks to Senator Ted Kennedy, folks who'd never heard of Martha's Vineyard suddenly wanted a piece of the place. My dad and Winnie's Uncle Joe did well. They did interior finish work on a whole lot of houses that were built back then." He ambled outside toward the truck, and Annie followed.

"So that's where you got your skills as a caretaker? From your dad?"

Laughing, he opened the passenger door. He waited until Annie got in, then he set the basket at her feet. "Hardly. My dad was a natural carpenter. I'm just a jack of all trades. Or as my irascible neighbor, Lou Morton, calls me, 'a jerk of all trades.'" He chuckled, closed the door, and went around to the other side. After buckling his seat belt, he turned on the ignition, then started to back out of the driveway. "Now," he said, "don't get upset with me, but I asked Frank, the *On Time* captain this morning, if he'd seen my wife's niece. I said she's about twenty, and would have been carrying a baby. I told him that most times she carries it in a woven basket. I figured the basket would be something he might remember."

Annie wasn't sure if she should be pleased that Earl was trying to help or upset that he'd risked exposing her secret—especially since he'd already agreed not to. She kept her eyes riveted on a snowbank. "You lied to him?"

He shrugged. "Call it a white lie. Claire doesn't leave Chappy without me, so if he asks about it in front of her, I'll say he misunderstood. But he won't ask. He barely says two words, even to me, and I've known him fifty years."

"So . . ." She paused. "What did he say?"

"He said, 'Nope.' Like I said, he's a man of few words. But I thought it was worth a try." He turned onto the main road, then after a minute, onto Narragansett. "Lots of places off the beaten path in here. It's not too far from your place, so she could have made it in the snow. She also might have thought no one would look for her over here."

Though Annie wasn't happy Earl had talked to the ferry captain, she reminded herself that she trusted him. If he didn't think Frank would repeat the conversation, then the man probably wouldn't.

The road was rutty and snow-packed, so Earl drove slowly. He glanced at houses on the left; she checked the ones on the right. A few places had old Jeeps or pickup trucks in the driveways, but Earl said he knew who lived there. Mostly, the houses were vacant. They looked like summer places; the driveways hadn't been plowed; they were modest, some even small, unlike the homes that faced the water.

"Rentals," Earl grumbled. "Some owners are here for a couple of weeks, others not at all. Imagine that. Having a place on the Vineyard—even just a cottage like one of these—but never using it."

The farther they drove from Annie's place, the thickets of scrub oaks grew more dense, their leafless arms twisting and knotting into one another's shadows. The land was more remote; soon it was clear that the young woman could not have trudged as far during the blizzard. Not if she'd been alone, and certainly not while carrying ten pounds or more of baby.

"Dang," Earl said.

"Yes," Annie replied, "dang, indeed."

"I don't suppose there's any point in looking farther out. Not without stopping at a house or two to ask. They're my neighbors, and I trust them, but you never know."

"Agreed. The fewer people who know, the better. Not unless—and until—it's necessary." She hoped she wouldn't have to keep reminding him of that.

He pulled into a driveway and turned the truck around. "I know it's getting late, but do you mind if we take a quick detour before I bring you back?"

"Of course not."

"It gets dark so early, and otherwise there won't be time . . ."

"Earl, it's fine."

"Thanks. Ever been to the Indian Burial Ground?"

It took her a moment to realize he was serious. "Well, no. Is it what it sounds like?"

"Yup. It's also called Jeffers Lane Cemetery. Chappaquiddick was once inhabited only by Wampanoags. Which you probably already figured. The official cemetery wasn't here until the mid–eighteen hundreds; I think some of Winnie's ancestors might even be buried there. There are only a couple of dozen original headstones, though, and not all of them are readable. Some field stones mark even older graves, though no one has any idea how old they are or who's buried under them."

"Are we going there now?" Annie asked. She wondered why, on Christmas Eve, Earl wanted to visit a Wampanoag cemetery.

"Yup. The land is precious, and the view is breathtaking, but at one time they opened it to a few other lucky folks. My parents are buried there. My great-grandfather's homestead was down the road, so my father's father and his father are there, too."

"Earl," she said, "how wonderful for you." He didn't know she'd been adopted; he had no way of knowing that being part of a family that had roots that could be traced back for generations—with graves they actually could visit—were an anomaly to her. She looked down at the basket at her feet and hoped that wouldn't be in Bella's future, too.

After a few short minutes, they arrived at the Indian Burial

Ground. There was no driveway; just a path that looked to have been cleared by a snowblower.

"Good," Earl said, "John's been here." He reached behind the seat and pulled out a small potted fir that Annie hadn't noticed before. It was decorated with a string of popcorn, small red birds fashioned out of birdseed, and a star that looked like it had been made from suet. He got out of the truck and, juggling the tree, started up the path.

Annie opened her door, picked up Bella, and joined him. If she ever planned to write another novel that took place on the Vineyard—specifically, on Chappy—this might be something she should see.

The headstones were no bigger than Annie's laptop. She counted a dozen: each read LYONS, followed by a first name, then birth and death years. Like Earl, there was nothing fancy about them. It was interesting, though, that they stood in a horizontal row, all facing the ocean. And even more interesting that the path had been cleanly plowed all the way down the row.

"Your son plowed this?" she asked.

"I was busy with the errands, so I didn't see him this morning. But, yes, I knew he'd be over to do it. The only one he remembers is his grandpop. But every year Donaroma's makes up a small tree for us just like this one, and I bring it on Christmas Eve. When John was a boy, he came with me. He can't always get here on account of his work, but he makes sure it's plowed out for me. It's a small thing, but it's how we pay our respects to our ancestors."

Annie watched as he set the tree firmly on the ground.

"They're lined up like this so they face the sunrise," Earl said. "Some folks think it's a tradition carried over from the Wampanoags. And though I can't be sure, my best guess is that one or two of my ancestors must have had Indian blood running through their veins."

He took off his hat, knelt in the snow, and bowed his head. Annie looked down at Bella, who began to softly coo, as if she were praying along with him. Annie realized that, as envious as she felt, she also found it fascinating that Earl continued to honor his ancestors, year after year, even the ones he'd never met, and that though Earl's son only remembered one out of the dozen, he continued to follow his father's tradition. Annie supposed that long after both his parents were gone, John would still bring a small tree every Christmas Eve. Annie suspected it was about more than plain tradition; it was about . . . roots.

Annie didn't know much about roots. She'd stopped by her parents' graves before she'd moved from Boston; she'd thanked them for the years they'd given her. She'd also gone to the large plot owned by Brian's family, but seeing his name chiseled into a large monument, one line of a list of his affluent ancestors, always left her cold. Murphy had been cremated, her ashes tossed into the North Sea, per her request.

Those were the only memorials—the only roots—to which Annie felt connected. They were hardly representative of a notable lineage.

When they got back into the truck, Annie said, "Thank you, Earl. For sharing this with me. It's nice that you still feel linked to your parents . . . and to the others."

He scratched at his whiskers, then drove away. "I know it's old-fashioned, but it's important to me. And I'm glad it's important to John. His ex-wife told him she was leaving because of all the people—the live ones and the dead ones—that he had around him. She said it was weird that he cared more about the Vineyard than he did about her."

"Did he?"

Earl laughed. "I expect he might have! I never thought she liked us very much. It's a shame, though, that John didn't have sons. No one to carry on the family name."

"Sometimes, today, girls keep their father's name whether they marry or not."

"Yeah, I know. It's a crazy world, isn't it?"

Annie didn't mention that in parts of Europe and Asia, and even in Quebec, it had been common practice for decades or more—in some countries it was the law—for a woman to retain her maiden name after she was married.

They were soon back on the main road, heading toward the cottage. The sun had begun to set, spreading a smoky, almost foggy blanket over the snow. Every so often, lights appeared in the window of a cottage—tiny, colorful lights, the markings of the season. A few chimneys puffed with life; a dog barked at a back door: Earl knew who lived in all of them. In spite of the cozy atmosphere, Annie was aware that the chances of finding Bella's mother were diminishing with every hour.

"What time tonight?" she asked as Earl pulled into her driveway.

"Six? I'll pick you up. You don't know how to get to my place, and it's a pain in the ass, pardon my French, to explain. Besides, it's pitch-dark out there. One of us can bring you and the baby home."

Annie was glad for the small bit of time alone. She put on black pants and a red cashmere sweater, fed and changed Bella, then slipped a CD of soft Christmas music into her small sound system. She held the baby while they sat by the tree, slowly rocking to the rhythm of the song.

"This is your first Christmas," she said in a low voice. "Thanks for sharing it with me."

She could have sworn she heard Murphy say, "My pleasure."

Annie laughed, then said to Bella, "If you heard that, it was our guardian angel. But as much as I'm glad she's here, I wish she could bring you something festive to wear, like a snuggly red onesie or a green elf suit with cute little pointed booties." She gently brushed back Bella's dark hair, then had an idea.

Setting the baby on the quilt, she went to the big container that held her soap-packaging needs: the labels, the netting, the ribbons. "I should have thought of this earlier," she said, pulling out a roll of red ribbon and a square of soft netting. She went back to the rocker and, through patience and persistence, she crafted a flower that looked like a corsage. She picked Bella up again then, and using two-sided tape, she attached it to the onesie, over the baby's chest.

Amazingly, Bella stayed very still while Annie then gathered her hair into a topknot ponytail and tied it with the ribbon. "There. You are the prettiest package of cranberry and aloe oil I ever could have made."

Bella gurgled, smiled, and wiggled her arms.

"No!" Annie laughed. "Don't even think about tearing it out of your hair!" She held her and rocked her and kissed her on the forehead.

Then she heard sounds on the front porch. A bang. Followed by clomping footsteps. She listened. The clomping didn't sound like Earl's. She held her breath. *Oh, God*, she thought. *I forgot to tell him the latch was broken. What if it wasn't him . . . what if it was . . .*

A knock on the door was loud. And firm.

Annie pulled Bella close, but didn't get up. *Could it really be Bella's mother, returning to get her on Christmas Eve? Could she look through the window and see them sitting there?* Annie knew she should welcome the girl, knew she should be relieved, and yet . . . well, the truth was, she'd looked forward to the evening, to being with the baby.

Then came a shout: "Annie? Annie Sutton? Am I in the right place?" It was a man's voice. Deep and resonant.

A man?

Annie didn't know what to do. Could it be Bella's father? Just because the visitor knew her name was no guarantee that he was there with good intentions. She sat motionless, hoping he couldn't see them.

"It's John Lyons," the voice said then. "Earl's son. He asked me to bring you to the house."

Letting her grip on the baby loosen, Annie muttered, "Oh, for God's sake." Then she stood up, hoisted Bella onto her hip, and went to let him in. By the time she reached for the door handle, she suddenly remembered that John Lyons wasn't only Earl's son—he was also the police.

Chapter 12

John looked taller than when she'd seen him from a distance. His dark hair was brushed with silver at the temples; his eyes were pearl gray, like his mother's. If Annie were younger, she might say he was close to being hot. If she weren't so nervous about the fact he was a cop, she might have needed to remind herself that he was younger than she was, and that she was not in the market for a man—any man. After Mark, she'd decided not to head down that road again. Maybe when she was much, much older, and only if her heart was strong enough never to break again.

"We're almost ready," she said, flashing a smile that she hoped masked her agita.

"Okay. I'll wait outside."

He spun around so quickly he'd barely looked at her at all. If she were to craft him into a character in one of her books, she'd have to describe him as aloof . . . and therefore unavailable. *Not a bad thing*, she told herself. Especially under the circumstances.

Hustling to pack up the baby and the gifts, Annie made it out of the cottage, but forgot her gloves. Rather than appear like a rattled, foolish woman, she decided to act as if she hadn't intended to wear them.

He was leaning against the passenger door, but his pickup truck was running, no doubt keeping the inside warm. He opened the door for her. "I glanced in your car and noticed you don't have a car seat. You need one for the baby. It's the law." He didn't know that might be the least of her legal issues.

"You're right," she replied as she did her best to situate the basket at her feet. She decided not to point out that at least she had a safe basket now and no longer used the "piece of crap" that was chucked in her back seat. "But this happened so fast. I'd told her mom I'd babysit, but she was rushing and forgot to leave me the car seat. She had to go off island, then the blizzard happened, and she hasn't been able to get back yet." The words tumbled out, unrehearsed, though sounding fairly plausible. Or so Annie hoped.

"A place in Edgartown rents them," John said. "They'll deliver what you need right to the *On Time*. You won't have to bring your car across to get it." He closed the door behind her and walked around to the driver's side. At least he hadn't asked questions, like who the baby was and why her mother had been in such a rush that she'd forgotten something as important as a car seat. Or why she hadn't been able to "get back yet" when the blizzard had ended what now seemed like eons ago.

Annie decided to divert the conversation before she needed to conjure up more lies. "Thanks for the ride," she said as he backed out of the driveway with remarkable precision. "I haven't been to your parents' place, and your dad said it's tough to explain how to get there."

John laughed. He had a nice, easy laugh, like Earl's. "He probably said it's a pain in the ass."

She smiled. "Why, yes, I believe those were his exact words."

She folded her hands in her lap and tried to pretend that they weren't freezing.

"Well, I was happy to get you. It's not often anyone lives on Chappy who I haven't already met."

She wondered if that was because it was an island, or because he was a cop. Was he trying to let her know he had his finger on the pulse of Chappaquiddick, that little happened there that he didn't know about? *Stop being paranoid*, she scolded herself. He was only being friendly, making small talk. After all, it was Christmas Eve, a time for merriment and joy, not undercover operations.

Staring at the dashboard, she noticed it was clean, free of dust, free of junk. In fact, the whole vehicle seemed surprisingly clean—for a man. *You know better than to make a character into a stereotype*, she could almost hear her editor bark. Annie had often thought that Trish was a stereotype herself: a New York literary woman—thin, attractive, yet slightly stooped— who dressed in understated black and always walked as if she were in a hurry.

"Are you just here for the winter?" John asked her now.

"No. I want to stay; I'm hoping that the Flanagans will let me rent the cottage year-round."

"So, are you starting over or in hiding?"

Annie blinked. "Excuse me?"

He laughed. "That was a joke. Most islanders think people move here for only one of two reasons: either they're starting their lives over, or they're running away from someone. Or the law."

If she weren't feeling guilty, she might have laughed, too. "I assure you, I'm doing neither. I'm a writer. A couple of my novels take place on the island. I've wanted to move here for years. I could finally afford to."

"A writer. That's right. My mother told me. I forgot."

Annie doubted that John Lyons forgot anything, though she wasn't surprised Claire knew what she did for a living. Earl probably didn't keep many secrets from his wife. Except, hope-fully, Bella's. "Since I've been here," Annie said, "I've also be-come a soap maker. Thanks to Winnie."

"Winnie Lathrop? She's great."

"She is. She's become a good friend."

"Do you know that even though they're Wampanoags, the name *Lathrop* came from one of the original Pilgrims who ar-rived on the island by way of Barnstable, or something like that? Anyway, it's an English name. It wasn't common back then for the Wampanoags to intermarry, but sometimes they did."

"Oh," Annie said, "I didn't know that." It was nice that John seemed to have his father's penchant for history. Earl had said that John's ex had accused him of caring more about the Vineyard that he did about her. Could that be true? Then Bella began to fuss. Annie wanted to pick her up, but didn't dare. Not when John had already said she needed a car seat.

"I dated Winnie's daughter for a while."

She wondered if that qualified as news: didn't he know that Winnie's daughter was married? "I've met her. She seems nice."

"So's her husband. I dated her long before they got to-gether. Long before I got married, too. She was a little too young for me, though."

Old news, then. Unimportant.

The heater churned, slugging warm air through the vent; Annie would have loved to ask him to turn up the dial. Instead, she said, "Your dad told me you have two girls?"

His nod was slow and deliberate, a mirror image of Earl's. "Abigail and Lucy. They're with their mother this Christmas. Up in Plymouth. But they'll be here for the weekend. I'm hoping they'll stay for New Year's Eve."

"That's nice."

"My mother agrees." He gestured toward Bella. "How old is she?"

Annie's fingers squeezed around one another. She hadn't

expected the question. "Um," she replied, "well, about four months, I think." Was that what she'd decided to tell people? That Bella was four, not three months? Had she already told Claire how old Bella was? Her palms started to perspire. She swiveled her gaze back to the window and stared out into the darkness. Where even the stars had enough sense not to come out in the bitter cold.

"I hope she enjoys her first Christmas Eve with the Lyons' family," John said. "Same goes for you."

Annie tried to smile in a way that would offset her case of nerves. "Thanks. I'm sure it will be lovely. At least it isn't snowing."

He turned onto a narrow road that, with no streetlight to mark the way, she never would have seen. He then turned down another and finally stopped. "Okay, here we are."

She was relieved the ride was over, though uncertain as to what lay ahead. Food, gifts, chatting with strangers. At least she had Bella as a conversation piece. And Earl would be there, so she knew that everything would be all right. As long as she could manage to keep her story straight.

Candles were lit; tree lights were on; the scent of evergreens and the sounds of holiday music filled the air. The table was set as if for a buffet—china, sterling, and crystal were lined up, an opulent display of treasured heirlooms. Annie wondered if they'd been passed down from the generations laid to rest at the Indian Burial Ground.

Unlike the tableware, Earl and Claire's saltbox-style house was only forty or fifty years old, hardly an antique. It was tastefully decorated with comfortable furnishings, full bookcases, and several pieces of art—mostly watercolors that looked like island landscapes. Local artists, she supposed.

The rooms were spacious, but not overly large: living room, kitchen, dining room, study, and bath were on the first floor; Earl told her there were two bedrooms and another bath upstairs. "We built it the year John turned ten. Back when we still called him Skippy." Earl snorted; John rolled his eyes; Claire tossed her husband a look of annoyance.

"You have a lovely home," Annie said.

Earl took her coat and disappeared; John took her bag of gifts and said he'd put them under the tree. She was left standing with Claire, whose eyes penetrated her from top to bottom.

"Thank you for including me tonight," Annie said, employing her finest manners, the ones she'd learned from the nuns at St. Thomas Elementary School.

"We like to have guests on Christmas Eve. And, of course, babies are always welcome. This one is very pretty. I was pleased when Earl said you were still babysitting." She was as tall as Earl. That night, she'd secured her wild white hair with a hairband; she'd highlighted her pale complexion with a touch of blush. Annie suspected that, in earlier years, Claire had been attractive. But though her words seemed friendly now, it was impossible to tell if the woman was still simply sizing her up, the way she'd done when they'd met on Dock Street. Unless having a baby in her house had softened her outer shell.

"Would you like to hold her?" Annie asked. "Her name is Bella."

Claire took Bella without hesitation. She was, of course, a real mother: holding a baby must feel natural to her. "Her eyes are quite big," Claire said, "and she has a precious little face. But I must say I'm surprised your friend let you keep her for Christmas."

Apparently she'd been faking her pleasant interest. Perhaps she was an accomplished gossip who knew when to act charming and understanding, but also when to go in for the kill. Annie had a nasty urge tell her that Bella's mother was Jewish. Or Muslim. Or that she worshiped Festivus, the comical, made-up holiday from an old *Seinfeld* episode. Any of those explanations would have snuffed out speculation as to how a mother could abandon her baby on Christmas. But they would also result in another lie that Annie would need to remember. So she only said, "I'm afraid the blizzard messed up everything for her. I hope she makes it back tomorrow."

Claire rubbed Bella's back; Bella started to fuss. "And you said she's from up island?"

"Yes." Despite Claire's nosiness, Annie didn't want to be rude—or worse, have the woman think she was trying to conceal something. She decided, once again, to redirect the conversation. "That storm was really something, though, wasn't it? Before I moved here I heard a rumor that there was hardly such a thing as 'plowable snow' on the Vineyard—that even if it did snow a few inches, the salt air melted it in a day. I can now attest to the fact that the rumor was wrong!" She laughed, maybe too loudly.

"John's girls are off island," Claire continued, ignoring Annie's weather remarks. "We'll have them here next year, I hope."

Maybe her earlier attitude had nothing to do with Annie after all. Maybe she was simply missing her granddaughters, and therefore both lonely and a little envious. *Think positive*, Annie thought.

"And you'll see them this coming weekend, Mom," John said, as he passed through the dining room, then disappeared into the kitchen. "Winter vacation," he called back. "Remember?"

"You and I both know we'll hardly see them. They'll stay with you in Edgartown, where they'll be busy seeing their friends and doing who knows what. Movies, skating, hiking—kids never run out of things to do." She shook her head and looked at Annie. "No, we'll hardly see them."

John returned, a cookie in hand. "They're teenagers, Mom. *I'll* hardly see them." He took a bite. "What time do we eat? I'm starving."

Claire heaved a deep sigh. "Everything's ready. Meatballs in the crockpot. Ziti in the oven. Seafood salad and deviled eggs in the fridge. Just waiting for your father to say when."

"Maybe everyone would like a cocktail first," Earl said as he entered from the opposite side of the room. "Annie? Cup of eggnog? Glass of wine? Fifth of whiskey?"

Everyone laughed, except Claire. Annie was relieved he had rejoined them. "Glass of wine, please. White, if you have it."

John said he'd have a beer; Claire said, "Nothing for me, thank you." She sat at the head of the table and bounced Bella lightly on her knee. At least she seemed to be warming up to the baby. Maybe it was true that Annie had misjudged her. Then she remembered Winnie's words: *Be careful.*

She smiled. "May I help you, Earl?"

"Sure thing," he said, so Annie followed him into the kitchen.

The cabinets were carbon copies of those in Annie's cottage, crafted from old-fashioned beadboard that had been painted white. As with the gray-shingled siding outside, Annie had seen enough places to recognize that the style was indicative of the island.

"Sorry if my wife's a little off tonight." Earl uncorked a bottle of chardonnay and poured Annie a generous glass. "She resents that John let his ex move his daughters off island, as if he had any say in the matter. The fact is, Jenny hated it here. She's a mainlander. Some of them can't adapt."

Annie deduced that Jenny was John's ex, the woman he'd married sometime after he'd dated Winnie's daughter. Annie was about to say it must be difficult for Claire not to have her granddaughters on the holiday, but a knock on the back door interrupted.

"Must be Santa," Earl said. He handed Annie the wineglass and made his way down the hall.

Annie picked the beer bottle up off the counter, returned

to the dining room, and held it out to John. Then she realized
he was holding Bella. Her hand stopped in midair; she muffled
a small gasp with a false cough. The last thing she wanted to
see was a police officer in charge of Bella, whether he was on
duty or not.

But before Annie could say or do something she might regret, Earl lumbered into the room, escorting a woman.

"Look who's here!"

As if the L.L.Bean parka and the knit cap in hand weren't
dead giveaways, Taylor's long auburn hair billowed over her
shoulders. The big difference in her appearance was that she
was wearing eyeliner and mascara that looked as though it had
been carefully applied.

Earl officially introduced them; Claire asked Taylor to stay
for dinner. "Absolutely," she replied, in the same husky voice
that had been part of why Annie had thought she'd been a
man when they'd nearly collided in the driveway.

John transferred the baby to Annie, took his beer, and gave
Taylor a bear hug. "Merry Christmas, old girl," he said. But as
Taylor fluffed her hair, Annie knew she was hardly an "old
girl." In fact, she was a very attractive, fortysomething-year-old
woman. *John's age*, she thought.

"Oh," Taylor said, her gaze drifting toward Bella, "you have
a baby."

"I do," Annie replied. "This is Bella. But she isn't mine; I'm
babysitting for a friend." The lie had grown familiar, the words
now sliding out like liquid silver.

"Well, you'd better be careful around this bunch. They're
baby lovers."

Everyone laughed, though Annie felt her gut tighten. Then
Earl asked Taylor if she'd like her usual. Apparently, she was a
frequent visitor.

Annie sipped her wine while Claire chatted with Taylor
about the health of her mother, the aftereffects of the storm,

and if they'd found that damn hawk that had been stalking the Alvords' coop. She was certainly friendlier to her than she'd been to Annie. Perhaps she was done pining for her grand-daughters.

Earl returned with two short, squatty glasses, each of which held a couple of ice cubes and a good amount of what looked to be scotch. "Cheers," he said as he passed one to Taylor, then clinked his glass to hers.

Taylor took a deep swig, then pivoted back Annie. "Oh!" she exclaimed. "Now I remember where I've seen you! You're down on North Neck. You and Earl were looking for your lost cat. Did you find it?"

Annie pulled Bella closer in the knee-jerk way she seemed to have adopted whenever she felt they were threatened. Her mouth went very dry. "Yes, we did," she replied because she had no idea what else to say. "And yes, I'm on North Neck. I'm renting the Flanagans' guest cottage."

Then Taylor's eyes gravitated toward Bella's basket, down on the floor. "And now I know where I've seen your baby! I remember the basket. And her beautiful eyes. I gave your niece a ride across the channel a week or so ago. Dropped her off at the turnoff onto North Neck. How's she doing? It's always confusing for folks when they come to the Vineyard the first time, let alone come out to Chappy."

Your niece.

Your *niece*?

Annie tried to smile, but her face felt frozen, as if she'd de-veloped lockjaw or was having a stroke. All eyes turn to her: Claire's, John's. Earl's. And, of course, Taylor's. Taylor, who, for some reason, thought Annie was Bella's aunt, who thought Bella's young mother was Annie's niece, who . . . *Oh God,* Annie thought. *Taylor had given the girl a ride over to Chappy in her truck.* If Earl's friend had been the ferry captain that day, it was no sur-prise he didn't remember the young woman—the stranger—

who'd come over with a baby. Taylor had been driving. The captain most likely had no reason to pay attention to her passenger. *Passengers*. Plural.

"Your niece?" Claire interrupted before Annie could think of a plausible answer and unlock her jaw. "I thought you said you were sitting for an up-island friend?"

"Can't be the same girl, then," Taylor said, taking another swig. "She said she'd never been to the Vineyard. I paid her four-dollar fare, because it didn't seem like she had much."

Annie's brain was frozen now the same way that her face was, the way her hands had been in John's truck without her gloves. The only movement she felt was the rapid thumping of her heart. She also felt John's eyes bore into her. And Earl's. Who'd turned out to be no damn help at all.

The next thing she knew her eyes filled with tears. "Families," she managed to say. "I'm sure you all know how tough those situations sometimes are." She looked to Claire, half expecting to see a snarl. But instead, Claire nodded gently. Then she reached out and took Bella from her.

And Annie just stood there, tongue-tied, again.

Chapter 13

*B*reaking into the cottage had been easier than Francine had expected. On the Vineyard, like on much of the Cape, no one seemed to believe in dead bolts. Maybe they thought the people who went there had enough of their own stuff and their own money and wouldn't need to steal anyone else's.

But right now, Francine really needed food. She'd been trying to come up with a plan about how to get some when she'd heard a pickup truck engine. She'd peeked out the upstairs window and saw that the truck had pulled into Annie Sutton's. After a few minutes it looked as if Annie left with whoever was driving. Francine couldn't tell if Bella was with her. But she figured it must be Christmas Eve.

At least she now had a way to get something to eat.

But she needed to be sure the cottage was empty.

So she waited a while. When she saw no further signs of life next door, she crept out of hiding and snuck through the trees until she found the path that led next door. It helped that Annie had left on the outside light . . . it reassured Francine that no one was home, in spite of the Lexus still parked in the driveway.

The porch door opened more easily than it had the night before when the latch broke. She tiptoed to a window and pressed her face to the glass: she saw a Christmas tree on one side of the room, its white *lights glowing. She got a big lump in her throat. A long time ago, back when she'd thought everyone had been happy, Christmas at her house had had a tree, too. A big tree. With lots of presents around it.*

Without letting herself give in to her feelings, she peered inside and confirmed that no one was there. Then she popped the front door open.

She went directly to the kitchen. It didn't take long to stuff a few things in her pockets: a hunk of cheese, a couple of brownies, a roll that smelled like cinnamon. She really wanted some of what looked like beef stew, but she didn't think it would be smart to steal it. After all, she didn't want it to be obvious that she'd broken in. Besides, she only needed enough food to last until she was sure Bella was okay.

Slipping out as quickly as she'd slipped in, she was careful to press the lock back in place so it would look the way Annie had left it.

Once outside, Francine meandered toward Annie's car. If the keys were in it, did she dare use it to get off Chappaquiddick? After all, the longer she stayed there, the greater her chances were of getting caught.

The car door was unlocked. She quietly opened it: the interior lit up, thanks to the overhead light. That's when she saw what was in the back seat: Bella's basket, carelessly thrown so it hung upside down, partly on the seat, the rest on the floor. The beautiful red bow was squished.

Francine stared at the mess: it was as if Bella hadn't mattered, and worse, as if Bella was in fact gone.

"Let's eat!" Earl said, and Annie thought, *Thank God*, because there was no way she wanted the conversation to continue to be about a fictitious, long-lost niece. "Annie? You want to leave the little one with Claire and come give me a hand?"

They went into the kitchen. Annie set her wineglass on the counter. As soon as she let go of the stemware, she saw that her hand was shaking. "Oh, God, Earl," she whispered. "What should I say? What should I do?"

"Jesus. Who knew that would happen? You want me to find out more? Maybe the girl told Taylor her name. Maybe she said where she was from."

"But if I was her aunt, I'd know those things, wouldn't I? How on earth did that girl find out where I lived? And, for God's sake, why? This confirms that I really was her target, doesn't it? Taylor dropped her off at my street." She wished she'd worn jeans so she could shove her hands in her pockets to stop them from trembling. "Why don't I just tell everyone the truth right now? What am I waiting for?"

"You're waiting because it's only Christmas Eve. And because you're hoping there's still a chance that Bella's mother will come back and get her."

"It's been almost a week. Do you really think she's still here? Or that she wants her baby back? Maybe I'm just being selfish. Maybe I enjoy pretending I'm a mother. Like I'm making up for the fact I never was one." She would not, ever, tell Earl about her abortion. Murphy was the only one who'd known about that. Murphy, and now Winnie.

He went to the refrigerator, took out a plastic-covered bowl of seafood salad and a pottery platter where a dozen deviled eggs were nested in perfect oval hollows. He set the dishes on the counter and folded his arms. "I can tell you one thing. Taylor is a good woman, but she's worse than Claire when it comes to wanting to know everyone's business. If you want to protect the little one from a boatload of rumors, stick to your original plan. Wait until Wednesday, then bring Bella to the police. Or tell John in private. There's no need to make a federal case out of this. Or what could become a very public one."

"Oh, Earl, I don't know anymore. I don't know if I've done the right thing."

"To tell the truth, neither do I. But I do know if you tell Taylor, you might as well tell the world. As it is, you've given yourself one more day before going to the authorities. How about if we spend tomorrow morning looking around some more? Check out a few houses out by Dyke Bridge? It could be that once the storm ended, she relocated over there. Maybe she's waiting until she thinks she can find a safe way back to Edgartown without calling attention to herself. What do you say?"

"Thanks, Earl. But I think it would be a waste of time. I really doubt she'd have gone all the way out there."

He nodded and lowered his eyes. "Yeah, I suppose you're right."

Then John appeared in the kitchen. "I don't know what's taking you two so long, but I say it's time to eat! Hurry up, before we all die of malnutrition."

Annie winced, but didn't dare look at Earl. She picked up the dishes of salad and the eggs, then followed him back to the dining room, her heart stuck in her throat for what felt like the ten thousandth time that night.

"I'll bring you home," Earl said and went to retrieve Annie's coat. They'd eaten and opened gifts—a jar of homemade chutney and a lovely wool scarf for Annie, a colorful picture book of *The Night Before Christmas* for Bella. Taylor had already left, having said good night, and offered Annie the hope that things for her niece would be resolved soon. Annie had gulped and said, "Thank you."

The truth was, she didn't remember much about what might otherwise have been a pleasant Christmas Eve. She had, instead, white-knuckled it through three worrisome hours.

"No, Dad," John said when Earl returned. He took Annie's coat from him. "I'll take her."

Earl shook his head, reached out, and grabbed the coat. "No. It's Christmas Eve. You should stay here and call your girls."

John stepped back, his grip holding fast. "My girls are with their grandparents tonight. Their *other* grandparents. I'd only be interrupting."

"Try anyway."

The tug-of-war continued.

"Stop it, Dad. I know you want to talk to the girls, too. We'll call them together. Tomorrow. As planned. For now, there's no need for you to go out again. It's cold, and Annie's place is on my way to the boat. I've got to get back to Edgartown. I'm on duty at midnight."

Even quick-thinking Earl had no comeback for that. Annie appreciated that he wanted to spend a few more minutes alone with her—no doubt to make sure she was okay. Or maybe he'd come up with an idea as to why Bella's mother had known exactly where she was going: to North Neck Road, to visit her aunt.

Then Annie had a sudden thought: *What if the girl's aunt wasn't fictitious? What if Bella's mother had merely gone to the wrong house?* Maybe she really did have an aunt—one who lived in a different cottage on North Neck, a cottage that Annie and Earl had missed. Maybe Earl didn't know every inch of land on Chappy the way Annie had thought he did.

All of which, she knew, was wishful thinking, and undoubtedly implausible.

However, she did know that right then there was no way she could turn down John's offer and force him to let Earl drive her instead. It would have seemed silly, and it would have been rude to John. Not to mention that Claire might start wondering if something was going on between Annie and Earl, which was the last thing Annie wanted her to think. She could not afford to have Claire Lyons as an enemy. So, standing in the living room while John and Earl wrestled with her coat, Annie did what she did best: she smiled. "John, if you don't mind, a ride would be great. Save your dad the trouble."

"It's no trouble," Earl said.

"I know. And I appreciate that. But it's on the way for John. And I bet you've had a long day."

"Well. Okay, then." Finally, Earl let go. "Do you have a flashlight?"

"In my purse. But I left on the outside light."

Claire stood up. "I hope you and Bella will come tomorrow for dinner. Roast turkey and fresh cranberry sauce. You can't pass that up, can you?"

The invitation came as a surprise. Annie hoped it hadn't been extended so the woman could keep prying. "Are you sure, Claire? Christmas Day is usually for family . . ."

"Nonsense. You and Bella can be our family for one day. In case you haven't noticed, other than John, the rest of ours is absent."

"She cooks enough for the whole island," John interjected. It was evident whose side he was on.

"Will two o'clock work for you?" Claire asked.

"I'll pick you up," Earl said. "I'll be out anyway. I have houses to check late in the morning." With no one else in her line of vision, he gave her a wink. "Besides, John's on the night shift, so he'll want to sleep in. No sense having him feeling rushed."

"As long as she doesn't drive," John said. "Not until she gets a proper infant car seat."

The plans were made without Annie agreeing, for which she was grateful. It saved her from having to struggle to think straight.

Bella's mother had showed up with her baby at the Holiday Crafts Fair where Annie had seen her. She'd asked the price of Annie's soap, but hadn't bought a single piece. The same girl had come from out of nowhere and deposited her baby on Annie's porch. In the middle of the night. In the middle of a raging blizzard. A nor'easter.

For some unknown reason, she'd picked Annie to take care of Bella. Even more confusingly, she'd known where Annie lived. How in God's name had that happened?

But as Annie gave Bella a bath and tucked her into the makeshift drawer-bed for the night, she finally accepted that there was no way the young mother had gone to Annie's by mistake: if the girl truly had an aunt, chances were she wouldn't have needed to sneak over during the storm, drop off the baby, then disappear. Even if the aunt hadn't known about Bella, if the baby had been a secret, she certainly would have known the grandmother whom the baby had been named after.

No, Annie deduced, it was more likely that Annie had been the actual target, that the cottage had been the girl's destination. Though Annie could not imagine why.

Sitting on the edge of her bed, she picked up the book from Earl and Claire and began to read aloud. "'Twas the night before Christmas, and all through the house . . ." She had barely reached the line about settling down for a long winter's nap when she saw that Bella was asleep.

Annie set down the book, returned to the living room, and sat in the rocker in front of the tree. She slowly sipped a cup of tea, wishing she'd asked Taylor if the girl had mentioned her name. Then Annie supposed that knowing her name probably wouldn't help find her. The fact that she'd said it was her first time on the Vineyard meant, as Annie had suspected, that she had not been in school with Winnie's nephew, Lucas. And that she could have come from anywhere.

But why?

Had she run away?

If so, why had she picked the island?

Did the baby's father live there?

She wondered if the girl had said anything else to Taylor, anything that might suggest where she had come from. Annie supposed she could call the woman and make up a story so she could sneakily ask questions, but she only knew her as "Taylor," which could be her first or last name. And besides, it was Christmas Eve. People didn't arbitrarily call someone at ten o'clock on Christmas Eve unless it was an emergency. A missing baby could be considered an emergency. Except that the most important person who might have missed her did not appear to want her. Not to mention that Taylor was an island gossip. A *rumormonger*, Annie's mother would have called her. "Tell Taylor . . . tell the world," Earl had said.

She set down her tea and rubbed her eyes.

God, how she hated when people disappeared.

And God, how she wished Murphy were there. Murphy would have reassured her that it was merely a coincidence that three people connected closely to Annie had chosen to vanish: her birth mother, Mark, and now the mother of this tiny girl. Murphy also would have said that the fact that all the people Annie had loved and who'd loved Annie back—her father, her mother, Brian, Murphy—had suffered early deaths was no reflection on her, either. Murphy would have told her she'd been chosen to be in their lives—not the other way around— because their lives were destined to be short, and that they had deserved the kind of love and support that Annie gave so freely. Murphy would have said those things, and part of Annie would have believed her. But part of her would have known her friend was full of crap. That she'd only been trying to make Annie feel better.

She stared up at the ceiling. "I miss you so much, Murphy. I hope you and my dad are having a toast to me this Christmas." She might have included her mother, but Ellen Sutton rarely drank. And Brian hadn't, either. He'd said it would have been a bad example for the kids that he taught.

Looking back to the tree, Annie surveyed the ornaments. She'd saved a few from when she'd been young: a star she'd cut out of yellow construction paper using children's round-tipped, dull scissors. A red pipe cleaner looped from the star onto the branch; it had once had silver glitter, but that had fallen off long ago, leaving a glue stain that had since faded. She knew that her mother had written on the back: ANNIE, AGE 4. Her gaze then traveled to a Styrofoam ball that she'd covered with strips of dark green velvet ribbon and, with the help of small straight pins, had bedazzled with pearls and crystals that reflected the lights from the tree. She'd been older then, but her mother had nonetheless attached a small label: ANNIE, AGE 12.

Yes, Annie had been lucky for an unwanted baby, a foundling. She'd been luckier than Bella. Or so it appeared.

Winnie had said that everyone had a story. Annie's writing teacher had told her that, too. "Every good guy, every bad guy, every guy—and girl—in between," was how he'd explained it. He'd added that most of us live in the "in between," and that that's where the best stories came from. Annie wondered what he'd suggest she should do about the characters in this situation.

"What I think doesn't matter," she could almost hear him respond, his beard, the color of parchment, bobbing up and down as he spoke. "What you need to do is turn it into a story. Put it on paper. That, you can do. That's *all* you can do. It's all you can ever do!"

She laughed now because, like moving to the Vineyard, meeting that teacher had also been thanks to Murphy, who'd been introduced to him at a function she'd gone to with Stan. "He does writers' workshops," Murphy told her. "It's time for you to take your writing seriously. I think he can help you have a real career." Annie's inner voice told her to believe Murphy. So she'd signed up, and she'd succeeded. And now, she listened to that inner voice again, the one reminding her that while she couldn't control things, she could ease the stress if she simply sat down and wrote.

"Okay," she said, standing up, gulping the last of her tea, and turning off the tree lights. "I get the message. I will stop overthinking this mess. I will sit down and work on my book. Maybe I'll weave Bella's story into the plot. Maybe one of my main characters will find a baby on the steps of the museum. Whatever. I sort of know how to write. Which is good. Because I sure as heck don't know how to do anything else."

She then reaffirmed her commitment to track down John the day after Christmas and tell him the truth about Bella. Maybe, when she saw him at Earl's for Christmas dinner, she would tell him then. She only hoped it wasn't too late, that the young mother wasn't already so far off island that no one would find her. Ever.

Retreating to the bedroom, Annie closed the door, set her laptop on a pillow, situated herself on the bed, and, five minutes later, was deeply immersed in the book she'd put off for too long.

In the morning, Annie was awakened by sunshine pouring through the window. Her head was half-hunched over her laptop; her neck had a terrible crick. She stretched, she groaned, she checked her page count: she'd written more than twenty-five pages before she'd fallen asleep at what must have been an ungodly hour.

Twenty-five pages, she thought as she pulled herself out of bed. *Maybe I can still write, after all.*

Turning to Bella's makeshift crib, Annie leaned down and smiled. Bella's eyes were open; it looked as if she were smiling back.

"Merry Christmas, little one," Annie said. She liked calling her that, the way Earl did. "It's your first Christmas. Let's make it a wonderful one." Hoisting the baby, she glanced over at the clock: ten twenty-three. Wow. She couldn't believe she'd slept so late. Or that Bella had, too.

She fed her and changed her, then sat on the rocking chair, holding her. She reached down and plucked the small gift wrapped in red tissue that was under the tree.

"For you," she said gently. "From Santa."

Bella touched the paper, and, when it crinkled, she giggled.

"That's funny, isn't it?" Annie asked. Peeling back one corner, she slowly pulled out the fleece lamb she had made. "Oh! Look! How pretty!"

The baby stopped giggling and, instead, examined the gift with questioning eyes, then deliberate fingers, as she studied each soft curve. When it seemed she was satisfied, she looked up at Annie and smiled.

"Do you like her?" Annie asked. "Well, I think she needs a name, don't you? How about if we call her Lily? Lily the lamb. Is that good?"

Bella looked back at her gift, touched the small red heart with her tiny finger, and made a sweet, gurgling sound.

"Okay," Annie said. "The trouble is, it's going on eleven now, and I have to get ready for dinner. Will you and Lily be all right if I put you back in your basket while I take a shower?" While she'd left Bella in her basket and brought it into the bathroom when she'd taken showers before, Annie wasn't sure if she should leave a stuffed animal with a baby. Hadn't she read somewhere that you shouldn't put toys in cribs? Or leave a baby alone when they had something they could chew on, choke on, or put over their nose and mouth and wind up smothering themselves?

"Okay. Change of plans," she said. With one hand holding Bella, who held Lily, Annie picked up her mother's quilt with her other hand and dragged it with them. As long as she could keep one eye on the baby, Annie figured everything would be fine.

But as she stopped to gather clothes, she spotted a truck coming down her driveway. Had Earl decided to check out the houses by Dyke Bridge after all? With Bella resting on her hip, Annie walked to the window. The truck stopped; the driver got out. It wasn't Earl; it was Taylor. And Annie had one of her gut instincts that told her this was not a social call.

Chapter 14

"Merry Christmas, again," Annie called out after she plastered on her biggest, brightest smile. She'd opened the front door, but remained in the doorway. There was no reason to walk out to greet her.

Taylor opened the screen door and stepped onto the porch. Her knit hat was back in place, her long hair crammed under it, out of sight. She looked like a man again. "You, too," she said. "Still got that baby, I see."

Annie ran her hand through Bella's hair. "For now. We hope her mom gets back today."

Though they were standing eight or ten feet apart, Annie could see Taylor's eyebrows raise as if she didn't believe her. "I was headed to Edgartown and decided to stop by for a minute. Something's been bugging me, so I thought I'd better ask."

Shifting Bella to her other hip, Annie pressed her lips together, not daring to say a word. If Taylor had figured out Bella didn't belong there, did it matter now? *Of course it does*, she told herself. Annie needed to be the one to tell John. Not Taylor. Or anyone else. She didn't want to be accused of kidnapping—not now, not when she was so close to turning Bella in.

"How may I help you?"

Taylor seemed to study the floorboards. "Your cat," she said. "Where is it?"

Of all the things Annie would have thought Taylor might ask, that wasn't one. She'd nearly forgotten about the lie that Earl had concocted. "Around," she replied with what she hoped sounded like nonchalance. "Hunting mice, I suppose."

"Gonna be tough to find 'em under the snow."

"I guess."

The woman strode to the end of the porch by the wood-pile. She peered into the corners.

"Is there a problem?" Annie asked.

Taylor looked back at her. "Maybe. I don't know what's going on here, but there's one thing I do know."

Annie stood. And waited. Willing her nerves to stay quiet.

"As long as the Flanagans have rented this place, one thing they've been strict about is not letting their renters have animals. No dogs. No cats."

It took a few seconds for the message to sink in. "Really?"

Taylor walked toward the other side of the porch. "Really. I'm sure it's in your lease."

"Well, actually, I don't remember." In spite of her wishes, her stomach started churning.

"I planned to take the critter off your hands if you wanted. So you won't get evicted. But I don't see a cat. Not even a sign of one."

Annie forced a laugh. "They're so independent. Never around when you want them."

"Well, keep it in mind when it gets back. Earl says you're a good tenant. Otherwise, I wouldn't bother to help." With that, Taylor meandered back to her pickup. "Have a nice day," she called as she raised one arm in the air, her back to Annie's front door.

★   ★   ★

Not for a second did Annie believe Taylor cared about her being evicted. And not for a second did Annie believe Taylor had showed up because she cared one hoot about her. At least she hadn't asked to see cat food or kitty litter or a scratching post, something to prove a cat even existed.

"Miss Taylor is a strange one," Annie said to Bella as they went back into the house.

After setting the baby on the quilt—not back in the basket—alongside Lily the lamb, Annie jumped into the shower, keeping the curtain half-open, wondering how in hell Murphy—and mothers everywhere—managed to ever take care of themselves while taking care of their babies, too.

She decided it was healthier to think about that than to obsess over the possibility that Taylor had somehow learned that Annie had a secret. If so, what the woman intended to do about it was one more mystery added to the heap of secrecy that had marched, uninvited, into Annie's life.

After finishing the fastest shower she'd ever taken, Annie dressed in her black cashmere dress and long red cardigan. She didn't think that Taylor would be at Earl and Claire's for dinner, so she didn't have to worry that her attire would be inspected for tiny cat hairs. Bypassing the black, high-heeled Pradas that she wore to book appearances in New York City, Annie slipped on simple ballet flats. "A little more appropriate for Martha's Vineyard," she explained to Bella. "And certainly for Chappaquiddick."

She tossed a small load of clothes into the stackable washer, then picked up the baby and dragged the quilt back to the living room. Retrieving her laptop, she settled Bella back on the quilt and sat in the rocking chair. With the baby seemingly content, Annie decided that, until Earl arrived, she should review what she'd written the night before. It would definitely be more productive than pondering any number of evil reasons that Taylor had stopped by.

The living room was bright; Annie's back was to the window. When she flipped open her laptop, the reflection of sunlight on snow glared off the screen. She blinked, turned her head, closed the lid. For a moment, she thought she'd been blinded. She shut her eyes and saw blurred silhouettes. She had a sudden flashback to when her father had taught her to drive through the Callahan Tunnel toward Logan Airport. It had also been a sunny day.

"Take off your sunglasses just before we go into the tunnel," he'd said. "Then blink—very slowly—three times. By the time we get into the darkness, your vision will have already adjusted to the change in light."

She blinked now—very slowly—three times. Then she opened her eyes and, sure enough, her vision had been corrected. She turned her chair so she was facing the porch; that way, direct sunlight wouldn't bounce off the screen. But as she readjusted herself and her laptop, she saw an odd smudge on the windowpane. Her first thought was that it was a handprint; then she realized that no, it was more like a . . . *well,* she thought, *more like a face print.*

"Well," she said to herself, "chalk that up to one more asinine thought."

But as she went back to her work, an ominous question crawled over her skin: Had someone been on the porch . . . trying to look into the cottage?

Her pulse started to race.

Stop it! she commanded her imagination. *Stop it this minute!*

But Annie was afraid; and when she was afraid, her body reacted. Fight or flight. Which meant that, right then, she wanted to race from the cottage, jump into her car, and drive . . . anywhere. Until the fear calmed down. Which it wasn't able to do. Not while her breath was shallow, going in and out in short, panicky bursts. She looked down at the floor; Bella was falling asleep. As badly as Annie wanted to run, she knew she couldn't. Not when there was a baby to protect.

Calling up all the courage she could manage, she pulled herself from the chair, set down the laptop, and edged toward the door. She hated that, except for a small curtain over the sink, there were no draperies or blinds on the windows. When she'd first moved in there, she'd thought it was a quaint Vineyard custom, a way of letting people know she had no secrets. But now she felt as if she were in a fishbowl.

She stood, perfectly still, in the same place where she'd stood only a short time ago making small, stupid talk with Taylor. And even though it was broad daylight, even though Annie could clearly see that no one was on the porch, she opened the door a tiny bit at a time. Then she squeezed through the space and slinked onto the porch.

She was right. No one was there.

Of course no one is here, she told herself. Still, she knew she must remember to ask Earl to absolutely, positively, fix the latch on the outside door. Maybe he could even add another lock. While it might cause others to snicker behind her back, Annie knew she might never be one of those islanders who felt safe enough to let everyone have easy access to her house. To her. And, for now, to Bella.

With her heart and her breathing calming to normal, she turned to go back into the cottage. That's when her gaze fell to the floor, onto a piece of paper.

It was over by the window where she'd seen the face print—or whatever it was. It was just a scrap, but its light color showed starkly against the dark floorboard. From that direction, it was easy to notice. If she'd gone out onto the porch when Taylor had been there, she might have seen it then. Unless whoever had dropped it had done so when Annie was in the shower. Or the night before. It might have even been last evening, when Annie was at Earl's. When John had brought her home, she'd rebuffed his offer to bring Bella inside, so the way she'd carried the basket could have blocked her view.

Fighting off a shiver that zippered up her spine, she took a few side steps toward the paper. But as she bent to pick it up, she saw, in an instant, what it was: an oval-shaped label from one of her soaps. The graphics showed an illustration of the island, along with the name of the natural ingredients—fox grape and sunflower oil. The typeface read: *Soaps by Sutton*. She turned it over: it was blank. It was not one of the labels that she'd signed at the fair.

But Annie knew where—and who—it had come from. It had been on one of the soaps that the girl with the sad, soulful eyes had examined. And when Annie had been distracted by the chaos that had ensued, thanks to the other women's rapid-fire questions about her books, the girl must have slipped the soap into her pocket. Some way, somehow, the label must have fallen off. And wound up on Annie's porch.

She had to get in touch with Earl. She couldn't wait until he picked them up for dinner. He had to come right away. If he were there, Annie might stop shaking.

Back inside, she shoved a kitchen chair against the door. Which, of course, made no sense. Bella's mother had apparently come and gone without causing any harm. Yet. Still, she unplugged her phone from its charger and quickly called Earl's cell number.

His phone rang. And rang.

"Answer it. Answer it," she pleaded.

Then it went into voice mail.

After the beep, Annie said, "Earl. It's Annie. Please come over now. She was here. Right on my porch. Please. Help me. And hurry." She knew she sounded desperate. Because she was.

With her eyes glued on the windows, Annie paced. Bella

was sleeping on the quilt on the floor. Annie knew she could not let her stay in the cottage. Not while her mother was . . . was what? Coming back to get her baby? Wasn't that what Annie wanted?

"Oh," Annie said. "Oh, God, I don't know what to do." She might have asked Murphy for advice, but Annie thought this time it wouldn't work. "Over my pay grade," Murphy would have said.

She stared at the phone; Earl was not calling back. Maybe he was on his rounds, checking the houses of his customers. Maybe he was outside and had left his phone in his truck. Or maybe he was home, taking a shower. He and Claire might have a landline at the house, but even if Annie found the number in the Island phone book, what should she say if Claire answered? It would be apparent from the quiver in Annie's voice that something awful had happened. Then she'd have to tell Claire about Bella before she was ready to.

If you want to protect the little one from a boatload of rumors, Earl had said, *stick to your original plan.*

That's what Annie would do. She would sit and wait for Earl like a sensible adult would. She would not overreact. She would have a lovely Christmas dinner with the Lyons family. Then, on Wednesday, she would bring Bella to the police. And tell John. She would not call the house now. She would not risk causing Claire hysterics. Or worse, she would not risk the potential melodrama of getting arrested, cops-and-robbers style. After all, Annie did not need negative publicity that would send her black-clad, fast-walking editor, Trish, into emotional convulsions and could bring Annie's writing career to a scandalous halt. And chances were, she could not make soap in prison.

She dropped into the rocker and took a few deep mental breaths. If only she knew why Bella's mother had come back. And when. Annie knew she might not feel as threatened if the young woman had simply knocked on the door and introduced herself. And told Annie why she'd come. Told her why she'd left Bella in the first place. Then Annie might have understood. But by having sneaked onto the porch, then sneaked away, the girl was not being nice. She was stalking.

One thing was for certain, though: no matter what the reason was for the most recent visit, the girl still was on Chappy. And she no doubt knew that Annie still had Bella.

Trying to talk herself out of her terror, Annie considered her options. She could quickly wrap Bella up, and—infant car seat or not—she could take her away. Off Chappy. As long as the *On Time* crossed the channel on Christmas Day. They could go up island to Winnie's—they'd be safe there.

Wouldn't they?

Or, Annie thought, slowly starting to rock, *she could go to the Edgartown police station and get this over with.* Once and for all.

But as she watched Bella sleeping, so silently, so trusting, she knew she couldn't do it. John had worked the night shift; he'd be off duty by now. It wouldn't seem right to turn Bella over to just any police officer. Not after he'd been so nice to them last night.

Besides, she reasoned, her happy-ending-foolishness returning, she couldn't just hand Bella over to the police if—now that Annie knew the girl was still on the island—there was any possible chance that she'd come back and explain. That she would not abandon her baby after all.

Over an hour later, Earl still hadn't called back or shown up. By then, Annie was in the car with the motor running, the heat churning, and Bella tucked into her basket on the floor of the passenger side—she'd barely stirred when Annie had transferred her from the floor into the basket. They'd been outside most of that time; Annie had decided she'd feel safer there. At least she'd remembered to put on her gloves this time. And she'd turned the car around, pointing toward the road, in case a quick getaway was called for.

She sat in silence, not wanting even the softest music to emit from the stereo, not wanting any noise to mask the sound of someone creeping up on her. On them. She prayed there was enough gas in the tank to last until Earl arrived. If he hadn't dropped dead, which might be why he hadn't returned her call.

She flinched. *God*, she thought, *forgive me for even thinking that.* Earl was such a good man, such a huge help to her. She would feel terrible if something had happened to him. He must, after all, have plenty of other people to worry about. Thoughtful people tended to worry about others. She had once done that, back when she'd had a real life, or had thought that she had.

She knew, however, that most people, Murphy included, would probably think she needed her head examined for what she was doing now. But Annie had decided that most people would have done things differently from the get-go. They wouldn't have kept a stranger's baby: as soon as the roads had been cleared after the blizzard and the ferry had resumed crossing the channel, most people would have brought Bella directly to the police station and dropped her off.

Goodbye.

Sayonara.

Hasta la vista, baby.

But most people, Annie figured, had not been adopted. She knew she was trying to give both the young mother and her baby a second, fighting chance, the kind of chance that Donna MacNeish—or Annie—hadn't been given. If Bella's mother had known that, she might not have wanted to sneak up on them, to have scared Annie half to death.

But in the car, with the engine running, Annie did, indeed,

feel safe. If the girl reappeared, and if Annie felt threatened, she could quickly slam the shift into gear and peel out of the driveway. Fast.

In the meantime, she studied the snow that had settled on the lawn; it had warmed and softened, and wasn't nearly as deep as it had been. Which meant there would be no evidence of footprints from a recent trespasser. As for the driveway, it was impossible to tell if the girl had walked up it, because most of the hardpack had already melted.

She thought about how it had been true that snow melted quickly on the island; much faster than in Boston, where the snowbanks held fast, sometimes as late as Marathon Monday, the third Monday in April. She supposed the quick thawing here might be why some seasonal people didn't bother to have their driveways plowed, much to Earl's irritation. What were the chances there would be an emergency in a house where no one was living? What were the odds, when even two feet of snow that had been dumped by a nor'easter were nearly gone a week later?

She thought about the neighborhood and wondered if there were any houses on North Neck that they'd left unchecked. Then she thought about the neglected house next door . . . where the driveway hadn't been plowed. Could Bella's mother have been hiding there? Right next door, all along?

Annie wondered if she should walk over to the house and check it out. Did she dare go alone? And what about Bella? Should she take her with her? She glanced over again at the sweet, innocent baby. And Annie knew there was only one answer:

Yes.

Yes. It might be Annie's last chance to find the girl while she still had Bella. It might be her last chance to find out why she'd done what she had done; her last chance to try to convince her to change her mind.

Yes. It was the right thing to do. And, what's more, Annie refused to be frightened. It was broad daylight, for God's sake. And Bella's future was more important that Annie's overactive imagination.

But as she turned off the ignition and opened the car door, a vehicle pulled in behind her. It should have been Earl. But it was John. And he was driving an Edgartown police cruiser.

Chapter 15

Annie's first thought was that she'd been right: something had happened to Earl. She bolted from the Lexus and ran to the cruiser before John had turned off the ignition.

"What's wrong?" She was out of breath. She stepped back while he killed the engine and opened the door, her pulse and her heart both racing. Again.

"Merry Christmas to you, too." His pearl-gray eyes looked almost iridescent in the sunlight. Shining, and unconcerned.

She gulped. "I thought your father was coming to get me."

John laughed. "Mom has him doing things. Peeling potatoes, cutting up squash. You know. Man's work."

In spite of herself, Annie laughed. "Right." She didn't ask if he knew why Earl hadn't answered his phone.

"You going somewhere?"

"Oh. No. Bella was fussy. If I take her for a ride it helps calm her down." She praised her fast recall that driving the twins was what Murphy and Stan had done whenever one of them was "crying up a Gaelic storm," as Murphy called it. She pointed to the cruiser before John had a chance to mention the car seat, or rather, her lack of one. "Are you here on official business?" She was beginning to realize that, unlike in the city, dropping by unannounced was acceptable on the Vineyard.

"I was. One of the good citizens of Chappaquiddick decided to be our guest in a cell for the night. I told the chief I'd bring him home. I thought I'd stop by and let you know I'll be picking you up instead of my dad. But, hey, why not come with me now? I'll return the cruiser, get my truck, then come back for dinner. The baby will have a nice long ride to keep her quiet."

"Oh," Annie quickly replied. "Thanks, but no. I'm not quite ready." She knew her answer was absurd: by the way she was dressed, it was probably obvious that she wasn't cooking or cleaning or making soap.

"You look fine to me."

"I haven't got Bella's things packed yet."

"I can help. I have experience, you know."

"No. But thanks. I'm not organized . . ." It was a lame excuse, and she knew it. By the smile on his face, she suspected he knew it, too.

"Just because I'm a cop, doesn't mean I bite. Come on. The ride on the water was always guaranteed to calm down my kids."

It occurred to Annie then that Christmas might be a hard day for him. Perhaps he was sad. And lonely. She hated that she was letting her silly, self-centered emotions get in the way of maybe helping someone else feel a little better.

"Okay," she said, returning the smile. "Give me a minute to get Bella's things."

"Don't forget her," he said, with a wide grin. "Is she in the car?"

Annie lowered her eyes. "Yes."

He bounded out of the SUV. "I'll excuse the lack of a car seat for today only. In fact, I'll get her while you're in the house."

Heading back to the cottage, Annie wondered if she'd lost her mind. Now was definitely not the time to share Bella's story with John. Not when she knew that the young mother was absolutely, positively, still on the island. And no doubt close by. But she knew that the more time she spent with John—especially alone—the more inclined she'd be to spill out the story. She reminded herself that, as nice as he was, he was not an ally. He was a police officer whose job was to uphold the law. Which might include placing her under arrest, then bringing her to Edgartown as a "guest" in a cell for the night. Or longer.

Still, she thought as she went into her kitchen, *it would be nice to be with him.* After all, it was Christmas. And maybe she was a little lonely, too.

"Should I say *I told you so?*" John teased once they were on the *On Time*, halfway across the channel, and Bella was sleeping soundly.

"Not fair. I'd already gotten her to stop crying."

They were the first vehicle on the ferry: the only thing between the cruiser and the water was a single, heavy chain wrapped in a three-inch strip of canvas that was strung from one side of the boat (the "motorized raft") to the other. It didn't seem like much of a barrier if the emergency brake let go or the tide suddenly surged. Annie closed her eyes and remembered that the dependable *On Times* had sluiced back and forth across Edgartown Harbor for decades with a near-perfect record—except for a few incidents caused by passengers themselves. Earl had entertained her with stories about those one morning over coffee and cinnamon rolls.

John looked at her sideways. "So. What about you?"

She blinked. "What about me?"

"I don't know. All you've told me is that you're a writer, and that you're not in hiding or starting a new life, although it sure looks like you are. Starting a new life, that is."

She smiled, but said nothing.

"Look, Annie. I'm not trying to be nosy, but my dad has probably told you all about me. That I went to college on the mainland. Got married. Came back to be a cop. Had two kids. My girls. Then my wife decided she hated living here." He shrugged, the way Earl often did. "End of story. So what about you? Do I get to hear a few juicy details about the famous writer who's moved onto the island and my father has be-friended?"

"Me?" she asked again. She told herself he wasn't hitting on her, that this wasn't a date, because, for starters, she was too old for him. Maybe he was interested merely for law enforce-ment reasons. Or maybe—just maybe—he was simply being nice. Neighborly. "Well," she said. "I could say you'd learn all about me if you friended me on Facebook or followed me on Twitter. But I'm afraid I'm a little lax in the social media de-partment." She had no idea why she'd led with that. She would have thought it was the last thing on her mind, the low rung on her ladder of importance.

But John was shaking his head. "I don't do that stuff."

"Good," she replied. "Me, neither. Or, my editor says, not often enough." She smoothed her skirt and smiled. "Before I became what you called a famous writer, my details aren't ter-ribly juicy. I was an elementary school teacher. Third grade. In Boston. I've been married twice. My first husband was killed in a car accident. My second . . . well, it just didn't work out. So now I write books. End of story."

"Family?"

"Not really." Then she thought about Taylor's announce-ment that Bella's birth mother was Annie's niece. "No one I'm very close to." It was not a lie. Technically, the only remaining "family" she knew of was Donna MacNeish, if she was still alive. And Annie certainly wasn't close to her. Still, Annie hoped and prayed for John's interrogation to stop.

By then they'd reached the other side of the channel. John

put down his window, said a few words to the ferry captain, saluted, and waited for him to remove the restraint strap. Then he steered the cruiser off the ramp and onto Dock Street.

They arrived at the police station in less than two minutes; in the mile-and-a-quarter it took them to get there, Annie saw only three other cars. She knew that the streets would look different by summer.

John ran inside to drop off the keys while Annie got out and carried Bella to his truck. He emerged with another officer; they chatted and ambled toward her. Her shoulders tensed; maybe it hadn't been such a good idea to be so close to the police station. Tomorrow would be soon enough.

"Got an infant car seat in that thing?" the other officer said as he pointed at John's truck.

"One's coming tomorrow, right, Annie? Unless your niece gets back first?"

Though the sun was shining, it was cold outside. And the wind had picked up. Annie hoped that the flush in her cheeks would be mistaken as being from Mother Nature, not nerves. "Tomorrow for sure," she replied.

John tapped the other officer on the shoulder. "Merry Christmas, man. Hope the day is quiet and uneventful."

"Right. Yours, too."

They got into the truck and said nothing more until John pulled out onto Peases Point Way and headed back toward the ferry. "Will she be here tomorrow?" he asked.

Annie knew she couldn't pretend not to know whom he meant. "To tell you the truth, I don't know. There's been a bit of an upheaval lately." At least she wasn't lying about that.

"Been there," John said. "Done that."

They went back to Chappy in silence, except for Bella's occasional gurgles.

★   ★   ★

Over dinner, Claire was more chatty and pleasant than she'd been the night before. She engaged Annie in conversation about the third-graders she'd taught, and even asked her if it was hard to write a novel. Annie asked Claire about her volunteer work at the Anchors, the senior center in Edgartown, a few steps from the *On Time*, and about the garden club, which Earl had once told Annie his wife was dedicated to because it was a terrific fund-raiser for the island. While they talked, Earl and John discussed several town ordinances and contracts they'd like to see get underway before the season began, which was still months away. Annie had begun to realize that winter was the best time for islanders to get things done.

Between the turkey and the baked Alaska, Annie finally had a chance to speak to Earl alone.

"Didn't you hear my message?" she asked. She'd gone with him into his study, ostensibly to look at old photos of Chappy: pictures of a magnificent inn that had been there in the 1930s, and of a renowned shop once owned by a Spanish contessa that had customers from New York City, Paris, and London.

"You called?" Earl asked. "I must have forgotten to turn my phone on this morning. I was busy peeling potatoes." He rolled his eyes, then gestured for her to sit on the small sofa in his study. His "man cave," he called it, because he admitted he'd grown too lazy to study much about anything anymore.

"She's still here. On Chappy." She told him about the night sounds, the face print, and the label that she'd found that morning.

"Holy shit," he said. "Pardon my French."

"I have a feeling she's next door to me, Earl. In the house where the driveway wasn't plowed. I think she was already in there, then the blizzard began, and that's how she got to me so easily when she brought Bella over."

"She was at the Littlefields'? Wouldn't you have seen footprints?"

"Not if she went back inside. The snow kept falling after that, remember? For another whole day. It must have covered them up. If she had supplies, she might have felt safe there. At the Littlefields', if that's their name."

"Yup, that's the place. The one that's been neglected by the kids. It would be a great hiding place. But you think that our little mother risked coming out?"

"I think so."

"But why now?"

"Maybe she wanted to be sure Bella is okay?"

"Do you think she wanted to take her back?"

"I have no idea. Maybe she's just scared, Earl."

"Maybe she is. I'll be damned."

"Yeah. Me, too."

He scratched at his whiskers, then smoothed his big eyebrows. "So now what?"

"I don't want John to know yet. I would love to talk to her first. Try and get her to change her mind. Maybe I can help her. Somehow."

Letting out a low whistle, Earl said, "That's a pretty high expectation. You don't even know the young lady. It sounds like she has—and I'm going to be politically incorrect here—a few screws loose."

"We don't know that, Earl. What we do know is that a child's life is at stake. Okay, maybe it's not life or death now, but, believe me, whatever direction the rest of Bella's life takes depends on how she'll feel if she's abandoned." Her voice cracked when she said those last words.

Silence draped over the room, across the books on the overstuffed shelves, the newspapers stacked in the corner, and the replicas of old whaling ships—some carved out of wood, some sculpted from metal—that had sailed in the late nineteenth century, when Edgartown was a bustling seaport.

Then Earl said, "You sound like you're speaking from experience."

Annie nodded. "I was adopted, Earl. But I was one of the lucky ones. My adoptive parents were wonderful, and I had a good life. They were both too young when they died, and I miss them terribly. But the truth is, I always felt a tug on my heart . . . a little hole in there, as if something was always missing."

He stared at her for a few seconds. "Sounds to me like something was. But good for your parents for raising you right."

"They did. And I loved them. I still do. But . . ." She didn't know what else to add. She could have told him about Donna MacNeish, about her chance to meet her birth mother, about how she let it go. About how she still wasn't sure that had been the right thing to do.

Then the door opened. "Baked Alaska," Claire said. "Come and get it before the glacial cap melts."

After dinner, John served coffee, then started to clean up the kitchen. With an afternoon spent entertaining the Lyons family, Bella had fallen asleep again. It was nearly dark, and Annie said they must really get home. But Earl suggested they retreat to the living room.

He put another log in the fireplace, and Claire retrieved a lone, plump package from under the tree. It was wrapped in green foil paper and tied with white ribbon. She handed it to Annie. "This is for Bella. In honor of her first Christmas."

Annie scowled, but took the gift. "But you gave her that wonderful book. I read it to her last night until she fell asleep." Neither Earl nor Claire said anything. Both of them simply smiled.

Sliding off the ribbon, Annie unwrapped the paper and took out the softest, tiniest white crocheted sweater that she'd ever seen. It had a matching white hat with tiny earflaps. They looked as if they'd fit Bella perfectly. "My gosh," Annie said. "These are beautiful. But how on earth . . ."

"Claire stayed up all night," Earl said, proudly pointing to his wife.

"You made these?" Annie asked. She'd never seen garments so perfectly stitched.

"I had leftover yarn from a sweater I made for John's Lucy. It was taking up space in the closet. I figured the baby might like something pretty."

Once in a while, if she was lucky, Annie was able to drop her guard, lower the wall she kept securely around her, and let out her emotions. One of those moments rushed at her then, and she knew she needed to act. She stood up, went to Claire, and hugged her. "This is beautiful, Claire. Thank you so much."

"Well, I didn't want your niece to think the folks here on Chappy don't take care of each other."

Annie bit her lip and went back to her chair. She picked up the sweater again. "Well, this certainly shows that they do." She blinked back a small pool of tears that had formed in her eyes.

"I miss having babies around," Claire said. "Do you think Bella will be with you for a while?"

So there it was. The big question. Annie couldn't very well say no, that Bella wouldn't be there after tomorrow, that this would no doubt be the last time Claire would see her.

"Who knows?" she said, after a moment's hesitation. "Life has a way of changing, doesn't it?" She got up again. "And now, I can't thank you both enough for such a nice day, but I really need to get Bella home. And me, too. I'm afraid I've eaten too much wonderful food, and I'm really, really tired." She laughed, but she knew it sounded like the kind of canned laughter used in sitcoms to make viewers think the actors were performing before a live audience.

Earl stood up. "I'll take you home."

"Here we go again," John said. "I heard what Annie said and was about to come in and offer."

"Sorry," Earl said. "But I have to drive by a couple of properties. I didn't get out this morning to check on them. I want to make sure they're locked up tight."

"Afraid of squatters? On Christmas Day?" John's sarcasm was not well hidden.

"Something like that," Earl said, then went down the hall to get their coats.

Francine was back in bed, wrapped up in the comforter, the warmest place in the house. All she could think about was how had she been so naive to think that a rich celebrity lady would have wanted to take care of Bella. Just because Annie Sutton had been adopted, just because she'd been raised by strangers and had obviously turned out just fine, was no reason for Francine to have thought she'd want to be bothered with Bella.

She should have known better.

Her stomach ached now. Last night, after sneaking next door, she'd eaten the cheese and the brownies. She couldn't get any water from the kitchen faucet, so she'd gone outside, packed some snow in the plastic baggie the cheese had been in, and sucked on it until it was gone. She'd meant to save the cinnamon roll until she got real hungry again, but she ate it.

She slept for a while, but then it was morning and Francine was afraid to go outside again. Afraid she'd be seen.

So she stayed upstairs, under the covers, wondering if she'd freeze to death. Which might be the best way to make everything go away.

Pretty much through it all—since she'd seen the basket that Annie had trashed in the back seat of her car—Francine had been crying. She'd bought the basket in a shop in Provincetown; she'd spent more than she should have. But she'd thought it was so pretty that it would help make someone want Bella.

But now Bella was gone. And Francine had no idea where. She only knew that it was her fault.

And, as if being alone on Martha's Vineyard at Christmas was not bad enough, she'd taken that little ferry across the freezing cold channel and now she was trapped on Chappaquiddick.

And she just didn't know what to do.

Closing her eyes, she felt tears run down her face again. Then, another idea slowly, finally formed.

And Francine knew it was her only way out.

Chapter 16

"Okay," Earl said, once they were finally out of the house and heading toward Annie's cottage, "here's the plan. You and the baby will stay with us tonight."

Annie toyed with the old onesie Bella had worn before she'd changed her into a clean one and the new sweater Claire had made. The woman was pleased to see how beautiful the baby looked—which was why Annie had done it. The sweater had been a thoughtful gesture, and the woman deserved to know it was appreciated. But then Claire spent so much time cooing over Bella that Earl got annoyed and told her to please shut the hell up and let Annie get home. He'd said it in a pleasant way, though. With a smile. And an exaggerated eye roll.

"What do you mean?" Annie asked now. "I can't stay with you and Claire."

"If you think I'm going to let you sleep in that cottage with the little one's mother snooping about, sneaking up on your porch in the middle of the night, you're wrong. No. I'll take you home now, and you can pack whatever you'll need for yourself and the baby. Then you'll come back to our house. I'll make up a story. I'll say the wiring blew out and the cottage has no power. Claire will be only too glad to have you; you and the little one can sleep in John's old room. Skippy's room," he added with a chuckle.

She wanted to say no, but the truth was, Annie was grateful. She hadn't been looking forward to trying to sleep; she knew she'd be waiting and listening, and that every creak in the house or swish of the wind would send her into panic mode. However, her intellectual brain told her she was a grown woman and should not be afraid of a young girl who probably only wanted to see that her baby was being well cared for. So, in spite of her misgivings, Annie said, "No, Earl. I can't let you do that. It's bad enough I've been lying to everyone. Claire will never forgive you if she finds out you've been in on this practically from the beginning."

"You let me worry about my wife. We've been married almost fifty years. I know how to handle her."

"But won't it be worse if Bella's mother comes to the cottage and sees that no one's there? That wouldn't be fair, would it? I mean, wouldn't she freak out? Wouldn't you, if you were in her shoes?"

"First of all, I would never be in her shoes, and neither would you. We have more sense than to do what she did. Second, I don't give a crap if she freaks out. She got herself into this mess; it's her own fault. Let her worry about where the baby might be. It might get her to think twice about what she's done."

But Annie shook her head. "I don't know, Earl. It just doesn't seem right."

He turned down North Neck Road, the light from his headlights skimming over what was left of the snow. "We could go over to the Littlefields' now, but, frankly, I'm too tired for confrontation. But that's the other piece of my plan. When I bring you home in the morning we'll pay her a visit. In the daylight. When it's safer. We'll see if she's been there all along. I said *we* because I'm going with you. If this girl is a nutcase, I'm not going to let you meet her alone."

"But we don't even know if she's there."

"Oh, I think you were right. It's the only place I know of on this road that doesn't have an alarm system. And, like I said before, that driveway never gets plowed anymore. Not to mention that people on the island who find themselves homeless always know where to go. As old as I am, I've never figured out how that happens, but it does. Maybe she knew, or maybe it was a good guess. Doesn't matter. What matters is that we'll check it out—together—in the light of day, and get whatever needs to be done, done. We can't have everyone falling in love with this little baby only to have her shuttled off to a foster home as if none of us cares." He pulled down Annie's driveway and turned off the truck. "Now, go get your things."

Annie sat for a moment, contemplating all that Earl had said. Then she sighed. "There's something else I didn't have a chance to tell you. Taylor came by this morning. She pretended she was looking for my cat."

"You don't have a cat."

"I know that. But remember when we ran into her the other day and you told her my cat had run away? Well, she came to tell me the Flanagans wouldn't let me have one, that it would have been in my lease. That if I get caught, I could get evicted."

"Oh, Christ."

"It seemed odd that she'd stopped by to tell me when she could have mentioned it last night."

Earl toyed with his keys. "She smells a rat. I should have known she would. She's a smart cookie. Not to mention that she's always had a crush on John. My bet is she sees you as competition for his affections. She'll probably do whatever it takes to get you off the island."

"Seriously?" Annie asked. "*Seriously?*"

"Yup. Which makes it all the more important for us to get this mess sorted out in the morning. Now, go get your things."

Annie knew not to argue any more: her dad had taught her the importance of knowing when to stop. *No point in picking up a book to read if someone's turned off the lights,* he liked to say. Which, of course, had been before the advent of e-books. In any event, Annie did as she was told now; she figured the fact that both Earl and Claire now cared about Bella, too, could work in her favor once she finally told the truth. Later, she'd contemplate Earl's suspicion that Taylor might be jealous.

Bella woke up early in the morning, so, naturally, Annie did, too. After quickly dressing, she changed the baby, scooped her up, and tiptoed downstairs, hoping they hadn't awakened Earl or Claire. Or John, who'd decided to sleep on the pullout sofa in Earl's man cave because he didn't have to work again until midnight on Wednesday.

Claire had been surprisingly kind when Annie and Earl had returned the night before. She agreed with Earl that Annie and Bella should not be expected to sleep in a house without electricity. "This isn't the nineteen fifties, after all," she said. From that comment, Annie had deduced that some homes on Chappaquiddick hadn't had power back then.

After instructing John—as if he were a teenager—to clean the junk out of his room and change the linens, Claire had heated a bottle for Bella and made a cup of tea for Annie.

Yes, she had been kind, which might have surprised Winnie, but it had seemed genuine. It was also why Annie felt terrible when she reached the foot of the stairs, rounded the corner, walked into the kitchen, and found Claire standing in her bathrobe, looking outside at a cardinal perched atop a tree branch.

"Oh," Annie whispered. "I'm so sorry we woke you up. I was afraid of that."

But when Claire turned, she looked wide awake, almost glowing in the early light. "Nonsense! I'm an early riser. I was up long before you two girls!" She laughed, so Annie did, too. "Coffee?"

Bella wriggled in Annie's arms. "First, I think Bella wants food."

"Let me feed her," Claire replied. "Please?"

"As long as you're offering . . ." Annie handed her the baby, took the bottle Bella hadn't finished the night before from the refrigerator, and set it in a pan of water on the stove to warm. Then she moved to the window. "What a peaceful morning. I've never been off the main road on this side of Chappy."

"I used to walk down to the water every morning. Now my back won't let me do that. Doc Ellis says I have to stick with yoga and Pilates—the kind of exercise that announces to the world that you're old. Not that I need a public proclamation. But I do take classes at the Council on Aging. Sometimes, it's even fun." As she spoke, she rubbed Bella's back, turning the baby's soft cries into little murmurs.

"My mom had back issues, too. That was before they recommended any kind of exercise. She mostly sat inside and suffered."

"Are you a walker?"

"I used to enjoy it. But other than walking back and forth to the *On Time* once in a while, since I've been here, I seem to be too busy."

Claire nodded toward the window. "Now's the best time of day. Go ahead. Have a nice walk. I'll take care of Bella."

Annie almost hesitated, then decided that was foolish. Claire would take good care of the baby. Or she'd have Earl to answer to. "Actually," she replied, "I think I'll take you up on that. I'll wait for coffee until I come back."

She found her coat and pulled on her hat and gloves. Claire directed her toward "the best path down to Wasque," and Annie headed out.

The morning was spectacular. The sun wasn't as glorious as the day before, but it cast a mellow peace over the earth. Small mounds of snow still huddled here and there among the scrub oaks, and the silence—the stillness—was like nothing Annie had ever heard. Or, rather, had not heard.

She made her way along a sandy path that twisted through the mini forest. It was carpeted with damp brown leaves—they seemed to have lost their crispness of autumn, no doubt from being tossed by winds and drenched with rain and snow. She was glad that, when Earl had brought her home the night before, she'd changed out of her ballet flats and into her boots and out of her cashmere and into her jeans.

It felt wonderful to walk. Annie had never thought of herself as much of an outdoorswoman. When she'd been a Girl Scout, she'd had fun when they'd gone camping, though the best part had been the ritual of sitting by the campfire, eating s'mores, and making up stories. But there was something about the Vineyard—the light, the land, the sea—that felt different. Peaceful. Whole. Even the blizzard hadn't frightened her the way the snow often had in Boston, when it made her claustrophobic, with neighbors upstairs, downstairs, and on both sides, and with the buildings squished too close together. Even the spacious apartment that she and Mark had lived in had made her feel squeezed in. She wondered now if it had been her marriage and not the rest that had been choking her.

The truth was, the only real thing that frightened Annie now was that Bella's mother was stalking her. She could deal with Taylor—or could leave it to Earl to deal with her. But if Bella's mother had changed her mind and wanted her baby back, why was she acting so secretive? So . . . creepy? What was she hiding?

The wind picked up; Annie pulled her hat over her ears. She was growing tired of trying to figure out what had been going on in the young woman's mind.

Turning around the next bend, she saw the Atlantic Ocean stretched out before her. The water glimmered its winter indigo; waves curled toward the shoreline in their endless, graceful dance. Annie stopped, watched, and breathed. Murphy had often said that everyone, in every moment, is exactly where she or he needs to be. Standing in the quiet, listening to the ocean's symphony, Annie certainly could not dispute that theory. Until she heard footsteps approach from behind.

She didn't know if she should turn around or run. If she weren't in boots, she'd be faster on her feet. Her hands started to tremble inside her mittens. *Maybe it's just a squirrel*, she told herself until she remembered that Earl once told her there were no squirrels on Chappy. Maybe it was the hawk that had been trying to get the chickens at the Alvord place. But she had no idea where the Alvord place was, and she didn't know whether or not a hawk was the kind of predator she'd want to come up against. Would it be worse than Bella's mother?

The footsteps grew louder, closer, sounding more . . . human.

She stiffened her shoulders so they were square and straight, the way her mother had taught her to do when, at twelve, Annie had begun to slouch because she'd grown taller than the boys in seventh grade. "Remember to stand straight as an arrow!" her mother barked every morning that year when she sent her off to school. Her dad explained that straight shoulders showed confidence. And that confidence would get her far in life.

If Bella's mother was sneaking up on her, Annie knew she needed confidence. She had to remember she was the one in control. After all, she was the one who had the baby.

Besides, maybe it was only Taylor. Surely, Annie could deal with her. Unless she was there to threaten Annie, too. Again.

Then, because she had convinced herself she was capable of taking control of the situation, Annie spun around with confidence—and came face-to-face with John.

She screamed.

He laughed.

Her hand flew to her throat. She looked away.

He touched her hand and said, "Hey, sorry, I didn't mean to scare you. I was just out for a run."

Was he? she wondered. *Really?*

"Didn't you hear me coming?"

She turned back to the water; he pulled his hand away. "You could have warned me," she said. "Called out my name or something."

"I didn't see you until I came around that last curve. Jeez, Annie, I'm sorry. I didn't realize you were the jumpy type."

What type do you think I am? she wanted to ask. Instead she shook her head. "It's okay. You startled me, that's all. I was deep in thought, mesmerized by the ocean."

He moved to stand beside her. "Yup. The prettiest place on earth, if you ask me. 'Course, those who live up island think the cliffs are the prettiest. And those in Menemsha think their harbor's the prettiest. And on it goes." He was a good five or six inches taller than she was; it had been a long, long time since Annie had wanted to lean against a man's chest the way she wanted to do right then.

"And on it goes," she echoed.

"So what were you thinking about?" he asked.

You don't want to know, she thought. *Or maybe you do. But I'm not going to tell you. Yet.* She shoved her hands into her pockets. "Nothing much. Life."

"I thought you were going to say you were thinking about the book you're writing."

"Oh, yes. Well, that, too, I suppose." Or the e-mails she'd yet to answer. Or the social media tidbits she'd yet to post. Any of those would have provided a believable answer, if only she'd thought of them.

"How's the writing going, anyway? There are so many writers and artists on the Vineyard, but I've never talked to any. Except maybe in the summers, when I've doled out my fair share of speeding tickets. I don't suppose asking, *Do you know how fast you were going?* could be considered conversation."

She laughed, grateful that her heart had resumed its normal pace. "Probably not."

"So," he said, "do you want to have dinner with me sometime?"

The fact that she'd been startled when he'd come up from behind her did not compare with the way she felt right then. Literally speaking, they'd had dinner together the day before. And the night before that. Was he asking her on a date? Could she do that? Could she go out with him and pretend she wasn't hiding a great big secret? And worse, what would Taylor do if she found out? "I . . . I don't know," she finally answered.

He shrugged. "Nothing fancy. Something casual. Like the Newes? Then again, most people know me there, which might make you uncomfortable. We might be better off to head to Vineyard Haven to the Copper Wok. Which is no guarantee I won't get sidetracked. Or we could go up island to . . . shit. Nothing's open up island now 'til spring. Then again, you haven't said you'd go, so I guess it's what you might call premature to pick a restaurant."

She thought about it. Briefly. As tempting as the offer was, how could she go out with him? How could she go anywhere with a man who might need to arrest her in a few short hours? "No," she said abruptly.

Silence cut the air.

"No?"

Maybe he wasn't accustomed to having a woman turn him down. "I'm sorry, John. It's just not a good time for me."

He nodded briefly. "No problem. I understand." He shrugged and waved, then ran off in the direction from where she supposed he'd come.

"Idiot," came Murphy's whisper from somewhere in the scrub oaks.

By the time Annie got back to Earl and Claire's, John's truck was gone. Earl was up and dressed, sitting at the table eating scrambled eggs and toast; Claire was sitting, holding Bella, whispering to her. Annie was not in the mood to smile.

Earl gestured toward the stove. "Help yourself to coffee. And there's more eggs in the pan. I asked Claire if she minded keeping the little one here while we go into town. You said you have errands; so do I. Might as well go together. Is that okay with you?"

Errands? Oh, right. She supposed that checking out the possibility that Bella's mother had been—was still—living next door to the cottage might be considered an errand. If the girl wasn't there, maybe Earl would drive Annie to the police station and get this over with. At least John wouldn't be working, so she would not have to face him. Which, unlike how she'd felt earlier, would no doubt be better. Quicker. Less entangled. After all, he must think she was strange enough already.

"I'm not hungry now," she said, "but thanks. And yes, I need to go into town. If you're sure you don't mind sitting with Bella, Claire? It would make things easier for me." Since Annie had left to take her walk, Claire had clearly found the time to shower, dress, fix her hair, and put the baby in the clean onesie that Annie had packed the night before.

"Do I mind?" Claire asked. "I wouldn't mind in a million years. This one is a sweetheart."

Earl brought his dishes to the sink. "Okay then, we'd best get going to avoid the after-Christmas rush."

Annie pretended to laugh because she knew it was a joke. With the holiday over and the tourists long gone—the last of whom no doubt had departed on the *Grey Lady* after Christmas in Edgartown—the Vineyard was desolate. Even, as she'd just learned, up island, where the restaurants were closed until spring.

Chapter 17

Annie convinced Earl to let her stop at the cottage and pick up some Christmas cookies for Bella's mother. "I want her know that we come in peace."

A slight guffaw urped from his throat, but he pulled into her driveway anyway. She ran inside, dropped half a dozen candy cane cookies into a plastic sandwich bag, and stuck a bow on top. Then she raised her eyes and said, "Murphy, I need a little help now, okay? Even though you think I'm an idiot?"

Back outside, Earl was standing next to the truck. "I think we should walk over. Otherwise, we might scare her off. In fact, we can cut through. I found a path that runs from the Flanagans' property to the Littlefields'."

"Which must be how she's come back and forth."

"More than likely."

Of course, that still didn't answer the questions of how she'd known where Annie lived in the first place, or why she'd picked her out of the hundreds or more women who stayed on the Vineyard in winter, most of whom were no doubt imminently more qualified to take care of a baby than she was.

Earl led the way. They ducked under a few trees and pushed back some brush, but the path definitely provided a gateway between the two land parcels. Once they reached the other side, Annie was stunned to see that, from the water, what looked like a magnificent place, had, as Earl had hinted, fallen into disrepair. Shingles, tree limbs, and litter were scattered across the lawn like seaweed and debris that had ridden in with the tide and had been left on the shore to rot. A hemline of shrubbery skirted the foundation of the house; bushes that once must have been lush were skeletal, remnants of snow clinging to their naked twigs. A broken rose trellis was slumped over, as if it had been shot.

"Wow," Earl said in a low voice, "it's worse than I thought."

"Now I understand why the driveway wasn't plowed. You were right: no one seems to care about any of it."

"Well, you know all about family discord. Thanks to your unfortunate niece." He grinned a toothy grin; Annie wanted to swat him. "Maybe we can get in through the sunroom on the side," he added. "But let's stay away from the windows. In case our young friend hears us coming."

They stooped, they shuffled, they duckwalked to a glass door. Earl reached up and tried the handle. It was locked.

"Damn," he muttered. Then he signaled Annie to stay behind him, and they made their way to the other side of the house. But the door there was locked, too.

Annie looked around. The sun porch was long, wide, and totally glassed in. It stretched across the entire back of the house. Inside, she could see an indoor swimming pool that had been covered. But unless she and Earl were willing to hurl a rock through a window, it didn't look as if they'd get inside. She scanned the area; then she noticed an alcove near what might be a kitchen. And another door. She tapped Earl on the shoulder and pointed in that direction. He resumed their furtive walking; Annie followed.

With a single, quick twist of the handle, the door opened.

"Well," he said. "That was easy."

Then he tried to stand up straight. "*Damn!*" he screeched, grasping his lower back. "*Hot bloody damn!*"

"Oh, God!" Annie screamed. "Are you okay?"

Between the screech and the scream, their "cover," if that's what it was, had certainly been blown.

Earl didn't speak for a few seconds, which Annie assumed was because he was an old-fashioned guy and wouldn't want to look helpless. Not in front of a woman. Then he groaned, "Damn. Stand by. Let me try to stretch. Crappy old legs. Sometimes they forget they're no longer thirty."

Annie held her breath. She hesitated to give him a hand; she wasn't sure if that would make him hurt more. Or bruise his ego. While she stood by, her eyes grazed the house. Then, just as Earl stretched upright and bent from one side to the other, Annie saw the blinds flutter in an upstairs window. The movement was swift and could have been her imagination, but . . .

"Got it," he said. "Okay, let's go in."

Taking a long breath of resolve, Annie tread lightly and followed him inside.

It was empty. They entered through what clearly had been a mudroom and laundry room: the lid of a boot box had been yanked off; the washer and dryer were missing; hoses and an air vent were strewn across the floor. A door that led into the kitchen was missing, its hinges sticking out at odd angles.

"Vandals?" Annie asked.

"Doubtful. From what I heard, the son thinks he's entitled. He probably wanted to piss off his sisters."

They went into the massive kitchen: some of the countertops had been removed, as had lighting fixtures that once hung above a sizeable island; if a table had been in the room, it wasn't there now. Nor were chairs. Surprisingly, the appliances remained. The only signs of life were vestiges of anger.

"What a mess," Earl said.

"It must have been a lovely place," Annie said, walking toward an expansive glass wall that mirrored the curve of the shoreline and looked out to the harbor and the lighthouse. There were only lower cabinets; upper ones would have obstructed the view. "Wow," she said, moving toward a large sink with elaborate stainless steel faucets that looked surprisingly intact. "This is incredible." Then her eyes lowered, and she suddenly froze. In the deep sink was an empty can of baby formula marked THREE TO SIX MONTHS. Just like the ones in the bag that had been left on her doorstep next to Bella. An empty plastic baggie was on top. Crumbs were scattered, mostly small ones. She touched one of the larger ones and held it to her nose: it smelled of cinnamon. Like the rolls Annie made for Earl. The crumb was still soft, which suggested it had not been there long.

Annie felt pummeled by a gust of island wind. She leaned on the edge of the sink to regain her balance, to pull together her thoughts. But all she could think of was: *The girl stole my food*. Which meant she'd been inside Annie's cottage. She'd been in her space.

"Earl?" Annie cried out in a hush.

He did not respond.

She turned; he wasn't there.

She almost shouted for him, but quickly changed her mind. Bella's mother had been in this house. Recently. If she were still there . . . and if Earl stumbled on her . . .

Then Annie remembered the flutter of blinds in the upstairs window.

Oh, God, she thought. *He doesn't know. And he's gone off exploring.*

She rushed from the kitchen into a great room. A massive stone fireplace climbed to the top of the two-story ceiling; the only furniture was an old sofa positioned haphazardly facing the front window. "Earl," she called softly, "Where are you?" If Bella's mother were still there, by now she must know that they were, too. Annie prayed she wasn't upset. Or scared enough to act out in anger. One good conk on Earl's head with a lamp or a vase would send him to his knees in hideous pain.

Moving from the big room, Annie stepped cautiously into a grand foyer where a butterfly staircase cascaded from the upper floor down to where she stood. Just as she was considering alerting John to come rescue his father, Earl rounded an upstairs corner and ambled down the staircase, one hand pressed against his lower back.

"Damn," he said. "Nothing. No one. A couple of bedrooms still have beds with blankets and pillows. I guess the son didn't need them."

Annie waited until he reached the bottom step. "No," she said quietly. "She's here. Or she was here." She led him back into the great room, keeping her tone low. "There are things in the sink, including . . . crumbs. She was in my cottage, Earl. There were traces of a cinnamon roll." She turned and, from that angle, she spotted something on the sofa. It looked like a book.

In that instant, even from several feet away, Annie knew what it was. She recognized the lavender cover, the thick spine that held the pages of a long and painful story. She stopped; her legs went weak. "Oh, God," she said. "Oh. God."

"What?" Earl asked. Then his gaze followed hers. "A book?" He walked into the room and plucked it from the sofa. He read the title: "*You Let Me Go*." He fell silent for a second, then he said, "Jesus, Annie. This is one of yours."

She was too shocked to nod. "That's the connection," she said, breathlessly. "It all makes sense."

"What?"

"It's why she picked me. I got into a conversation with some of my readers at the fair. Someone asked if I was living on the Vineyard now. I said I was on Chappy. For God's sake, I might have even said I was on North Neck. I do remember that someone asked if I was writing an autobiography. I said the closest I'd ever come to that was in my first book. And then someone else asked if that was the one where my character was adopted. God, Earl, the girl was standing right there. She knew where I lived and that I was adopted. She must have thought I'd be sympathetic to taking Bella in."

He opened the front cover. "This is a library copy."

Annie blinked. She walked over and took the book from him. She scanned the volume, then handed it back. Knowing that the girl could still be in the house, that she could still be listening, Annie simply said, "Well, good for her. She's a reader. Come on, Earl, let's leave well enough alone. The poor girl has been through enough."

He scowled until she gestured toward the door. Then she motioned for him to bring the book with him: she dropped the bag of cookies onto the sofa where it had been.

"What the hell was that about?" Earl asked once they were outside again and out of hearing range.

"We need to go to Edgartown," she said. "To the library. Maybe they know who checked out that book. Maybe when she got a library card she had to give her name . . . and her address. I don't know if they'll tell us, but it's worth a try."

He tap-tapped the lavender cover. "A brilliant deduction, Sherlock. But right now my judgment might be clouded because I am so pissed. The girl stole one of your cinnamon rolls. That's one less for me."

Virginia was behind the counter; Annie knew her from the Wednesday night film programs she put together, and from the fabulous desserts she always served. When Annie had first arrived on the Vineyard, she'd introduced herself there, and Virginia had kindly made sure they had a good stock of her books.

Now, Annie stood impatiently next to Earl while the woman scrolled through the computer, searching for information about when Annie's first book had been most recently checked out. When Virginia said it was library protocol not to release the name of a patron, Annie had said that just knowing the date would help. If Virginia found that, Annie would tell her the whole story. If she thought it would help her learn more.

"Hmm," Virginia said. "Hmm." Above her eyeglasses, her brow was set in a visible frown.

Annie leaned on one foot, then the other.

Earl drummed his fingers on the countertop.

"No," Virginia said. "Nothing."

"Nothing?" Annie asked. "It can't be. The label on the cover is clearly marked EDGARTOWN PUBLIC LIBRARY."

"Sorry," she said, still perusing the screen. "But let's check the shelves. See if our copy's there."

Fiction was upstairs.

Earl said his back was still dicey and that he'd take the elevator and meet them up there.

Annie followed Virginia up the wide, open staircase; all the way up, Virginia said she couldn't imagine how the girl had obtained their copy, that none of the other branches in the CLAMS network had borrowed it, that they no doubt had their own. "You're a popular author on the Cape and Islands," she said with a pleasant smile.

The compliment was nice, but not what Annie needed right then.

By the time they reached the top, Earl was there. It took a minute to find the authors whose names started with an S. Annie, of course, would be at the end; usually, only a few S authors followed Sutton. The three of them huddled together, reading the titles from one shelf to another. Two of Annie's last four books were there; two had been checked out. But her first book was missing.

"Maybe it's in the wrong place," Earl said.

Virginia nodded. "Our volunteers are very good. But once in a while, things do get misfiled."

They hunted the shelves, side to side, top to bottom. *You Let Me Go* was nowhere to be found.

"Wow," Annie said, "I'm so confused!"

"Well," Virginia said once it was apparent their mission had failed, "there's only one answer."

"Somebody stole it?" Earl asked with a sarcastic laugh.

"Exactly," the librarian replied. "It's rare, but it happens. Maybe she was in a hurry and didn't want to bother to get a card. Or maybe she has a backlog of fines. Whatever the reason, if a book can't be traced, it's usually because someone has merely helped themselves."

"Especially," Annie added, "if the thief did not want it traced back to her."

The three of them stood, speechless.

Then a gentleman in a wool vest, white hair, and glasses emerged from the stacks. "Are you looking for one of Annie Sutton's books?"

Virginia introduced them to Nils, the library's research director. Annie hadn't met him before.

"Oh, hello, Annie. Nice to meet you," he said. "You might want to know that I spoke with a young woman . . . I think it was just before the blizzard. She came in looking for your books."

"She was around seventeen or eighteen? Big, dark eyes?"

"That's her. She had a baby with her in some sort of basket. She said she was a relative of yours. She knew you'd moved to

Chappy and that you were out on North Neck Road. But she wasn't from the Vineyard, and she didn't know which house you were in. She wondered if we might be able to tell her."

Annie's mouth went dry. She looked at Earl, then back to Nils.

"I told her we don't give out that kind of information," he continued. "She said never mind, that she'd check the town hall. Or ask at the ferry. She said someone on the island would tell her. I remember she said, 'Celebrities aren't entitled to privacy, you know.'" He harrumphed, as if he did not agree.

"And that was it?" Annie asked. "She left?"

Nils nodded. "Yes. She and her baby left."

It didn't matter how Bella's mother had learned that Annie was renting the Flanagans' guest cottage. As she'd informed Nils, someone at the town hall could have told her what house she was in; someone at the *On Time* who, like Earl, probably knew where everyone lived; or, Annie supposed, even someone from the pizza shop. Annie had had a few deliveries in the fall; she'd paid extra for them to cross the channel and drive out to the cottage, because she'd been immersed in making soap and hadn't wanted to leave.

Then, as Annie and Earl walked out of the library and climbed back into the truck, she had another thought.

She buckled her seat belt and dropped her forehead onto her hands. "God, Earl. She told Nils that I was a 'celebrity,' so she must think I'm rich." Annie laughed. "Clearly, she does not know my ex-husband." She was glad Earl didn't ask her to elaborate, because Annie was tired. Bone tired. Her adrenaline had been in overdrive the past few days. "She must have thought that she'd struck gold. She must have seen me as the perfect patsy to take her baby: a rich woman with a good reason to be an old softie about a motherless child who needed to be adopted. Who knows what she'd planned to do before I literally fell into her lap?" She sighed. "Can you bring me back to get Bella now? Then take us home? If her mother pokes around my place again, all the better. I'm ready to confront her. But first, I might be older than Bella, but I really need a nap."

"And I," Earl said as he backed out of the lot and drove toward the *On Time*, "really need ibuprofen."

Chapter 18

By the time Annie and Bella arrived back at the cottage, dense clouds had thickened the sky, and the temperature had fallen below freezing. She added more logs to the fire in the woodstove just as sleet began to pelt the roof.

Bella seemed to have had a terrific time with Claire. She'd been smiling and content; she'd had a bath and smelled snuggly sweet. Claire had wrapped her in a pink, quilted romper that she said she'd put away after John's younger girl had outgrown it. She'd also brushed Bella's hair into an adorable topknot and added a pink bow, the same color as the ribbon Annie used to tie her beach roses and cream soaps.

And now, as Bella slept contentedly in her basket, Annie sat in the rocker. She knew she should take advantage of the quiet time and get back to work on her book. At least she should reply to an e-mail or two, maybe let Trish know she was making progress on the manuscript. Or perhaps she should send a HAPPY NEW YEAR post to her patient fans. But instead of opening her laptop, Annie picked up a pad of paper. Sometimes she simply could think better with a pencil in her hand instead of something electronic. Now that she knew Bella's mother had specifically chosen her; now that she knew the girl was—or had been—living right next door; now that the girl had twice said—once to Taylor, once to Nils—that she did not live on the Vineyard (a fact that seemed reinforced by Nancy Clieg's comment that the poorly made basket had come from the Cape), Annie wondered if she had any options left before she called the police.

She clicked her pen and began to write:

Option 1: Return to the Littlefield house and go through it room by room, hoping to come face-to-face with the girl. She chewed the tip of the pen for a few seconds, then added: *Bring Bella.* Maybe if the baby—not Earl—were with her, the girl would come out of hiding. Then Annie wrote: *Offer to help her find a way to keep her baby.* At the moment, however, Annie had no idea how to do that. Or if the girl would even want to.

She looked down at Bella, so pretty, so peaceful, and tried not to think about what her life would be like if Annie didn't succeed. If only she knew something about Bella's mother . . . something like her name, where she was from, something, anything, that might help her figure out how to connect with her. Chances were that she'd come to the island recently, on the *Grey Lady* with the throng of Christmas in Edgartown shoppers, or on the big boat that went from Woods Hole to Vineyard Haven, which was near the upper tip of the triangle that formed the island's curious shape, and was a twenty-minute drive from Edgartown. As far as Annie knew, the only other passenger boat that came to the island in winter was the *Patriot,* a small, rough-and-tumble thing that was best known for bringing the newspapers in the wee hours every morning and for shuttling a handful of passengers back and forth from Falmouth to Oak Bluffs year-round.

No matter how the girl had found her way there, she might have been scared.

Then Annie had another idea.

Option 2: she wrote. *Call the* Grey Lady *office in Hyannis. See if there's a way to find out who the passengers were that weekend. Then call the* Patriot. But as soon as Annie wrote it down, she knew it was a long shot. If the people at the library wouldn't disclose private information, chances were that security in mass transportation would be even more rigid. Unless . . .

She clicked her pen again.

Option 3: Go to Vineyard Haven tomorrow; ask Winnie to check the ferry manifest. Because they'd inadvertently learned from Taylor that the girl did not have a vehicle, Annie didn't know whether or not she would have had to show an ID when she'd bought her ticket—no matter what boat she'd taken. Even if she hadn't, maybe she'd paid with a debit or credit card: maybe there was a record of her name. Annie had no idea if Winnie could get the information, but she sensed it was her best option. At least if she knew the girl's name, she could call out to her if she sneaked, uninvited, into the cottage again.

Last, but maybe not least, was the grandmother. Bella. There might be a chance the woman lived on the island, and for whatever reason, the girl hadn't looked her up. Maybe she'd been ashamed to have a baby—and to be alone. But Annie had no clue where to start looking for the grandmother, so that really was not an option.

She looked down at the pad, at her notes filled with *maybes*. Such a frustrating word. Still, she thought it made the most sense to see Winnie first. Once she learned the girl's name, it would make it easier for the police to track her down, too.

The police. *Right.* She had meant to go there that day.

But now, with the sleet and all, it would have to wait until the morning.

After she'd seen Winnie.

Because Annie could not give up yet, not when she now

knew that Bella's mother was most likely right next door. And that she'd trusted Annie to take care of her baby. *Please*, she had written in the note.

Annie stayed awake until the sky was awash in orange morning light. The next thing she knew, Bella was crying; it was past ten o'clock. The young mother had not stopped by during the night—or if she had, she'd left no evidence.

Quickly reviewing her notes, Annie knew that before she trekked to Vineyard Haven, she should call the *Grey Lady* terminal in Hyannis. She would say that one of their passengers had left some baby items on the wharf in Edgartown, and that Annie was trying to locate her. If they said they'd put out a lost and found notice, or if they asked for Annie's name and address, she'd have to hang up. Still, it was worth a try. And it would be a simple enough thing to check off her list if she struck out.

She looked up the number and, while feeding Bella with one hand, dialed her phone with the other. She warned herself not to view this multitasking as proof that she was now skilled at being a competent mother.

The phone rang six times, then voice mail kicked in. "You've reached the phone line for *Grey Lady* service from Hyannis to Martha's Vineyard and Nantucket. Our regularly scheduled boats run between Memorial Day weekend and Columbus Day weekend. Please check our website for the upcoming schedule." Click. Annie hung up without making a note of the web address.

When Bella was done with her breakfast, Annie called the *Patriot*. "Sorry," a nice man said. "We can't give out passenger information."

So she focused on Option 3, starting with calling the place that rented car seats. No sense annoying John if she ran into him while she was en route to Vineyard Haven.

Somehow, she managed to have both Bella and herself presentable by noon. Shortly after that, she wheeled the Lexus off the *On Time* and onto Memorial Wharf, where a yellow van waited. It was buttercup yellow and sported a huge, multicolored logo that read BABY RENTS. A cheerful young man jumped out. He was helpful and friendly, even to Bella, and in only a few minutes, Annie was headed toward the Steamship Authority with Bella safely ensconced in the back in a rear-facing car seat. At first, the baby fussed and cried, but once they reached the smooth straightaway of Edgartown-Vineyard Haven Road, she fell asleep.

Fifteen minutes later, Annie reached the terminal. The noon boat from Woods Hole had arrived after its forty-five-minute journey: it belched out cars and SUVs, and trailer trucks from Stop & Shop, Cape Cod Express, and Cottle's Lumber. Several dozen people toddled down the boat ramp and walked straight into the crowd that was going to board. Between vehicles waiting to pick up walk-on passengers and those dropping them off, Annie did not see a place to park. She drove to the end of the street, where she spotted Winnie's van in a reserved employee space. So Winnie was there. At least the trip would not be completely in vain.

Once the incoming traffic had cleared and the outgoing had filed into the ferry's gaping mouth, Annie circled back to the public lot and quickly found a space. She got out, happily freed Bella from the car seat, and went into the terminal in search of her friend.

"She's not here," the man behind a glass window said, then turned back to his computer screen.

Annie gazed around at the maps on the walls, the hand-painted decorations, and the racks of brochures that were nearly empty, not yet replenished from last season's onslaught. She looked back at the man. "Her van is."

Removing his bifocals, he eyed her with suspicion. "She's on a break. Try the Black Dog."

With a cordial smile, Annie left the terminal and threaded her way through the queue of cars awaiting the signal to board. She then walked toward a cluster of buildings where the Black Dog Tavern and its web of retail shops were headquartered. She decided to aim for the bakery, mostly because it was the closest, and because carrying ten pounds of baby on the crook of her arm wasn't terribly comfortable.

Winnie was not in the bakery, because, Annie huffed, that would have been too easy. She walked around back to the clamshell-covered ground and climbed the stairs to the clothing shop. She wasn't there, either.

Passing the gear shop, she went directly to the gray-shingled tavern that sat by the water and offered a great view of the comings and goings of the boats. Winnie was walking out, chatting to a woman Annie didn't know.

"Annie!" Winnie said as soon as she saw her. "Are you here for lunch?" She introduced her to her companion, whose name Annie promptly forgot.

"Actually, I was looking for you, Winnie. I hoped you might have a minute to talk."

Winnie said goodbye to her friend and suggested they sit on a bench by the front door. It wasn't August, but the sun was out, and for once, it wasn't windy.

Annie wasted no time asking for help. "If the girl paid with a credit card, you must have her name. If not, is there a way to trace someone who paid cash? Especially if that someone had a baby with her?"

Winnie patted her hand. "I'd do a lot of things for you, my friend, but I'm afraid I can't prowl through our files. That information is confidential; I can't jeopardize my job. I can, however, tell you that children under four years old don't need a ticket, so she must have purchased only one. Beyond that, well, I could get fired for sharing anything else. I hope you understand." She looked down at Bella and made small clucking sounds, at which the baby laughed.

"Oh," Annie said. "I'm so sorry, Winnie. I should have thought about that. I must really be desperate." She told her she'd learned that the girl had been living right next door, and that apparently she'd sought Annie out intentionally. "She knew where I lived: I'd blurted that out at the fair. She also heard—from me and my big mouth—that I was adopted. She stole my book from the library and learned the gory details about that. I think she picked me because she guessed I'd be sensitive to her situation. It looks like she guessed right." She saw no reason to mention that the girl might also have thought Annie was rich.

Winnie let Bella grab onto two of her fingers. Then she asked, "What about the taxis? Have you thought about asking the drivers? Or the bus driver? This time of year, most of them are the same. Maybe someone remembers them." She stood up and hoisted Bella's basket. "I'll walk you over to where they park. Then I have to get back to work."

They wove their way around the waiting vehicles, then to the far side of the terminal, where a bus and three taxi vans sat.

"Good luck," Winnie said and gave her a hug. "Let me know how it goes." She leaned down, kissed Bella's forehead, and handed Annie the basket. Then she disappeared into the terminal.

Annie raised her chin, squared her shoulders, and approached the first taxi.

No, the driver had not taken a young woman with a baby in a basket anywhere.

The second driver, a woman, claimed she did not understand what Annie meant.

The third one was asleep.

She decided not to bother him and, instead, went to the bus.

The driver smiled and opened his eyes wide. "She had beguiling eyes," he said. He had a light Jamaican accent and shining white teeth.

Annie's heart began to race. "Really? You remember her?"

He nodded. "And the baby. Is that the same baby?"

"It is," she replied. "But I've lost track of her mother, my niece. I let her take one of our cars, but I think she got lost. She left her cell phone at the house." Annie had no idea where the lies had come from or where they were headed, but decided she didn't care. "I know she has a friend here, but for the life of me, I can't remember her name. Is it possible you know where my niece got off the bus?" She held her breath, fully expecting him to say, *No.*

"Sure," he said. "She asked if I knew the Thurmans in Edgartown. I had a neighbor named Thurman, which is probably why I remember. Anyway, they weren't the ones she wanted. 'Cuz I live in Oak Bluffs."

Annie tried to conceal her excitement. "She asked for the Thurmans in Edgartown?"

"Yup."

"You probably don't remember what day that was, do you?"

"Sure. It was the Saturday of Christmas in Edgartown. I remember because I hated driving into town when it was so crowded. I knew it would be as bad as it is in July. And it was. Oh, yeah, it sure was. Anyway, I asked her why she hadn't come over on that special ferry they ran this year. I told her she could have gone right into Edgartown and not wasted her time with a bus ride. But she said she hadn't heard about it. Only that someone on the Cape told her to get the boat out of Woods Hole."

Annie's cheeks flushed. "Thank you. Thank you." She'd left her purse in the car or she would have offered him money. Or soap, if she had any with her. But her head was spinning, so she simply said "thank you" again and ran back to the car, with Bella swinging back and forth on her arm.

She planned to go to the library and check the Island Book for the name and address of the Thurmans in Edgartown. Then she'd be able to find their house and maybe find them before heading back over to Chappy.

Then, Bella started to scream. Annie knew it was not from the car seat; it was because she was hungry. In her haste to get to Vineyard Haven, she'd never thought to warm up some formula and pour it into the thermos instead of using it for coffee for herself. She was, indeed, a long way from being a competent mother.

Changing course, she headed toward the *On Time*. If she went home now, she could get Bella fed and changed, look up the Thurmans in her own Island Book, and save a trip to the library. All she needed was a little patience. Which she could practice first by releasing her white-knuckle grip on the steering wheel.

But when she turned from Simpsons Lane onto North Water, then down Daggett Drive to the *On Time* slip, she slammed on her brakes. In addition to several vehicles waiting in line, two police cruisers sat, their blue lights flashing. Behind them, a number of people had gathered and were facing the water, watching. The *On Time* arrived, and the Edgartown Fire Department ambulance disembarked, its red beams arcing over the wharf, the crowd, and the channel. As soon as it turned onto Dock Street, its siren began to blare.

Annie bit her lip and surveyed the scene. She spotted John Lyons standing by the slip, talking with a couple of men.

The ferry wasn't loading. Instead, someone was putting the canvas strap back into place, blocking the loading space. Something had happened. Something bad.

She got out of the car and walked down toward John. She hoped she would not get a ticket for leaving Bella in the back seat alone.

Not wanting to interrupt, she waited for him to notice her.

His face was drawn, his expression somber. "Annie," he said after a minute. "There's been a strange accident."

If there really were such a thing as her gut instinct, a wave of it washed over her then. "What?"

"A young woman. She got on the ferry on the Chappy side, then, in mid-channel, she climbed over the restraining strap and jumped off the back."

Annie couldn't speak.

"She went right into the water. The freaking, freezing cold water. She damn near drowned."

"She's . . . she's okay?"

"I wouldn't exactly call it 'okay.' She went under. She wasn't conscious when they pulled her out. But she was alive. Hopefully they can keep her breathing from here to the hospital. Then the docs can take over."

It wasn't the time to ask what the young woman looked like—if she had dark hair and sad, soulful eyes. It wasn't the time for Annie to vomit, either. But in spite of herself, she did.

Chapter 19

"You okay?" John was beside Annie in a flash. She was still bent over, holding her stomach, wishing she could curl up in a corner of a dark room. And maybe die. The last time she remembered feeling so sick was the day she'd realized that Mark was not coming back.

"I'm okay." Her words quivered. "It must be something I ate." Her body rocked back and forth. "Will you please check on Bella? She's in the car . . ."

He left Annie leaning against the shrubbery that separated the narrow lane from the elegant North Water Street houses.

If only she could remember what Bella's mother had worn. Or how tall she was. Or something significant, like if she had a scar. Or a tattoo. Or a dimple on her chin, the way Bella did. But all Annie recalled were those two words: *How much?* Had the girl intended to buy the soap for someone named Thurman? Someone who might be her grandmother?

Resting one hand on her stomach, Annie straightened up with tedious caution. She felt as if she'd been smacked to the pavement, run over by one of the pickup trucks that still waited in the *On Time* line. She inhaled, exhaled; her belly started to relax.

Then she saw John striding toward her. He was holding Bella tenderly, comfortably, as if she were one of his own.

"Better?" he asked.

She nodded. "A little." She touched Bella's cheek. The baby giggled.

"Once this mess clears, I can drive you home. I'll have a car follow us so I can get back."

"Thanks, John. But there's no need to go to any trouble. We'll be fine." She wasn't, however, sure she believed that.

"It's no trouble, Annie." His smile was genuine. If her stomach weren't roiling, she might have thought it was sexy.

"But I expect you have enough to do right now." She looked back to the water and to the small ferry. "Does this kind of thing happen often?"

"Not at all. A few years ago a truck drove off the end when the ferry was boarding. That's happened more than once over the years. And we've had a few people go overboard. But that's been in summer, and alcohol was always a factor. Don't think we've ever had a jumper."

Though her thinking was hazy, she remembered Earl's stories of summer carousing. "Do you know who the girl was? Like, was she someone local?"

"Sorry. But the incident is under investigation."

Annie smiled back. "Right. You can't release any information yet. I know how that goes." The police had said that about Mark's disappearance in the beginning.

John cocked his head as if he were going to ask how she knew that. "That's true," he said. "But the fact is, we don't know anything yet."

She quickly reached over and took Bella. "All this aside, I am disappointed about something. I thought you'd commend me for having the car seat." It was a weak attempt to shift the conversation.

His grin turned smug but was endearing. "I fully expected

you'd do as I recommended. You don't seem the type to ignore the law."

One of the trucks in the line began to move forward. The canvas strap had been dropped; ferry service to Chappy appeared to be resuming.

"I'd better get back to the car," she replied. The timing, she knew, could not have been better. The last thing she wanted was to engage in speculation about whether or not Annie Sutton was a law-abiding citizen.

"Wait," John said. He reached inside his jacket, pulled out a small card. "My cell number. In case you need anything. Someone to watch the baby if you don't feel up to it but my mother is asleep or at her garden club meeting. Call me. Or text me. Anytime. Okay?" He seemed sincere, and for that Annie was grateful.

She slipped the card into her pocket without looking at it. "Okay. Thanks again." She went back to the car, got Bella situated, then sat behind the wheel. She wished she could go to the hospital and see if she could learn anything. She wished she could have asked John if he knew the Thurmans. She might have done either, except she genuinely didn't feel well. *Home first*, she thought. *Rest*. Maybe after a while she'd be able to think straight. After all, she had absolutely no concrete reason to believe that the young woman who'd jumped off the ferry was Bella's mother. No reason at all, not even a clue from Murphy. Annie only had her god-awful gut instinct. But, reliable or not, she knew that her gut was not in the greatest shape at the moment.

When Annie was, at last, back at the cottage, she turned off the engine, but stayed in the car. She wasn't ready to go inside, make lunch for Bella, make tea for herself. She wasn't ready to move.

From the way she'd pulled into the driveway, she had a clear view of the thicket of naked scrub oaks where she and Earl had crept through the path that led to the house next door. With no visible foliage, she was able to see a blur of the house, its gray shingles muted against the pewter sky.

How she wished she could see inside. How she wished she could look to an upstairs window and see the blinds waver again, see some sign of life. How she wished she had climbed the butterfly staircase and looked for Earl, had searched and searched until she'd found Bella's mother, had let her know she would help.

She would have offered to do anything. Take the baby. Keep her until the girl was on her feet. Raise her, if that was what was needed. Yes, Annie would have done anything to help solve the problem. Anything to have helped avoid something like . . . this. If it really had been Bella's mother who'd jumped off the *On Time*. And now lay in a hospital bed. Or worse.

The longer Annie studied the house, the more of a blur it became. Then Bella started to fuss.

With painful resignation, Annie got out of the car, retrieved the baby, and headed into the cottage. But when she went up the three steps onto the porch, she noticed that the door wasn't latched. Again. She supposed there was no point now in telling Earl it needed fixing. Not if she'd no longer have a visitor skulking around in the night.

Once on the porch, Annie shifted the baby in order to open the front door. As she lowered her head to put the key into the lock, she saw a small piece of paper parked on the doorstep where Bella's basket once had been.

At first, she thought it might be another label from her soap, something else the girl had dropped when she'd been there. But it was too big. And it wasn't oval. She reached down

and picked it up: it was a bookmark from the Edgartown library, a list of titles of the documentaries that Virginia planned
to show on Wednesday evenings throughout the winter.

Annie frowned. Had she—not Bella's mother, but herself—
taken one of these when she'd been at the library? Had it fallen
out of her pocket? She supposed it was possible. *And probable*,
she admonished herself. It was her own doing. Nothing sinis-
ter. Nothing more.

With Bella in one arm, she dropped the bookmark into
the side pocket of her purse. Then she and the baby went inside.

A while later, Annie felt better, so she made tea and ate a
few nachos that she hoped would help settle her stomach the
way saltines did. Mark once told her that saltines helped curb
seasickness. He had loved sailing—or, at least, he'd loved the
social part of sailing: rubbing elbows with those who had way
more money, way more things than they did, though God
knew he'd done his best to keep up. Among other "necessities,"
he'd bought a boat, one of the many toys that Annie later
learned he'd owed more on—correction: that *she'd* owed more
on—than it was worth. She'd ended up using the proceeds
from her second novel to cover that debt.

She crunched another nacho and remembered the reason
he'd told her about the saltines was that she'd been having
morning sickness, though she'd told him her doctor said she
had a small ulcer. As the years passed, during those times when
she regretted the abortion, she took some satisfaction from
knowing that she'd kept a secret from him, after all the ones
he'd kept from her.

With a small sigh, she wondered about the Thurmans now,
and if, whoever they were, they had any idea that Bella's
mother had been looking for them. If the girl had jumped off
the ferry, maybe she'd had an ID in her pocket, one that hadn't

been ruined by the water. Maybe the police had found a connection to the Thurmans by now and had already contacted
them. Maybe the Thurmans—whatever roles they had in the
story—had rushed to the girl's side and were at the hospital, so
she wasn't alone.

Maybe! Annie shook her head at her persistent need for a
happy ending. Murphy once told her it was why she'd make a
good novelist. But Annie often wondered if it was because she
was still searching for her own.

With that thought, she laughed. At herself. At her foolish-
ness. Then she went to her bookcase, took out the Island
Book, and brought it back to the table. A small phone book,
with both white and yellow pages, the book also had green
pages that held all sorts of data about each of the island's six
towns; it had been heralded by the Chamber of Commerce
as essential reading for those who lived there year-round.
Opening the book, Annie also realized that, as with most
books, she now needed glasses to look up the Thurmans' name
and address. She reached around the back of her chair where
she'd hung her purse and pulled out her glasses. The bookmark
from the library slid out with them and fell to the floor.

Strange, she thought as she bent to get it. She really didn't remember having taken it from the library; she must have picked
it up off the counter when she and Earl were waiting to find
out who'd checked out her book. Annie had been so nervous
then, it was something she could have done subconsciously—
something to do with her hands while Virginia scoured the
database.

Setting the bookmark on the table, she put on her glasses
and opened the Island Book. But her gaze was drawn back to
the bookmark . . . it had landed upside down on the table;
there was no printing on the back except for three handwritten words:

I trusted you, it read.

Chills swirled through Annie's body the way the snow had swirled during the storm.

Bella's mother must have left the bookmark on the doorstep when Annie was in Vineyard Haven. She must have messed with the latch on the outer door, which was why, that time, the door hadn't shut firmly at all. It was clear that she'd left the message for Annie. Then she'd walked down to the ferry. Gotten on it. And jumped off.

Worst of all, Annie was now to blame.

She let out a scream that startled Bella and set her to screaming, too. Annie wanted to be wrong. Oh, how she wanted to be wrong.

I trusted you.

Had the girl thought Annie had ratted her out? That she'd shipped Bella off to a foster home? Hadn't she seen the little lamb Annie had made? It was on the rocking chair right where she had left it.

"Oh, God," Annie cried, picking up the baby and wrapping her in her unsteady arms. She sat on the rocker, and the two of them rocked, cried, and rocked some more.

There was no other explanation. The girl had accused Annie of not taking care of Bella as she had begged. And she'd used three simple words that were unmistakably portentous. And, apparently, meant to be final.

After a few minutes, Bella settled down. Annie dried both their tears and tried to think about what her next step should be.

First, she needed to be sure that the girl in the hospital was Bella's mother. The best way to do that was to hear it from John. If they could talk quietly together, she might get up the courage to tell him the whole story.

She reached into her pocket and pulled out his card. Then she picked up her cell phone and dialed. His voice mail kicked in.

"John?" she asked. "It's Annie Sutton. I'm feeling so much

better now. And I've been thinking about your offer for dinner. I've decided to take you up on it after all. My treat. It's the least I can do for how you helped me today. Let me know when. Hopefully your mother will watch the baby."

She set down the phone and hugged Bella more closely. "Oh, little one," she whispered. "Oh, you poor, poor little one. What have I done to you?"

Chapter 20

Annie ordered chowder and a salad; John, the bangers and mash.

"I suppose it's not the healthiest thing for a guy of my advanced years," he said, then gestured to the next table, where a man was diving into the British Cumberland sausage. "But, man, it looks great."

So did he. Dressed in jeans and a charcoal sweater, he might have been a lover instead of a cop. Or instead of the father of two teenage girls, who were scheduled to arrive the next day to spend a long weekend with their father. Which was why, when he'd replied to Annie's message, he'd suggested that they go out that night.

Clearing her throat, Annie sipped her chardonnay. "Your years aren't so advanced. Not as advanced as mine."

"Forty-eight," he said. "Forty-nine in April."

A Taurus, like Murphy, Annie thought. She pushed back the fantasy that it might be a good omen for compatibility. And the fact that a two-year age difference was fairly insignificant. "I still win."

"Not by much," he said. "I Googled you."

Her laugh was sudden and unexpected. "You use Google? I would have thought you'd have a covert search engine. Like VitalStatistics-dot-com, if there is such a thing."

He cocked one side of his mouth into a smile. She liked how he looked when he did that. "I didn't want to feel like I was a stalker."

She came very close to saying she'd already had one of those. She decided, instead, to choose to be flattered. Then she set down her glass and reminded herself this wasn't a date. Not to her. This was her chance to learn about the girl who'd nearly drowned. "I'll take that as a compliment. But I'm not here for those. I really did want to thank you for helping me out today. It was not my finest hour."

"No problem. Lots of people have reactions when they get near death, even when someone's had a close call."

"Does that mean she'll be okay?

Toying with a mug of local beer, John said," All I can say is she's in critical condition."

"Did you find out who she is? Or if she lives here?" Annie wondered if she sounded frantic. *Slow down*, Murphy's voice whispered in her ear.

He smiled. "She's in critical condition."

A waitress arrived, a different one from the one who'd taken their orders. She was paying attention to balancing a tray until she set the chowder and salad in front of Annie and then spotted John. "Johnny!" she cried. "Haven't seen you in a while. How are those girls of yours?" She wore a maroon T-shirt with the Newes logo and black pants that hugged her thin body as if they were leggings. Her over-bleached curls were anchored by a sparkly headband; a fake tan accentuated whitened teeth.

"Hey, Michelle. The girls are great. They'll be here for the weekend."

She put the bangers in front of him. "Be sure to bring 'em

round. Speaking of girls, I heard there was some excitement at
the *On Time* today."

He paused, as if carefully forming his words. Then he said,
"Yup. You could call it that."

"Bob Morton said she jumped right off the back."

"Yup. Pretty much." He lowered his eyes and took another
drink.

"He said she was a wash-ashore. None of the captains remembered bringing her to Chappy."

He lifted his beer mug. "You know how it is. This time of
year there are so many tourists, it's hard to remember faces."

The girl named Michelle stared at him a moment, then let
out a laugh. "Oh, John Lyons, you're such a kidder. It's December. Nobody's here. Even in high school, you were a kidder."

The fact that the waitress was flirting with him did not slip
past Annie.

"This is my friend Annie," John said. "Annie, meet Michelle."

Michelle nodded at her. "Seen you here before. Well, enjoy
your meals!" She turned to go, then pivoted back to John.
"They said she has a baby."

Annie blinked.

The waitress continued chattering. "They said she muttered something about a baby when she got on board. Such a
shame. I sure hope the kid's okay." She shook her head and
walked away, her bleached curls bouncing in her wake.

Picking up her spoon, Annie poised it over the chowder,
but her appetite had disappeared again. The young woman was
Bella's mother. She was sure of that now.

"What you just heard was not an official comment," John
said. "It was island gossip. In case you haven't noticed, there's a
lot of that around here."

She tried to smile. "It's hard to stop people from talking."
She set down her spoon, picked up her fork, and poked at the
greens on her plate as if she were a child. She could almost

hear her mother's stern words: *Young ladies don't play with their food.* Yet Annie could not stop. The next thing she knew, John's hand was on hers.

"Annie? Has all this talk upset you? Would you like to leave?"

It was the right time to tell him. It was absolutely the right time. But Annie could only think about Bella being taken away from her and shoved into a foster home. The way she once had been. She had no way of knowing why the girl thought Annie had gone against her wishes, but she couldn't worry about that now. *The bottom line,* as her practical, straight-to-the-point dad would have said, was that the girl had trusted her to take care of Bella, and, legal or not, she was going to do it. As long as she could. She took her napkin from her lap and set it on the table. "Yes, I'm upset," she said. "And I'm sorry. But I need to leave."

John pulled back his hand and stood up. "I'll get take-out containers. We can do this some other time."

They walked down the hill, because John had left his pickup on the Chappy side. As a police officer, he probably always got a free ride, but Annie supposed he wouldn't take advantage of that. She wondered if he would have held her hand if she hadn't folded her arms at her waist and walked with her head down. After all, it would not do his career any good if he got too close to her. Especially since she was now withholding evidence about an investigation.

Once on the boat, the cold, clear night enveloped her. Though she knew that a billion stars must be visible, Annie did not look up. She didn't want to think about Murphy then, or about her dad, who might be disappointed in her for keeping such a secret. Instead, Annie sat next to John on the bench and kept her eyes fixed on her feet, on the knockoff Ugg boots she'd bought at Trader Fred's last fall. They weren't fancy, but they were warm. And staring at them seemed preferable to looking at the canvas strip that Bella's mother must have stepped over before she'd gone into the water. God, it must have been freezing. The only consolation was that because she'd done it in the daylight, maybe she'd wanted to be noticed, maybe she'd wanted someone to stop her. If she'd jumped off in the darkness, chances were she wouldn't have been found until it was too late. If it weren't already.

"How deep is it here?" Annie asked John in a whisper.

"Around twenty-five feet, I think."

"The girl could have killed herself."

"Sure. But I'd like to think she would have changed her mind. I mean, if someone jumps into the water—even if they fully intend to drown—won't their first instinct be to swim? Of course, this time of year, hypothermia kicks in pretty fast."

She didn't know what to say, so she said nothing.

He took her hand. But because they both had on thick gloves, she felt no warmth from his fingers or palm. "Annie, I have to ask you something."

They'd reached the halfway point across the channel; the current was strong, forcing the captain to veer slightly north in order to safely dock once they reached the other side. The *chug-chug* of the motor rose; Annie wondered if she could pretend she hadn't heard John above the increase in sound.

And then he squeezed her hand. "Annie? Are you afraid that girl who . . . who did this is your niece?"

Of course, she'd forgotten all about her long-lost relative. Worse, she couldn't think straight enough to know how to respond. So she pulled her hand from his and entwined her arms below her breasts. "I don't know."

John folded his hands as if she hadn't brushed him off. "Once she's stable, I'll bring you to the hospital to see her. If we haven't ID'd her by then."

So he'd admitted they didn't know the girl's identity. Not that Annie needed further proof of who it was.

The *On Time* docked between the pilings. Annie and John stayed seated until the captain unhooked the restraining strap— *which,* Annie thought wryly, *had not restrained Bella's mother*—then John helped Annie up. "My mother wouldn't mind if you want to keep the baby at their house tonight," he said as they disembarked and walked toward his truck.

"No," Annie quickly replied. "Thanks, but I'd rather have Bella home tonight."

One more night and one more day might be all Annie needed to somehow change the course of Bella's future. If only she could do it before John learned the truth.

When they stepped into Earl and Claire's kitchen, the lights were on. Earl sat at the table, a coffee mug in front of him; Claire was in her wool plaid bathrobe, knotting and unknotting the long belt as she paced.

"What's wrong?" Annie cried. "Is Bella okay?" Her words burst out before she could swallow her guilt.

"She's fine," Earl replied. "Upstairs. Asleep." His words, however, did little to mask the pallor in the air, the colorless, toneless energy that made Annie's stomach tighten again.

Claire moved from the kitchen sink and marched directly toward Annie, her white hair wild, her eyes the same, her forefinger flapping at her like a child's broken toy. "How dare you!" she snarled. "Earl has done so much for you. And I treated you like one of ours. How dare you, Annie Sutton!"

Annie stepped back.

John shot between them. "Mom. Stop. What the hell are you doing?"

She glared at Annie, then caught her breath. "Well, one thing I am NOT doing is harboring a kidnapper. That's what she is, aren't you, Ms. Sutton? Ms. Big-Shot-Goody-Two-Shoes coming to our island, as if you're doing us a favor? Well, how's this for a favor? You're going to be arrested. Arrest her, John! Arrest her this minute!"

Annie was so startled she could barely breathe. "Claire . . ." she started, but the woman cut her off.

"No! I will not listen. Earl told me how Bella arrived on your doorstep in the middle of the blizzard and how you kept her—*you kept her!*—as if she was yours to keep. As if she were a batch of Christmas cookies or a loaf of homemade fruitcake. Well, you're the fruitcake, missy. And you need to get out of my house!"

Earl was suddenly behind Claire. He grabbed her hand. "Claire. Stop. Your blood pressure . . ." He looked back at Annie. "I'm so sorry, Annie. But she kept grilling me . . ."

"Grilling you?" Claire screeched and turned to John, her finger still flapping at the air. "As soon as Taylor said the baby's mother was this . . . this *kidnapper's* niece, I knew something was fishy. Annie told me she was sitting for a friend. An *up-island* friend." She twisted back to Annie. *"I gave you the benefit of the doubt! I believed your cockamamy lies. I let you spend Christmas with my family!"*

"Mom," John said again, "no one can understand you when you're screaming."

Claire wiped her mouth, lowered her voice. "Then Taylor came by today. She said she didn't trust you. She said you don't even have a cat like you said you do. She knows you've been lying. I've known that woman since she was born. I've only known you three days. Who was I going to believe? Who? *My husband,* that's who. So I asked him. I'm not stupid, you know." She vigorously shook her head. "No. I'm not stupid."

"Mom," John interrupted. Then he took both her arms and quietly said, "No one said you're stupid. Now please, calm down. I'll take care of this."

Claire's words came out in a whimper. "She won't leave

here with that baby girl. She'll take her out of here over my dead body."

Letting go of his mother, John wheeled around and took Annie by the shoulders. "You," he said. "With me."

He edged her toward the study. Once they were inside, he closed the door and locked it. "Sit," he said, so Annie sat on the small sofa in the corner. He took the chair at his father's desk, removed his gloves, and raked his hands through his hair.

"Jesus," he said.

Annie looked around the room at the framed photos on the walls, some in black-and-white, that captured happy times. One showed a much younger Earl standing with a large pig and a sign in the background that read: AG FAIR. 1981. She wondered if one of his many "trades" had once been raising pigs on Chappaquiddick.

"John," she said, "I want to explain." She was surprised how calm she felt. Maybe it was the kind of relief some people felt once they finally shed a secret that they'd harbored for years, or had let out a grievance gnawing at their insides. Depositing her gloves into her coat pockets, she unwrapped the wool scarf around her neck, folded it, and set it in her lap. "I never meant for you to find out this way."

He let out a giant sigh.

Then, starting with when she'd opened her front door and seen Bella's basket at her feet, Annie told him the story. She told him about the note in which the mother asked her to take care of Bella only for a couple of days. She told him about Winnie's help. She told him about how, once the "couple of days" had passed, she and his father figured out that the girl was staying next door to her cottage. She told him about the library book. Annie even told him that she'd been adopted, so she'd been the ideal choice, the perfect patsy.

Annie told him all those things. She did not, however, mention that the bus driver remembered the girl, or that she'd asked him about the Thurmans. She had no way of knowing yet if there really was a connection, so she decided not to create more island gossip. With Claire Lyons no doubt listening at the door, she feared that could happen.

"When I got home this afternoon," she continued, "I found another note on my front porch. It simply read, *I trusted you*. I might be wrong, but it seemed ominous to me, as if Bella's mother thought I'd done something terrible with her baby. Like that I'd turned her over to foster care. I'd planned to tell you everything at dinner. But when the waitress mentioned 'the baby' as if Bella's mere existence made the story juicier, well, I couldn't. Bella *is* just a baby, John. Someone needs to protect her. No matter what her mother's done."

He sat quietly. He had not interrupted, not even once.

Annie wrung her hands. "I was only trying to watch over her. To do as her mother asked. I hoped she'd come back. In the meantime, I wanted to find her and get her to change her mind before you intervened and put Bella God knows where. But now it seems clear she's the one in the hospital . . ."

Her words trailed off. They sat in silence, except for the ticking of the ship's clock on the wall.

After taking a long breath, she asked, "So, are you going to arrest me?"

He ran his hands through his hair again. "I don't know what the hell I'm going to do with you. Aside from everything else, you've been withholding information. If you'd told me right away, we might have prevented what happened this afternoon."

Guilt flooded through her. Pieces of her heart began floating away. "I know."

He leaned forward, propped his elbows on his knees, tented his fingers together. "Look, Annie. I'm trying to be fair.

Who knows what anyone would have done if they were you? Right now my mother's angry because you've been lying to her."

She tried to smooth the wool scarf on her lap, tried to align the edges so they'd be in perfect symmetry.

"However," he continued, "my father thinks you're wonderful. And it sounds as if he was in on this cover-up pretty much from the beginning. So if I arrest you, I suppose I'll have to arrest him, too." His eyes drifted down to his hands, which were strong and sturdy, like his dad's. "If there's a funny part to this, it's that if my mother had known about this early on, she probably would have tried to help, too. She would have seen it as a heroic act of social justice." He looked back to Annie; his eyes were clouded over. "But you're right. This is about a baby. And, for what it's worth, the only reason her mother is still on the island is because the doctors don't think she's stable enough to be airlifted to Boston. They don't think she'd survive the trip."

Another piece of Annie's heart broke off. She bit her lip and tried to hold back tears. She wondered if she really wanted him to answer her next question: "Is she going to die, John?"

He shrugged; he averted his gaze. "Maybe."

Maybe, Annie thought. There was that word again.

The clock ticked, then chimed two bells. Nine o'clock, ship's time.

"What are we going to do?" she asked.

He scratched his chin the way Earl did when he was thinking. "Unlike what my mother said, technically, you haven't kidnapped anyone. Do you still have the note where the mother asked you to take care of the baby?"

She nodded. She'd tucked it into the box that held the long-ago letter from Donna MacNeish. Storing it there had seemed appropriate.

"That indicates you had permission. On the other hand,

the baby's mother knew nothing about you. And there are laws that protect children from being handed over to strangers."

"I know a lot about child protective laws. I used to teach third grade." She thought she'd already told him that she'd been a teacher, but right then, it hardly mattered.

He stood and paced the room, the way Claire had been pacing, but without anger fueling him. "My mother won't like it, but you should take Bella home tonight. That's where her birth mother left her, with permission. Tomorrow I'll talk to the chief. I'm sorry, but we'll probably have to turn the case over to the Staties—the state police. They help handle our complex cases."

Annie stood up and looked into his eyes. "What about Bella's mother? Do you think I can see her?"

"Like, now? At the hospital?"

"Well. Yes."

He took her by the shoulders. "Not a chance," he said. "Be grateful I didn't put you in handcuffs."

Murphy would have loved the prospect of that; she would have made a suggestive comment that, later, they would have laughed about. Once the dust had finally settled and a happy ending was assured.

Instead of laughing, Annie gave in to her tears and let the salty wetness drizzle down her cheeks.

Chapter 21

"Mommy?"

"Mommy?"

Francine didn't know if the voice was hers or Bella's. She only knew her eyes were closed and she was warm and weightless and that the crying was coming from somewhere far away.

"Mommy, are you there?"

When John brought Annie and Bella home, he made sure they were safely inside, then said a perfunctory "Good night." She had not expected a kiss, even on the cheek, and she didn't get one.

She put Bella to bed, grateful that Claire had fed her, given her a bath, changed her, and dressed her in soft jammies that must have been another hand-me-down from one of John's daughters. Annie didn't know whether or not Claire had done that before Earl had revealed to her what was really going on. But Annie didn't, couldn't, blame him. His wife might sometimes be "difficult," but like she'd said, she wasn't stupid.

From now on, Annie would keep Earl out of this. He shouldn't have to suffer any more because of her.

As for John, if he learned the rest, there was no telling what he'd do. If he did not arrest her, he could still make her life so miserable she'd have to retreat back to Boston under a dark cloud of publicity that would no doubt affect book sales in the wrong direction. It was a frightening thought, but Bella was more important. And, right or wrong, Annie was even more committed now to doing whatever it would take to stop the baby's life from being torn apart.

Starting with finding the Thurmans, whoever they were.

She moved to the table, put on her glasses, and picked up the Island Book. It took only seconds to find the name. There were three listings:

Thurman Clark 7 Deep Forest Rd Ed
Thurman Laureen 181 7th St VH
Thurman Stephen & Bonnie 12 Scallop Cove Rd Ed

She ruled out the one in Vineyard Haven, because the young mother had specified the Thurmans in Edgartown. She booted up her laptop and Googled the first location. She tap-tapped her fingers on the edge of the keyboard while praying for that elusive thing called patience. The indicator went around and around. She tried to remember it was just the un-predictable island connection and not a conspiracy between the Internet and a malicious force—like Claire Lyons or Taylor what's-her-name—working against her.

Finally, the home screen appeared.

Deep Forest Road was out by the transfer station, affec-tionately called the dump, though Edgartown's trash was no longer just dumped but hauled off island. The street would be easy to find. Annie then went to Zillow and learned there were only nine houses on Deep Forest Road: a two-bedroom ranch was for sale, the asking price three hundred twenty-five thousand—a pittance for Martha's Vineyard. She wrote down Clark Thurman's address, as if there was a chance she'd forget it.

Then she searched for Scallop Cove Road. No houses on that street were listed for sale. The last transaction, for number twelve, had been in 2009, when it was purchased for five hundred twenty-five thousand dollars. It was now worth eight hundred seventy-five.

Two different Edgartown addresses in two different socioeconomic locations: Annie wondered which Thurman, if either, was connected to Bella's mother.

"Tomorrow will be here soon enough," she told herself as she banked the fire in the woodstove for the night and got ready for bed.

She couldn't sleep. Thoughts of Earl and Claire collided with anxiety about what John would do and how soon it would be before he—or the "Staties"—took Bella from her. Just because she had the note from Bella's mother didn't mean Annie was entitled to keep her forever.

She supposed she should have told John that Bella had been named after her grandmother. Unlike Annie had been free to do, the police must be able to access information at the town hall. A couple of data entries and two or three clicks would probably reveal all island women who were, or ever had been, christened "Bella," and every derivative of the name.

It was doubtful they would wait for the girl to get better—or die—before they started their full-fledged investigation. More than likely, they'd go next door to the Littlefield house first thing in the morning. They'd look for fingerprints, traces of DNA, whatever they could find to help identify the girl. They'd also search for things she'd left behind: personal items, a cell phone, an ID.

In the darkness, Annie blinked.

An ID.

Of course!

She bolted upright, her pillow careening to the floor. *The house!* If the girl had no ID when she'd jumped from the ferry, she must have left it there.

If only Annie dared to go over there now. When she and Earl had gone inside, Annie had known the girl was hiding, had known she'd had to be the one who'd peered out the upstairs window. The empty can of formula in the kitchen sink and the piece of cinnamon roll certainly had proved it. But when the girl had not come forward, and then Earl had found the book, Annie's first thought had been not to scare her off. So she'd insisted that they leave. She'd never thought to look for an ID. A purse. A phone. Something.

Snapping on the lamp atop her nightstand, Annie tried to quiet her racing thoughts. *Could she—should she—go back to the house and look around before the cops arrived, before they took everything, including Bella?*

With her heart doing its dance again, Annie looked up at the ceiling and shook her fist. "Help! You're the one who got me into this mess! You're the one who made me move here! So, help! Please!"

She was being ridiculous again, but Annie didn't care. Murphy had often been adventurous, sometimes even daring. She might have told her to take a shot now, to go next door and see what she could learn. But Murphy had her husband and her boys . . . she had a support system. Unlike Annie, who had no family who loved her so much they would be there for her, even if she'd done something wrong.

And yet . . .

Annie looked over at Bella, who had woken up without a stir and was staring back at her.

"The hell with it," Annie said, then hauled herself from under the covers.

In less than ten minutes she had winterized them both and, armed with the LED lantern she'd bought for the nor'easter, she ventured outside into the night.

After having lived there for four months, Annie had finally grown accustomed to the stillness of the Vineyard and the darkness of the nights. It often made her think about the early settlers who'd come from other lands, who hadn't known about the beauty and serenity that awaited them. Sometimes she thought about the Wampanoags, the people "of the first light," who had been there for countless generations, for thousands of years, and who'd depended on the earth and sea to sustain them—from the deer and rabbits to the fish and fowl and all the berries, herbs, and edible plants that they gathered.

Sometimes, Annie thought about those things. But not that night.

As she traipsed through the scrub oaks, lugging Bella on her hip to avoid having to lug the basket, too, Annie thought instead about the bond between a mother and her child, the special glue created by nature that surmounted caution, trepidation, and, occasionally, logic. Apparently one didn't need to have given birth to feel that tight connection.

The side door was still open. With the light from the lantern casting a not-so-subtle path, they went inside. Annie wondered if Bella might remember having stayed there—if she would remember the sights, the smells, the sounds.

Once in the living room, she swung the light toward the sofa: the candy cane cookies that she'd left were gone.

"Hope you enjoyed them," she whispered into the room.

Turning the corner, she headed to the staircase that looked as if it belonged in a grand plantation home, a place bustling with voices, footsteps, laughter—not in a house that was unoccupied from September until June, as if it, too, had been abandoned. Annie didn't miss the irony of that.

She climbed the stairs, then went into the bedroom that was closest to the landing, which would be where she'd have gone if she'd been in Bella's mother's shoes. She moved the light around: nothing seemed out of place. There was no comb or brush, no makeup or purse on either of two bureaus; there was no backpack on the floor. No phone. But a puffy, white comforter was spread across the mattress of a high brass bed: it looked somewhat rumpled, as if it had been put there in haste, not straightened by a housekeeper.

It was the kind of detail that a man—Earl—might not have noticed.

Two other doors were in the room: one led to a large walk-in closet, complete with remnants of shelving that had been removed, but nothing else. Annie tiptoed toward the other door: a bathroom. As in the bedroom and the closet, there were no personal items. So far, other than her book and the trash in the kitchen sink, the place lacked any indication of recent human interaction. The cookies, after all, could have been carried off by a four-legged critter.

But as Annie turned back toward the hall, something snapped under her foot.

She stopped. She beamed the lantern to the floor. A small disk of what looked like clear plastic rested there. She might never have seen it if she hadn't stepped on it. Bending down, she picked it up, glad that she was wearing gloves. She held it up, close to the light.

"I'll be damned," she said.

If she hadn't had the experience of the last week or so, she never would have recognized the plastic in her hand as the ring on a baby's pacifier.

Pulling Bella higher on her hip, Annie squatted. Then she slowly peeled back a corner of the comforter to try and see if the rest of the pacifier was under the bed.

It was. So was a large vinyl purse.

If anyone had asked Annie what she remembered about Bella's mother from the ten seconds that they'd interacted at the fair, the last thing she would have said was that the girl had been carrying a vinyl handbag, let alone a big one. But now, as Annie slid it from under the bed frame, she recognized it immediately: it had been hanging over the girl's shoulder on the opposite side from where she'd carried the baby's basket.

Annie sat down on the floor; Bella began to fuss, as if being in the room was upsetting her. Perhaps she sensed her mother.

Gently rocking the baby, Annie murmured low, shushing tones. But as she sat in the shadows cast by the flashlight, comforting the tiny baby who'd been born to a mother so frightened or depressed that she'd try to kill herself, Annie knew she couldn't do what she'd intended: she couldn't dig into the handbag and search through the girl's personal things until she found a cell phone, an ID, whatever might be there that would reveal her name and might tell the story of why she'd come and who she'd planned to see.

No. Annie couldn't do it.

She could not invade the young woman's belongings; she couldn't scrutinize her life. It would feel too much as if she were being a busybody, like Taylor. And maybe a bit like Claire.

Trying to find the Thurmans would be something Annie could do for Bella's mother. But snooping through her things seemed like a violation of her privacy. *I trusted you*, her last note read. No matter what she'd meant, Annie didn't want to break that trust. She didn't want to forget that, beneath the layers of the whys and wherefores, Bella's mother was just a girl who'd *gotten into trouble*, as the old saying went, as it had gone for years and years and no doubt had been whispered about Annie's birth mother, too.

Besides, Annie reasoned, if she prowled through the bag, she would, without a doubt, be tampering with evidence, so she'd have John to answer to. Again.

Tucking a lock of Bella's silky hair under the soft hat Claire had crocheted, Annie pushed the purse back under the bed. "Let's leave this for your Uncle John," she said.

As either luck—or Annie's guardian angels—would have it, she'd barely gotten back inside her cottage and unwrapped Bella from her toasty covering when streaks of red and blue broke through the darkness, illuminating the scrub oaks and the pines. From her kitchen window, she saw a parade of law enforcement driving down North Neck Road: three police cruisers—two from Edgartown; the other, state police—and the Edgartown ambulance. The disco-like reflections paused, then turned into the Littlefield's driveway. Within a minute, floodlights bathed the house's exterior. Through her closed windows, Annie heard the officers shout to one another, though their words were muffled and unintelligible.

Then the inside of the house lit up, too. Annie hadn't known the power was on. From what Earl had told her, the Littlefields weren't concerned about caretakers or housekeepers.

But apparently, she mused, the police had decided not to wait until morning to start their investigation. Now that she'd told John where Bella's mother had been living, it was his duty to learn everything possible about her. After all, he'd made a commitment to uphold the law. And there was a baby who needed protecting.

Chapter 22

Earl didn't stop by in the morning for coffee and a cinnamon roll. Annie was disappointed but not surprised: she knew he must feel trapped between his wife and her, and maybe between his son and her as well. His allegiance would be, should be, to his family. And though John had been nice to her, for all Annie knew, it had only been part of his role as a police officer. A public servant. A steward of the island community.

She'd stood at the window until well past midnight, watching the scene play out next door, trying, unsuccessfully, to figure out what was happening. When she'd finally gone to bed, she'd stayed awake another hour or more, her thoughts about paying a visit to the Thurmans flip-flopping like a bad politician.

Should she?

Shouldn't she?

As hard as she tried to tell herself otherwise, Annie's heart kept saying: *Yes.* Although she hadn't met the girl who now lay in the hospital, she felt she owed it to her to carry on with her mission. There was a chance, of course, that the girl had found the Thurmans and been turned away. Maybe they—not Annie—

had been the real trigger for the suicide attempt. Annie wondered how they'd react if she, a reasonable adult—or one who used to be reasonable—went to them instead. She could start by asking if they'd heard about the girl who'd tried to end her life.

From her kitchen window, she could tell that the police were gone; she couldn't see if they had circled the Littlefields' house in yellow DO NOT CROSS tape. No matter what they had or hadn't found, she had to meet the Thurmans. If John didn't like it, she'd deal with him later. After all, she was only following through on a hunch based on the memory of a bus driver. Unlike the purse, it wasn't tangible evidence. Or . . . she didn't think that it was.

Less than an hour later, Annie boarded the *On Time* with Bella safely in the car seat in the back. The captain—it wasn't Martin, but a woman—gestured up to the low clouds and said, "Better not be out too long. Looks like another storm is on the way." She said "another" as if it ended in an *A*, the way folks said it in Boston, the way Annie's mom and dad had talked, and she had worked hard to avoid doing.

Annie smiled, but thought: *Oh, great. I wonder what this batch of snow will bring.*

Once off the boat, she headed toward the Scallop Cove Road property, because it was the closest, in the Katama section of Edgartown, out by South Beach. She turned left at the fork, where the only signs of life were three llamas and a donkey that roamed the massive, manicured lawn of the harborside property that she'd heard belonged to a Boston car dealer. Otherwise, there was no sign of life; it was as if now that Christmas had passed, Edgartown had settled in for its long winter's nap.

In less than a minute, her GPS announced: "Turn left," followed by: "Your destination is on the right." Annie stopped the car.

Number twelve Scallop Cove Road was an oversized Cape Cod–style home that looked like several of its neighbors. It was gray-shingled with pale yellow trim and sat on an average-sized, treed lot; there was no garage, which was not unusual, due to, as Annie recalled with a half smile, the rare "plowable" snow events. Two vehicles were in the driveway: an old white Toyota and a black panel truck with white lettering on the side that read: THURMAN'S HOUSE PAINTING, EDGARTOWN. A phone number was listed below that. The only sign of life on the street was an elderly woman who was walking a yellow lab.

Then, as Annie deliberated bringing Bella with her, a young man bounded from the house, leapt into the Toyota, and backed down the driveway. He spotted Annie, gave her a quick wave, then drove off before she got a good look at his face.

"Is that your daddy?" she asked Bella. He seemed to be in his late teens—the perfect age.

That question, however, made her realize she had no idea what to say once she was at the door. If Bella were on her arm, Annie could say, "Hello, I'm looking for the father of this baby," which, of course, would sound bizarre, not to mention confrontational. Then she remembered the grandmother. Bella's mother hadn't specified which grandmother she'd been named after; maybe that would be a safe introduction. But, "Excuse me, does an older woman named Bella live here?" also sounded lame.

At least it looked as if the Thurmans lived there year-round. And now Annie knew they had a boy who might also be a baby daddy—whether any of them knew it yet or not.

She decided to check the other Edgartown address before making any accusations. But as she left Katama and headed west, Annie had another thought: *the boy in the Toyota looked about the same age as Winnie's nephew, Lucas.* Maybe they knew each other. Maybe Lucas knew if one of his friends had recently become a teenage father.

Deep Forest Road was easy to find, too, though pinpointing which house was number seven proved difficult. Of the few cottages, none had visible street numbers. And all looked as if they'd seen better days, none of which were recent. They were small and boxy, no more than one or two bedrooms, and had unkempt yards filled with treasures that looked to have spilled over from the transfer station that abutted the road. A couple of rusted cars seemed to have legitimate state license plates, but otherwise, the street looked vacant and forlorn and gave Annie the creeps.

She quickly went back to the main road, where she knew if she turned left it would bring her up island to Winnie's.

So she did.

"She's in Vineyard Haven today," the woman who Annie remembered was Winnie's sister-in-law said when she opened the door. She was dressed in cotton scrub pants and a colorful top: Annie remembered that she was a nurse and worked at the hospital.

"Of course she is," Annie said, feeling foolish. "It's a weekday, isn't it? Most normal people are working."

"Which does not imply that all people who work are 'normal.' But you drove up from Chappy? Can I help you with anything? Do you want to come in? I'm Barbara, by the way."

Annie laughed. "Right." Except for Lucas, she'd forgotten the names of Winnie's clan, remembering only their occupations. "I'm so sorry to bother you. But, yes, I wondered if I might have another look at Lucas's high school yearbook. You're his mother, right?"

Barbara stepped out of the way so Annie could angle Bella's basket through the doorway. "I am. As it happens, it was only yesterday I asked him to put the yearbook away. It's been sitting in the living room since you were here. Odds are, it still is." She shook her head as if to say, *Boys.* "Come in. Sit. I'll get it."

Annie went into the kitchen and sat at the big table that held the soul of the family deep within its wood. She set the basket on top, adjusted Bella's hat, and put the pacifier into her tiny mouth.

"How's the book coming along?" Barbara's voice called from the other room.

It took a few seconds for Annie to remember she'd claimed she needed to see the yearbook for research. "Oh. Great. Finding bits and pieces can be time-consuming, though."

"Well," Barbara said as she returned to the kitchen, "I hope this helps." She set the book in front of Annie. "Would you like tea?"

Annie politely declined, saying she'd only be there a minute. She opened the book, searched for the seniors, and quickly found Thurman. She'd been right; they'd been in Lucas's class— "they" referring to two. Twins. Like Murphy's boys, though not identical. And these were named Caleb and Michael. She couldn't tell if either boy was the one who'd waved from the Toyota. However, Caleb had a dimple in his chin that looked exactly like Bella's.

Trying to hide her excitement, Annie glanced through a few more pages until she landed on the section that showed a teacher speaking in front of a class that gave a good view of the room, which was what she'd claimed she needed. Then she said, "Perfect. A little behind the scenes color—what it looks like in a classroom, the corridors, that sort of thing."

"Right. I guess it would be pointless to go and ask for a tour. What with them being closed for Christmas vacation and all."

Annie felt the color in her cheeks flare. She hadn't considered that, to an outsider, visiting the school would have made more sense. Or that not visiting might seem questionable. She quickly stood and picked up the basket.

"Has the baby been with you through Christmas?" Barbara asked.

"Yes. Her mother's away." Then she had another idea. "You work at the hospital, don't you?"

Barbara pushed back her long dark hair. "Midnight to eight last night."

"Wow. That must be tough."

"Sometimes."

Annie paused. "I was at the ferry slip when that young woman jumped off the *On Time*. Did you hear about that? She was my neighbor. It was horrible."

Barbara nodded. "It's so hard to know what goes on in these kids' minds today. It's not like she was on drugs or anything."

"That's good to know. Have you seen her at the hospital? Is she doing okay?"

"I think she's still in ICU. I'm in maternity. But from what I've heard, she's in and out of a coma."

"What a shame."

The two women were quiet a moment, then Barbara said, "You asked that for another reason, didn't you?"

Annie blinked. "What?"

"I have a feeling that the girl who jumped off the boat is more than your neighbor. The way Winnie was so concerned about you and the baby, well . . ." She softly smiled and said, "Sometimes I hear more than words that are spoken. The girl in the hospital supposedly has a baby, too. I wonder what happened to it."

Annie sat back down at the table. "You know what? I might have tea after all."

She told Barbara the truth because she trusted Winnie, and so she trusted Barbara, too. Besides, the police already knew, so Annie supposed she could stop trying to cover up the real story, in case there was a chance to get some answers.

"I'd really like to find whoever might be connected with Bella before the police take her away." She took a long drink of savory tea; it was a mixture of up island herbs, like the ones Winnie gave her for Christmas. "At Winnie's suggestion, I talked to a bus driver. He remembered Bella's mother and that she asked him about a family named Thurman. In Edgartown."

"Which Thurman?" Barbara asked.

"Before I came here, I didn't know. But Bella looks a lot like Caleb Thurman. Her dimple is like the one in his picture." She reopened the yearbook to the section on seniors and showed Barbara the photo.

"It sure is," she said. "I suppose dimples can lie, but . . ."

"Do you know him? Or the family?"

"No. Sorry. I only know Laureen. Clark's ex-wife."

"She lives in Vineyard Haven? He lives on Deep Forest Road?"

"Yup. He's near the dump." Her facial expression was neutral, but the tone of her voice suggested that the location was a real shame.

"I went by his house before I came here," Annie said. "I'll admit I'd hoped Bella didn't belong to whoever lived there. But I don't think she does. Not after seeing this."

Barbara shrugged. "Clark's had a tough life. Damn near killed him when Laureen up and left."

It was not a scenario Annie had expected. "How old are they?"

"Midthirties, maybe. Laureen's an aide at the hospital."

"What does Clark do?"

"He's a fisherman. Longline. Gone most of the time. That's what got to Laureen. She's young. She wanted more of a home life than a fisherman could give her." She thought for a moment. "Oh, I almost forgot, Clark is Stephen's kid brother."

"Stephen? Caleb's father?"

"The same. I think Clark's about ten years younger, though."

Young enough to attract a teenage girl? "May I ask how well you know Clark? Like, do you know if he has a dimple, too?"

She frowned. "I only met him once. At the hospital cookout a couple of years ago. I might have seen him around after that, but I never paid much attention. I guess he's sort of average. Dark hair. Kind of tall. That's all. Sorry."

Annie stood up again. "Don't be sorry. You've been a huge help. Please tell Winnie I stopped by." She had turned toward the door when she had another thought. "Barbara? I know I shouldn't ask, and I will completely understand if you can't tell me." She took a deep breath again. "You said you work in the maternity department?"

"I do. I have. For twelve years."

"I have no idea how many babies are born there every year, but I assume it's not a lot?"

"You'd be surprised. We've become an obstetrical go-to place."

"I think Bella is around three or four months old."

Barbara nodded. "I'd agree."

"I don't think she was born on the island, but her name might be memorable. Can you remember if a baby was born at the hospital in August or September who was named Bella?" She knew she might be putting her in a terrible position, but . . .

"You're right," Barbara replied. "You shouldn't have asked, because I can't tell you. Privacy laws, you know? But I think it's safe to say I don't remember a baby with that name. Not that I could tell you if I did, of course." She winked, then gave Annie a hug, wished her good luck, and said she was welcome to stop by anytime.

On the drive back to Edgartown, Annie mulled over the possibilities. She knew she still had no clear answers, but she now felt certain that Bella's mother was not an island girl. And she felt as if she was getting close to the truth about the rest. Very, very close.

She wanted to stop at the Deep Forest Road address and find out if Clark Thurman was at home or off fishing somewhere.

She wanted to return to the Scallop Cove Road address. Maybe she could talk to someone. Ask if they knew anything about Bella. Or about the young woman who now was "in and out of" a coma.

She wanted to learn as much as she could before calling John. Once he had all the facts, he might not be as inclined to take Bella away if there was someone who wanted her. If someone could prove that they were her family. Her *birth family*. Annie knew the term well.

But as soon as she reached Beetlebung Corner and turned

onto South Road, it started to snow. The drive back would take more than thirty minutes; by then the roads would no doubt be slippery. If it became a full-blown storm, John might be inclined to wait to take Bella away. As long as he knew that she was safe and warm and being taken care of.

So Annie decided to wait another day.

Chapter 23

By daybreak, the snow had stopped. Only a few inches had accumulated on Chappy, most of which had been blown helterskelter, leaving barren patches in some places, deep drifts in others. A cold wind was still whirling.

Annie decided that rather than calling or texting Earl, she would try and find him at one of the properties where he was the caretaker. She didn't know all the places he watched over, but he'd pointed several out when they'd been on their meanderings. Still, it meant bundling up, packing up, loading Bella—again—and driving around, but Annie wanted to tell him face-to-face about the Thurmans and ask if he'd go with her to meet them. For all Annie knew, Earl was a friend of the Thurmans or of their fathers and their fathers before them. Maybe his presence could help buffer the news that Caleb was a father—if they didn't already know.

But when she pulled out of her long driveway, the Lexus nearly crashed into a pickup truck that was barreling up the road. She slammed on the brakes; Bella let out a screech. The pickup swerved and wound up in a gully of scrubs on the right side of the road.

Annie snapped off her seat belt, jumped out, and ripped

open the back door. Thanks to the car seat, the baby was fine. Like Annie, she merely seemed startled. Still, Annie undid the restraint, picked her up, and cuddled her closely. She walked a bit, her back against the wind, rubbing the baby's cheeks and whispering, "Shhh, little one. It's okay, it's okay."

Then she looked over and saw the driver of the pickup walking toward them. It was Taylor—one of several people Annie could have done nicely without seeing right then. Or ever again.

"Well, damn, I am so sorry," Taylor said. Her apology might have been believable if it didn't look as if she was smirking. "This time of year, I forget that other people are on Chappy. I was listening to my music and . . . well, I was going lickety-split when I should have been paying attention. You okay? What about the baby?"

Small island. Annie heard her father's voice that time, not Murphy's. *Must try to get along with everyone.* "We're fine," she said and smiled through her teeth. "A little surprised, that's all."

Taylor looked genuinely apologetic. She was a terrific actor. "Well, I sure am sorry."

"No harm done. Honest."

Bella, however, was not being magnanimous: her screech had turned to crying, tears and all. Her arms had sprung free from the blanket, and her fists were making tiny punches at the air. Maybe she, too, sensed that Taylor was probably trouble.

Taking a few more steps toward them, Taylor touched one of Bella's hands. "Quite a little fighter, aren't you?" Bella opened her fist, grabbed Taylor's finger, pulled it into her mouth, and chomped down on it. Taylor winced; Annie tightened her lips to ward off a wave of laughter. Then Taylor asked, "How's your niece doing?" The question was so sudden, Annie was not prepared.

"Um . . ." she replied. "Um . . . well . . ." Her words sounded like the stammers of her former third-grade student Jerry Ferris. One day she'd asked him to tell the class about his family's trip to the maple sugar shack in the Berkshires, and the poor boy grew so nervous he not only stammered but he also wet his pants. Annie had hoped that sharing a fun experience might help him get over his public speaking anxiety; instead, she'd provoked humiliation. Jerry would be a grown man now, almost thirty; she wondered what had happened to him and if her well-meaning attempt had scarred him for life.

She blinked back to the awkwardness of the present.

"Sometimes family things take time to iron out," Taylor went on. "I have a brother no one ever thought would straighten out, but today he owns a restaurant up in Boston. First-class place, too, not one of those chain things. Can you imagine?"

No, Annie could not imagine, nor did she care to. But she smiled again and said, "That's wonderful."

"Your cat ever come back?" Taylor asked, and, yes, she was definitely smirking then. Clearly, the woman enjoyed toying with Annie.

"No," Annie replied. "It was a stray, anyway. I'd only been trying to help it." She had an uneasy suspicion that Taylor now knew the secret about Bella. Claire might have told her. Or maybe she'd coaxed information out of John while she was being flirtatious. Before the woman could make Annie feel even more uncomfortable, she asked, "By the way, have you seen Earl this morning? I think a few shingles blew off the roof last night. I decided to drive around and look for him instead of calling, because Bella likes the fresh air." She was getting good at lying now—a trait she hoped would be short-lived.

"He's probably at the Jackson place. I heard their alarm go off this morning; if I know Earl, he's checking every nook and cranny. Anyway, it's the big yellow farmhouse on Old Indian Trail. Just past the fire station. You know the way?"

Annie said she did, which she would have said even if only to get away from the woman and her smirks. She went back to the car and secured Bella in the car seat again.

"You sure you're both okay?" Taylor called out as Annie got behind the wheel.

"We're fine. You swerved so fast you avoided an accident." It was a backhanded compliment, but Annie didn't think Taylor would notice.

"Well," Taylor added with a sneer, as if she had an overwhelming urge to have the last word, "we do need to keep that baby in one piece in case her mother ever decides to come back." Then she trudged toward her truck, turning up the collar of her red-and-black-checkered wool shirt as if declaring a warped kind of victory.

As Taylor had predicted, Earl was at the Jackson place. He was walking to his truck when Annie pulled into the driveway. She waved; he hesitated for a second, or maybe two, then he sauntered over.

Annie put down the window. "Good morning."

He nodded. "Everything okay?"

"I saw Taylor—she told me where to find you."

"Bit of a problem out here with the alarm. Must have been from the winds. Happens all the time. Damned if you have 'em, damned if you don't. At least they keep the bugs down in summer. The winds, that is. I doubt if bugs give a crap about alarms."

Small talk was a decent icebreaker, but right then it was not what Annie wanted. "Earl," she interrupted, "I'm so sorry if I've caused trouble for you in your family. With Claire. With John."

He rubbed his chin—he was clean-shaven that day—and shifted his gaze up to the blue sky, over to the farmhouse, down to his boots, then back to her. "Claire's okay now. She said she hated being lied to; I told her you hadn't really lied. She said that was true, but that you hadn't been forthcoming, which sometimes is just as bad. Anyway, I told her more about you, how you were adopted, so protecting Bella means a lot to you. I hope that was okay."

"If it helped mend fences for you, of course it's okay."

"It did."

"Good. Because I . . ." She was afraid she was going to start stammering again. She thought about Jerry Ferris. Like he had been, she was among friends; well, one friend, anyway. She cleared her throat and found her confidence, the way she'd hoped Jerry could have done. "Earl, I've learned more information. It might be my last chance to find Bella's family. I know that foster care sometimes has a good outcome, but once she's in the system, who knows what it will take to get her out." She paused, she knew, for dramatic effect, which she hated that she'd stooped to, but thought it might be essential. "Anyway, I sure could use your help. I need to go to Edgartown and find out if I'm right or wrong. I think it would be better if I didn't go alone."

He leaned against the roofline of the Lexus, looked back up to the sky. "You're asking if I'll go with you?"

"Yes."

He exhaled loudly. "I can't, Annie."

She toyed with the steering wheel. "I understand."

"It isn't you," he said. "Like I said, Claire has a real thing about people holding on to secrets when they know damn well they shouldn't. Those are her words, not mine."

"I do understand. If it's any consolation, I don't think I've ever not been forthcoming, as you called it, in my entire life. Until now. But so much is at stake. For the baby. For her mother."

That time, he didn't respond.

"I know it's a lot to ask, Earl. But aside from Winnie and her daughter-in-law, you're the only one on the island who I trust." It wasn't the right time to mention her encounter with Taylor, whom she did not trust for a single, solitary heartbeat.

"Are you going to tell me what you plan to do in Edgartown?"

"I need to see a family named Thurman. Stephen and Bonnie. And maybe Stephen's brother, Clark. Do you know them?"

Earl nodded. "Stephen's a house painter, like his dad, Billy, who was my friend. Billy died a while back, six, seven years ago. Accident. Fell off a ladder." He shuffled his feet again. "Stephen and Bonnie have twin boys."

"I know," Annie replied. She was grateful that, as she'd hoped, he knew the family—and the boys.

Earl thought a moment, then said, "Oh, no. You don't think one of them . . ."

"That's what I need to find out."

"Damn," he said. "Damn. They're such good kids."

"It's either one of them or it's Stephen's brother, Clark."

"I don't know Clark very well. He's a lot younger than Stephen, and he's a loner. From what I've heard he doesn't leave the island except to fish. I guess he's never been interested in anything else. Cost him his marriage. Which caused Stephen and Bonnie to split up for a little while, too, on account of Bonnie sided with Laureen, and you know how that goes."

"Families," Annie said, as if she knew much about any of them.

"No," Earl continued. "I really doubt it's Clark. But . . ."

"But what?"

"But I suppose you never know, do you?"

"No. You never do."

"Damn," he repeated. "If it's one of Stephen's boys . . ." He sighed again, stuffed his hands into his jacket pockets.

"Well, we don't know that yet. Maybe we could start at Clark's house? I drove by yesterday, but it looked vacant."

Earl paused, his eyes moving around again. "Would you be insulted if we took two vehicles across? That way . . ."

"No problem. I don't want to cause any more trouble for you, Earl. But I really would appreciate your help."

He tapped the roof of the car. "I'll meet you at the parking lot behind the library," he said. "In about twenty minutes. We shouldn't take the same trip across."

She knew he meant that they shouldn't board the *On Time* together. Gossipmongers, after all, could be lurking anywhere.

"Besides," he continued, "in this wind, you'll be more comfortable in your car. The higher the vehicle, the more it rocks and rolls when you're on the water."

"It's fine, Earl. I'll meet you at the library." Annie smiled at his need to come up with a justifiable excuse for them to travel separately, as if they were having a sordid affair. Which really would give the island something to talk about.

"Want to tell me how you came up with this link to the Thurmans?" Earl asked after they'd met on the other side of the channel and he'd climbed into the passenger side of Annie's car. He'd been right about the wind: despite the sunshine, the ferry crossing had been like a ride at an amusement park. Annie had been a little frightened, but the motion had eased Bella into sleep.

Driving west along Edgartown-West Tisbury Road, she explained about the bus driver and the rest.

"I know it would probably be better for everyone if Bella's father turns out to be Clark," she continued, "but I have to tell you something else: I looked in the high school yearbook and saw photos of Stephen's twins. Caleb has a dimple in his chin that looks identical to Bella's."

Earl let out a low whistle. "But you said it doesn't sound like Bella's mother is an island girl? That the bus driver thinks she came over the same day as the fair?"

"He said he was sure about that because he hated driving into Edgartown because of the traffic that weekend. He also asked the girl why she hadn't come over on the *Grey Lady* and gone right into Edgartown, but she said she didn't know about that boat. Which isn't surprising. My best bet is that the special trips were marketed to women as a shopping adventure for the holidays—like the stroll on Nantucket or Kennebunkport's prelude. I doubt that the ads would have meant much to Bella's mother, even if she had seen them. After all, she didn't come to shop. Or sip cocoa with Santa at the Harbor View."

"I take it she's still in bad shape?"

"As far as I know."

After a few minutes, she turned onto Deep Forest Road. "His house is number seven," she said. "But I couldn't see any numbers."

"Enclave," Earl commented. "These houses were built for year-round laborers. Housing is such a problem here; it keeps getting tougher for regular working folks to afford a decent place to live." He pointed to one of the small ranch-style homes, where a man was getting out of an old SUV, a grocery bag in his hand. "Stop the car," Earl said.

Annie stopped.

Earl got out, approached the man, and nodded at him in a friendly, neighborly way.

Annie cracked her window so she could hear the conversation.

"Looking for Clark Thurman. He around?"

"Nope," the guy replied. "Been gone a couple of weeks. Think they were headed to Georges Bank for tuna."

"Thanks." Earl started to walk back to the car, then turned back. "Can you tell me which place is his?"

The guy pointed across the street. Although it was an equally small house, it seemed better cared for than the others, with no debris strewn around the yard.

"He has kids, doesn't he?" Earl asked. "Or am I mixing him up with his brother, Stephen?"

Annie wondered if Earl might be pushing his luck. In Boston, no one would have told anyone anything about a neighbor.

"Clark's got two. Boy and girl."

Annie gulped. She hadn't considered that Clark might have a son who could be Bella's father, too.

"How old are his kids?"

The guy shook his head and went up his steps. "I have no idea." He seemed exasperated now. "Little kids. In middle school. Not as old as mine." He opened the screen door just as a gust of wind whipped past and nearly ripped it off.

"Thanks," Earl said again and trotted back to the car. "Like I said, it's hard to believe that Bella might be his," he said as he buckled his seat belt. "I expect he never goes anywhere where he might have met her. And his son's a little kid, so Bella darn well isn't his. Yup, Clark's wrapped up in himself. Always was. Always too busy to help his father. Never home to be a father, either, or at least that's what I remember hearing."

She didn't want to ask if he'd heard that from Taylor or from Claire.

"So," he added, "let's go to Stephen and Bonnie's. And get this over with."

Less than ten minutes later, Annie turned down Scallop Cove Road and stopped at number twelve.

"I suppose I should do the talking," Earl said.

"If you don't mind. At least if you could start the conversation."

He pulled open his door. "You bringing Bella in?"

"I don't know. What do you think?"

He shrugged. "Proof is in the pudding."

It seemed to take an hour to undo the car seat and situate Bella back in her basket. Then, because Earl said front doors were only meant for company, they walked in silence to the side porch. Annie said a quick prayer for help to Murphy, then tacked on an extra one to her dad.

Chapter 24

A woman who looked to be in her forties opened the door. She wore a muslin apron that was too tight for her plump body; her hands were covered in white flour; her cheeks were pink, perhaps from the heat in the kitchen. "Earl Lyons!" she greeted him happily. "What brings you way out here on such a fine and blustery day?"

"Hey, Bonnie," he said. "Long time, no see. This is my friend Annie Sutton. She's living over on Chappy."

Bonnie attempted to straighten her chestnut-colored hair and then said hello to Annie. "Yes, I recognize you. I think I saw you at the fair. Please excuse the mess. Today is baking-bread day. I'm finally catching up after making enough Christmas breads to choke an elf."

Annie supposed that most of the town ladies had been to the fair. She would have liked to ask if Bonnie had seen her soaps and if she'd noticed a young woman hanging around her table. But that wasn't why they were there, so she simply said, "It's nice to meet you, Bonnie."

Bonnie let them out of the cold and into the kitchen. The aroma of fresh, warm bread perfumed the room.

"Stephen home?" Earl asked.

She leaned against a large center island with clean, white-painted cabinets on the bottom and a slab of ebony granite with silver flecks on top—the same cabinets and counters that lined the room. "He's working. Doing the interior at the new post office."

"Yeah," Earl replied. "Who'd have thought they'd ever get around to building one? With twice as many clerks behind the counter. Or so I hear."

She carried a large earthenware bowl to the sink. "You going to tell me why you're here? Somebody die?" She turned on the faucet, twisted her hands together under the stream, then dried them on her apron. She was a no-nonsense woman, direct but not rude, the kind of woman Annie respected and, under other circumstances, might want as a friend.

"Nobody died," Earl said.

Bonnie nodded, walked back to the island, leaned on it again.

Bella started to fuss.

"You've got a baby there," Bonnie said.

Annie smiled, tried to look compassionate.

Earl fidgeted with the zipper on his jacket. "That, we do."

Annie could tell he was having trouble finding the right words, so she blurted out, "Her name is Bella. And she's the reason we're here. I was told someone named Thurman might know something about her."

Bonnie frowned. "Something like what?"

Sucking in her breath, Annie said, "Like who her father might be."

Bonnie watched her for a moment, then turned her gaze back to Earl, who had closed his eyes as if this were too painful for him to deal with. Annie felt guilty for having dragged him there, for having used him to help her gain entrance to the house.

"Well," Bonnie said, "let's have a look, then." She crossed the room to where Annie stood just inside the doorway. Looking into the basket, she peeled back a corner of the fleece to get a good look at the little face. "Oh," Bonnie said. "Oh."

Annie let the woman process whatever she was thinking. Then she quietly asked, "Oh, what?"

"Oh, God," Bonnie replied, not pulling her eyes from Bella. "She looks just like my Caleb, doesn't she?"

Caleb was home, Bonnie said. He was downstairs with his brother, playing video games. Earl moved a bowl of fresh fruit from the kitchen table; Annie set down Bella's basket. They sat across from each other while Bonnie went to the basement door.

"Caleb!" she shouted. "Come up, please. Now." She walked back to Annie and Earl. "They're both on their winter breaks. Michael goes to UMass Amherst; he's majoring in sports medicine. Caleb's at Northeastern for business."

"Smart boys," Earl said.

Like Murphy's, Annie thought.

Bonnie looked into the basket again. "I used to think so." Her complexion had turned pale and powdery, like the remnants of bread-baking that dusted her apron. She sat next to Annie, wearing a look of disbelief that Annie supposed parents wore when they saw their children's dreams—and their dreams for their children—take an unexpected turn—a *crash-and-burn*, Murphy used to call it.

Bonnie glanced toward the basement door. "Caleb! Now!" She looked back at Annie. "How old?"

"We're not exactly sure. Three or four months."

Heavy footsteps thundered up the stairs. The basement door opened; a tall, handsome boy clomped into the kitchen, pushing a tangle of black hair up off his brow. He had on torn jeans and a blue plaid flannel shirt that his arms had outgrown by a couple of inches. He wore a wide grin. "You saved me, Mom. Michael was destroying me."

When no reaction came from his mother, Caleb's grin faded. That simple act carved a dimple into his chin, emphasizing the unmistakable genetic link.

"Come here, Caleb," Bonnie said. "You remember Earl Lyons."

"Sure," the boy said, his expression hardening into a heightened state of alert. He looked from Earl back to his mom, who had lowered her gaze. He squared his shoulders, then walked to the table and shook Earl's hand. "Hi, Mr. Lyons."

"Caleb," Earl said.

"And this is Earl's friend Annie Sutton," Bonnie said.

Caleb gave Annie a small smile. Then his eyes traveled to the basket.

"Have you seen this baby before?" Bonnie asked. She was not only direct, but had an admirable steadiness in her voice. *A strong woman*, Annie thought.

Bella gurgled as if on cue.

Caleb raised his shoulders; his dark eyes widened. "I don't think so. Why?"

"Why?" Bonnie asked. Her voice grew louder. Her hands, which had been resting on the table, now curled up tightly. Her composure seemed to dwindle. "Well, for starters, she looks a little like you, don't you think?"

He did not turn pale the way his mother had. Instead, he frowned, his lower lip jutting out as if he were legitimately confused. "Well, no. Not really."

Bonnie reached out and grabbed his hand. "Caleb. She does. She looks exactly like you."

Like Earl, even Annie had to look away. She didn't want to witness the boy's reaction. Doing so seemed intrusive. And mean.

"Mom?" Caleb asked. "Are you saying somebody thinks I'm this baby's father?"

No one replied.

"Jesus," Caleb said, then plunked his angular body onto the last empty chair. "Are you fucking kidding me?"

"Caleb," Bonnie snapped. "Language."

"Sorry. But Jesus . . . seriously?"

Bella's gurgle turned into a soft cry. Which was exactly what Annie had hoped wouldn't happen. The adults sat in silence, staring at the basket. Annie finally reached over, picked up the baby, and held her.

"You said you think she's three or four months?" Bonnie asked. "When was she born?"

"August or September. We're not sure where, though. We don't think the mother lives on the island."

"This is nuts," Caleb said. "I haven't even had a real girlfriend since Mia Stimson broke up with me after prom last spring. Tell them, Mom. I don't have a real girlfriend. This baby can't be mine."

Bonnie reached over, took his hand again. "Caleb, please. We'll figure it out. Nothing is certain yet."

A timer dinged.

"That's the bread," Bonnie said, but stayed in her chair as if waiting for permission to get up and tend to it. When permission didn't come, she stood and went slowly to the oven.

"Son," Earl said quietly, "we're just trying to find out who this poor little one belongs to. She was left on Annie's doorstep during the blizzard. It turns out the girl's mother came over on the boat a few days before and asked the bus driver if he knew the Thurmans."

Caleb's eyes widened. "Maybe it's Uncle Clark's."

"It doesn't seem that way. You know he rarely leaves the island except to fish. And, besides, Bella's mom is young. About your age."

As if knowing they were talking about her mother, Bella stopped crying. Annie turned her sideways, resting her in the crook of her arm so Caleb could see Bella's tiny face. She fixed her pretty sweater—the one Claire had made—and let Bella hang on to her finger.

"Tell them," Bonnie said from across the room.

"Tell them what?" Caleb asked.

"You're the math whiz, Caleb. Figure it out. If that baby was born in August or September, the girl could have gotten pregnant during your Christmas vacation last year. Tell them how you and Michael went to the Cape with your dad. Remember? Your last 'boys' only' adventure before you two went off to college? Tell them, Caleb."

His eyes shot back to Earl.

"Where'd you go?" Earl asked.

"Wellfleet. My dad knows a guy there."

Annie bounced Bella gently. She moved forward on her chair, eager to ask a hundred questions. Instinct, however, told her to keep her mouth shut. Let Earl and Caleb discuss this man-to-man. There'd been enough finger-pointing from the women.

"How long were you there?"

"The week between Christmas and New Year's."

"Did you meet a girl?"

Caleb's eyes widened, then dropped to the floor. "I did, yeah, but it wasn't like that."

Bonnie clattered the bowls, the utensils, the cooling racks. "Mom. Please."

She rattled another rack. "*Mom? Please?*" she mimicked her son. "Caleb. What in God's name have you done? What in God's name did you do?" She yanked off her apron, tossed it on the island, pulled at her hair. "God," she said, though Annie couldn't tell if it was a plea for help or just a gut reaction.

Caleb stood up quickly. The chair wobbled beneath him.

"This kid isn't mine," he said. "Where's her mother, anyway? Why you don't find her? Why don't you ask *her*?"

Earl sighed. "She's in the hospital, son. She tried to kill herself."

"What?" Caleb cried. "Are you fucking kidding me? Am I supposed to be responsible for that, too?"

Bella started to cry again. Annie lifted her to her shoulder, rubbed her back. "Caleb," she said, because she could no longer hold back. "The girl you met in Wellfleet. Do you know her name?"

"Francine. She was a waitress at the Sunrise Café. I hardly knew her. She served me toast and eggs that were pretty crappy, but there aren't many places open in winter. We were friendly. *Friends*, you know? One time we went for a walk. But I swear, we didn't do anything."

His mother dropped something that clanked into the sink. "One week," she seethed. "You 'hardly knew' a girl a week and you had sex with her."

"Were you listening, Mom? I said we didn't . . ."

Bonnie left the kitchen.

Caleb inhaled a heavy breath, let out a stream of pain. "Jesus," he said again. Then he went back to the basement door and disappeared down the stairs.

Annie and Earl—and Bella—went out to the car and sat for a few minutes.

"I'm sure you noticed he didn't beg for a DNA test," Earl said.

"Maybe it hasn't occurred to him yet." She turned on the ignition. "Is John working this afternoon?"

"I think so."

"Okay. I'll drop you off first. Then I'll bring Bella to the police station."

"You sure?"

She nodded. "I guess Caleb could be Bella's father. No matter what he claims. What do you think?"

Earl nodded. "I think one of the few things in life that never changes is that kids can be stupid. And that even the best of them can lie if they're backed into a corner." He shook his head. "Do you want to go home to Chappy first and pack Bella's things?"

A lump the size of one of her soap scoops suddenly felt lodged halfway down Annie's throat. Her vision grew watery. Her heart felt thick and heavy. "No. If I bring her to the cottage, I'm afraid I won't want to let her go." She winced at her choice of words. "I'll get her things to John later."

But as she drove to the lot where they'd left Earl's truck, his cell phone rang. He fished it out of his pocket, looked at the screen, then at her.

"It's John. Should I answer?"

Annie blinked. Then nodded.

"I'll put him on speaker. To make it easier." He clicked on the phone and set it on the console. "Yeah, John. I'm here with Annie."

"She's awake," came John's reply.

"What?" Annie sat up straight.

"Bella's mother is fully awake."

Tears instantly welled.

"Does this mean she'll be okay?" Earl asked.

"The doctors aren't committing. All they said is her vitals are good."

Annie felt a smile inch across her trembling lips. Bella wasn't going to lose her mother. Her mother would survive. One crisis had been averted.

Then John said, "I was calling to ask you to go to Annie's, Dad. To let her know about Bella's mother. I didn't know you'd be together."

An unpleasant queasiness crawled into Annie's stomach. Why hadn't he called her himself? Did she disgust him so much after what she had done?

"I'm at the hospital, Annie," he continued. "I wanted Dad to ask if you'd come over here. The girl is awake, but she won't speak to anyone. Not to the doctors or the nurses, and for sure, not to us. I thought if you brought the baby . . ."

"You think once she sees Bella, she'll talk?"

"That's the idea. We have to start somewhere. And, right now, you're our best option."

Chapter 25

Annie dropped Earl off at his truck so he could go back to Chappy. "As much as I'd like to be with you," he said, "let's face it. I'd have to tell Claire where I am, and she'd want to stick her nose in. I mean that with love, of course."

"Of course," Annie said with a smile. "I'll call or text you if anything important happens, so don't forget to charge your phone. And leave it on. Okay?"

He opened the car door and started to get out. "Annie? I just want to tell you something in case you don't already know it. I think what you're doing—all that you've been doing—for the little one has been terrific. No matter what other folks might say, including my own wife, I think that little girl was lucky that she ended up at your door." His blue eyes grew misty; he nodded and got out. "I'll keep the phone charged and turned on. That's a promise." He waved, then closed the door, and Annie drove away, so filled with love for a dear friend, there was no room left in her for anxiety as she headed toward Oak Bluffs.

On the way, she glanced into the rearview mirror and said to Bella, "Your mother's name is Francine. Did you know that, sweet girl? And now you're going to see her again. Which is wonderful, because I know she must love you very much. In spite of all that's happened, she wanted you safe and taken care of."

"Francine," she whispered to herself. If only the guy who'd gotten her pregnant had bothered to ask for her last name.

Annie had never been in Martha's Vineyard Hospital, but it was hard to miss. It sat up on a hill, overlooking Vineyard Haven Harbor, and she'd been told had been designed so every patient room had a water view. *Prime real estate*, she thought. She only hoped that Francine was happy to be there, grateful that she'd been rescued.

She found a parking space in the lot, gathered herself and Bella, and was quickly inside the large foyer. The receptionist gave her directions up to the intensive care unit.

Walking toward the elevators, Annie looked around the wide corridor. It was empty and still, occupied only by large prints of famous people—Dylan, the Stones, a young Barack and Michelle Obama—curiously interspersed with a palette of island landscapes—fishing boats in Menemsha Harbor, pastel Victorian cottages in Oak Bluffs, the picturesque Gay Head Cliffs. Annie saw no white-coated doctors or scurrying nurses, no patients on gurneys or parents with children, thanks in large part, she supposed, to the comfortable incubation of off season.

Whenever possible, Annie avoided hospitals and the memories they evoked. Her dad had been rushed to one via ambulance through the streets of Boston during the night; by the time she'd arrived, he was dead from a massive coronary. All she remembered were the cavernous hallways, the murmurs of doctors and nurses, the blank stare of her mother's eyes. And she remembered that she was cold. *Bone cold*, she recalled.

Six months later, she'd gone to the hospital every day for
the short time her mother was a patient for acute leukemia.
Annie had dressed in a crinkly paper gown, a hat, and a mask
for every visit in order to protect her mother from any germs
she might bring in. The precautions made little difference: her
mother died anyway. Annie was at her bedside: she turned off
the overhead lights and sat, alone, holding her mother's hand,
the soft hues of dusk leaking into the big window, the end of a
day, the end of a life.

By far the worst time had been the night Brian had been
killed. She'd stood outside, nearly catatonic, the big red letters
of the emergency room sign glaring at her, the double-wide,
automatic doors opening and closing, opening and closing,
each time an ambulance arrived and another stretcher was
wheeled inside.

But when she reached the elevator now, she reminded herself this was not one of those times; this was a feel-good event,
not one that would upset her life. Not if she didn't let it. It was
about other people, and it would not hurt her.

A small, artificial Christmas tree stood on a counter at the
nurses' station. A string of garland decorated the half wall; greeting cards had been clipped to it in a neat, colorful row. Annie
wasn't sure if such festive decor was still allowed in hospitals on
the mainland—in *America*, she often heard it called now.

A nurse in a lavender tunic and blue scrub pants sat with
her back to the counter, engaged in watching a small bank of
monitors. Annie did not want to interrupt her, so she stood,
waiting. She wanted to set down Bella's basket, but didn't dare
put it on the hospital floor. Though it looked highly polished,
she'd read too much about germs when her mother had been
sick.

"You made it."

She turned and saw John approaching. His uniform and his walk suited both his frame and demeanor: striking, professional, masculine. "I did."

He glanced at Bella. "The patient is in room three. She still hasn't talked."

"I'll do my best."

"I'm sure you will. I think she's scared, though. Maybe you should go in alone first; I don't want to make her feel like we're ganging up on her. I'll take the baby to the waiting room. If you can at least get the girl to tell you her name, that would be a big help."

Her name is Francine, Annie could have said. But she wanted to wait before giving him the latest details. She wanted to gain Francine's trust, to let her know that she cared. But first, she needed to convince herself that John would be there when she returned, that he wouldn't take the baby away without telling her.

He held his hand toward the basket. And Annie realized that no amount of trying to convince herself would matter: she had no choice but to hand Bella over.

She smiled. "Take good care of her while I'm gone," she said. He took the basket; she took a last glance. Then she went down the hall to room three.

It was worse than she'd imagined. The lights were harsh and glaring, digital screens hung from the ceilings, wires snaked from them to electrical sockets, IV poles stood in wait. Countless boxes and packets of gloves, assorted gauze pads, and various pieces of equipment—for uses Annie did not want to guess— were lined up in an orderly manner on sterile-looking counters. All four walls were glass; an ominous syringe—Adrenalin, Annie guessed—was taped, about chest-height, to one. Below that was space for a single bed that wasn't there now.

She hurried from the room back to the nurses' station. "She's gone. Room three. The patient's gone." She tried not to sound anxious.

After one, two, three seconds, the nurse turned around. "Excuse me?"

In spite of her resolve, Annie had a hard time catching her breath. "The patient. In room three. She's gone."

The nurse smiled. *She smiled!* "She's downstairs. In radiology. Her doctor ordered a couple more tests. It might take a while."

"Oh," Annie said, wilting like a wildflower after it had been picked. "Okay. I'll wait. In her room. If that's all right?" With her words clipped and staccato, she sounded even more ludicrous than she felt.

The nurse nodded, returned to her task, and Annie went back to room three. She could have gone to the waiting room and told John it would take a while, but she didn't want to have to deal with him right then. Not until she had something to tell. Not until she could be sure she would not overreact again.

Back in the room, she sat in a lone chair, facing the window with the promised view that she hadn't noticed before. It must have faced west, because, thanks to the shortened daylight of December, the sun was already starting to set, spreading cantaloupe streaks across the cold, purple sky. She sat and waited, trying to think only positive things, like the nice words Earl had said to her, how he thought that what she'd been doing with Bella was terrific, and that Bella was lucky to have landed on Annie's doorstep. Those happy thoughts helped tone down the resurfaced memories of past hospital visits. Gratitude, she knew, was always guaranteed to make the world a little brighter.

Closing her eyes, she reviewed the long list of the blessings in her life. Within moments, the veil lifted.

The next thing Annie knew, it was pitch-dark outside: she must have dozed off. When she looked out the window, all she saw were reflections of the digital screens, the boxes of supplies and equipment, and a bed that was being wheeled in. The squeaking wheels must have jarred her awake.

A young man steered the bed into position, locked it into place, and left. Under the sheet, a patient in a blue cotton johnny lay on her back, motionless. Her head was straight; her eyes were open; she stared up at the ceiling.

"Hello," Annie said. She dragged her chair close to the side of the bed. Though Francine looked familiar, she was much different than Annie remembered: her complexion was pasty; her big, dark eyes, without expression. Her short hair was askew.

A nurse swept in. "I'll just be a minute," she said, then proceeded to connect various monitors and tubes to the patient. Electronic beeps and digital graphs sprang to life; Annie looked away. After a couple of minutes, the nurse said, "All set," and whisked out of the room as quickly as she'd whisked in.

Annie sat, as unmoving as the girl in the bed. Finally, she said, "I understand you're doing better. How do you feel?"

No answer came, no acknowledgment that Annie was in the room. Yet Annie saw her blink. She looked smaller than she had at the fair, maybe because she was without the winter jacket she must have worn then, not that Annie could recall it.

With the long, settling breath of a mindful observer, Annie said, "I thought it was time for us to meet properly. I'm Annie. Annie Sutton."

Beeps and clicks hung in the air. The girl's eyes flicked to Annie, then shot back to the ceiling.

"You'll be glad to know Bella's fine," Annie continued. "She's still with me. For now, anyway. She misses you, though. Babies can really miss their mothers. I read an article once that said a baby knows its mother's voice at the instant of birth, that it can tell its own mother apart from all other women." She'd forgotten she'd read that. It had been years ago, not long after she'd received the letter from Donna MacNeish. At the time, she'd tried not to give it credence.

More than anything, Annie wanted to reach out now and touch Francine on her shoulder; she wanted to let her know she wasn't alone, did not have to be alone. But she was afraid it would startle the girl, scare her. So Annie kept her hands in her lap and her voice low. "I know you must have been through a terrible time. But on the Vineyard . . . well, whether by accident or intention, you've come to the right place. People take care of one another here."

No response.

She hadn't wanted to play her trump card, but Annie could tell nothing else was going to work. She leaned close enough to the bed so she could rest her hands on the sheets. She glanced around to make sure no nurses—or, worse, police—were in sight. If she whispered, maybe the nurse who was watching the monitors wouldn't hear her. "Francine?"

The girl blinked, but remained silent.

"That's your name, isn't it? Well, Francine, I know more than you might think. I know you're from Wellfleet, and I know about Caleb. But I haven't told the police. I wanted you to have a chance to give Bella a family . . . with you as the most important person in it. You know from my book that I was adopted. I was lucky—I went to a good home; I had a good upbringing. But I'd be lying if I told you I never thought about my birth mother. Or that I never longed to know the woman who . . . who gave me up." The last thing Annie had expected was that she—not Francine—would start to cry. And yet there she was, silvery tears sliding down both of her cheeks. Genuine tears. For the mother she'd never known—or worse, hadn't acknowledged when she'd had the chance.

She took a tissue from her purse, wiped her eyes, tried to regain her composure. It would be helpful if the girl responded to Annie's confession, but she did not.

"Francine," Annie said again, "I don't know how things will work out for you with the Thurmans, but I want you to know I will help however I can. You might think I have a pile of money, but I don't." She laughed. "That's a long story I'd be glad to share one day over a cup of hot tea." Then she stood up. "But there are other ways that I—and others—can help. If you let us. I'm going to go now, but I'll be back tomorrow. And the day after. However many times it takes for you to know you don't have to go through this alone."

Annie left the room then, tears glistening again, leaking from the dark cloud that had covered her heart. For once in her life, her true feelings had wrangled their way out, and she hadn't shut them down by pretending to smile.

She quietly walked down the hall to the stairwell outside the waiting room. She wasn't ready to see John; she didn't feel like talking yet. She knew she needed to tell him about the Thurmans now and that the girl's name was Francine, but Annie was tired. Exhausted, actually. Maybe she could use the baby as an excuse: she could pick her up, pat her bottom, announce that Bella needed a diaper change, then make a quick dash for the ladies' room, where she could sit for a few minutes and be alone.

With her luck, however, John would have already changed the baby. A smart guy like him would know how to do that.

Instead of going into the waiting room, she slipped around the corner and snuck into the ladies' room alone. She slumped against the wall and tried to think about what she had done.

Had she offered Francine financial support? A family? A home? It didn't look as if Caleb Thurman had any intention of accepting the role of a father. Chances were, he'd simply go back to college and move on with his life. The best Francine could hope for might be some financial support. Maybe at some point Bonnie Thurman would step in and assume some type of role in Bella's life. Maybe not.

As for Bella, well, Annie had been around a long time—she'd taught several students from single-parent homes. Some did okay; some did not. It never seemed to turn out as easy as young women thought it would—even for those who had a good support system and the best of intentions.

And what about Annie? She was fifty years old. In a couple of months, she'd be fifty-one. She was just getting back on her financial feet. Was she ready—or willing—to take on the responsibility of a young mother and a baby? Especially after she'd worked so hard to create a new, unencumbered life?

Glancing into the mirror over the sink, she tucked her hair behind her ears, widened her eyes, and studied them. She didn't know if she'd started to look her age yet; she didn't know what her age was supposed to look like. She wondered if having a baby in the house who needed attention and a young mother who clearly had problems would put more stress on Annie than even Trish and her crazy deadlines could do. Would subsequent age lines come faster than necessary?

Did thinking that way mean Annie had grown selfish?

John had survived having two daughters and, though two years younger than Annie, he certainly didn't look as if stress had taken a toll on him.

Stretching out her arms, she rolled her head from side to side, hoping to relax. When that didn't happen, Annie gave up. It was time to forget about mundane things like age lines, which probably would show up when they wanted. It was time to stop procrastinating and face the final, major hurdle. It was time to face John. Before she got too far ahead of herself.

When she reached the waiting room, John wasn't there. Neither was Bella.

At first she thought she must be in the wrong place. But a quick look around confirmed that it was the waiting room, the only one nearby. Her mood started to plummet; her pulse sped up. She told herself that John must be in the men's room. Would he have taken Bella in there? Annie had no clue about today's restroom protocol.

She checked her watch. Six thirty.

Where was he? Where were they?

She scooted back to the nurses' station. "Excuse me . . ." Her voice was suddenly weak, as if she were the one who needed to be hooked up to something. Or shot with the Adrenalin stuck to the wall over Francine's bed.

The nurse spun around. "You must be looking for your baby." She reached under the counter and brought out the basket. "Here she is, sleeping like an angel."

Annie let out a huge, unladylike sigh. "Thanks . . . thank you. But . . ."

"Oh, and Sergeant Lyons left you a note." A Post-it was stuck to a monitor: the nurse peeled it off and handed it to Annie.

Sorry, it read. *Had to run. Accident duty. Later. John.*

Damn. She had hoped they'd go down to the cafeteria and have coffee and a long talk. She had planned to tell him everything—about the bus driver, the Thurmans, and Francine. She'd hoped that he wouldn't hate her for not having told him sooner. But no matter what, it would have been a relief to purge the rest of her secrets.

But she was there and John was gone. She tried to come up with an alternative plan. When that didn't work, she dropped the Post-it in her purse, picked up Bella, and walked away, trying to ignore the fact that her pulse hadn't slowed down.

Chapter 26

If she had any strength, she'd get out of bed and get out of there. She'd get away from Annie Sutton, get off of Martha's Vineyard, where, for some weird reason, everyone wanted to help everyone else.

You couldn't even kill yourself without people jumping in to save you.

At least Bella was okay.

She listened to the beep-beeps coming from somewhere behind her head. She smelled the antiseptic smells. She saw that every wall in the room was made out of glass. She was in a fishbowl. Even if she were stronger, she couldn't get out undetected.

Tears leaked down her cheeks. They did that so many times these days, she wondered if something had gone wrong with her eyes. She took a corner of the scratchy bedsheet and dabbed at the wetness before anyone saw it and decided to ask questions.

Annie took the elevator downstairs and walked toward the exit. She had almost reached the entrance when Bella started to cry—not her kitten-like whimpers, but a full-blown wail.

Hunger.

Diaper change.

Attention.

She ran through Murphy's list of three reasons a baby cries. She settled on hunger, because it had been a long time since Bella had eaten.

Where her oversized purse once held notebooks and pens, and more recently, jars of soap-making ingredients, it now held diapers, pacifiers, and a bottle. And formula. That would need to be warmed up.

Stopping at a large campus map mounted in the lobby, she located the café at the junction of the physicians' office building and the hospital. She turned and went back down the hall, past the portraits and the landscapes and seascapes again, while Bella kept up with her nonstop insistence for food. Annie prayed they weren't disturbing others—especially patients, who were probably not happy to be there in the first place, in spite of their view of the water.

The café was easy to find, but the door was locked. A sign read: OPEN MONDAY–FRIDAY. 6:45 A.M.–10:30 A.M.; 11:00 A.M.–3:00 P.M.

Annie stared at it and stifled a scream as loud as one of Bella's.

Just then a man hustled around the corner, yanking his arm into the sleeve of a heavy parka. Though obviously rushing, he stopped. "They're closed on weekends," he said.

"I noticed. Too bad the baby can't read. Or doesn't care what it says."

"Hungry?"

"I have formula, but no way to warm it."

"Yes, you do," he said, pulling on gloves, his car keys jangling. "Upstairs. Maternity. I'll bet they'd be glad to help." He trotted down the hallway and disappeared out a back door before Annie could thank him.

She toted Bella back to the elevator and pushed the button marked 2.

Once upstairs, she went directly to maternity and begged for assistance.

"Absolutely," a nurse replied. She had light brown hair, barely touched with gray and pulled back into a ponytail. Most importantly, she didn't seem ruffled by Bella's noise. She was holding an iPad and a stethoscope: a blend of the new world and the old. "But you're not breastfeeding?"

Annie almost laughed. "Thanks for the compliment, but I'm afraid I've aged out of having babies. I'm just sitting for a friend."

"Well, okay then, we'll get you set." She took the formula and the bottle, then escorted Annie to a comfortable chair while she left to heat up Bella's dinner.

While sitting, waiting, Annie realized she was still terribly weary. *Done in*, from head to toe. She would have loved to close her eyes again, but Bella was not going to allow that. Maybe she was as tired and cranky as Annie felt thanks to the emotional roller coaster of this charade.

When the nurse returned, Annie held Bella, who ate—and ate—with frenetic spasms. "Slow down, little one," the nurse said with a chuckle. "Or you'll have gas pains all the way home."

Then Annie had an idea—*perhaps,* she thought, *the best one she'd had all day*. She smiled at the nurse. "I know you must be sick of doing this, but would you feed her for me? I'm new at this, and it's way over my pay grade. I'd love to see how it should be done." She noticed the woman's name tag: HELENE. Helene said she'd be delighted.

Bella settled into Helene's arms and continued her meal at a more leisurely pace. Annie couldn't imagine feeling more grateful.

Then she said, "Oh, gosh, I just remembered. My friend Barbara works here. In maternity. Actually, her sister-in-law is my friend. Winnie Lathrop."

"Barbara's the best. I'm noon to eight; Barbara's midnight to eight. Part-timers trade off eight to midnight and eight to noon. Which is more than you need to know. I don't suppose you'd care to sit here until midnight to say hello?"

Annie laughed. "Five hours? I'd love to see her, but no thanks. It's been a tiring day, and Bella and I both need to get home." She said the word *home*, as if the cottage was Bella's home, too.

"Bella," Helene said. "What a beautiful name. I was in school with a girl named Isabella Wright. Sometimes we called her Bella."

It took a second to process what she had said. Then Annie asked, "Here? On the Vineyard?"

"Oh, yes. I'm an island girl. She was, too. Class of nineteen ninety-five. She left right after graduation, though, when her family moved to Minnesota. I always wondered how a girl from an island could stand being trapped in the Midwest. Anyway, we were all upset; she was the first one in our class to move away."

Minnesota. Had Francine traveled all the way from Minnesota to Cape Cod, hooked up with Caleb Thurman in Wellfleet, gotten pregnant, had the baby, bought an "inferior" basket to use as a carrier, then landed on the Vineyard in search of support? The prospect seemed convoluted, even to Annie, who made a living by making stuff up.

But Isabella Wright had had friends here. It was over twenty years ago, but could it be the island connection?

After searching for words that would sound like small talk and not interrogation, Annie said, "Losing touch with classmates often happens over time. Did you and Isabella keep track of each other?"

"For a while. Then she went to college, got married, you know, the usual."

"Did she ever come back?"

"Once, for a reunion. Her husband's family was in some kind of banking. I got the impression they were pretty well off."

"Did she have kids?" Annie felt compelled to ask, though if Isabella's in-laws were in "some kind of banking," it seemed doubtful that she'd had a daughter who'd wound up as a waitress at the Sunrise Café.

"Probably. I don't remember. We did lose touch after that. I looked for her on Facebook once, but came up with nothing. Probably because I can't remember her married name. I asked a couple of friends, but they couldn't, either."

"Well. It's interesting that you called her Bella."

"Only when we were small. By the time we reached high school she let it be known she preferred Isabella."

Oh. Darn. "But she never moved back?"

"No. Like you said, it happens."

Annie knew it also happened that her imagination could accelerate until it went out of control. The fact that she'd learned that a woman named Isabella had once been called Bella and had been raised on the Vineyard didn't mean anything. Anything at all.

Did it?

Helene finished feeding the baby and said it was time for her to check on the two patients who were waiting to deliver. But first, she insisted on giving Annie a few extra diapers. "I think you'll find these will fit better than the ones you've been using."

Annie thanked her and finally left, impatient to get home now, eager to talk to John in the morning. She'd tried to learn as much as she could, but her mission was over. And she was worn out from conjuring complications where they most likely did not exist.

Outside, winter blasted the parking lot with frigid gusts that whooshed up from Vineyard Sound and sprayed ice crystals across Annie's face. Grateful that Bella was asleep, she quickly snapped her into the car seat, closed the door, then jumped behind the wheel and cranked up the heat. It was after seven thirty: maybe if she took the shortcut down County Road, which was inland, the driving might be easier. Now that it really was winter, she didn't know how late the *On Time* did its back-and-forth run, but she hoped she'd make it before they shut down for the night. If they hadn't already stopped running because of the wind.

She passed a house that was lit up with a blaze of holiday lights, evergreens, and miniature houses—a Christmas village, Annie guessed. Cars lined both sides of the street: a chalkboard stood at the entrance to the driveway and read: COST OF ADMISSION—A CAN OF SOMETHING FOR ISLAND FOOD PANTRY.

Annie smiled. Her love for the island seemed to grow more every day, in spite of its quirks and entanglements.

When she reached the end of County Road, she went left onto Edgartown-Vineyard Haven Road. She didn't get far before a ribbon of flashing red lights stopped her in her path. A police cruiser and a tow truck blocked the road: an officer stood attentively, as if prepared to detour a vehicle if one came along. It was John.

He motioned for Annie to pull off to the side.

She put down her window. "What happened?"

"It's over now. SUV flipped. Went off the road. Speed. Alcohol. Ice grazing the pavement. Amazing the guy wasn't hurt. How'd you make out with our girl?"

As much as she wanted to tell him, she didn't want to do it then and there, not with so much to explain. "She wouldn't talk to me, either."

John sighed, then rubbed his hands together though he was wearing gloves. "Too bad our manpower is down because of winter. We might be able to get to the bottom of this faster."

Annie watched the white puffs of air that formed when his breath hit the cold. She knew if she held back now, she might be crossing the line into something that might be illegal, and definitely wouldn't be fair. It was time to tell all. And she knew it. She looked straight ahead. "John, I've learned a few more things that might help."

"Like what?"

"Let's not get into it here. Will you be around tomorrow?"

"I have a better idea. I'm off duty at eight. Meet me at Linda Jean's? I'll buy coffee."

The driver of the tow truck shouted something at John. He gave her a quick wave and went back to his duties.

Linda Jean's was a restaurant on Circuit Avenue in Oak Bluffs that was favored by locals for its casual atmosphere and good, basic food. Annie set Bella's basket on the bench in a booth and sat beside it. Thankfully, Bella was asleep and had barely stirred when she'd been moved.

Realizing she was hungry, Annie was gazing at the menu when John came in and sat down across from her.

"You were at the hospital a long time," he said. "Especially if you did all the talking."

"She was in radiology. They took her down for more tests."

"Did they bring her back?"

She closed the menu. "Yes. Her eyes were open. But she played possum."

He didn't bother with the menu. "You hungry? They close at eight, but I texted ahead. It's amazing how being a cop helps out sometimes."

Judging from what little time she'd spent with him, Annie doubted if he bent the rules too often. "The truth is, I could use a sandwich. I haven't eaten since this morning."

"Done." He called the waitress over. Annie ordered a fish sandwich; John, the meatloaf dinner.

"What about your daughters? Shouldn't you be home with them?"

He waved his hand as if brushing the thought away. "Change of plans. Teenage girls. What can I say." He had obviously mastered the art of concealing emotions. Annie recognized the behavior.

"Your mother must be upset."

"She'll forget about it once they're here next weekend. A week late, but she won't care." He leaned forward. "But enough about me. You need to tell me what you know."

Yes. She did. "John," she began, "I told you I was adopted, and that I've figured out that's one reason why Bella's mother picked me. I guess it's also why I've been on this quest to keep her out of foster care. If there's a chance to reunite her with her mother, I've wanted to do that before you had to place her with . . . strangers." She didn't remember how much of that she'd already told him, but decided it wouldn't hurt to repeat it. Then she told him about the bus driver at the ferry terminal, about looking in the high school yearbook for the Thurman boys, and about the picture of Caleb and the dimple in his chin. She saved the part about going to the Thurmans' house for last. And Caleb's denial that he was Bella's father, for last. Just as she finished, their supper arrived.

"I wish you'd told me before you went to the Thurmans'," John said as he started in on the meatloaf. "You shouldn't have gone alone. Who knows what might have happened. Stephen and Bonnie are good people, but in these situations—"

"Your father was with me."

John chewed. Swallowed. "Oh," he said. "Well. Guess I'll have to deal with him later."

She hoped he knew not to "deal" with Earl in front of Claire.

Her sandwich was terrific: the fish, fresh and flaky; the tartar sauce, the perfect amount. She delighted in it a minute before she said, "At the hospital just now, I found out something else. It's probably not connected, but apparently there was an islander named Isabella. The kids called her Bella in grammar school. In the note Francine left me, she said Bella had been named after her grandmother."

John set down his fork. "Who?"

"Bella's grandmother. If her real name was Isabella—"

"Not her," he answered flatly. "Francine. Who the hell is that?"

Annie blinked. "Oh. I forgot to tell you that part." She filled him in on the details of Caleb's story: that he'd met a girl who was a waitress at the Sunrise Café in Wellfleet, and that they'd gone for a walk one day, but that they barely were friends. "He did, however, remember that her name was Francine."

"And when did you learn this?"

"Um. Well, this afternoon."

"So you agreed to go to the hospital and told me you'd try and find out her name even though you already knew it?"

It was quiet in the restaurant. They were the only diners, and most of the help had no doubt gone home for the night. It was even quieter because John had stopped talking. Then he reached into his pocket, pulled out a couple of twenties, dropped them onto the table, and stood up. "We're done here," he said. At first she thought he must be talking to the waitress, but the waitress wasn't in sight, and he was looking straight at Annie.

"What?" she asked.

"I said *we're done.* You had no business getting involved any more than you already were. I was willing to risk a lot so you could keep the baby with you, mostly because my father wanted me to. But this time, you've gone too far. I don't know what you're up to, or why you're up to it, but this is not a story in one of your novels; it's a police investigation. You've abused our friendship. Go home, Annie. Someone will pick up the baby tomorrow."

He walked out of the restaurant without saying goodbye.

Chapter 27

The fire was out. If Bella hadn't been with her, Annie would have let it go, would have frozen to death during the night and not cared. No matter what her dad had taught her, sometimes a simple smile did not make the bad things go away. Especially when they were your fault.

After tucking the baby into her makeshift bed—knowing it was the last time she'd be allowed to do that—Annie took a shower, then wrapped up in a long flannel nightgown and a warm quilted robe. Because she hadn't arrived at the wharf until after nine, she'd had to wait nearly an hour for the next *On Time* to Chappy. At least now she knew that after six o'clock in the evening in winter, the ferry only ran on the hour until eleven; later than that, only for emergencies, until regular crossings resumed at six forty-five each morning. It had not been a good way to learn the schedule.

While waiting, she'd left the car running with the heat turned up; she'd brought Bella to the front seat where it was warmer. John would never know: he wouldn't have followed them there. He no doubt never wanted to see her again.

Despite the heater, Annie hadn't been able to shake the chill that had permeated her whole body. She'd sat in the darkness, holding Bella in her arms, gently rocking back and forth, her heart aching all the while. By the time the ferry appeared and she made her way home, she was numb inside and out.

She slipped into her big, fuzzy slippers now, went into the kitchen, and brewed a pot of tea—chamomile, which might or might not help her sleep.

Finally, she moved the rocker away from the Christmas tree, faced the woodstove, and slowly rocked, staring into the flames, wishing she could talk to Murphy. But even Murphy had deserted her now. Who could blame her?

Annie couldn't believe she'd been so . . . what was it? Reckless? Arrogant? When had she decided she was both entitled and equipped to control an important police investigation, or that John Lyons would appreciate her butting in? Had she become too impressed with Anne Sutton, best-selling novelist, who'd come to Martha's Vineyard, made quaint soaps for fun, and lived in a cozy cottage—a perfect press release for fans? Had she changed that much? And would her behavior now jeopardize her happiness on the island?

She'd changed when Brian was killed. Her soft edges had hardened, which was why she'd married Mark. It had been easier to dance and laugh than feel too much emotion, the kind that came with real love. When Mark had left, he'd taken what little had remained of her ability to be loving, trusting, vulnerable.

Until now. Until this.

Murphy had promised that one day Annie would find herself again, that she would *feel* again. Until now, she'd been able to do that only on paper, only in her books. Despite Earl's flattery about what she'd done for Bella, Annie had feared she'd been trying to become the heroine of her own story, the one who saved a baby from losing its mother. But she now knew that, in truth, she'd been trying to right the wrong that had been done to her.

And she had screwed up. Big time.

Staring up at the beamed ceiling, she sighed. "Well, Murphy, it looks as if I opened up my life and I got hit—smack, right in the face. *Right in the kissah,* as my dad would have said. I'm afraid I'm not very good at this thing called living. Not on my own. Not all alone." Tears rolled down her cheeks. Then her cell phone rang.

She almost didn't pick it up; no name showed on the screen. But she'd learned that a call at such a late hour often meant something bad had happened. So she clicked on.

"Annie? Did I wake you?"

Her stomach knotted; she recognized the voice. "Winnie?"

"Yes. I only have a minute. I'm using Barbara's phone because she gets better reception."

It took a second for Annie to remember who Barbara was. Winnie's sister-in-law: the nurse who worked at the hospital. In maternity. "Are you okay?" Annie asked. "Is everybody okay?"

"Yes. And I can't give you any details, because Barbara couldn't tell me. All that privacy stuff, you know?"

Annie took a sip of tea, hoping it would clear her head. "What is it, Winnie? What's wrong?"

"Nothing's wrong. Not really. But it's about that girl in the hospital. Bella's mother."

Setting her mug on the floor, Annie sat up straight. "Francine," she said. "Her name is Francine."

"Well, Barbara thought you should know something important. She said to tell you that everything is not as it seems."

Annie shook her head. "What's does that mean? Has Francine talked?"

"I don't know anything else. But it must really be important, or Barbara wouldn't have told me that much."

"That isn't much."

"I know. I hesitated calling, but she thought you should know."

"Because *everything is not as it seems?*"

"Her exact words."

Annie thought for a moment. "I saw Caleb Thurman today. He denied that he's Bella's father. Do you think that's what she meant?"

"Maybe. I don't know." Then she said she had to go, that Barbara was leaving for work and needed her phone.

Annie thanked her and hung up. Then she sat staring at the Christmas tree again, at the flickers of gold and red and sparkling silver, wondering what the cryptic message had meant and how she could possibly stay out of it now. And if she did not, what would be the worst thing that could happen?

In the morning, she dressed Bella again in the sweater Claire had made. After all, John—or someone else, like a be-spectacled, concerned social worker—would no doubt show up any minute to take her away: making sure the baby looked her best was the least Annie could do.

As for herself, Annie threw on an old, gnarly sweater and worn-out sweat pants—her go-to outfit for the messy art of soap-making. She brushed her teeth and hair and washed her face, but did not bother with makeup. After all, she wasn't going anywhere. During the long, restless night, she'd decided that, against her inclination, she would not get involved.

Her decision hadn't been easy: if she told John about the mysterious message that had come via Winnie from Barbara, she'd risk getting her friends into trouble. If Barbara had learned something, chances were that John—if he was half as competent as he appeared—would find out on his own. As for Annie, she'd already caused enough chaos, especially if Caleb wasn't Bella's father. She tried not to think about how upsetting her accusation must have been to the whole Thurman family.

And now, while Bella was on the quilt, playing with the fleece sheep, Annie filled a bag with diapers, formula, and the rest of the baby things. Then she retrieved the red ribbon from the original, supposedly inferior basket in her car, shaped it back into a bow and fluffed it, then tied it to the handle so it looked as festive and perky as it had the night Bella arrived.

In addition to not getting further involved, Annie decided she was not going to hand Francine's note over to John, in case she ever needed proof that Bella had been "given" to her, that she had not been a kidnapper. Who knew what John might do; who knew what anyone might?

No matter what, Annie was done meddling. The Vineyard was her home now; she was too happy there to want to rock whatever boat was in the harbor. She only hoped that, in time, Earl and Claire, and maybe even John, would forgive her for having been such a fool.

The sounds of tires crunching down the clamshell driveway broke into her thoughts. Which was fine. She needed to be done with this.

After taking a few slow breaths, Annie stood up, went to Bella, picked her up. "Come on, sweet girl," she said. "Time to face your future, whatever it might hold."

But when Annie opened the door, she didn't see an Edgartown police cruiser. Her visitor was Earl, not John. Perhaps he'd stopped to wish Bella goodbye. Or to do John's bidding for him.

She welcomed him in.

He took off his cap as if he were in a restaurant or a church. Maybe even a funeral.

"Did John send you to do his dirty work?"

He looked perplexed. "Depends on what you call 'dirty work.'"

"Taking Bella. Isn't that why you've come?"

"In a manner of speaking, yes."

Her heart cracked again. She was surprised anything was left inside of her to break. "She's almost ready."

With Bella riding on her hip, Annie went into the bedroom, took the white fleece blanket from the bureau drawer, then turned to head back into the living room. Earl was standing in the middle of the doorway.

"You're coming, too," he said.

She stopped. "What?"

"John called this morning. He's going to bring Caleb to the hospital for a meet and greet with Bella's mother. He said it might go better if Bella was there. But because nobody knows how her mother will react, he thought it might be easier for the baby if you went, too. If you were holding Bella. You know?"

"Me?" Annie asked. "He wants me there?" She knew she must sound daft. "But last night . . ."

Earl offered a dismissive wave. "John told me about the mix-up. That you told him about our visit to the Thurmans. He was put out with you; I think he was mostly jealous that he hadn't found out about them first. That, plus the fact that this case is extra hard on him on account of it hits home for him. Because his ex took away his girls. I pointed that out to him."

Annie had a suspicion that he'd done more than "point that out" to his son. She looked down at her clothes. "I should change."

"You're fine. He wants to get this done. Before Caleb can sneak off island. We were lucky it was windy last night—the big ferry shut down its last few runs. John went to the Thurmans' before the crack of dawn and took Caleb to the station to question him about Francine's suicide attempt and to find out what he knows about Bella being abandoned."

Endangered, Annie remembered from her teaching days was the word social services would have used.

"Not that John thinks Caleb did anything illegal," Earl continued. "But I think he's trying to scare the kid into telling him what he knows. They'll meet us at the hospital. So get your coat. Time's a-wastin'."

On the way out, Annie grabbed mascara and a tube of lipstick and stuffed them into her purse.

They were the first ones there. Annie and Earl sat in the waiting room where Annie had been the night before. A different nurse was behind the counter; she was young and pretty, with neatly braided hair and stunning aquamarine eyes. She nodded when they entered as if they were expected, but turned back to her work without saying a word.

Earl scratched his chin stubble; Annie knitted her fingers; Bella fussed, wriggled, cried.

Twenty minutes later, after Annie had tried, failed, succeeded, then failed again to keep Bella quiet, Caleb arrived. John followed closely behind as if ready to pounce if the boy dared to move one way or another. Another officer walked behind John, one hand on his belt, resting next to his gun. Annie wondered if he was preparing to shoot Caleb, Francine, or her. When they reached Annie and Earl, John touched Caleb's shoulder; the three-man procession halted.

"All set?" John asked Annie, forgoing a *hello*. He looked grim and a little gray. Maybe he'd had as little sleep as she'd had.

Annie stood and picked up Bella's basket. Earl remained seated.

But as Annie, John, and Caleb stepped toward the corridor, the nurse behind the desk bolted up. "Stop right there," she barked in a tone that sliced the silence and caused them—even the uniformed police officers—to halt. "Two at a time," she added. "No exceptions. And five minutes. That's all."

Caleb looked dazed, but then, he had since he'd walked in.

John's jaw tightened; the cords that stretched down both sides of his neck protruded. "Gail," he said, "this is official business."

She shook her head and returned to her chair. "Sorry. No exceptions."

With a small twinge, Annie wondered how well John knew the nurse.

After a heavy sigh, John went around the counter. He leaned down and spoke to Gail in low tones that Annie couldn't hear. The nurse blinked, then flicked her eyes from John's, her gaze landing on Caleb, who was staring, blankly, at her.

Well, Annie wanted to say to Earl with a hint of sarcasm, *we're off to a pleasant start.*

John came back and told Annie she and Bella could not go in. "She's making too much noise."

But Annie didn't want to be left out of what was about to happen. "Maybe if I hold her?" She scooped up the baby and brought her to her shoulder. As if Bella knew the importance of their visit, her cries turned into soft whimpers.

John handed the empty basket to Earl, then motioned for Caleb and Annie to follow him to room three. Annie walked swiftly, patting the baby on the back, half-expecting Nurse Gail to bark at them again.

They made it without further disturbance. Inside the glass-walled room, Francine was in bed, staring out the window. Her breathing seemed steady.

"Francine Gardner?" John asked.

Annie was startled. She had no idea how he'd learned the young woman's last name.

Francine didn't move.

"Francine, I am Sergeant John Lyons, Edgartown Police Department. I understand you're feeling better. We only need to bother you for a few minutes. First I need you to identify your baby. Then I need you to identify her father."

Annie wasn't sure if John was overstepping legal authority by trying to get the girl to identify the father of her baby—maybe he wanted to determine if the couple had conspired to endanger Bella. Then Annie remembered that John knew what he was doing. And that he hadn't pretended he was actually going to arrest anyone. Yet.

Still, Francine didn't move.

John looked at Annie, who couldn't imagine how atrocious she must look despite the mascara and the swish of lipstick she'd put on in Earl's truck. She walked to the other side of the bed and stood between Francine and the window, in the girl's line of sight.

"Hello, Francine," she said in a hushed voice. "I think Bella wants to see you."

The girl looked more tired than she had the day before. Her lower lip trembled; her huge brown eyes became glossy.

"Please?" Annie asked. She held Bella down so Francine could see her clearly.

A small gasp slipped from Francine's throat; she made eye contact with Annie. Then she pulled her arms from beneath the sheet. Careful not to jar the IV needle on the back of her right hand, she reached up and took the baby. She drew her to her chest and closed her eyes. Bella stopped whimpering.

"Francine?" John asked again. "Caleb is with us. He's come to see you. Will you say hello to him?"

She turned her head toward them.

"Hey," Caleb said. "Remember me?"

Annie couldn't see Francine's reaction.

"Please?" Caleb pleaded. "Will you please tell these people I'm not that baby's fucking father?"

Before the girl could answer—if she were going to answer—
a woman walked into the room. She wore a crisp white coat.
"I'm Dr. Richards," she said. "This woman is my patient. I understand you refused to adhere to our regulation of only two
visitors per room."

Aha, Annie thought, *John wasn't so convincing after all.*

"Police business," John said. "Right now we're reuniting a
baby with her parents."

The doctor's lips pursed, and she squinted. "I don't think so."

"Please—" John began again, but the doctor raised her
hand.

"I believe you are mistaken. And whatever story you come
up with won't work, Officer. Believe me, we've heard them all."

"That's *Sergeant,*" John replied, his cheeks coloring with a
dark shade of annoyance. "Sergeant John Lyons. And, no, there
is no mistake." He pointed to Bella. "This baby is your patient's
daughter. And this young man"—he pointed to Caleb—"is its
father."

The doctor grinned. "As I said, you are mistaken. Now,
please leave."

"She's right," Francine said suddenly, her voice weak and
raspy. All eyes in the room swiveled to the bed. "I've never had
a baby," Francine continued. "I'm not Bella's mother." Her eyelids closed.

The silence that followed was punctuated by the beep-
beep of a monitor.

Then John cleared his throat. "Francine?" he asked. "If
you're not Bella's mother, who is?"

But the girl stayed perfectly still and didn't, wouldn't answer.

"Bella does not deserve this," John said emphatically. He
put his hands on his hips as if daring her not to reply.

Though Francine didn't move, her small chest started to heave. Then it stopped. And started. And stopped. Completely.

An alarm screeched, like a piercing, electric jolt. Green numbers flashed on the digital screens that were hooked to the wires connected to Francine's arms. A bell rang. And rang.

"Out!" the doctor yelped. "All of you. Get out right now!"

Chapter 28

It made no sense.

Back in the corridor, John told Caleb to go home. "But don't you dare leave the island, or we'll have your butt."

Caleb lopped away, a boy who had been scolded for doing . . . nothing, apparently.

Annie paced back and forth, trying to calm Bella, who'd started screaming when the alarm went off.

"Come on," John said, "let's get my dad. I'll send Lou back to the station—he's on duty, but I'm not. Let's go to Linda Jean's and try and figure this thing out." He rushed toward the waiting area, leaving Annie stumped.

Let's get my dad?

Let's go to Linda Jean's?

Was this the same man who, mere hours ago, had told her she'd abused their friendship—a friendship she didn't even really know that they'd had?

"Bella," she murmured, "one word of advice from your Auntie Annie. Be wary of any man's word. *Any* man. Except, of course, your father . . . if we ever find him."

She realized this must have been what Winnie's odd phone call had been about. *Everything isn't as it seems*, Barbara's message had been. It now looked as if that was true. Annie had been so focused on trying to find Bella's father, it hadn't occurred to her that Francine might not be her mother. But Barbara was a nurse. Right there at the hospital. Down the hall, around the corner. Perhaps she'd learned that Francine hadn't had a baby. Perhaps that was why she'd told Winnie the message was important.

Wow, Annie thought, as the news started to sink in.

She supposed this meant that the island woman named Isabella—Annie's far-fetched deduction—wasn't Bella's grandmother after all. So much for simple solutions. And so much for Annie thinking she could be a sleuth.

"Annie?" John called from the far end of the hallway. "Let's go."

They sat in the same booth where they'd sat the night before, which now seemed like eons ago. Earl had convinced John to let him take the baby back to Chappy: he'd said that two heads would be clearer than four, on account of one of the four being a fussy baby. No one pointed out that by then Bella was napping. Annie suspected Earl's real motive was to make sure John and Annie had some time alone—maybe John had told Earl more about their "mix-up" than Earl had revealed to Annie. She was beginning to realize that, though the island often held sacred secrets for generations, the everyday ones were sometimes up for grabs.

She toyed with her napkin, a little shaken by whatever had happened to Francine, hoping that, whether or not she was Bella's mother, the girl was going to be okay.

"I'm sorry I overreacted last night," John said after they'd ordered coffee and scallops that the waitress promised had come from off Cape Pogue early that morning. "Most of all, I never should have said the part about you abusing our friendship. Because I don't feel that way at all."

Annie toyed with her water glass, wishing she weren't stuck on the Edgartown side of the harbor in her soap-making clothes, with hardly any makeup, and without her car. "I only wanted to keep Bella safe as long as I could. But you were right, John. I never considered the legal ramifications. I got too close to the situation, and I let my emotions get in the way." It would have been nice if he contradicted her confession, but he did not. She supposed she couldn't blame him for that, either. "Anyway, it seems now as if it's all been for naught. We're right back where we started, with absolutely no clue as to this baby's history, except that she showed up on my doorstep in the middle of a blizzard and looks a lot like a young woman who isn't her mother and like a boy who's not her father."

John shook his head. "No. Thanks to you, we have much more."

The coffee arrived. Annie no longer used cream or sugar. Though she always had coffee and tea on hand in the cottage, she'd given up lamenting that the Chappy store was only open in the summer. Instead, her taste buds had adapted to going without the extras—which was more convenient than taking the trip to Edgartown if she ran out. "What do you mean you have more?" That time, she was careful to say *you* without echoing his *we*. The more detached she could get, the better off she'd be.

"You know the girl's name is Francine. Which, by the way, I already knew, because my team found her purse and her ID at the Littlefields'. That's how I also knew her last name is Gardner. And, yes, she's from Wellfleet, or at least, that's what it says on her driver's license. We know that most likely because you are adopted she brought the baby to you; that maybe she thought you'd be more understanding than someone else. What we didn't know was her link to the Thurmans. To be honest, I'm not sure how, or if we ever could have learned that. You also told us that, whether or not Caleb is the father, he does, in fact, know her. He knows her, and, good God, the baby really does look like him. As a cop, I don't—I can't—believe in coincidences." He stirred in a couple of spoonfuls of sugar. "No, Annie, you've been helpful. You really have."

She sipped her coffee, wondering if she would challenge his renewed opinion of her if she told him about the other piece of information that had seemed minor at the time. Then she decided that since they didn't know who Bella's mother was, it was more important to worry about the baby and not about herself. "Speaking of coincidences," she said, "I might know something else."

John leveled his pearl-gray eyes on her; his jaw tightened, and his lips slammed shut as if he were afraid of what he might say.

"When it happened," Annie continued, "I discounted it. Even more now that I know you found her ID. But a woman in Menemsha named Nancy Clieg makes baskets like the one Francine carried her in." There was no need to drag Winnie into the drama, especially since it would only add to the confusion. "I went to see Nancy even before I told your father about Bella. She said the basket was too shoddy to be one of hers."

John snorted, as if he knew the woman so her reaction had come as no surprise. "Go on," he said.

"She'd been told that someone on the Cape had been making fakes and selling them in Provincetown. That was one of the things that led me to the ferry terminal, where I found the bus driver who confirmed that Francine had come from there. Once I knew she had, the story about the basket seemed insignificant. But now that we know Francine isn't Bella's mother, well, whoever bought it no doubt bought the basket in P'town. Which, as you probably know, isn't far from Wellfleet. Maybe Bella's real mother bought it. Or her father. Anyway, maybe you could track them down that way."

He drank his coffee, then set down his mug, while Annie's heart started to thump-thump again. "We could have used that earlier."

"I know. And I'm sorry. But I never considered that Francine wasn't Bella's mother."

Pausing another moment, John looked around the restaurant. Annie couldn't tell if he was assessing the facts, or if he was planning to bolt from her again. He turned back to his mug of coffee and sighed. "Anything else?"

The scallops arrived, giving Annie another minute to gather her thoughts. "Yes." She focused on her plate so she wouldn't have to look him in the eyes. "I told you that, in Francine's original note, she said the baby was named after her grandmother. Last night, after you left the hospital, I went to the maternity department. Bella was hungry, and I needed to heat a bottle for her. A nurse named Helene helped me out. While we chatted, she said she'd been in school with a girl named Isabella Wright—and that they'd called her Bella in grammar school. She moved off island with her family right after her high school graduation in 1995. Anyway, Isabella could be Francine's mother—she'd be the right age. When I saw you later, I didn't think it mattered anymore because, well, I still thought Bella was Francine's daughter."

He lowered his eyes and dove into the scallops. "Doesn't matter what you thought. You should have told me."

She looked down at her plate, but her appetite had waned. "I know. And I'm sorry, John. I should have told you everything. I should never have tried to solve this myself—I might have wound up costing Bella a lot. At least Francine is still alive, but you've lost precious time."

He nodded. "But that's how a case goes sometimes. There are often lots of details that don't seem related. Sometimes they are; most times they aren't. That's why we put them all into the file. But it's okay, Annie. We'll figure this out."

She appreciated his words, though his voice was a tad flat and unconvincing.

Then he added, "I still need your help. Will you go back to the hospital? Hopefully, whatever happened with Francine—a seizure, an 'episode,' or whatever it was—wasn't serious. I still think you're our best chance to get her to talk. In spite of all that's happened, she trusted you enough to leave the baby with you. Besides, once the doctor says she can leave the hospital, where's Francine going to go? We can't just give Bella back to her. For one thing, she tried to kill herself. We don't know how unstable she is. Also, she left her on a stranger's doorstep in the middle of the blizzard. Which screams 'child endangerment.' "

Yes, Annie thought, that was the term she remembered. As much as she might want to disagree, Annie could not. And she was eager to check on Francine. No matter what—or who— the girl was to Bella, Francine didn't deserve any more pain.

Besides, how could she refuse John? She needed to make friends, not adversaries on the island. Her only choice would be to go back to Boston. But there was no longer anything— or anyone—waiting for her there.

After they finished their meals, John brought Annie back to the hospital. He said he'd go to the station and write up the rest of the information she'd provided, and then he'd start working on the leads. But he told her to call him if she learned anything. Even if it seemed insignificant.

She promised she would.

She went upstairs to ICU, where she was met with a surprise: the nurse at the desk said Francine had been transferred downstairs to a regular room. Annie frowned. "Didn't she have a problem this morning?"

"She's fine," the nurse replied with a small sneer. "She held her breath so the monitor would go off. She said it seemed like the fastest way to make all of you go away." Either the nurse

didn't care about the patient's privacy, or she was annoyed that
Francine had been devious.

The good news, however, was that Francine had talked.

Annie thanked the nurse, went down to the first floor, and
found the girl's room. The television was on, but the sound was
down. And Francine was sleeping, peacefully, as if she were
Bella. Annie dropped onto a visitor's chair in the corner of the
room, half hidden by a curtain. She folded her arms across her
gnarly sweater and waited.

The room was barren except for sterile-looking hospital
things, though not as many as were in the ICU. There were no
flowers, no cards stuck to the corkboard under the TV, no personal items like slippers or a robe. There was only the small girl,
asleep in the bed, without friends—without anything, as far as
Annie could tell. She wondered if the staff had laundered her
clothes and hung them in the narrow closet. If not, perhaps she
could offer to do that. Francine would need clothes when she
went . . . where?

Annie sat, quietly thinking, considering what she could do
to help the girl. She was so quiet that, when a young man entered the room, he didn't see her in the corner. She had no
idea who he was.

He was fairly tall for a teenager. His buzz cut revealed dark
hair; his sneakers looked new; his blue parka had ski lift tags
fastened to the zipper pull. He moved close to the bed and
bent down. "Francine?" he whispered.

From where Annie sat she could see Francine's eyes flutter
open. "Go away," she said.

"Do you remember me?"

No answer.

"Jesus, you have a baby."

She didn't reply.

"What are you going to do?"

"I don't know."

"Are you going to tell?"

Annie stayed as still as a stone, as immovable as one of the ancient geological formations up island at Lucy Vincent Beach, hoping beyond hope that she wouldn't be noticed.

Francine gave no response.

"You'll ruin everything."

Francine was silent. Then she said, "Everything's already ruined. My mother's dead. My father is, too. I have no one. Except Bella. A baby shouldn't have to live with a loser like me."

The boy shuffled his feet on the polished linoleum. "I'm sorry your mother's dead."

She didn't answer.

"Please, Francine. I'll get you money. I don't know how, but I'll figure something out."

"Money isn't going to help. I'll still be alone."

"Money helps everything. That's what my mom always says." He reached up and ran his hand across his buzz cut. As he did, he caught sight of Annie. He snapped his head toward her; she saw his face clearly. "Holy shit," he said and darted from the room.

But Annie hadn't needed to hear his crude language to know who it must be. Though they weren't identical like Murphy's twins, the boy resembled Caleb Thurman. In a flash, the pieces swirled as if in a kaleidoscope. Then they formed a total picture in Annie's mind.

Without hesitation, she pulled out her cell phone and called John. She wasn't going to withhold this kind of information. Not for a second.

When Francine heard Annie's voice on the phone, she raised up on one elbow. She stared across the room at her, her sad eyes locked with fear. Annie told John to pick her up at the main hospital entrance. She added that he should not come alone. Then she hung up and went over to the bed.

"Francine," she said softly, "you don't have to say anything.

But I want you to know that this will be all right. You'll be all right. And so will Bella. No one will hurt either one of you. That's a promise."

She went out to the hall and ran upstairs to check out one last detail. It only took a minute to confirm her suspicion.

Then she walked briskly toward the main entrance. She didn't know if John had figured it out yet, too, but Annie was now certain she knew who Bella's mother—and her father—were.

Chapter 29

Annie climbed into the police cruiser, no longer caring what her clothes or her makeup-less face must look like. She was blissful that she finally knew the answers.

"Where are we going?" John asked.

"Are you alone?" she asked, disappointed. She'd been concerned they'd need some sort of backup like in the cop shows on TV. She suspected that few people enjoyed a confrontation with law enforcement.

"Tomorrow's New Year's Eve. A couple of revelers already went crazy out on South Beach. Hank and Lou are taking care of it."

Small town. Small police force that swelled in summer months in tandem with the heat and crowds. As John had already told her, until then, the force was stretched thin. "Okay, then," she said, "let's hope for the best."

John smiled. "I certainly will, once you tell me where we're going."

"To the Thurmans. You know the address."

His eyes narrowed. He squinted. "But Francine said . . ."

"I know what she said. That she isn't Bella's mother. So we

now believe that Caleb told the truth—he isn't the father. That is correct."

John took his foot off the brake and drove down the hill to the road. "You think she's the brother's baby? What's his name . . . Michael? Well, if Michael's the father, who's the mother?"

"Michael came to visit Francine this morning. They had an interesting conversation. They didn't see me in the room."

"And? Did he confess?"

"He does resemble Caleb, though he does not have the dimple. And though I know beans about DNA, I suppose it's possible. Or, of course, Bella could have gotten the dimple straight from her father."

"Oh, God," John groaned. "Well, we know for sure Bella's father isn't Clark. We got confirmation this morning that he was out on the *Jean Marie* fishing at George's Banks most of last winter. He wouldn't have had time to be over on the Cape."

Annie let it slide that she'd already discounted Clark as Bella's father. "No. She isn't Clark's daughter."

"Then . . . ?"

"Well, though I've never met him, I'm willing to bet that Caleb and Michael's father—Stephen—has a dimple on his chin."

John blinked. "Stephen? You think Bonnie's husband is Bella's father?"

Annie nodded.

"Wait a minute. If Stephen's her father, who's her mother?"

"That's the easy part. Bella's mother is Francine's mother, too. I think Bella and Francine are half sisters. Which accounts for why the baby has Francine's sad, soulful eyes."

John turned south onto County Road. "You sure about this?"

"Completely. I told you about Isabella Wright—the woman I learned about from the nurse, Helene, in the maternity department. Isabella moved with her family to Minnesota right after high school graduation in 1995. Helene had said all the kids had been upset. After I left Francine today, I went back to maternity. Helene was working. I asked if she remembered the first name of Isabella's mother. She said it was also Isabella, which was why she'd called her daughter Bella until the daughter refused. Then I asked if Isabella, the younger one, had a boyfriend before the family moved. She did. It was Stephen Thurman. And he was really upset when she left. I don't know the details, but I'd be willing to bet Stephen does."

"Holy crap," Sergeant John Lyons said with a broad grin. "So there's a definite connection with Francine being from the Cape and Stephen going there with his boys . . . but how did Isabella and Francine get there from Minnesota? And why?"

"I have no idea. I know that Isabella married a guy whose family was in banking. Based on Francine's age, she must have been theirs. But that's all I know."

"Okay, we know for certain that Francine was living in Wellfleet a year ago. So let's start with that—and the Sunrise Café." He picked up his phone and called the police station. He fired off a few questions, then asked for a callback, ASAP. When he hung up, he turned back to Annie. "Let's go. I'll question Thurman, but jump in whenever you want. I'd love to see him grovel to a woman. I can't stand the son of a bitch."

Annie laughed. "Seriously?"

"Stephen convinced his father, Billy—who was my dad's friend and a great guy—that he should let Stephen take over the books for the painting business. He'd taken an accounting class somewhere off island and thought he knew more than God about finances. But he was cheap. He screwed both seasonal people and islanders. And he wouldn't let Billy buy new equipment. When the old man fell off a ladder and was killed, it was because the damn thing was too old to still be in use. In-stead of taking any blame for his dad's death, Stephen collected a boatload of insurance and bought the house on Scallop Cove Road. He never could have afforded the place otherwise. Or to send his kids off island to college. On top of everything, he's a crappy painter."

By the time they turned onto Scallop Cove Road, someone at the station called John back. He said "Yes" and "Uh-huh" a few times, and he nodded. As he pulled into the Thurmans' driveway, he gave Annie a thumbs-up sign.

And Annie knew that Stephen Thurman was about to be brought down a notch. She was happy she'd be there as a witness.

Bonnie opened the back door. "Again?" she asked. "Which one do you want now?"

Annie knew that the woman would not like John's answer. "Is your husband home, Bonnie?"

She let them in but didn't ask them to sit down. Then she disappeared from the kitchen.

Annie and John stood in the doorway that led into the kitchen. They didn't speak. It was interesting to Annie that John had what she'd heard was called an "island grudge." She supposed there were plenty of those scattered around, like the one Winnie had with Nancy Clieg.

Stephen arrived. An angry shade of red tinted his cheeks; his hands were shoved into the pockets of his jeans. Annie hoped he didn't have a gun in there. She was, however, able to see a distinctive dimple in the center of his chin.

"John," he said directly. He did not address Annie.

John removed his hat and pushed back his hair. "Hey, Stephen. I suppose you know why we're here."

The man pulled his hands from his pockets—thankfully, there was no gun—and folded his arms across his broad chest. "Actually, no. Except I heard you've been accusing one of my boys of knocking up some girl from the Cape."

"The girl has a name. Francine Gardner. I believe you met her last Christmas when you took the boys fishing in Wellfleet? She was a waitress at the Sunrise Café?"

Stephen emitted what could have been a guffaw. "A waitress? Jesus, John. Is that the best you can do? Do you know how many girls have waited on me over the years?"

"Well, you might not remember her, but perhaps you knew her mother?"

Annie couldn't stand keeping quiet another second. "Her name was Isabella," she said. "You knew her years ago on the island. When her name was Isabella Wright."

The red tint of his cheeks washed out to a gray pallor.

Annie stepped forward. "I understand you were high school sweethearts?"

Before he could agree or deny it, John interrupted. "It was too bad when Isabella moved away, wasn't it? Then she got married. After her husband died, she moved to the Cape. Where she was the manager at the Sunrise Café. In Wellfleet. Where it just so happens you took your boys last Christmas vacation." While he talked, John's gaze penetrated Stephen's body language and every flinch that the son of a bitch's eyes were making. Then he looked at Annie again. "Annie, would you do the honors and tell Mr. Thurman about Bella?"

Annie smiled. "My pleasure. I think we'd all like to know, Mr. Thurman, if you knew that you'd—how did you call it?—knocked her up? Not Francine, but Isabella? Did you know you are the father of her baby? A sweet little girl named Bella. After her grandmother. Oh, perhaps you didn't know that Isabella Wright had been named after her mother, who turned out to be Bella's grandmother. Don't you love how island folks respect tradition?" She knew she sounded snarky, but she couldn't help it.

Bonnie shoved Stephen out of the way and pointed a finger in John's face. "Get out of my house," she hissed. "Both of you. I'm sick of you people and your accusations. Unless you have a reason to arrest anyone, get out of my house right now."

The four adults stood there, eyes jumping from one to another.

Annie had a hard time believing that this Bonnie Thurman was the same woman who'd been so nice when she'd been there with Earl.

John turned to leave.

Then Stephen held out an arm and stopped him. "No," he said. "Wait. It's true. It's all true."

Bonnie's fists clenched. Then she shrieked, rolled one shoulder back and then forward, and socked her husband in the jaw.

"Whoa," John said. He moved quickly and grasped Bonnie's arm. "Maybe the four of us can sit and talk about this like civilized people?"

Bonnie glared at John; John glared at Bonnie, his grip remaining on her arm. She turned her eyes from him; he let go and relaxed.

They moved into the living room. Stephen led the way, rubbing his jaw where Bonnie's punch had landed. John walked behind him, one arm resting on Bonnie's shoulder. Annie went last.

They breathed. They sat. Stephen sagged into a big leather chair. John and Bonnie took the sofa. Annie perched on a small ottoman, because laundry was piled on the other chairs.

Stephen put his hands on the armrests and began to pick at the tightly rolled piping along the edges. "I had no idea. Not 'til this morning."

His wife said nothing.

"It was when we split up. Remember? Last Christmas?"

"As if I could forget," Bonnie seethed.

"You told me not to come back."

"But you did. You bastard. After you'd been fucking a . . . a *waitress*."

Annie was embarrassed now, as if she'd walked into a domestic scene that she had no business being in.

"Once," Stephen replied. "Only once."

Bonnie laughed. "Only once? The same way you fucked Laureen? Your own brother's wife?"

Good Lord. Annie would have done just about anything to slip out the side door unnoticed then, to leave the Thurmans to disentangle their very personal issues.

Then Bonnie's eyes narrowed with piercing accusation. "Do our boys know? God, Stephen. Did you flaunt this in front of them?"

Stephen stood, walked to the fireplace, and pressed his forehead against the mantle. "They did. But none of us knew about any baby."

Bonnie put her hands up to her face and bent forward, almost down to her knees.

The back of Stephen's neck was crimson now. Annie wondered if he might grab the poker, whip around, and lash out at them all. Would John be able to yank his gun from its holster and stop him before it was too late? Before their skulls were bashed in or their faces disfigured? She knitted her fingers together and tried to breathe slowly, tried to calm her overactive imagination. Then she said, "I know this must be difficult for both of you. But can we please remember there's an innocent baby involved?"

A moment passed before Stephen said, "Where's her mother? Where's Isabella?"

"She's dead," Annie said. She took grim satisfaction in the silence that filled the room.

After a few seconds, John said, "Did you know that Francine Gardner—Isabella's other child, the one we guess was her dead husband's daughter—is the girl who jumped off the Chappy ferry? That she tried to kill herself because she didn't know where to go or what to do with the baby now that her mother's dead?"

Stephen turned around and drew his hands down his face. "Jesus."

Bonnie started to cry.

"You've probably heard that the courts frown on birth fathers who shirk paying child support. Chances are, it will be easy for me to get a warrant for your DNA," John said. "So you might as well tell us what happened. You knew that Isabella was in Wellfleet, didn't you? Please don't insult us by saying it was a coincidence."

Stephen moved to the wide window that looked over the lawn and out to the cove. "Yeah. Isabella has an older sister named Marty. Marty hated it in Minnesota. Within a year after they moved, she came back east to the Cape. Didn't come back to the island, though. She said she no longer wanted her life to be at the mercy of the boats. Anyway, she met Bill Hastings— the guy who owns the Sunrise. Meanwhile, in Minnesota, Isabella married some wimp. A rich boy who never measured up to his daddy's standards. When the daddy died, they learned that he'd been cut out of the will. The guy even gave away all his assets so they couldn't contest it. The rich boy was no longer worth shit. So he killed himself. They had one kid— Francine. By then Isabella's father was gone, too, and her mother was a pain in the ass. So Isabella moved to the Cape to be near Marty. She needed a job; Bill gave her one. When Francine got a little older, she worked there, too."

"When did all this happen?"

Stephen shrugged. "Five, maybe six years ago. Francine was twelve, I think, when they arrived. She's a quiet, mousy little thing. Must take after her weasel of a father." He guffawed, as if he were a bully.

"Did you know that Isabella got pregnant?"

"Hell, no. My boys told me this morning. The way I figure

it, she kept it from me because she didn't want to screw up my marriage. Not that it was in any great shakes at the time. But Isabella was like that. She really liked my boys and didn't want to mess them up. She was real thoughtful. She always had been."

Bonnie stood up and left the room.

John took a long breath. "It sounds like you'd seen her more often than last Christmas."

His shoulders slumped; his head now drooped. Stephen Thurman actually looked smaller than he had before, as if his conscience might have shriveled his bravado. "Look. She went through a lot. We had a good thing when we were kids, you know? Her folks didn't like me; they said I wasn't good enough for her, but the wimp was." He waved an arm around the room. "Like this wouldn't have been good enough? Christ, I paid six eighty-five for it, and now it's worth over a million. That wouldn't have been good enough for his precious daughter?"

Annie decided that, no matter that he was Bella's father, Stephen Thurman was a jerk who had even inflated the valve of his real estate as if they could not learn the truth. She silently praised John for not commenting that the money for the house had come from the insurance from the painting business.

"When I started taking the boys fishing over there on school vacations, Bonnie was glad to be rid of us."

"And you were glad to reconnect with Isabella," John said.

He shrugged with nonchalance. "That was how it started. She called to tell me when she and her kid got to the Cape."

Annie wondered where men like him came from and how they often managed to have a decent family that they took for granted; a wife like Bonnie; boys like Michael and Caleb, who'd been willing to protect their father from his indiscretion. She also wondered what on earth Francine's mother had seen in him. Then again, Annie's own parents might have asked the same thing about Mark if they'd still been alive when he'd come into her life. They'd loved Brian, but they would have had a hard time even liking Mark.

John stood up. "Well, Francine is in the hospital if you want to bother to see her. She's going to be okay, not that you asked. As for your daughter, she's safe for now. Where she'll end up is yet to be determined." He turned to Annie. "Come on, Annie. I've had enough of the stink in this house."

Some people prayed to God. But Francine prayed to her mother. "Please, Mommy. Get me out of here."

Then she cried again, because she no longer believed that her mother—or anyone—was listening.

Chapter 30

"I need a drink," John said, once they were back in the cruiser and heading into town.

"I have wine at my house," Annie said. "And clean, decent clothes. I'd give just about anything to change into clean, decent clothes."

He laughed. "Let's pick my truck up at the station. Then get the hell over to your place." On the way out of the house, he rested a hand on Annie's shoulder. They walked to the passenger side of the cruiser, and he opened the door for her as if she were a real lady and not a woman in gnarly, soap-splattered clothes.

"I bought all this before the blizzard," Annie said, showing John her collection of chardonnay. "I guess I'd feared I'd be snowed in 'til April."

She'd called Earl and Claire to be sure Bella was all right. Then John had taken the phone and told his dad everything that had happened and that Annie had figured out that Stephen Thurman was Bella's father. "So we decided to celebrate," John said. "Would you and Mom keep Bella for the night? We might stay out late." He thanked him and hung up, then looked at Annie. "I thought you might need a break from the baby. Besides, you shouldn't drive to Mom and Dad's to pick her up if you've been drinking."

Annie laughed and handed him a corkscrew. "I'm going to get cleaned up. Glasses are to the right of the sink."

She took her time changing into jeans, a soft white sweater, and thick wool socks that were casual, but more stylish than her fuzzy slippers. She felt no need to rush—rushing about anything was not the island way. Then she added what she hoped was enough makeup so she looked attractive without sending a message she didn't know if she was ready to send. When she went back into the living room, John was sitting on the love seat. She noticed that he'd added wood to the stove and had turned on her Bose stereo—one of the few things she had kept from her life with Mark. Low strains of Thelonious Monk filled the room.

John handed her a glass of wine. "I kept the stereo on the same station where you had it. You're a jazz aficionado?"

She sat down, squeezing in beside him, his sturdy build and casual sprawl filling more than half the sofa. "Sometimes. You?"

He laughed. "Nope. I'm a country music boy." His honesty was endearing.

She clinked her glass to his. "Well, here's to music of any kind. And to solving Bella's brief, but mysterious past."

They took a drink, and then he asked, "You have no kids. That's surprising, watching you with Bella. You seem like a natural mom."

"Me? Well, hardly. Except for when I was a teacher, if that counts for anything."

"Did you want kids? Couldn't you have them?" Then he pressed his fingertips to his forehead. "Jeez. I can't believe I asked you that. Sorry. It's none of my business."

Annie was startled by the question, but not offended. In

fact, sitting in the cozy room, watching the fire glow and hearing the quiet jazz, she decided to tell him.

"I did want kids," she said. "But my first husband died too young. Our lives together had hardly started. And my second husband—well, I thought we both wanted them. I was wrong." Then she told John about the abortion, and decided to add something she'd never told anyone because it had been too humiliating. Like the letter from her birth mother, Annie hadn't even told Murphy. They were the only two secrets she'd kept from her best friend.

"When a couple of years had passed," she said, "I broached the subject about having kids with my husband again. That time, he agreed to try. But it never happened. I blamed myself; I figured the abortion had left me unable to have kids. I stayed with him, though, hoping God would forgive me. As for Mark, well, he was more interested in making money. After he disappeared, I found an old insurance document stuck in with his papers. It was a printout for a surgical procedure. A vasectomy. He'd had it soon after my abortion. But I never knew if he'd found out what I'd done."

The room was silent; Murphy, apparently, had no comment.

John took her hand. "God, what a creep."

"My sentiments exactly."

"And then he disappeared?"

"We were together almost ten years. I wasn't happy, but I was too confused to realize it. He left me with a ton of debt. That's when I started writing. I was lucky it worked." Her hand felt nice inside of John's. Nice. Safe.

Then he leaned over and kissed her. On the lips. Before she'd barely had a chance to breathe. She touched the corners of her mouth and laughed. "Well, that was unexpected."

"Unwanted? Or just unexpected?"

"Just unexpected."

"Good," he said. "Because I've been wanting to do that since the first time I saw you."

The kiss had been gentle, sweet, arousing. It had been a long, long time since she'd felt that way. And yet . . . and yet . . .

"John," she said, "I think you're terrific guy."

He groaned. "And here comes the 'but.'"

"But nothing," she replied. "But nothing at all. Except maybe can we take this slow? I was so burned by Mark . . ."

"I don't burn."

"I believe that about you."

"For what it's worth, I was burned, too."

"I thought as much."

He took a drink. "Okay. Slow is fine."

She nodded. "Thanks. Because I don't want to make any more mistakes."

They sat watching the fire while Thelonious serenaded them. Then John said, "Do you have some idea of how long you mean by 'slow'?"

Annie laughed again. "You are such a man."

"Yup. That I am."

"And once we start . . . well, this is a small island."

"Yup, it is."

"A small town, really."

"Yup, that, too."

"There are so many things to consider. Once people know . . . well, they'll know."

"Yup, they will."

She took another sip of wine and smiled a real, honest-to-goodness smile. Her heart began to pitter-patter, which was so much nicer than thumping. "How about now?" she asked. "Have we waited long enough?"

Before John could reply, footsteps clomped across the porch, and someone knocked on the front door.

It was Earl.

"Come in," Annie said, because what else could she do? The pitter-patter had slowed; reality had intervened in the form of a red-and-black-checkered wool shirt and a scruff of day-old whiskers. "Would you like a drink?"

"No, thanks. I promised Claire I'd get right back after I talked to you. I didn't mean to . . . interrupt."

She dragged one of the kitchen chairs to the living room. Earl sat, and Annie took the rocker across from John.

"Talk about what, Dad?" John asked.

Annie reminded herself there were no longer any secrets, that Earl was not going to tell her something that might hurt. She hoped.

"About the girl. Francine. What's she going to do when they release her? And what's going to happen to Bella? If the Thurmans don't take her, will she be handed over to the state?"

John leaned forward, placing his elbows on his knees in a way that seemed to help him think. "We haven't gotten that far, Dad. This only fell into place today. But Francine's history might be a problem. Because of the suicide attempt."

Earl took off his cap and smoothed the brim. "Well, your mother and I . . ." He looked at Annie. "Claire and I have a proposition. Our house is pretty big, you know. Too big for the two of us. And our granddaughters seem to be at the age when they'd rather stay off island. Maybe someday that will change, and we sure hope it does." He looked at John, then back to Annie. "But right now it seems to Claire and me that Francine and Bella might need a place to live. We figure it would help them if they had a solid home, and we've got that. Annie, you can spend a lot of time with Bella if you want, but we know you've got your soap-making. And, of course, your writing."

Oh, Annie thought. *Right. My writing. I must get back to that one of these days.* At least her editor hadn't called to bug her; she must have gone away for the holidays.

"We're around most of the time. Maybe Francine could get a job in Edgartown. Start a new life, you know?"

Annie was speechless. She remembered John's remark that people only moved there if they were in hiding or wanting to change their life.

"Well, Dad," John said, "that's quite a generous offer. Have you considered that she might have lots of emotional baggage?"

"Everybody's got some of that, son. And besides, this was your mother's idea. Sometimes she gets depressed, hanging out with an old coot like me. I think it would be good for her to have Francine and the baby to fuss over."

Annie almost asked, "Hey, what's wrong with me? Why can't they live with me?" But she knew Earl was right. The cottage was too small for both Francine and Bella, and unless the Thurmans stepped up, which seemed fairly doubtful, Earl and Claire had the best arrangement for them. Not to mention, it was time for Annie to get back to her life and her career. Besides, she'd see them often. And she could always babysit. Maybe John would join her, and, while Bella was asleep, they could sit in the living room and kiss as if they were schoolkids.

"I'll tell you what, Dad. How about if you and Annie go to the hospital tomorrow and see what Francine thinks? If she agrees, I'm sure we can at least work out something temporary."

Earl nodded and got up. "Annie? How about if I pick you up at eleven?"

She agreed.

Earl smiled, looked at John, and said, "I hope Francine wants to do this. It would be nice for me, too, to have some young energy scampering around the house again." He said goodbye to Annie, patted John on the shoulder, then went outside and climbed into his truck.

"Well," Annie said as she closed the door, "that was a surprise."

"Not really. Not if you think about my dad. And you might not have seen my mom's best side yet, but she's a lot like him. Wanting to help most anyone who comes along." He stood up, went to her, and slipped his arms around her waist. "I do think their idea is a good one for everyone concerned. Now . . . where were we?" He leaned down and kissed her again.

Annie lingered that way a moment, feeling the pitter-patter rise again. Then she pulled away and smiled. She touched his mouth with her finger, tracing the outline of his lips. "I believe we were discussing if we'd waited long enough."

"And?"

"And . . ." she stepped back, sliding from his grasp. "And I think your father's timing was perfect. I do need a bit more time." She paused. "Okay?"

"Nope. It's not okay. It sucks." But to his credit, he smiled. "So I guess I should leave now?"

She folded her arms. "I guess. Are you working tomorrow?" His eyes were still on hers; it was hard to let him go. But Annie knew she had something else to do. Something more important.

"Noon to eight."

"Okay. Then . . . well, I guess we'll talk soon?"

He gulped the last of his wine and put on his jacket. "Count on it," he said.

She bit her lip and watched him walk toward the door. Then he stopped. Turned. And took her in his arms again. And kissed her for a long, long time.

After John was gone, Annie waited awhile. She'd decided to catch the *On Time* crossing at nine o'clock, which gave her enough time to get over to Earl and Claire's first. Earl warned her to be careful not to miss the last ferry heading back, but they both knew her mission shouldn't take long.

Bella was sleeping soundly when Annie carried her into the hospital. She hadn't bothered with the basket; she didn't want to have to keep resettling her.

Like the baby, Francine was asleep.

Annie had scooted past the nurses' station undetected, and now she stood watching the girl. Moving closer to the bed, she leaned down, then rested Bella near Francine's arm. Without opening her eyes, Francine reached out, put her arm around the baby, and drew her close. Bella never even whimpered.

Annie sat in the chair where she'd sat before.

Several minutes passed before Francine awoke.

"Bella?" she whispered.

"It's her," Annie replied. "I think she wanted to see you."

Francine looked over at Annie. "You know the truth now, don't you?"

Annie nodded. "About Stephen and your mother, yes. But I was hoping you'd like to tell me about her. I have a feeling the two of you were close." She drew the chair closer to the bed.

"My mother died."

"How?"

"She got sick after Bella was born. It was a bad infection. She was forty-one—not too old to have a baby, but she had a heart condition. The doctor said the combination contributed to her . . . death."

"And you were left alone."

Francine smoothed the hair on the crown of Bella's head. "She smells so sweet, doesn't she? Like she hasn't lost that new baby kind of smell."

"You're right. And she is beautiful."

"My mother didn't want Stephen to know. But I didn't know where else to go. I couldn't support her on my own. It's winter . . . I was hardly making any money."

"What about your mother's sister? Her husband owns the Sunrise Café, doesn't he?"

Francine shook her head. "He sold the restaurant last spring. My mother's mother—her name was Bella, too—well, she got Alzheimer's, so Aunt Marty went back to Minnesota to look after her. My uncle sold the Sunrise and started another restaurant out there. I stayed and worked for the new owner; there was no way me and my mother were going back to Minnesota."

"What about your mother's father?"

"He died a few years ago. My other grandparents did, too. But that grandpa was not very nice."

No wonder the poor girl felt alone.

"Well," Annie said, "I wanted to come tonight to tell you that I'll be back tomorrow. And I'll be bringing someone with me. He's a good man; his wife is a good woman. They have a wonderful idea about your future. And Bella's, too."

"What?"

Annie smiled. "I'm going to leave that up to him to tell you. But I wanted to let you know ahead of time. It can change your life—in a good way—if you say yes to him. If you think you like it here on the Vineyard. Okay?"

Francine looked at her. "Why is everyone being so nice to me?"

With an exaggerated shrug, Annie simply said, "Oh, honey. Why not?" Then she took Bella from her. "We'll be here before noon. For now, I must get this little one to bed."

As she started to leave, Annie stopped and turned back. "Francine? There's one more thing that I've been curious about. Why did you come to the holiday fair? Did you know I'd be there?"

She shook her head. "I Googled Stephen Thurman on my phone and found out his address. It wasn't too far from the center of Edgartown, so I took the bus into town. Then I walked from there."

"Carrying Bella."

"In her basket, yes."

There was no need to mention that the bus usually went all the way to South Beach and probably drove right past Scallop Cove Road. Or that the original basket had been a danger to Bella. "So, Stephen wasn't home?"

"Nobody was. But I saw a lady walking a dog—a yellow lab. She told me Stephen's wife was at the fair, selling her baked goods. She said it was at the school, so I found my way there, too. But when I saw his wife, I chickened out. She was so nice and seemed so friendly, and I knew I'd freak her out."

So the reason Bonnie Thurman had recognized Annie was because she, too, had been a vendor at the fair. "Was that when you decided what you were going to do?"

Francine shook her head. "I read a lot. There's not much else to do on the Cape in the winter. When I heard those ladies talk about your books, I realized I'd read a couple of them. But not your first. Not the one about you being adopted. That's when I got the idea. When I left the fair, I went to the library."

"And you found out where I lived."

"You said you were on North Neck on Chappy. I found a big house that was unlocked, so I camped out in there and checked out the neighborhood the next day. Your place wasn't hard to find; you said you were in a cottage, and yours was the only one on North Neck that had a car in the driveway. Where somebody obviously was living. I couldn't believe you were right next door."

Francine was clever, there was no doubt about that.

"I was going to wait until Christmas Eve to bring her to you," she continued, "but when the blizzard came, I knew I was stuck. It was cold in the big house, too cold for Bella, so I had to stop procrastinating and bring her over to you. I almost knocked on your door and asked if I could stay, too, but . . ." She did not finish the sentence.

Annie smiled. "And then you stalked me."

"I didn't mean to. But when the blizzard was over, your car disappeared overnight. I got scared. I thought you took Bella away."

That must have been the night Annie had stayed at Winnie's.

"The next day you came home, but then you left with some guy in a pickup. I broke in to get food . . . I was so hungry. That's when I saw Bella's basket tossed into the back seat of your car. And I figured you really did get rid of her. That you'd taken her to Boston or somewhere and left her at one of those hospitals where nobody asks any questions."

"Oh, Francine . . . I am so sorry. That basket got wobbly. I bought her a new one . . ."

"I bought the red bow because I thought it made it special. And that it made Bella look special, too, so you'd want to keep her."

Annie's eyes quickly filled with tears. "Oh, Francine, she is special. You have no idea how special she is to me."

"It's okay," Francine said. "None of this was your fault." Her big eyes got teary, too.

"It wasn't your fault, either," Annie said, then walked back to the girl, picked up her hand, and squeezed it. "Everything will be fine now. You'll see." It was clear that Francine was as much a victim as little Bella. Annie knew they both would be well cared for in Earl and Claire's home.

Then she said good night and made it back to the *On Time* for its ten o'clock crossing, one more mission checked off her list.

Chapter 31

"My wife's a real good cook," Earl told Francine the next day after he had explained the plan. "She didn't come today because she said she didn't want to smother you. And I'm the one who knew about Bella first. Well, after Annie, of course. Taylor tried to figure it out, but, well, you'll get used to her. And Claire already loves the baby. She made her the new white sweater you might have seen her in."

"I love her, too," Francine replied. "She's all I have, you know."

"Not anymore," Earl said. "If you wanted to be lonely, you came to the wrong island."

The girl smiled; she had a lovely smile. Annie was glad she'd come to see her the night before; glad she'd prepared her for something good that was finally going to happen.

"The doctor says I can be discharged as early as tomorrow," the girl said. "Is that too soon for me to come over? If it's okay with the police?"

Earl's smile was warm and welcoming, as Annie knew it would be. "You let me worry about the police. You're over eighteen, so there's a good chance that, in time, you'll get custody of Bella, if Thurman doesn't want her. But let's look on the bright side: a new year starts tomorrow. Seems like a perfect time to start a new life, don't you think?"

She lowered her eyes. "They want me to come to the hospital three times a week for counseling. On account of what I did. Or rather, what I tried to do. To myself."

"No problem," Earl replied. "I'm over this way at least that much." It wasn't true, of course, but Francine did not need to know that.

Annie watched the two of them. She was filled with hope for them; filled with hope for Bella. Bella's birth mother might be gone, but she still had her half sister. And new people in her life who would love her very much.

Then she thought about Donna MacNeish. She wondered if her birth mother was still alive, and if she'd thought Annie hadn't answered her letter because she had new people who loved her very much.

Then the text bell dinged on Annie's phone. She glanced into her purse; the message was from Winnie. Annie excused herself and skipped out into the corridor.

TONIGHT IS NEW YEAR'S EVE, the note read. WANT TO COME UP ISLAND FOR FIREWORKS ON THE CLIFFS? THEY START AT NINE.

Annie thought for a moment, then texted back: MAY I BRING A FRIEND?

John's shift ended at eight o'clock. After bringing Bella back to Earl and Claire's for the night, Annie met him at the police station, because it took a long time to get up island to the Gay Head Cliffs. He jumped into the passenger side of the Lexus. Then he closed the door and gave her a lovely kiss, which wasn't easy, because they were both wearing heavy, winter-weather parkas.

"You're going to let me drive?" she asked with a wide grin.

"Of course. That way I can get drunk."

She blinked.

"Kidding," he said. "The truth is, I'm exhausted."

"Oh, that's right," she said. "I keep forgetting about your advanced years."

He laughed and told her to start the car. He opened his jacket in order to put on his seat belt: she didn't ask if he'd gone home on his dinner break to change into the navy sweater and jeans he now wore. He did, indeed, look handsome. Murphy would be pleased at Annie's choice for helping open up her life.

The ride to Aquinnah passed quickly. John kept his arm on top of her seat back; they talked and laughed while she maneuvered around all the hills and curves in the deep, secluded darkness.

When they reached the lighthouse, cars lined the circle all around the point of land. Annie parked and they got out, walking hand in hand, up past the Wampanoag gift shops that were closed until spring, and out to the lookout point. Winnie spotted Annie right away.

"Well, hello, you," she said to Annie.

"Hi, Winnie. Thanks so much for inviting us. I think you know John Lyons?"

"I do," Winnie replied with an inquisitive smile.

"We have a lot to tell you," John said as he shook her hand.

"So it seems. Well, when the fireworks are done, we're having a clambake down on the beach. I hope you brought blankets." She smiled, waved, and walked back toward her family.

Annie and John stood side by side, his arm around her waist. They looked up at silver stars, millions of shining specks of hope and wishes for the new year. Then the fireworks began, splaying their vibrant colors across the black velvet sky, then floating down into the water, reflecting in the surf.

"Happy New Year," John said, and kissed her, even though it wasn't yet midnight.

Annie laughed. "Jumping the gun a bit?"

"Trying to make a good impression so you'll think we've waited long enough."

She hugged him and rested her cheek against his chest. "Too bad it isn't summer. There are lots of dunes around us."

"Where we could sneak away from the crowd?"

"And do whatever we liked."

"Yup. It's too bad it isn't summer."

She leaned closer against him.

"Of course," he said, "the advertisement for this jacket said it was good down to fifty below zero."

Annie laughed. "It's not that cold tonight."

"And I bet we can find a perfect place . . ." He took her hand and led her from the cliffs, past the rocks and the sea grass, through an ancient pathway that cut through clusters of low-growing sassafras trees, away from the noise and the people and the fireworks, until finally they found a small sheltered dune, where John lay his jacket on the windswept sand and, at last, they made slow, perfect love.

It was after two a.m. when Annie sat in her living room, in front of the woodstove in her flannel jammies, wool robe, and fuzzy slippers, grateful that John had pulled some strings to get them back late on the *On Time*.

They'd made love again, that time in her big, warm bed, where he was sleeping now. She'd sneaked away once she'd heard his steady breathing.

As she sipped tea now, watching the tiny white lights on the tree and the magical way they glinted off the colorful ornaments, Annie realized she was not dwelling on Christmases past or Christmases future, but only on the present. This had been such an unexpected roller coaster of a year: now a new one was beginning, and she felt filled with contentment. She was missing her dad, and, yes, her mother, too, but she was filled with gratitude for having been so lucky to have had them. Most of all, Annie knew she was finally ready to accept the cycles of life that came and went in their time, not hers.

She missed Murphy, too, but something had changed.

The cottage was quiet, except for John's gentle breathing. Looking up to the ceiling, Annie knew that Murphy was no longer hiding up there. She was where she belonged now; perhaps she, too, knew that their cycle was complete.

"I will miss you, old friend," Annie said, raising her mug in a toast.

Then, whether it came from her heart or was a last message from Murphy, who no doubt knew everything now, Annie knew there was one thing left to do. And she knew that a handwritten note would be better than one typed on her laptop.

Spotting her purse slung over a kitchen chair, Annie retrieved it, sat back down, and dug out her notebook and a pen. After twenty years of not knowing what to say, it seemed odd that the words came so quickly.

Dear Donna, her letter began.

It's taken me a long time to answer the letter you sent years ago. I am so sorry for that. I wasn't ready. Tonight, however, I realized I finally am. I'm ready, really ready, to open up my life. And I hope you are still open to wanting to know me.

She continued writing, page after page, thought after thought. She had no idea if her birth mother would receive the letter, if she were still at the same address, if she were even still alive. But Annie knew the time had come. After John left in the morning, she would go to Edgartown and put it in the box at the post office. It didn't matter that it would be New Year's Day and no mail would leave the island until the following day. In Annie's mind, it would be en route.

Then she'd stop at the hospital and see if Francine was ready to leave. She'd bring her home to Chappy, to Earl and

Claire's, where she'd start her new life—a real life—with Bella, the sweet little one. Annie would suggest that they keep Bella's things—her lamb, the book, the wiggle biggle—in the original basket, that was so much like the one her aunt had used to hold skeins of yarn. Her aunt had been Ellen Sutton's sister, and Annie had treasured both of them. Because she knew that families—both the originals and those that had been gifted—had plenty of love to go around.

Francine had waited until the clock read midnight. Then she'd closed her eyes. It was New Year's Day. Her brand-new life was about to start.

Maybe Mommy had been listening, after all.

Epilogue

The weekend after New Year's, Annie got around to taking down her Christmas tree. It had been a busy time: she'd helped Earl and Claire get Francine and Bella settled into their new home; she'd helped John get ready for his girls, who'd finally arrived the day before. She'd answered some e-mails and sent a HAPPY NEW YEAR post to her fans. She'd even called her editor to tell her that she was progressing.

Best of all, she'd gotten back to work. She named her main characters Emma and Maggie. They were transparent clones of Annie and Murphy, even more than they'd been when she'd started. She channeled Murphy's wit and wisdom throughout the pages—it was her way of sharing her friend with her readers, who surely had best friends that they loved, too. Best of all, it helped Annie feel that Murphy was still with her after all.

Amazingly, Saturday was sunny and warm, almost sixty degrees. It was a perfect day to transport what remained of the blue spruce that had been decked out for Christmas up island to the beach. Winnie had told her that several beaches, like Lucy Vincent, had suffered loss and erosion during the blizzard; the used trees would help capture blowing sand and create new dunes. Pleased to learn that the infernal winds were at least good for something, Annie decided to contribute to the effort.

She'd dressed in jeans and a flannel shirt that she'd picked up at Trader Fred's—FAMOUS NAME-BRAND CLOTHING AND EVERYTHING ELSE!—in Edgartown last fall. She was wedging the tree into the trunk of the Lexus when the sound of tires on clamshells diverted her attention.

She doubted it was Earl, because he rarely stopped by for coffee and cinnamon rolls on Saturdays now: his weekends were busy with Francine and Bella. Besides, the *crunch-crunch* sounded too light for a truck.

With the last branch jammed into the car, Annie closed the lid—and saw that another Lexus had parked behind hers. That one, however, was a sports model.

The sun flashed off the windshield so she wasn't able to see who was behind the wheel. The license plate was from Massachusetts, but was without a special designation like the MARTHA'S VINEYARD ones that so many people, even Annie, had now.

She started to walk toward the car when the driver's door opened and a silver-haired woman got out. She was tall and slender, dressed in jeans, a cropped wool jacket, and boots. She slid her sunglasses up onto her head. And Annie knew right away who it was.

"Donna?" she whispered.

"Annie?"

A long time ago, Annie had read that it was rare for individuals to truly see themselves in another person. The article had noted that a person hardly ever looked into a mirror and said, "Wow, I look just like Aunt Shirley," or "Man, I look like Cousin Cindy." But Annie didn't need a mirror to know that, despite the hair color, she was the image of her birth mother.

"God," Donna said, "it's really you."

"I look like you," Annie said.

Donna bit her lower lip. "Very much."

Annie laughed. "You drive a Lexus."

Donna laughed. "So do you."

Then they looked into each other's eyes, the same hazel—not blue—eyes. One of them reached out first to hug the other: later they would not remember which one it had been. It didn't matter. Mother and daughter were reunited—another circle connected, like the willow hoop of a Wampanoag dream catcher.

Be sure to look for Jean Stone's new novel

A VINEYARD SUMMER

On sale in July 2019
in bookstores and online

Read on for a special preview. . . .

"You have to leave."

Annie Sutton stood in the doorway of the cottage on Chappaquiddick. Her jaw went slack; her thoughts tumbled into one another.

Her landlord, Roger Flanagan, pressed his thin lips together as if attempting an apologetic smile. "I'm sorry, Annie. You've been a wonderful tenant. But my grandson, Jonas, is moving to the Vineyard." He averted his eyes and stared off toward a cluster of scrub oaks in the side yard. "He recently completed the master's program at the Art Institute of Chicago; he's an exceptional artist, so it makes sense for him to live here, what with the growth in tourism and an uptick in disposable income among the seasonal residents who are also discerning collectors . . ."

Blah, blah, blah.

She barely heard a word he said after his opening line. It was already the end of June. The entire island of Martha's Vineyard was about to launch into its high season—July and August—which meant it would be nearly impossible for Annie to find a year-round rental. She'd heard that the feat was tough enough off season.

"When?" her voice quaked. If he'd already said when she'd need to go, her brain hadn't processed it yet.

His smile morphed into a sheepish look. For a seventy-plus-year-old man that *Forbes* Magazine had proclaimed a hedge fund piranha, he looked oddly embarrassed. "Technically, your lease was a winter rental. It expired June first. After that, we'd agreed you'd be here month-to-month, with a thirty-day notice required by either party. So shall we say mid-August? That will give you a couple of extra weeks to find something else. Jonas can live in the main house until then."

A couple of weeks of "extra time" would hardly make a difference. As much as Annie wanted to say, "No! This is my home!" Roger Flanagan was right: *technically*, she had no choice. She'd known from the beginning that renting the cottage might not be long-term. She had not, however, chosen to believe it.

"Thank you," she said, without meaning it. "The extra time will help." Before she could add something polite about wishing Jonas success, Roger folded his arms.

"Big wedding here on the Fourth. Hope we won't disturb you."

She leaned against the doorjamb. With the Flanagans in New York most of the year, she'd lived alone on the property for such a long time—nearly ten months and counting—she'd almost forgotten the place wasn't hers. "Weddings are nice. It's for our daughter."

"Dana. She's all we have. Dana and, of course, Jonas."

Of course, Annie's mind echoed with a twinge of disdain. Then she realized it must mean that Jonas was Dana's son. Annie had seen the woman flit by the cottage once or twice, but was surprised she was old enough to have a child out of college. The master's program at the Art Institute of Chicago, she corrected herself. "Well, don't worry about disturbing me.

I grew up in Boston. I'm accustomed to living with noise." Besides, she sensed that any sign of protest would be pointless.

He tipped his Tilley hat and shuffled away in his Tevas.

Closing the door, she slumped against it and said, "Damn." She loved the little cottage. She loved Chappy, where she'd landed when she'd traded city life for the peaceful island. She'd made friends, connections with people she now cared about and who cared about her. She did not want to be forced to leave.

"Damn," she said again.

At age fifty-one, Annie had lived long enough not to envy anyone with a life of privilege. As a writer, she knew that every individual, every family, had a story (often a dark one, an *underbelly*, her old friend Murphy used to call it), and that having *beaucoup bucks* (Murphy again) was no guarantee of happiness.

"But money helps when you need a place to live," she said out loud now. Then she did what she did best in times of stress: she put the kettle on for tea.

While waiting for the water to boil, she plunked down in the rocking chair and stared at the wall.

Correction: she stared at the bookcases that stood against the wall, the ones she'd bought when she'd moved in, then packed with her favorite volumes. Along with the corner desk, the bookcases fit perfectly into the snug space and created an inspiring nook where she'd finally been able to settle in and conquer her writer's block.

Where would her things fit now?

She was almost finished with her latest novel—*Renaissance Heist: A Museum Girls Mystery*—but with less than a month until her publisher's deadline, she needed time to focus. How the heck could she do that if she had to hunt for a place to live and then actually move? Should she simply shove everything but her laptop, her thesaurus, and a suitcase of clothes into storage? She'd have to blow her budget by renting even a quiet, single room (shared bath, kitchen privileges) at an exorbitant summer rate, but at least she could get the book done. Then, come September, she could begin a realistic housing search.

It was a lousy plan, but the only one she could come up with at the moment. Her priority, after all, had to be *Renaissance Heist*, as her editor, Trish, often reminded her. Aside from the deadline stipulated in her contract, Annie had been counting on book sales to replenish her savings now that she'd finally paid off the huge debt her former husband had bequeathed her when he'd disappeared. But how could she be creative with this new crisis disrupting her thoughts?

"Damn," she said for the third, self-pitying time. She hated that at her age she needed to worry about how and where she would live. Mostly, she hated that her idyllic, dream-come-true world was about to come crashing down.

She gazed out the window. The view from the cottage was of the scrub oaks, not the water. Ocean views were reserved for the Flanagans of the world, the "haves" in a world of "have-nots" like Annie. Unless she got really lucky. Really fast.

The kettle whistled.

"You can move in with me," John Lyons said over dinner that evening, a concoction she'd created from fresh bass and the last of winter's root vegetables from Slip Away Farm. He was handsome—tall, dark-haired, and *well-muscled*, Murphy would have said—with soft gray eyes and one of those magnetic smiles that made people instantly trust he was on their side, although Annie wasn't sure if anyone he arrested would agree. Even better than his good looks, John was kind. Caring. Sensitive. And Annie adored him. They'd been dating since New Year's Eve: things between them were still wonderful, sexy, fun. Yet she'd wanted to linger a while longer in the lovely beginning of their relationship—that magical time when all things were new and exciting—before making any kind of commitment.

And she certainly didn't want to feel forced into one because of the island housing crisis.

She toyed with a carrot slice. "I think it's too soon for that, don't you?"

He cocked his head and grinned the half grin that made Annie feel like a fifteen-year-old girl with a crush on the best-looking boy in the school. "Maybe. But I can't pretend I haven't thought about it."

Neither could she. But before she spoke the words, he added, "Of course, you might not want to be too picky if you're going to wind up being homeless."

Annie knew he was joking, but his remark stung. "Right," she said. "It will be tough to finish my book if I have nowhere to charge my laptop."

"You can always camp out on the sofa in my father's study. You know you'd be welcome there."

"I do know that. And it's a good feeling. But your parents have a busy household now, complete with a beautiful, but sometimes fussy, baby. Which isn't conducive to writing, ei-ther."

He set down his fork, reached across the table, and took her hand. His expression turned serious. "Look, Annie, what-ever you decide, I'll do what I can to help. The last thing I want is for you to have to leave the island."

It was the last thing Annie wanted, too. But she'd had enough ups and downs in her life to know that just because she wanted to stay on the Vineyard didn't mean it would work out.

Just then, John's cell phone rang.

Annie forked a piece of fish while he checked the call. Born and raised on the Vineyard, John was a police officer in Edgartown and did not turn his phone off. Ever. He looked back to her and mouthed, "Sorry," then stood, walked toward the front door, and stepped out onto the porch.

"Hi, honey," she heard him say. She deduced it was one of

his teenage daughters, who lived off island with their mother. They were only up in Plymouth, but John once said that having a wide girth of water between his ex and him had been essential after the divorce. Annie had not been surprised. She couldn't imagine what it would be like to live on an island with a former spouse, having to run into him at the supermarket or the post office or even at the movies, where she often went to quiet her stress. As wonderful as life was on the Vineyard, there were simply few places to hide.

"What does your mother say?" he said into the phone.

She hated feeling as if she were eavesdropping. But her one-bedroom cottage was not built for privacy, and he had not shut the door behind him. She took another bite of the fish.

"That's not acceptable, Lucy. You know that."

Oh, dear, Annie thought. Lucy was the younger girl—thirteen going on thirty, according to John.

"Put your mother on the phone." His voice was stern but not threatening; Annie would bet he was a soft touch when it came to his girls.

"When will she be home?" He paused; he sighed. "Never mind. I'll call her myself." He did not say goodbye.

The screen door opened. He walked back to the table and sat down. He stared at his dinner plate.

"Everything okay?" Annie asked, though, clearly, it was not.

Picking up his fork, he poised it over his dinner. "Consider yourself lucky that you never had kids." Then he closed his eyes and shook his head. "Oh, God. I'm so sorry."

Annie smiled. He, of course, had forgotten how close she'd been to becoming a mother, that the abortion had been one of two life choices she wished she'd handled differently. The other bad choice had been to marry her ex-husband in the first place.

Then John's cell rang again. He glanced at it and muttered,

"Crap." He let it ring twice, then said to Annie, "I hate to do this, but I gotta go. It's Jenn."

"I understand," she said, but her words dissolved before she knew if he'd heard them: he was too busy standing up, pulling his truck keys from his pocket, and going back out the door while asking, "What the hell's going on?" to the woman he had once married. Then he disappeared into the night.

Annie tried to finish her dinner, but couldn't. She set the leftovers aside for the compost bin and reminded herself that she was on her own now. She tried to believe that she'd find somewhere to live, and that it would be fine, because she was resilient and had learned how to land on her proverbial feet.

If only she could shake off the feeling that this time there was much more at stake. Maybe she'd feel more hopeful after a good night's sleep.

Donna.

The thought of her birth mother's name jolted Annie from the edge of a dream.

Of course! She bolted upright, her heart softly pounding. *Families help one another out.* Or, at least, her adoptive parents had helped each other. Blood relations would, too. Wouldn't they?

She switched on the lamp on the nightstand and smiled. She'd met Donna just a few months ago. The woman was open and ebullient and seemed truly happy to finally meet Annie. But she'd recently sold her antiques shop on the north shore of Boston, had happily retired, and was now on a long-awaited, four-month world cruise with her current gentleman friend. "We're almost seventy," she'd lamented with a grin. "Please don't call him my boyfriend."

But Donna wasn't due back until the middle of August; far too late for Annie to make a decision.

She wanted to stay on the island, wanted to live and breathe and keep writing there. She also wanted, very badly, to continue her relationship with John, wherever it led. And she wanted to perfect the craft of soap-making that she'd learned from her friend Winnie Lathrop, who was part of the up island Wampanoag tribe.

She didn't suppose she could live in Aquinnah with Winnie and her family, because Annie's roots were Scottish, not Native American.

She wished she could ask Donna for advice. She also wished she could talk to her adoptive parents, the Suttons, who had known her in a way Donna never could. Which Annie still found disturbing, to think that a mother did not really know her child.

"It will take time," Donna had said the day she'd arrived on Chappy after Annie had finally responded to the woman's letter that had begun with the powerful words: *I am your birth mother . . .*

Donna had stayed with Annie nearly a week, camping out on an air bed on the living room floor. They'd talked and talked about important things and about nothing special. They'd walked for hours, exploring the dirt roads of the island, getting used to each other's presence amid the sounds of the waves and the occasional cry of a gull. It had been January. When most folks had the good sense not to be there. But for Annie, the togetherness had been like a warm quilt.

Annie looked like her, or at least she had before she'd traded her designer clothes for jeans and flannel shirts and had stopped having manicures that weren't conducive to harvesting herbs, plucking wildflowers, and making soap. They had the same dark, almost black hair, streaked with silver, though Donna admitted to having more streaks than her stylist allowed her to show. They had the same long-legged, lean body, the same careful stride, the same happy laugh. The same hazel—not blue—eyes.

Mother and daughter. The tree and the apple.

Donna promised to return after the cruise; they'd agreed that the Vineyard would be a wonderful place to build their new bond. Which was one more reason it was imperative that Annie found a damn place to live.

There was always Kevin, she supposed. But she was still getting used to the idea that her birth mother was now in her life, let alone that she had a half brother who was nine years younger than she was. She'd met Kevin only once—over lunch, in Boston—when he'd joined her birthday celebration with her birth mother. He'd recently sold his construction business, and, like Annie, was single again.

"I spent all of an hour with him," Annie said now with a laugh. "It might be a bit presumptuous to ask if I could move in for a while."

Still, she had his phone number.

She could always send a friendly text.

If she knew what to say.

Or how she thought he could help.

She punched her pillow to rearrange the fluff, then snapped off the light again. *Tomorrow*, she thought. *I'll think about it to-morrow.*

Or the day after.

Then she closed her eyes again and prayed that sleep would come quickly.

Connect with Us

Visit us online at
KensingtonBooks.com
to read more from your favorite authors, see books
by series, view reading group guides, and more.

for sneak peeks, chances to win books and prize packs,
and to share your thoughts with other readers.

facebook.com/kensingtonpublishing
twitter.com/kensingtonbooks

Tell us what you think!

To share your thoughts, submit a review,
or sign up for our eNewsletters, please visit:
KensingtonBooks.com/TellUs.

Printed in the United States
by Baker & Taylor Publisher Services